To Senn
Semper Fi
[signature]

SitRep: Viet Nam

By

John W. Newton

DEDICATION

To The Warriors of Viet Nam
To The Marines of Echo 2/5
To "Pumpkin"

CONTENTS

CAMP LEJUNE: First Lieutenant Horton Sills was found dead today, the victim of an apparent suicide. One of the first MPs on the scene said, "I've never seen anything like it. He cut his own head off with a chain saw. I took one look and threw up. There was a half empty bottle of Dram Bouie on the bureau with one of those little tiny glasses and a note taped to the mirror. It said 'It's the stuff dreams are made of, kid – Bogey'"

1 QUANTICO – JULY, 1968

Full alert; I watch.

She sits in the dark rocking back and forth in the small stuffed 'lady's chair,' lady's because of its size and the ornate flower pattern on the cover, lilacs I think, and because that's what she says it is. She is silhouetted against the smoothing hang of wisp-peach curtains backlit by a predawn smoky glow seeping through the window behind her and she watches me sleep. The chair smiles her delicate sleepy scent. She runs her slender fingers through her short waves of brown hair and then across her perfectly rounded forehead letting her thumb drag across one cheek in search of freckles. Her hands, artist's hands she calls them, slide down the front of her night gown pausing here and there on one of the small purple flowers that decorate the gown. Even with child birth she remains slender on the verge of frail delicacy. The image fades. I hover over the room.

The thrashing stops and now I rest across the bed on the sweat swamped sheets that she will strip and wash later today once I am awake and gone off to the base to work. And while she washes my sweat from the bed clothes she will pause mid task and remind herself of how much the lingering smell of 'him' meant to her when I was gone. She clutches the shirt and shrinks away into a round spiraling shining dot.

I tense, and in a single jerking motion jump and land on my knees next to the bed - "whoa, shit" – I was looking down the wrong end of an M-14 into the frightened eyes of young steel fingered Lance Corporal Bates standing guard on the roof of his bunker. I am awake and huddled up next to the bed bewildered, trying to figure it out. I look first at the shambles of sheet and blanket; her pillow punched and wadded into the small space between the mattress and the footboard, and then across the room to the small chair where I know as sleep fades and my thoughts begin to clear the horizon I will find her.

"Couldn't sleep?"

"You fought the war again last night so I just sat and listened for the passing of the brown car." she says without emotion looking down at her hands, nestled sleeping birds in her lap. I look at her for a moment and then turn to leave, pausing at the door.

"It always starts with a small field full of tiny white flowers and littered with thin broken crosses whose names I can't read, and then it fades and I don't remember what comes next."

"So you've said."

"What brown car?"

She looks into and through my eyes with a slight smile that says 'you must remember' and then turns to the window without answering. I know it makes no sense to wait for an answer because she knows I know what car. Still, no matter how many times she tells me of the brown car I always manage to forget it's ugliness by the next morning.

I look down and smooth at my clinging red white and blue striped boxers, my green tee shirt now grown transparent and colorless. I flick my moist hand hoping to will it dry and shutter slightly.

"I've got to get out of these. I'm soaked."

2

She looks back up and watches me leave.

"Don't wake the Gerald," she whispers into the darkness.

I turn on the bathroom light and close the door. I strip down, kick the clinging soggy clothes into the corner and step into the shower. Hot water tumbles over me. The small cube fills with steam. I know what she is doing now, now that I am gone from the bedroom. She is listening for baby sounds, but she won't hear any, only the gentle easy hiss of the shower. Now she is looking down at her resting hands and closing her eyes to follow them back into sleep to dream of parading brown cars.

I close my eyes and turn my face into the rhythm of the shower. July. In a couple of days it will be the Fourth. Another special day set out in the calendar like a booby trap with those little knuckleheads at the base running around throwing firecrackers in every direction. July Fourth, and tonight we've got that fucking party. The pulsing beat of the water on my face sweeps the thought away and the steam and the heat wrap around me and drive me an unwilling passenger back through the past twelve months; back to the echoes and screams of the voices of Nong Son.

SitRepUnknown: Men climbed here bringing stars up to a place where the dark sky already teems and they smiled because the height and the sheer fall to the valley below made them feel safe. They hung their stars on the summit and they left smiling still, because they were here. They left dropping blessings safely here and there in their wake. Everyone was warm and happy.

Like the river, I watch them.

Like the still water in the paddies, I watch them as they come up and as they go down.

Like the gently flowing streams, I watch them as they draw up in their Fourth-of-July chairs to sup in happy places and they toast themselves-contented.

Like the fall of the rain that drips drop by drop through the leaves of the jungle, I watch too as small quiet shadows inch toward the top to sweep the summit in a torrent leaving thirteen to die and two others to forget for a moment what men call life and that it is their job to go on living.

'I shot him,

'I shot him no more than from me to you in the guts, and he smiled.

'He fuckin' smiled at me as he died, he looked down at his hands where they held him together, and when he saw that it would not work, when he saw that too much was running loosely through his fingers to stay alive, he looked at me and he smiled. They're not suppose to smile when they die. They're not suppose to smile.'

'I grabbed for my trousers and it fell between my legs, it was small. It was small, very small between my smooth bare youthful legs, very small. I clutched my trousers hard because I knew, I knew when I saw it why it had come. I knew, I waited, I clutched my trousers and I waited for it to greet me, and when it didn't, it left me with only my trousers and the pressure in my arms holding them tight into my chest.

'I still clutch them and I wait for the small hard object between my legs to speak in a thunderous smoke filled voice.

'"Grenade," someone shouts.

'It remains silent.

'It remains silent but the pressure in my arms increases.'

There will be medals I suppose as there always are when someone has made a mistake. There will be medals given by those who made the mistake to those who paid the price, to the one who wouldn't be driven from his machine-gun until finally he died.

And they will be presented quite properly and quietly to retired whores standing on lush stages of green. There will be medals and there will be speeches and the retired whores will cry and blush because with it all there will be cameras.

There will be medals I suppose.

And as the rain continued, I watched the next morning when the men who brought the stars returned. I watched them and I knew them when they came, by the newness of their boots and the smell of their starch and polish. I knew them and I watched them as they bent to pick up their scattered stars and looked carefully around so that no one should see the tarnish that had gathered

4

there. I stood quietly beneath them as they waved their smooth little fingers in strange rapid ways seeking someone to blame and I watched their eyes when they learned that a 14th had perished in an accident and that he must lie for two days crushed beneath the metal of his truck before he can safely be borne away. I watched and I listened as heads were hung and soft sorry words were mumbled and I wondered as the puffy eye attached to the night took on color because of it.

And then they were gone.

Like the water of the rivers and sea, I remained to feel the stake driven into my heart to bear the skull of one who brought the fire found dead in the wire, its flesh boiled off in a pot, ripped loose from the shoulders in the hands of a child to remove the stink, its putrid lips parted to make room for a cigarette. They grew quiet then and they walked away leaving only the occasional crack of a rock as it fell off the western edge into the deep distant valley below.

I turn off the shower and step back out into the bathroom, gripped in a chill in spite of the heat saturated air.

I pull a towel around my waist and lean forward on the sink pushing my face into the mirror still fogged from the heat of the shower, until I'm sure I still recognize the person looking back. I wipe at the mirror with my hand scratching a small circle of clarity in the steam shrouding my image. Bates. I hadn't thought of him in almost a year. Skinny kid, young with big round Irish eyes. With three months left, he thought of his wife and his son and he was suddenly frightened. He said to himself that he was tired, too tired for any more of it, and he asked Piggy, his assistant gunner, his ammo humper to take him out of it. Piggy said yes because he would do anything for Bates and he did it. He smashed Bates' fingers in the breech of the gun with the bolt over and over until they were bloody, limp and broken. He did it because he was serious and thoughtful and because he liked Bates, he would do anything for him and he wanted him to go home and be safe with his wife and his baby. Bates left with his hand and fingers lashed to the limbs of small wire tree and he smiled through the pain, and after he was gone, the ones that didn't know about it who was mostly me said "goddamn" and I was glad that he made it out for his wife and his child and his youth.

I rub at the mirror again with the back of my hand, my fingers still intact. Through the heavy air it looks like I still have my youth. My face is mostly unchanged, maybe a little pale on the upper lip where my 'been there' mustache had been but everything else still the same, still reflecting my ID description; red hair, hazel eyes, Protestant, blood type AB, 5 foot 9, 180 pound Sam, master of the P38 C-rats can opener that hangs on a chain around my neck Sam, Lieutenant Sam, Second Lieutenant Sam, USMC, once brand new, still green, one each, came through it all without a scratch and still A-OK Sam, 094952 Sam, trying to keep the story straight, trying to separate the true parts from the parts that may slip into fantasy, trying to figure out why during a war it's often hard to tell the difference between what's real and what's a dream, separating dreams from dreams only to discover that it's all dreams, dreams inside dreams inside dreams...

I survey the night stubble on my chin. But still, perhaps there is something different now, something around the eyes, darker, fewer lights there to dance, something that escapes photographic capture, something down in my gut, or something that was once there but no longer is. They fill with tears.

I try to remember. It was winter. We had been together for more than a year. I was a reporter for the small local paper and in my spare time wrote short pieces of doggerel and lengthy descriptive things. I was 21.

Warm water fills the sink while I lather to shave. Steam re-coats the mirror and fills it with the darkness of a deep narrow tunnel. Out of the steamy swirl the shape of my head begins to re-emerge, recognizable by the set of my ears, one just a little lower than the other. I pick up the razor and lift my chin.

How the hell had I gotten to this place? It was January 1966 when the letter arrived that set the avalanche of crap on its way down the slopes of what I thought was going to be a pleasant outing, the downhill run of my life. Only two years ago, but it seems so much longer.

"You are to report for a physical," it said, "pursuant to induction into the armed forces of the United States of America." I

6

passed. Then, in February of the same year, the avalanche gained momentum. "Greetings, you have 90 days to get your affairs in order after which you may be called to active duty."

"We can go to Canada," Pumpkin shouted in an urgent voice that was really saying 'this is not a good thing, grab your stuff, we've got to get out of here.'

But I decided to stay.

Small rows in the lather showing the path of the razor begin to line up together on my neck. I rinse the razor and lean in close to the mirror again.

Joining the reserves was a good idea I explained. After six months active duty it was only one week-end a month and two weeks a summer and it was a short run to the unit meeting place in Parkersburg. Besides I assured her six years would travel faster than a speeding bullet. And anyway, everybody had to go. I was lucky; really, to get a spot in a safe haven of week-end warriors when they were being snatched up by every well-connected college grad in sight; and it sure beat the hell out of going to jail.

"But it's the Marines," she whined.

And on that she was right. The 104th Rifle Company of Parkersburg, West Virginia, USMC. But what could possibly go wrong?

Well, for one thing, they closed the freaking unit five months later, and for another the unit I had to go to was 297 miles away. And to really make it hurt they met once a week for three fucking hours. That's what went wrong.

I bring the razor up out of the now tepid pool in the sink and continue to drag an inch and a half of finely honed steel across my throat. If I knew then. But it was all bullshit. I thought I knew then. Even after I decided to go on active duty because the prospect of a 600 mile round trip once a week for six years seemed untenable. Even after I decided to take the OCS route for four years instead of two as an enlisted Marine because I was sure it

7

would be a better life. I thought I knew exactly what I was doing and what the consequences were. But I didn't know shit.

I pull the razor down next to one ear so that now the line where hair stops and beard begins flows to invisible.

And by then of course it was too late and the avalanche continued on bouncing and bumping down the slope, a series of little things that one-by-one stole the light that had danced in my eyes.

I lift my nose between finger and thumb and hack at the small emerging crop on my upper lip careful not to knick myself again as I have already done twice to my chin. Well fuck. Two more small patches of red well up at the corners of my mouth. I throw the razor down into the sink and rinse off the remaining drifts of lather. I pull small pieces from the toilet paper roll and set them on the stinging cuts to stem the flow of blood. Complete, I step back and take another look at the self inflicted damage before turning off the light. I am at the bottom of the hill neck deep in a shit avalanche.

I go back into the bedroom quietly. My face decorated like a field of small white flowers. Pumpkin is asleep.

2 PHU BAI – FEBRUARY, 1968

It was TET and I couldn't get out of that fucking place fast enough. Three more rockets screamed in with rapid military precision, distant, impacting on the far side of the air strip in blossoms of dark blue, black streaked with crimson. When they landed they sounded like the violent slam of a car door.

How long had it been now two days, three, five? I'd lost count but it seemed like the whole goddamn country was in flames as rocket after rocket poured in on the sprawling Marine compound. No, it was five. The first ones came in five days ago just hours after we got back from Hue. Hue, was it only five days ago? Jesus. When the Colonel asked me if I wanted to take a fire team up to the Seabee pumping station on the southern bank of the Perfume River it sounded like a good idea and I jumped at the chance.

"You're short," he said. "It'll be a good day to get some pictures of the city, the ancient city, the imperial city."

So I went. I grabbed the new fire team and together we rattled up Highway 1 leaving Phu Bai mid-morning. Telephone poles marched along next to us punctuated by occasional bill boards advertising beer and cigarettes. Small, clay roadside shrines, like the ones back in the world made out of old bathtubs stood up and planted on end, crowded in from the lush undergrowth. Unlike those at home, these were decorated with flowers and cheap beads that had been tossed on them with no particular plan in mind.

On the way I made the driver stop by the old abandoned train tunnel. It had to be half a mile long, the far end no more than a spot of simmering light. I took several pictures of the sabotaged twist of steel rails and dark ties, tossed and forgotten pickup sticks. I grabbed a stone from the rail bed and threw it into the darkness where the detail of the rails disappeared. When it finally clattered to a stop I said "Boom," and then returned to the waiting PC. Other than the interruption of rail, the war had managed to miss this small arc of highway that circled tight up against the tunneled mountain. "If there's one thing I will remember about this place it's looking down fucking tunnels in the rain." I climbed back into the PC and we continued north.

At the pumping station the four debarking Marines laughed at their departing counterparts shouting at them while they tumbled their gear down off the truck. The ones they replaced put a month of soft living and glowing night memories along with back packs and rifles into the back of the truck and clambered on behind.

"Four weeks crapped out on the banks of the Perfume River while you all gonna be humping back in the bush by sundown, bro. Man, it gets no better."

"Enjoy it asshole," one of the departing called from the truck. "Your ass'll be back in the bush too and your pecker will be drippin' just like mine soon enough."

The driver gunned the PC and we headed back toward the main road, crossed the bridge and pulled into the crowded narrow streets of the city of Hue. For the rest of the afternoon we rode slowly through the clatter of pre-Tet preparation. I took pictures, a Shell station, a new hospital under construction spidered with vacant slender bamboo scaffolding and everywhere small clusters of Vietnamese men in uniform, who smiled and bowed as we passed. Some saluted and others waved. When the sun began its headlong plunge into the lips of the Western horizon, I put my camera away, adjusted my shoulder holster and we crossed back over the Perfume River bridge, pulled into the flow of holiday travelers crammed into and on tiny swaying busses on Highway 1 and headed south. That evening, before we had completed the eight mile run back to Phu Bai, Hue fell. Overrun by smiling clusters of Vietnamese men in uniform. The Imperial City bled into shallow graves and a new celebration began. All the smiles were gone. By morning the members of fire team I had dropped off along with the Seabees they were sent to protect were all dead, their hacked and mutilated bodies tossed into the Perfume River. The celebration of TET was underway.

But that was then. Now it was Tet plus 5, and no shit, I had to get back to the world and be a hometown hero mo ricky tic, but these bastards were for some reason still trying to kill me.

The last five days really sucked and the most recent few minutes proved to be no exception. The perfect end to a miserable year of walking hunched over in the heat and the rain waiting to get shot with big eyes and standing neck hair. And now, in celebration of my departure, every few minutes more 122 mm rockets fired from west of the city continued to slam into the tarmac on the airstrip or into the hooches that stretched in web-like rays out away from the strip forming the huge Phu Bai combat base. The sirens had blown nonstop all day and counter mortar fires roared out of the gun pits circling the strip throwing freight trains of high explosives into the erupting countryside.

That last hostile bucket load of shit was close, too close. The first rocket hit by the fuel dump mingling its explosion with the shriek of the warning sirens cranking up all over the base again. Before the next one started its arched approach to the base I was sucked into the scramble of office Marines and swept into one of the zigzag sandbag bunkers that stood next to each of the baked plywood hooches. There was a flash and the ripping sound of a thousand crashing waterfalls as a second rocket piled into the hooch next to us, releasing a wave of heat that pressed me deeper and deeper into the dirt floor of the scant bunker. It was followed quick on by the snarling splash of splintered plywood and screen mixed with lethal shards of corrugated roofing and shrapnel that rained down over and on our heads and hissed like hot fangs into the sandbags of the bunker. When it was over, the settling dust cleared like a quiet morning shower and I peeked up over the top of the bunker. The heavy air was saturated with the smell of spent explosive and smoke that wove its way up from the wreckage. My sea bags sat untouched by the surrounding destruction leaning into one another for protection in the middle of the road where I had left them stranded in a violent thoroughfare of confusion. 'Cross at the green, not in between or you could get hurt,' rattled around in my memory while I cautiously looked up and down the narrow alley-way that separated the hooches in neat orderly rows, left, right, left, and left again.

"For Christ sake."

The Colonel ran down the alley toward us with a bewildered Lance Corporal in tow. Even at a distance he was unmistakable. Taller than most and slightly bent forward at the waist like one of those spindly birds that when placed next to a glass of water bobbed up and down for a drink. As he ran he pointed from side-to-side into the bunkers shouting, "purple heart, get his name." At each one, the Lance Corporal stopped, scribbled the information shouted back to him over the heads of kneeling corpsmen and then ran on to catch up with the swiftly moving Colonel who, if he wasn't a warrior, would be playing basketball. He stopped now just feet away from where I stood in the waist deep bunker wreckage and gave me a long hard look.

We knew each other. A hero at Inchon, he had replaced Teapot. We had been on operations together, -Essex, Union,- and slept in shit together, ate shit together, been in the shit together. It was more important to him to be a Marine than a Colonel and I admired him for that. He paused and surveyed my two companions who moments before had been pressed up against me in the bunker.

"Get their names," he said turning his attention back to me.

Now, for the first time I saw blood. Their blood. It began to ooze around the small bits of metal that burrowed deep into their skin and spread out through the weave of their jungle utes linking together like a chain of small brown lakes. Peppered. I looked at the Colonel and he shook his head. Not a mark. I shrugged and the Colonel continued on down the row of shattered hooches looking for more wounded. I watched him grow smaller as he strode down the alley followed by the harried Lance Corporal who found it necessary to take three steps for each one of the Colonel's.

I hopped over the rubble that littered the broken lane passing the Colonel and mumbled to myself as I ran along, as I continue to run now. Why in the hell those two got whacked and I didn't was a mystery. But then that was the hallmark of my tour. Thirteen in the bush with one day to go and not a mark. Funny. It had to be just dumb luck. But whatever it was it sure as hell wasn't conducive to sleep.

The warehouses were right next to me now, moving past in slow motion emerging and disappearing in the dust filtered light. I slowed to a jog dragging my worn and bleached once green sea bags behind me in the swirling dust down the row of metal warehouses and looked for a place to stash them while I waited for the plane that was scheduled to take me to Da Nang for further connection to CONUS. Magic. Continental United States. The world. The promised land. Pumpkin, I'm on the way home. The buildings were close to the flight line and the terminal and thanks to their size there was shade and a good place to rest.

Around me I heard the hum of war administration, that a moment ago was silenced by the most recent attack, resume. I aimed in on the building closest to the strip. Like the smouldering piles of tin and screen I ran out of seconds ago, these too had flanking zig-zag trenches and that was a good thing.

I pulled on the first of the large plywood sliding doors. Locked. I continued on to the next.

Last night wasn't much better. I spent it in a ditch drinking shit gook rice wine from a passed around bottle, wondering where the fuck do we get this stuff, and to hold my own ghosts at bay, tried to scare the shit out of some poor new greenie bastard with war stories by the rockets' red glare. And while I drank, all over the base Marines lay out in the dirt fucked up, but it didn't matter, with one night left I was too frightened to sleep, too frightened to sleep per chance to dream, too frightened to give a shit. Ha. Even the security of time left to count was gone. To even risk the thought of one day, the thought of tomorrow and home and her was frightening and unlucky to boot. 'Too short, too short, too short.'

At first light this morning I woke up draped across a gritty rack with a bowling ball perched on my shoulders. Somehow I'd managed to crawl out of the trench and into a rack that I wasn't sure was mine but at least I was alone. I packed up all the gear I could carry, stuffed it into my two sea bags and went directly to the Major I worked for and said, "I'm getting out of here." The Major, getting ready to move north into the rubble of Hue said, "If you can get out of here, God Bless you."

Now, I was just inches away and if they gave the C-130 a window to land this afternoon, I wouldn't be short, I'd be gone and all the shitty fucking memories of this place would be left here on the ground. Or so I hoped. In the meantime, I needed an open door. I came to a stop in front of the last one the one closest to the air field. A sign on the door said 'Refrigeration – Keep Secured.' This was just the one.

I leaned into the door and it move easily. I slid it open far enough to slip into the heated darkness. As my eyes adjusted, I saw the rows of stacked metal coffins.

Jesus, it was the fucking morgue.

A little further in and the thick musky smell jerked me back toward the open door and for a minute I thought I was going to throw up. Fucking dead people smell. Man. Funny, that was the one thing I worried about before I got here. I'm going to see broken bits of body and brain and shit and I'm going to get sick and what will they think of me then. "Where's the Lieutenant?" "Oh, he's puking his gut out over in the bush." But it never happened. It was all like walking through the butcher shop at the market back home. No feeling, no nothing, and that's funny and maybe a little scary too. Dreams inside dreams. But now, I thought, Christ, why is this place so hot?

I groped along the inner wall for a light switch. When I found it I flipped it up and down several times. Nothing. No power, no lights, no refrigeration. Gooks. Happy fucking New Year. Five days of TET by the rocket's red glare and the power on this side of the base was as dead as these.

I held onto the wall to steady myself and then plunged farther into the dim filtered light. On either side of me the smooth sides of the caskets piled four high gave the passage the feel of a tunnel crafted with care.

"You guys must be in here somewhere," I whispered into the darkness. My eyes adjusted to the dark and I tried to read some of the name tags clipped onto the ends of each casket. It was no use. Night vision or not, it was still too dark.

I shook my head. Stupid. They've been home now for months. Had it really been months? It always seems so close to the surface of the pool of my memory. But I can't think about that shit now, not now, maybe later in a different dream. Right now I've got to get my young ass out of here or I'll be a floater in my own fucking pool.

I moved back past several rows counting as I walked. At number five I turned and followed down the row to its end at the wall and dumped my sea bags in the shadows and then headed back out the way I came toward the light.

"Damn."

I turned and ran back to the nested sea bags. Pushing the top one aside, I unclipped the clasp of the second reached down into the bag and pulled out the remains of a broken and bent but still wrapped cigar. Securing the bag for a second time, I jammed the cigar into my breast pocket and headed back up the aisle once more sighted in on the slim line of light reluctantly peeking through the slightly parted sliding doors. Before I stepped through the door I turned and saluted.

I'll be back.

I backed out into the mounting heat and pulled the door closed behind me. I walked the short distance down to the airstrip to check on the time of the next incoming flight that would take me to the promised land, the world. That way I knew how long crap out time would be.

"It's coming in now, Lieutenant, you get on this one or you sign up for another tour."

"Bullshit."

I looked out of the low cramped concrete building that served as the military terminal. There it was just coming clear of the mountains that separated Phu Bai from Da Nang, a small dot and growing.

I looked back toward my warehouse.

Just enough time to get my stuff.

As the plane approached the incoming sirens began to wind up again, once more sending Marines back up in office-vill scattering to the still smouldering bunkers. There were a couple Marines less in the scatter this time. I paused, looked up at the distant plane, thought a moment about the two stashed sea bags. Was there really time? I judged the distance and then continued on, running now, back to the warehouse.

I had taken only a few more steps when another cluster of rockets whispered into the compound engulfing my large warehouse in fire and swirling debris. I froze and watched as the twisted smouldering wreckage of aluminum canisters and body parts rose up in front of me like a fountain.

Holy shit, no use going back there now, they're gone.

For a moment longer I watched the black flames flick up out of the burning building. I couldn't believe it. Other than the complaint of the stubborn sheets of corrugated metal as they melted into the blast and the distant sound of sirens, it was quiet, and then I heard the approaching plane.

I turned away and headed back for the flight line a second time to join the small knot of the also departing as they emerged from the bunker built up against the terminal. There was nothing in the sea bags that I needed badly enough to miss this flight, the first step on my return to the world, by pawing through that mess.

"Jesus...,"

Behind me more ugly flame laced plumes erupted and climbed up over my shoulder. I picked up the pace with every step.

"...how necessary was that. Those poor bastards were already dead once, wasn't that enough? Christ, what shitty, fucking luck."

By the time I reached the strip, as close as it was, I was dripping with sweat. I slowed to a walk and joined the other Marines headed to Da Nang. As a single unit we edged toward the line of departure. No one talked, we just listened and watched the sky, focused on the life saving plane. We rooted it on with our eyes and sucked it down with wishes. When we reached the edge of the tarred airstrip, the clumsy aircraft had just begun its final approach. Shading my eyes with my hand from dust and sun I watched the descent with tingling anticipation. Back in the warehouse area incoming rockets continued to cook off and dance between the buildings; but now judging from the sound they began to slide slowly toward the air strip, a stealth move toward a new tempting target, a descending aircraft. But none of that mattered now I was beyond the point of no return, you can't get me now, I'm headed out.

The big C-130 touched down at the far end of the strip, and as it did the rocket barrage leapt from behind me to the strip. Goddamn it, it had been waiting to pounce the first brave pilot, my pilot, willing to make this risky landfall. In celebration of the holiday it greeted the new arrival with yet another bouquet of 122mm rockets flowering into the airstrip to its front, just off to the left and safely away from the wing. The first was followed by another and then another, a colorful lei tossed up over its nose to drape over the fuselage. We all pushed into the bunker. Unlike the first one up in the office area, this one was large enough for a squat stand and had a roof. From the darkness of the bunker, relieved, I saw the 130, its roaring four engines at full throttle, accelerate and lift up to safety out through the columns of black, flame-laced smoke.

"The TET cease fire is going rather well don't you think?"

The shadows shoved up against the damp sandbag walls behind me shifted uneasily.

No one answered.

I stepped up closer to the mouth of the bunker and watched the plane carve a wide circle high over and away from the airstrip and then, a tiny drop against the hot leaden February sky just about to evaporate in the mist; it turned and began a second approach. Again the plane touched down and again another rocket barrage greeted it with a tree line of smoke, flame, shrapnel and twisted bits of air strip. A second time the pilot throttled up and lifted the big air craft up and out of the broiling arm of fire.

Where the fuck are the counter mortar fires?

From the terminal, the PA system crackled loudly above the roar of the four straining engines.

"He's coming one more time touch and go, if you get on you get on, if you don't, well, we don't know when he'll be back, or if."

I jumped out of the bunker again and jogged back down the few steps to the edge of the airstrip along with the rest. Watching the others dragging baggage, I congratulated myself on having had my sea bags vaporized in the initial explosions. The 130 was now a dark but recognizable smudge on the horizon as it lumbered toward us for a third time growing larger and larger off the end of the strip.

"Third time's a charm."

We began to run. Those running with me left a scattered trail of sea bags and small web slung containers behind them. I watched over my shoulder as the plane grew closer descending onto the metal strip. Anticipating touchdown I angled toward the middle of the strip. Now I didn't see anything but the plane. If there were people still running next to me I was unaware of them. Every muscle strained toward the plane that seemed to accelerate as I crept closer. The roar of the aircraft crushed any other sound.

The ramp on the back of the plane lowered in a silent screech of hydraulics, and now the plane was taxing past. I ran toward the ramp as the plane began to pick up speed. It was flowing past me in a blur. Faster. Faster. I wasn't going fast enough. I ran harder. All I heard was the plane and the pounding of my boots or maybe it was my pulse that I heard beating in my ears like a drum, or maybe another shower of rockets. The air was on fire. My arms pumped higher and higher grabbing for small outcrops of air to pull me along more quickly to the plane as it closed in with increased speed. Faster. Soaked in rivulets of my sweat I lunged through the thick swirling dust toward the accelerating aircraft. Closer. The large tires streaked by and then the fat camouflaged body and now the ramp. My lungs were about to explode. I was running as hard as I could. I...was...not...going...to...make...it. And then a hand reached out to me from the darkness of the plane. I jumped for the ramp and took hold of this sinewy, outstretched, miraculous hand. My life was saved.

The still warm flesh slid gently from the charred bone in my grip. Now, other hands reached out of the darkness, burned flesh black as soot and the smell, the horrible, horrible smell, grasping at my jacket my boots shredding my jungle trousers, snatching at bits of my hair. I released the hand and felt myself falling backwards off the ramp under the cold stare of countless glittering eyes. The back of the aircraft filled with smoke and flames and the explosion rocked me loose. I was falling back, back toward the tarmac, back toward my sea bags surrounded by hundreds of broken silent aluminum boxes and bits of smouldering smiling flesh, falling, drowning in a river of my own sweat.

"Lieutenant..., Lieutenant.., it's okay. You looked like you were dreaming."

I sat up rigid gripping the arm rests and then relaxed slowly back into the soft seat and the soothing hum of the jet engines pulling me on a heading due east. I was soaked again. Was I ever going to dry out? The smiling stewardess looked down at me while I placed myself back in the present.

"It's okay, It's over now, you're headed home."

I smiled back at the stewardess, turned my head toward the darkness of the small cool window thinking of home and of her and closed my eyes.

3 DA NANG – JANUARY, 1967

Sitrep Jan071330H: I waded into the crowded Da Nang terminal and found a place to sit, to wait. Like most of the old city buildings that from the air created an impressionist pallet of pastels, this one was probably French, or at least European. It was cooling masonry construction that no doubt protected the people of the colony from the blistering swelter of tropical summer heat. It was skimmed with a faded yellow pigmented stucco coat that now carried the soot of time and neglect and flaked off in shame. My two, brand new sea bags stood where I put them on the floor in front of me, a barricade blocking out the push and noise of the large smoke filled room. Pigs ran freely through the building's part dirt, puddled floor while Vietnamese women sat next to complaining caged chickens stacked three, four, and sometimes five high adding to the cacophony and the phenomenal smell so heavy and pungent I could taste it.

The Marine liaison said it would be an hour maybe two before a plane headed south for the 13 minute ride to An Hoa. It couldn't get here soon enough. I shut my eyes and tried to close it all out, the combined high pitched hum of Vietnamese and livestock punctuated by the screech of the P.A. system calling out the arrival or departure of another Air Vietnam flight causing a swarm of arms and legs in a dusty swirl to rush first in one direction and then another, the memory of where I had been and what I had left behind, the lurking fear of what was yet to come.

'Too young for this shit.'

I smoothed at the broken down starch in my pants, trousers that's the Marine Corps way, sissies wear pants, and rubbed my neck stiff from travel. I ran my hand against the stubble of closely cropped hair on the back of my neck and across my jaw. I needed a shave. I wondered what she was doing right now, whenever now was. My inner clock was all screwed up. I closed my eyes to hide away the fear and thought back to the going away party.

He's 'D-R-U-N-K' one of the girls whispered to the one in the wheelchair as I rolled from her lap to the floor, seriously gored by the bull who stood next to me breathing heavily, his hair hanging wildly over his eyes reaching down to help me up and then both of us spinning off through the basement room kicking our feet up and snapping our fingers high up above our flushed ears and roaring heads stopping only to fill the glasses and a momentary huddle for a dirty story whispered quickly so, as not to be heard and then erupting in laughter and spinning off again until someone shouted 'A race to the pond,' and we bolted the house and ran across the yard and over the fence out through the deep grassy field toward the pond at the bottom of the gently sloping hill, and then the race back, I catching my toe on the top rail of the fence and flying headlong to my back where I lay laughing while the others ran up around me and flopped down in the grass laughing and shouting 'let them eat cake, let them eat cake.' 'too late' another called, 'for the cake is smashed, the face is shattered.' 'Alas,' I shouted, 'and he was my friend, my very, very, good friend, my very, very, very good friend, alas, alas, it grows cold here in the grass, and the women, I fear, despair for us and there are songs to be sung and laughing, much more laughing,' so we dashed back to the house, pushing and cursing and laughing still, we thundered down the stairs into the dark cellar and turned again to the punch they called it and as we poured, the laughing died off easily around me until I was the only one who laughed while the rest looked into their glasses and listened to my very good friend ask me if I was ready to kill, my very, very good friend and listening still to see the answer in my eyes and hear me say it as quietly as I could, but there are no answers tonight and it rather lies there doesn't it, and to think this is my party, motherfucker, 'MY party, MOTHERFUCKER, we go, goddamn it now, we go, my friends, I leave you here with your stinking stupid questions and the reasons

you ask them. I'll drive, goddamn it all I'm fine, I'm fine, Jesus, God, sonofabitch, it takes you all, it takes you all my friends, my very, very good friends, the devil take you, take you straight to hell, to his very hell indeed,' I shouted over the brickly road while you drove and I fell asleep in the seat next to you.

'It's not good for you,' you said in the morning, 'and I wish you wouldn't, you don't need it and I worry when I see you like that.' 'I feel badly about the girl in the wheelchair,' I said 'and my head is sore, but you don't need to worry, see how I can smile.' The smile cracked loudly in my head and I winced slightly, so that you might smile and feel sorry for me, which you did. 'But I don't understand why you do it,' you said and I looked down at the floor quietly and said nothing. 'I don't understand why you feel you must do it.' 'I can party with only a few,' I said 'but I can get drunk with anyone. The less there is to the party the better I want to feel about things inside, and besides, there was the thing about the cake too; it was my party, it was.' 'I know,' you said, 'but I still don't approve. You were funny,' you said after a pause, reaching to feel my forehead, 'and you're funnier now.' 'How did the cake taste?' I said, still looking at the floor and feeling her cool touch across my brow. 'I don't know,' you said, 'because you knocked the table and the cake slid off to the floor and had to be thrown away.' 'Too bad,' I said, 'but it was nice of Buzz to make the cake, it's a shame he couldn't be there, I might have acted differently if he had, I enjoy his company better than the rest.' 'It isn't really an excuse,' you said. 'No,' I said, 'but it was my party and other things happened, too, that seemed to make it all alright.' 'What was it?,' you said, and I said 'I'd rather not say,' but you pursued and so I told you what they had said, what they had wanted to know, as it worked out, even as we had first walked in. 'They said that?' you asked, and I said 'yes' and continued to look at the floor while we both sat there quietly listening to the pounding in my head until you said at last, 'I understand now, and I'm sorry that your head hurts.' 'I'll get over it,' I said, 'but it still hurts when I smile.' The sun had shifted while we spoke and the heat of the shaft through the window felt good on the back of my neck. 'They won't forget you anyway, you were really quite dramatic,' you said, and I, who had been thinking while you spoke said, 'they don't understand that it's easier to go than not, to be afraid of something real than something like a maybe that is hard to grasp, they don't understand it and it is a shame. I'm sorry we missed Buzz, he would have seen it all in a glance and the question would have remained unasked and we, the three of us, would have talked quietly while he poured good wine into long stem glasses. I'm glad you're not mad, but that's not right, what I mean is angry, angry is the correct word, because I'm sure in the end we're all quite mad.'

"I wish I could answer their question," I said out loud, "but right now, right this minute, I'm afraid it might be 'no.'"

Someone sat down next to me on the hard wooden bench, leaned up against my shoulder and sighed. I turned and looked into the face of an old man, probably older than anyone I had ever seen. He had a smell of dead fish. The old man smiled and nodded slightly. I stiffened and instinctively shrank away from the closeness trying to increase the distance between us. He stared momentarily and then turned away. And then the old man turned back and sighed again.

"I speak English," he said.

I looked back at him and as I did so I reached down to my sea bags and pulled them closer to my feet.

"Sir?"

"I speak English," he repeated. His voice was brittle and dry.

I nodded and met his old man milky squint with a slight smile. Attention to small detail. His long white hair was pulled straight back tightly, smoothing the skin of his forehead, and cued in a long braid that snaked down the middle of his back. His wrinkled cheeks ended on a thinly stretched chin that boasted wisps of fine spindly white hairs like proud pennants highlighted with light brown crusted streaks leading from the corners of his windswept cracked lips. His eyes folded nearly shut. The collar of his heavily patched and stained black jacket that gathered in lumps over his waist, shielded his neck and throat hiding their antique frailty. His pants, also black and puckered up around his middle drawn together with a piece of rope, ended in tatters just above his ankles.

He wore no shoes. His large feet were flat and broad with the texture of leather left too long in the rain. If someone tried to push him to the ground they would spring him quickly back to vertical like a child's blow up clown.

A dead starkly veined leaf blown weightless and flat and brittle but of the same dark brown color as dirt with the smell of one that had rested in brown, pooled, walked in water mixed with the bouquet of mid-decay fish. A leaf that had been dead for more seasons than it had been alive.

It was several moments before he spoke again.

"You are new to this country."

I nodded and turned to lose my face in the folds of the roaming terminal crowd. The old man continued.

"I have lived here for many years."

"Difficult to do in this place I would imagine, stay alive that is."

Now I was trapped, stuck ankle deep in a conversation I really didn't want to have. When I turned back he was speaking again. His lips were not only cracked but thin, thread-like, and slightly parted. What remained of his teeth were stained a deep brown red and appeared to be the headwaters of the small brown rivulets slipping over his chin.

"My name is Ông Già Dòng Sông."

For the next several minutes the old man said nothing. He pulled a small round quid from his pocket, popped it into his mouth and closed his eyes as he began to chew.

He leaned back tipping his face toward the high open ceiling from which single light bulbs dangled precariously on slender long electrical wires like aerial artists, and let the warmth of the chew spread through his body. Most of the bulbs had long since given up. He opened his eyes and turned to me. Now he began to speak again and as he spoke the timber of his voice billowed in the breeze of the terminal moving his words ahead in a swollen torrent, as if

25

driven by a storm. I was not expected to join in conversation but rather to serve as an audience.

The old man said:

"My ancestors were children of the dragon and lived always in the waters of the South even as we do today. We draw our soul from its quiet ripple our strength from the roar of the swollen river. We share our lives with the life of the river and the stream and the paddy. We learn from the placid flow of the great rivers cutting up and dividing the land. We live in harmony with its depth and raise families in the moist warm eddies. From the water we take peace. But it is from the water too that we have fought many wars and we have won many victories. During the ancient times, the fertile daughters of my father the dragon rose from the rivers rushing down from the mountains in torrents to the still paddies below to drive our invaders north and into the dripping jungles where they perished and sank from sight. And when the fighting was done, the daughters returned to the water to live quietly spreading the seed of the dragon through the springs and streams and they became one with the land and the sea. Our people grew, flowing over the dams and dikes as a giant river. And always they came from the water. As others came to invade, again the water overwhelmed them pulling them down, seeping deep into the weave of their skin until they vanished beneath the surface of the still paddies to decay and feed the slender young rice shoots that in turn fed our people. And our people, generations of people, children of the dragon, grew strong. Again and again our enemies came and each time they were driven away. And when they were gone, the people once more returned to the ways of the paddies and the rivers and the sea. They remain there today knee deep and tied to the banks, pulling fish in their nets, cutting the slender rice with hand wrought hooked knives, living their lives, waiting. The water. To the children of the dragon it is life; to all the rest it runs deep into their spirits, and their spirits drip into the hard earth to drown; and they never forget."

"Lieutenant, your plane is just coming in, grab your gear and head out to the flight line."

I jumped and looked up to the voice trying to focus on where the liaison officer was pointing. I grabbed and slung my sea bags quickly and started for the large garage-like door of the terminal that emptied out onto the flight line. I was anxious for the smell of fresh air and the quiet of outside. As an afterthought I turned to nod to the old man but he was gone.

I scanned the terminal, shrugged, and pulled the collar of my field jacket against the rain that now fell in sheets and headed for the flight line.

It was going to be a long 13 months.

4 AN HOA – JANUARY, 1967

SitRep Jan071945H: There were 14 others living intermittently in the long house that they, the ones living there, called the hooch, and later the "Q" and still later, "Number Nine;" a tribute to the number of Marine officers that had walked in only to be carried away moments later in crates and boxes of small meaningless trinkets.

Of the 14 only four were there on the night I arrived. The others were at war somewhere out in the bush.

I stood awkwardly in the middle of the room. The men there sat quietly with their thoughts on the boxes and on cots littered around the walls. The Personnel Officer, acting on behalf our friends and neighbors, had placed them there earlier. Felt board cutouts anchored in place casting shadows on the wall.

The Personnel Officer introduced me.

A week ago I felt lonely and isolated as my departure date drew nearer and I climbed into myself alone with my thoughts, distant even from her. But now, to find others here comfortably ahead of me I was mildly surprised. I felt tricked somehow, and as I looked from one disinterested face to another I was mildly irritated that they had wasted my time on Okinawa with talk of tropical snakes. This is what I should have been told, that although when I began I would be beginning alone, I wouldn't be the only one here. And if not that then at least it was time I should have spent with her.

I took several more steps into the room and dropped my dripping sea bags in front of me.

Moments before, the men that lived here sat and hid and waited and while they waited they listened to the rain drive harshly into the tin on the roof and they watched absently toward the door hoping for it to open on something new, a face, the mail, the command to saddle up and move out, anything. They waited for me. They watched the door and they waited and they read and reread the sign posted just above it. "Fuck Communism" it said, "Fuck Communism" in red, white, and blue.

Tonight finally, their vigil bore fruit. The door opened and for a brief moment they lowered their gaze from the sign. They looked to the door as it opened on me and the body count went to fifteen and then they looked away without interest.

From the darkened far end of the hooch tall slender Captain Delpert emerged, his hand extended. Next to him a young German Shepherd came forward with caution, sniffing, straining for a recognizable smell.

The water poured into the mud from the eaves. I glanced nervously around the cramped room; attention to small detail. The roof reached down to the soggy earth masking the two-foot ribbon of screened window that ran along both sides of the building and made it impossible for a standing man to see out. Below the screen, there was a narrow band of plywood that gave the building shape and from the outside looked like an artist's pallet of rain-splashed mud. It was a solid block pasted against the darkness that dissolved into the mist for safety. A door at each end held shut by pieces of inner tube struggled to hold the darkness and the rain outside at bay. When it rained, as it was now, the tin amplified the impact making it sound larger than it was and it made the room sound empty even when we were all there, me hiding behind my sea bags, and them hiding behind cracked ponchos and scraps of canvas pilfered from the Seabees. The tattered pitiful shelter halves that hung over the tropical screening that served as windows were unable to deter the penetration of the wind driven mid-January cold that rode in on the constant sheets of filtered mist and rain. How the hell did they stay warm? Even when they huddled together they must have been cold. There was no electricity, no plumbing, no heat.

Dirt complained under my nervous shifting feet. It had infiltrated as mud concealed in their deep cleated jungle boots and clotted on the stained plywood floor as they walked where it dried and was then ground to fine dust in their restless traffic. It accumulated in brown gritty trails that ended at the different racks in the night, obscured in the feeble light of their small sputtering sentinels, candles, each privately owned and each sitting carefully fixed in its own waste guarding the detail of the clutter of cots, blankets and military equipment, web gear, that filled the small room, C-rations cases, and overpowered it giving the whole place the look of soggy sand paper. In the fluttering light the cots revealed their lost comfort, gone with the missing cross braces required to make them taught.

The place smelled. It was an agonized brew of wet wool blankets, stale tobacco both spat and smoked, and spent and scorched tallow. Over the clutter and the dirt and the smell a comfortable damp established itself as a welcome long term guest. A co-conspirator that joined with the rest as soft rot folded into the tapestry of their days. Together they invaded clothing while it hung on nails beaten into the two-by-fours that supported the roof, with the butt ends of .45's and K-bars. They assaulted mine while it hung from my shoulders. They joined with the daily endless sweat and burrowed into the weave of the jungle fabric, the open sores, and gave a delicate warmth and sweetness to the medley of misery. It was the quiet misery of decay. Attempts to dry would surely fail until the end of March. The moist memories would linger far beyond. I thought of the old man.

SitRep Jan072130H: I sat on my new rack. A few minutes ago it belonged to someone else but it was mine now because the person it belonged to wouldn't be back tonight. He wouldn't ever be back. He was dead. So now we all sat there quietly with our thoughts in boxes and bags and on cots clinging to the walls. The rain increased and settled in. I shuffled through my belongings with no particular goal in mind. The Personnel Officer was gone and now with the introductions complete no one seemed inclined to conversation. Captain Delpert, the Company Commander had gone back to sleep after shaking hands and of the others, two wrote while the third in the rack next to mine sat quietly gazing into the flames of his candle. I focused on the beat of the rain. It was a universal sound, a familiar hook that lifted me out of the building and helped me begin to settle in.

I am the gentle Adirondack rain that falls through a hole in the explosive July sky wrapping folded tired valleys in stillness and gray and the sound is that of I splashing into the tense quiet of a lake.

I am the harsh mountain rain that beats through the leaden shield of the gray October sky snatching remnant bits of color once green and alive and the sound is that of life beaten into the depths of a lake run dry.

I shifted in the sandpaper-gritty canvas of my new rack and now for the first time I noticed the sign over the door, 'hatch' I corrected myself, it was no longer a door. "Fuck Communism." At first glance it was a quiet announcement that, other than the obvious meaning of the two words, seemed to convey the thought that nothing else needed to be said. But on second thought, was it what I am here to do here or was it just a statement, an angry sentiment that because of it I am here in the first place. I leaned back against my sea bag and fished for a cigarette. A Marlboro. God, how I loved Marlboros. I hadn't had one since I stepped off the plane in Da Nang and now I was ready. A pack-and-a-half left, and then what. I had to go slowly and make each one a memory. I didn't even know if they had Marlboros here. I lit up and blew the smoke up toward the sign. Fuck Communism, in red, white and blue.

The flame-gazer next to me was First Lieutenant Wellington Wick of Atlanta, the Company XO. He wore only skives but seemed not to notice the chill. My blanket, because there had been none in the mound of abandoned gear called Battalion Supply, came from the rack directly across from mine. It belonged, I was told, to Second Lieutenant Horton Sills, the Company Artillery Forward Observer. But 'Horey' wouldn't give a shit it was explained because he was probably down at the battery drinking beer and would either spend the night there or come back half fall-down drunk. In either case he wouldn't miss his blanket for several days. Second Lieutenants Harry Bings from somewhere in West Virginia and Frankie "Boots" Boogatti recently from Chicago nodded in agreement and then returned to their noiseless pre-sleep rituals. Boots turned on a small battery operated radio and fanned through the numbers on the knob looking for Armed Forces Radio. Lulu singing "To Sir With Love" suddenly filled the small space.

"Ah, shit."

"Jesus Christ, turn that fucking thing off."

"Can you get the Beatles?" I asked.

"The Beatles!" Boots looked across at me with radiant distain, "Why the hell would I want to hear the Beatles?"

"I fell in love to the Beatles."

"Holy shit, you just got here and you're fucked up already.

"This isn't love, this is war. We go to war with the Stones."

"No bugs, no rocks, I'll take Brenda Lee." Lieutenant Bings joined the conversation without looking up from the pile of mail in his lap.

"Brenda Lee, you're as crazy as he is, but you got one thing right you goofy old bastard."

"What's that?"

"Brenda Lee sure don't give no satisfaction and she sure as hell ain't got no stones."

There was an uneasy hummm from Captain Delpert's darkened corner.

Boots smiled at Bings, turned off the radio and blew out his candle.

"No fucking thing to listen to anyway."

Soon, both were under their blankets and asleep while the smoke from their extinguished candles swirled around them in the breeze blowing in through the partially covered screening. In the darkened corner, away from his Lieutenants, Captain Delpert returned to his easy stammerless sleep with little sign of his earlier wheeze. Polo, his dog, slept fitfully under his cot. Now, Wick, sitting on his gear box leaned back against the wall. At his flip-flopped feet was a half-gone case of San Miguel Beer. It was warm, the warmest thing here, and although it was made somewhere in the Philippines it had a tolerable taste especially here, and especially now.

"Crazy bastards...,beer?"

"Thanks." I reached for the can.

"Because there ain't no '0' Club here, we get to buy this shit beer by the case out the back door of the snuffies club." Wick said. "Asshole beer and warm on that, but I guess that don't make it no less beer."

"No, I guess not."

Wick remained silent while he watched me fumble my beer open with the C-ration can opener he had tossed to me. I watched him open one quickly and easily making two opposite incisions in the can's top and then prying one of them open with the flat end of the small opener. Although it had looked easy, experience now told me it was a practiced art.

Wick spit on the floor and produced the nub of a cigar from somewhere under his rack. He lighted it in his candle and leaned back again spinning it slowly. He began to speak around it, softly, his drawl crackling and dry as though the smoke from his cigar has started his tongue smouldering and his mouth might soon burst into flame. He was lean and muscular and although he was short, his leanness made him appear to be taller than he really was. His hair was long by boot camp standards but by any other, short, clipped clean well above the ears. His head was nearly marble round and his face made of clay; sunken cheeks pinched in below a straight narrow nose and serving as pediments to lazy but alert blazing eyes.

"This here's a bad-ass place," he said. "Yeah, a bad-ass place. Tocsan gooks out there. We stepped in the shit Christmas Eve. Jesus, got hell shot out of us on Christmas Eve. Most everybody in the damn Company got hit.

"We was in the south first down by Chu Lai, it was all right there but we been here two months now and I been hit twice already. That there was the last one. Shrapnel. Christmas Eve. Boots didn't even get here till the next week. So far all he's done is get lost in the fucking dark in the next ville over trying to set up a midnight ambush."

He looked back from the easily heaving mound of Boots and pointed to a Band-Aid mid-way up his muscular thigh and watched me carefully. I nodded and sucked at my beer. Wick spun the cigar around again and turned his attention to the blue smoke that rolled out of his mouth and as it rolled, he followed it, watched it flow into the yellow flicker of the candle and then break. He drew another deep breath of smoke and sent a perfect ring out across the hooch. All the while his fingers worked absently over the Band-Aid on his leg and for the moment he remained silent. Delpert moaned in his sleep again. Polo sat up, looked for a moment into Delpert's tranquil face, stood, stretched in a bow toward the cot, circled in place several times and lay back down. Wick paused gazing into the darkened corner, shook his head and then turned back to continue. But before he could speak...

I jumped and spilled my beer as the thunderous echo of the report drifted away and into the hills that surrounded the An Hoa basin.

"Jesus...!"

"Artillery, H&I's," he said quietly. "They fire them all night to harass and interdict the gooks so they can't get any sleep. Must be about 2200. That's when they usually start. Been a long time since I been interdicted but I'm harassed most of the time."

He smiled just slightly at his joke and watched to see if I'd gotten it and then he handed me another beer.

"Yeah, tacson gooks out there all right," he said at last returning to a quiet study of his smoke. "And you know those bastards we replaced here didn't say shit about nothing. Jesus. But I'm getting short so fuck it."

Another round raced across the camp.

"We don't get much fucking sleep either."

SitRep Jan072347H: The H&I's continued into the night and while the others slept undisturbed, I laid awake harassed and interdicted waiting for the next mission to fire.

SitRep Jan080300H: At three a.m. I had to take a leak. I wandered around in the dark for a few minutes trying to find the piss tube without luck and finally pissed on the ground, the deck, outside the hooch. It was cold and I could feel mud oozing in around my half-laced boots. The breeze that blew through the night off the river that flowed past to the north of the camp, stiffened to a pre-dawn wind that riveted the fine mist that the rain had now become into my bare arms sending shivers and goose flesh to my shoulders. Back inside, my rack continued its grinding complaint roughing up my skin when I moved; sleep in the cold, for which I had also been unprepared, was completely impossible. Now, piss free in the haze of half-sleep I gave up and tried to put order to the events of the past several hours since my arrival at Battalion at An Hoa.

A darkness in motion who I assumed was Horey came in and dropped to the rack across from mine.

"Cold, fucking cold," he said, and then he was quiet.

Dear Pumpkin,

Will they care in the morning that I pissed on the ground here? I suppose lots of them can't find the piss tube in the night and I suppose even if you find it it's hard to hit a half buried artillery casing in the dark and most of what you got to do goes on the ground anyway. Funny I found it easy enough earlier when we walked over to this place, the hooch, me and the Personnel Officer. He stepped around it and I got it right in the shins. Jesus. 'Piss tube,' he said and then he threw open the do.., the hatch to the hooch, the hooch hatch, and I was in the middle of the room holding hands with the C.O. Captain Delpert and all the rest were watching me like some audience that was waiting awhile for the show to begin and all I could think about was how much my damn shin hurt and how come the Personnel Officer didn't tell me it was there. Then I began to take a closer look at this Delpert and I wondered does he always curl his lip back over his gums when he smiles like in his sleep and does the pause in his speech always hide behind guttural things in his throat that escape in ahems and stammers and was it easy to be so damn tall. Wick, the XO talked about the CO's dog. He said he's got a dog and he said it like there was not much else to say about Delpert. He said Delpert's got this goddamn dog from the MPs because that's what he use to be and probably that's what he should be still. A goddamn MP. He said the goddamn dog's a pain in the ass. He talked about it after Delpert was asleep. Still Delpert seemed like a friendly guy. He named his dog Polo and while we talked I was sniffed from every direction. Finally he curled up under Delpert's rack. Other than Wick they don't talk much here but when they do it's to say how much they like the Stones and Brenda Lee. Christ. Most of what Wick said came from behind the glow of a cigar. The Colonel I met this afternoon when I first got here he could talk. Colonel Teapot, the Battalion Commander talked and talked and talked. He had silver leaves on his collar but his attention kept drifting to the eagles in the little plastic box on the corner of his desk. Watching him eyeing them was most all I could think about while he was talking. He was all eyes. They were alive moving out of his body flitting back and forth between me and the birds. Made me think that maybe they should get a room. The others are all eyes too; faintly here, faintly there and faintly somewhere else. When the plane that brought us here touched down late this afternoon it hit the rain soaked tar of the airstrip and fishtailed just like a car on a wet highway. The Captain sitting across from me in the plane had some eyes. They got big and jumped out of the seat ahead of him and were sitting again before he could get to his feet. And then there were the eyes that greeted the mud I splashed on them when I stepped down from the plane; Harry and Boots, the music experts, left their eyes outside tonight and Wick's eyes are hard to see. Delpert's eyes, I guess they're nestled in next to the dog and Teapot's are full of stars. I wonder about my eyes and if I'll be able to see them when they're closed. I would rather have known about that, not the snakes that they talked about in staging. I noticed that everybody here has a rubber mattress but me. I hope I can take care of that in the morning. Jesus its cold here and the mud could swallow you and time seems all messed up. So far though war's not bad although I still worry about seeing somebody's insides outside and Boots got lost. It's easy loving someone orange. And, oh, remind me to tell you about this old man.

Sam

I got up again to see what was scratching on the door. I pushed it open a crack and Delpert's German Sheppard bounced into the middle of the hooch.

"When did you get out?"

He sniffed at me again, shook violently leaving a fresh layer of water soaking into my front and trotted off wagging his tail, to the corner where Delpert continued in undisturbed sleep.

"Son-of-a-bitch."

Wick was right. The goddamn dog.

SitRep Jan080645H: In the morning Wick and I walked the several hundred sloping sloppy yards to the Company area. The dog raced down the hill ahead of us to the Company hooch turned and ran back jumping up on Wick and embracing him with large mud laden paws. Wick kicked at the dog but missed and the dog raced off again and made the turn for a second strafing.

"Fucking dog."

Wick grabbed a stick and threw it over the dogs head. The dog stopped and raced off in pursuit. Wick scraped the mud from his field jacket.

"Fucking dog," he said again.

As we approached the Company area, I could just make out the sign 'Fightin' Echo' nailed over the hatch of the Company hooch. The whole area was masked in a thick black smoke that blew from several oil drum halves midway down the slope. The drums appeared to be guarded by two shirtless men who infrequently prodded at the stout chewy flames with long blackened sticks. From a distance the sticks looked like extensions emerging from their arms in place of hands. With every stirring, the reluctant smoke belched from the sizzling fire and flames, danced and licked the length of their bare arms.

"They're burning the shitters," Wick said, and he spoke their names as we approached spitting them into the ground as though they left a taste born in the bubbling mess they tended. "Trent and Stepps. The black one, Trent, calls himself 'Lonely.' You'll see why in a minute."

I nodded but said nothing. They were dirty and thin and the black smoke smudged on their faces and arms. That that missed them snapped into the air and breathed for what was up close a sunday-bacon gurgle in the fires. It was substance. It had not only smell but taste as well.

"So, you're our new Lieutenant, huh?"

Lonely pulled the stick out of the smouldering mass, leaned his folded dark skinny arms across its top and studied me from the ground up.

"Welcome to the Nam. Man, I forgot things could be that green. You better get rid a' those nice shiny leathers or you'll be walkin' in flip flop soles in a week. I thought they just treated us draftees that way." He nudged his partner and laughed. The other grinned and rocked back nearly falling from the force of Lonely's poke. Lonely grabbed him by the shoulder, still laughing and rubbed him on the top of his spiky bald head. The grin vanished and Stepps pulled away pushing at Lonely's hand and again nearly tipped over.

"No shit man," is all he said.

Wick scowled at Lonely.

"Oh yeah..., Sir."

Lonely's laugh resigned itself to a smile but it continued to dance in his eyes like hot rivets against his soot smeared coffee completion.

"Pvt Stepps and laughing boy, Pvt Trent," Wick said once again spitting the words into the mud.

"Lonely…" Trent said pushing his stick back into the bubbling can. "You can call me Lonely, stirring up the shit again cause stirring up the shit is what I can do real good… Sir."

"Shitbirds," Wick said as we passed between them. "But they're all yours." He paused. "And like Lonely says, now you're all theirs."

Soon there were more, some alone cleaning weapons, others congregated in small groups talking and laughing and smoking cigarettes and playing cards. Like the two stirring at the burning drums they were skinny. Their loose fitting jungle utilities amplified the lean hard thinness of their necks and faces and arms. Somewhere from one of the hooches "Let's Live For Today" played on the radio.

As we passed through them, I met them. In twos and threes, Wick called out their names. "Good man," he said, or he said nothing. At one point he said "Fifty-five bodies, that's what you got, fifty-five bodies."

Just bodies; scrawny, hard, cruddy, mumbling, I met them. They saluted wearily, looked at me from behind long hair by Marine Corps standards, watched me quizzically, mumbled their names and their rank, told me what they did as they had told others before me, followed me with their eyes when I moved on and then faded into the background of the smoke filled muddy slope. Another, and the same, and finally I had met them all. Fifty-five bodies tagged with fifty-five names, more or less, that I had already forgotten. I wondered about the few that had said little but greeted me only with a lingering smile.

"These three commin' up are your squad leaders: Balen the young one with the big strong lookin' bent over shoulders on the left, Rico the stubby brown Mexican, and Wescott the older lookin' guy with the big smile that looks like he just snuck a cookie and you ain't gonna get any. All three of 'um were with us on Christmas. They did alright but they was lucky, didn't one of 'um pick up a heart. Right now that tall one over there leaning up against the hooch who looks like he's asleep, he's your platoon sergeant. But he might's well not be, he's leaving in two days which means you don't really have one. So don't expect too much from him. He's shorter'n me."

While Wick spoke his eyes wondered off to the horizon beyond the airstrip. The pauses between sentences grew longer and each sentence was spoken more quietly than the one before it.

We walked to the perimeter wire past the Company hooch and across the air strip. We stood next to one of the sandbag bunkers where two Marines dozed on the roof while a third was propped up over a machine gun in the aperture looking out across the wire. In each direction from where we stood muddy shreds of a well beaten dirt trail linked the bunkers into a lethal necklace around the throat of the camp. Triple concertina barbed wire bounced out in front of the thin line of defense. Tangle foot wire laced into a twelve foot woven spread lay in front of the concertina and before that low lines of comwire hung with brown C-ration cans filled with stones and signs warning of mines, completed the array. The bunker beside us was worn. Tears in the bags released slender streams of sand and the bags began to sag.

"We man these bunkers on the line when we're back in out of the field."

He walked to the nearest and leaned on it looking out across a small field to the refugee village. I came up beside him. The dozing Marines stirred, mumbled brief military curteousies and returned to slumber. In the distance across the small field the yellow masonry building that served as the district headquarters looked out of place, surrounded by the small thatched huts that made up the adjoining village. But it was the field that startled.

"Amazing. I don't believe it in the middle of all this, a small field covered with a blanket of beautiful tiny, white flowers."

Wick looked down at me for a moment and then said, "Come on. "

Later, following a silent trek from the wire, we got back to the Company hooch. We were greeted by the tail-wagging Polo. In its excitement and to the amusement of the nearby Marines, Polo mounted Wick's leg.

"Get the FUCK away from me. I'm gonna shoot that fucking dog."

5 NONG SON – JANUARY, 1967

SitRep Jan090500H: Just before dawn of the following day, Company E moved out. Echo Company, composed of 183 bodies; 183 little echoes rattling in quiet harmony between the hooches of the still sleeping camp, shucking in the mud past antenna guy wires and piss tubes, pulling at shoulder straps from which hung backpacks and web gear belts festooned with canteens and grenades and magazines full of ammo, heaving shoulders forward under flak jackets draped with bandoleers, straining from side-to-side in their cocked unbuckled helmets, moved out. Shifting for touches of private cherished things, records, radios, battery operated phonos, photographs and recent letters from home, 183 easy echoes spoke the password and passed out through the barbed-wire display and the mine field beyond that circled the camp. Once through the wire, we struck south on a road that ran through a steep pass and then bent to the flow of the river that it followed on its way to the mountains forming the Laotian border. In the darkness, the rutted wet clay road proved difficult, and me in my shining, new jungle utilities but as yet without jungle boots, I found that I was frequently about to fall. It was a seven-mile hump to the mine.

"It's a someday mine" Wick said at last night's meeting. "They say that someday it'll produce coal and that someday that coal'll turn turbines in what will someday be an industrial complex at An Hoa and that the turbines will someday produce electricity and that someday this shit-hole of a country will be civilized with lights and cold beer and have industry and that someday there'll be somebody here that gives a shit, although I doubt it. Right now as a nowadays mine, it ain't much. What comes out in a year could fit in a spoon. So while we wander around and get shot at, the gooks get to work in an empty someday mine in safety."

Delpert stood quietly at the map listening to Wick and while he listened he scratched the dog's head and when Wick finished, he gave the order of march. He called the dog Polo, and left.

The Third Platoon under Harry's command had the point in the line of march. I had the First Platoon. We followed safely in the second position and Boots with his Second Platoon brought up the rear. Captain Delpert walked at the head of the column with his radio operators. Wick walked at the very end of the column with the Gunny and listened in silence as his radio operator responded to the frequent sit rep requests from Delpert, the Six Actual.

Harry fell back through the ranks to the rear of his platoon and joined me where I struggled at the head of mine.

"You'll like Nong Son," he said. "It's quiet there and right on the river."

I staggered with the weight of my gear and the unsureness of foot while Harry walked and talked easily beside me. He was slight and older than everybody else in the Company except the First Sergeant and maybe the Gunny. He spent most of his youth and all of his adult life in the Corps coming in three years after Korea to escape a life in the mines just outside of Moundsville and he intended never to go back. Now he was Lieutenant Harry Bings who reached his commission up through the enlisted ranks. Now he was an officer and all the smart-ass shitty remarks about hillbillies and West Virginia could go to hell. "Maybe," he said, "I will finally go home after all and walk right down the middle of Main Street because now I am sure that none of the coal dust that fills the air will stick." Now he had status. Because of it he was hard on the troops. Later I learned they called him Lieutenant Asshole.

"The engineers there speak English that they learned in France where they went to school," Harry continued. "And their wives give parties. It's nice."

SitRep Jan090736: Harry looked up the column. "You fucking dirt bag Marines better spread out or you'll get a boot up your ass." Slowly the interval increased.

He turned and smiled at me.

"That's all it takes," he said and then he moved back up through the gauntlet of a column of twos staggered and resumed his position at the head of the Company just behind Delpert's command group.

Echo moved slowly on the road where it pinched in between the river on the west and the mountains that swept up to the east. Polo ran sideways and forward in the mud ahead of the Company, or she ran back through the column smiling from face-to-face with her tongue searching for recognition and an opportunity to wag and jump. Few spoke to her. She ran to the end of the column and tried once again to jump up on Wick's leg.

"The Skipper's dog has got a sweet thought for you, Lieutenant."

"She's gonna have a sweet fucking hole through her head if she doesn't stay off my fucking leg Gunny."

When Captain Delpert could no longer see her from his place at the head of the march and decided that she had been gone from view long enough he slowed the march and called. She raced to his side, bumped her head against his leg and walked there for several minutes before running on ahead for several yards and then turning, bolting through the sweating Marines to the end of the Company to jump up on Wick and the Gunny. This time it was the Gunny's leg that Polo approached.

"What is wrong with this queer bitch," he said kicking her loose.

"Two-timing bitch," Wick said smiling at the Gunny's discomfort. "Maybe you got the 'fucking leg' this time Gunny."

During the time when he knew where she was, Captain Delpert chatted slowly over the radio with Wick at the end of the Company. Wick answered in single syllables and walked beside the Gunny, Gunnery Sergeant Elgin Pickwick, Gunny Pick, from Aroostook, Maine. Together they watched the rise and fall of the mountains and quietly cursed at the muddy pawed Polo.

"Somebody ought to shoot that fucking dog," The Gunny said without emotion. "The son-of-a-bitch would feed a village for a fucking year."

The gray dawn broke off 15 years of whitewalls. Daily shaving had whetted the Gunny's sharp Yankee features and honed the thin bridge of his nose and the drop of his cheeks until they gleamed like the glossy edge of a nearly new hatchet. When he spoke, his voice was soft and lispy but his accent and the meanings of the things he said were rough and hard edged as well, and when he walked, he carried his right hand jammed deep into his hip pocket. This was his second war and because of that he wore the trappings of conflict, - his .45, his flak jacket, his helmet - with ease. If there was one thing he had learned it was never look at your feet when you move in the combat zone. As they moved past a gaping valley entrance he paused for a moment and then moved on.

SitRep Jan090752: The sun, still hidden from view by the thick veil of clouds, cleared the mountains and filled the river valley with dull light and heat.

Two miles out and Echo reached what was left of the first of two bridges to be crossed on the way south to the mine. Polo sat at its edge, panting. Only the rusting skeletal steel I-beams that once held the planking of the bridge remained spanning the sullen non-reflective murk that wound on into the river. All the rest had been blown away by explosions of unknown origin. Movement stopped. Silently, Echo tried to dissolve into the sparse growth on either side of the road. Set in facing outboard and kneeling, they waited. Polo whined. The sound of her complaint carried down through the valley seeking out the restless members of the Company. She refused the beams.

"Come!" Delpert said.

Polo sat and looked away out toward the river panting, her tongue lolling out over her sharp canines.

Other than the light vegetation, the area where we waited was uncomfortably open to the steep lift of the mountains on both sides of the river. And from the thick vegetation that fringed the river's far shore a round could travel across the sullen flow unimpeded into our midst causing one echo to slump and drift away while the others went to ground at the report a moment too late.

"Come!" Delpert said again. Polo continued to look away and whine. All else was still. Again, Polo refused.

Now Captain Delpert smiled and the pink of his gums flashed in the humid tropic clutch. He stooped, cradled the dog in his arms and crossed the beams.

The Company reformed, resumed the road and moved. Wick had chewed through the end of his dead cigar while he kept a close watch on the far bank. Now he spit it into the ground. Gunny Pick stood stretched and moved up beside him. His eyes had not left the mountains. I stood and moved with the rest, moved to the beams and crossed.

"One shot," the Gunny said, "right between the fucking eyes."

"I thought you liked that dog, Gunny," Wick said.

"Just when it's on your leg, Lieutenant, just when it's on your leg."

Once across, I stood with my radio operator Corporal English, and waited until the last of my platoon was across. Nodding to Boots on the far side, I turned and with English hurried; sliding through the slurry in my smooth soled stateside boots, back to my position at the head of my people, my bodies, my little echoes, my steamy sweaty scrawny hot little echoing bodies.

Breathing heavily, I looked over at English who in spite of his size and the weight of the radio seemed unaffected by our trot through the muddy trace of the road.

We continued. Soon the second bridge was crossed without incident. I lowered my eyes. We had stopped and now stood loosely coiled at the edge of the river looking across to the far shore. Minutes earlier, we passed through the small village that was now directly to our rear. In my memory I heard its vague clatter, smelled it, but concentrating my attention to the high ground and sore feet, I had seen little of the movement beside me. Now tracing back along the path we had just covered I looked more closely at the rotting thatched huts, trying to place the sounds and smells with their source. Children from the ville mingled with us as we passed through and now they teased for cigarettes. As with the village, I had missed their initial assault but now fully aware of their presence, I moved among them as if they were shadows. I looked, instead, steadily across the river. And while I watched, small plumes of dialog erupted between my scattered troops and the braver of the children.

"Hey Marine, you got one cigarette?"

"Hey, you want my sister? Number one first class boom-boom – you give me ten cigarettes."

"Hey, you take her right here in bushes."

"Five cigarette you have number one blow job with pretty face girl."

"You show me, you little shit," Lonely shouted.

"She my sister, she number one boom-boom right now. You give me three cigarettes I show you."

Lonely walked up into the small knot of the short hustlers scattering the more timid ahead of him but who soon closed in behind in his wake.

"Bullshit, your sister's VC. VC number 10. You give me sister and five cigarettes."

"Naaw, sister no VC. VC number 10. Sister number one top boom-boom, give number one blow job you see."

"You VC, you little shit."

"Hey, me no VC, no, no. Sister no VC, sister number one. She love Marines. Only take seven cigarettes."

"No way, you little bastard. I'll give you two cigarettes for your mamasan and your sister."

"No way, Marine, you number 10, fuck you Marine."

Lonely laughed and pushed the tallest away with the butt of his rifle.

"Hey, Marine, Fuck, you number 10"

'In red, white, and blue.' I turned and looked back across the silent river. Golf Company mirrored us on the opposite shore, milling around, waiting to cross and start the trek back to An Hoa. Behind me I could hear Gunny Pick.

"All right, all right you girls get away from these goddamn kids and get set up in a column of twos and get the fuck off to the side of the goddamn road. This is a fucking war, not a whore-house. Lonely, I said get your sorry black ass away from those goddamn kids. This is fucking Echo Company, not like that Chinese cluster fuck across the river. Goddamn it, you girls better get your ass squared away or you won't be a part of my goddamn Company."

Gunny Pick walked back up toward the village from the shore.

"All right, I'm tellin' you girls, knock this shit off, don't be fucking around with these little shits." He took a menacing step toward the small knot of children. "Get the fuck out of here you little bastards." He reached down to his .45 and the knot quickly dissolved into the safety of the shadowy hooches in a cascade of shouts and squeals.

"Marine number 10 fuck."

"You no good, you no Marine."

"You number 10 dogface GI."

A shallow draft barge moored on the far bank grumbled, then fired and waited as the first elements of Golf Company filed in. When it was full to the point that one more might sink it, it started across. The sucking of its engine spit out black smoke and evaporated the noise of the children still clamoring within our ranks and from the shadows and made it easier to ignore them.

"And another thing," the Gunny's voice sliced through the noise. "When those gomers from Golf get here, this ain't no goddamn reunion. You let 'um pass through to buy some boom-boom or any other damn thing, but you girls keep your eyes outboard and on the high ground until I tell you to get in the goddamn boat."

The barge was slow and before it was half way across, its wake had rippled smooth on the far shore. I watched it lap weakly and then die. As the barge approached I wandered my gaze up the far beach past the clusters of waiting Marines and across the small flat area that led to a splatter of colorful masonry patches like those in Da Nang, that broken by the dapple of veiled half light and vegetation, were barely distinguishable as buildings. No more than three or four, as far as I could tell, they were pulled back into the cover of a ridge that sprung from the river two hands to the right of the beachhead and ran steadily up for what looked like a mile or more to a brown scraped slash in the deep green growth. From there it angled sharply and jumped to the summit over the spotted treeless ground that made up the several hundred meters of the remaining slope.

"That's it."

I turned and looked into Harry's deeply sunken cheek.

"The mine," he said, pointing to the ridge I had been studying. "It lies in around behind that nose in a draw, there."

He moved his finger along the ridge.

"That's a position on the top and there's another one part way down that you can't see from here. It's by that brown slash there. Then there's another one just up behind those houses there back in the trees. The trail that connects them all runs right along the top of the ridge line, there."

The barge returned for its second trip, lowered its ramp and emptied another segment of Golf Marines who quickly engaged the scrambling children, and waited as Harry followed by me at the head of my platoon stepped in. The helmsman singled us out from the others easily, bowed slightly and lifted a dirty, yellow cloth rain hat with a delicate spider-like hand. I nodded slightly, and Harry, who now leaned his pack against the bottom of the closed ramp, bit out a chunk from his damp plug of tobacco dug from one of the deep thigh pockets of his jungle utilities. He peeled back the cellophane banana-style and attacked the plug like a hungry man. I declined Harry's drizzled offer and noticed how the mountains in this part of the country seemed to squeeze the sky.

It cooled when we moved out onto the river and into the shadow of the mountain and the huff of the engine made me feel sleepy. Condensation, starting midway down the metal sides of the hull, marked the waterline and made it appear that the barge because of use and antiquity was unable to hold back the endless flow of the river which now seemed to ooze through the porous metal. For a moment I thought of the old man again and wondered what life moved under us in the placid river as it continued south and disappeared into the increasingly rugged mountains. Like the river, the thought passed. With it, the notion that the river pulled me toward it with long, thin, sinewy fingers, ebbed slowly away. I shifted my weight around to get better footing in the crowded barge and brushed hard up against the bulkhead driving the condensed moisture deeply into my trousers and sending small streams of water running down my leg.

Behind us, shadows moved from the valley onto the road that passed south. Watching for a moment, they studied the deep tracks of the Company's passing, noted that there has been a dog, and then moved back into the wet folds of the narrow valley.

SitRep Jan090915H: The mountain was known by more than one name by those who humped the road that ran the ridge to the top. On the map it bore only a number in meters, 1218: the names stayed below among the trees where it was cool and peaceful.

The road ached up the face of the mountain, a slick churning sinus. Dank greenery crowded in from the sides and grew over us as we moved up the nose. Soon the road trickled off into trail. My platoon was assigned to the two positions near and on the summit. The air was heavy and musty, stiff with the stink of the ripe and the rotting. Like our gear its weight demanded our attention, demanded that it be shouldered like a soggy pack and carried to the top. Through it, slender green razors snatched in at our arms pulling small bits of flesh away and leaving thin stinging cuts.

My chest felt crushed from lack of use and conditioning as I struggled up the slope. Under my helmet my thoughts melted and flowed together like hot wax. Large black splotches began to move through my vision. Skipping the rigors of Los Pulgas in the winter was a mistake. While the rest of my transit unit humped the hills, I humped their paperwork in a busy office mainside. A gift to me from the other two officers assigned to push the replacement Marines through thirty days of pre-combat training because I was married and they were not. An opportunity to spend more time with her, to avoid the cold mountain nights and lie next to her quietly, curling around her like smoke and quietly slipping away. Now I paid for it.

About 300 meters from the top I reached the bald dome I had seen from across the river. From here the canopy of grass dwindled and the muck of the trail became a solitary clinging challenge to the final sprint up the sharp rise to the summit. I paused for a moment gulping in the swollen air. Behind my eyes I could see the Hill Trail snaking almost straight up through the humid OCS Quantico woods and hear the chirp of my hyperventilation as I struggled to keep up with the Marine ahead. That day, during the stress of the march I wondered who the chirping candidate was. Later they told me it was me. I assigned Rico's squad to this lower position. I stood quietly by while they divided up the area into a loose circle of defense and began to stow their gear in the vacant fortified shelters.

"All set Sir," Rico said once they were all in place.

I nodded. I adjusted the straps of my pack, pulling them forward and down and slid on toward the top.

A brief saddle formed the top of the mountain. Around it a loosely connected tattered necklace of sandbag bunkers slipped off the shoulders in an apparent random toss. Like the road and the trail and the barren summit, they were brown. I sat on the first bunker I came to and stripped off my pack and helmet. I watched as my remaining two squads gained the summit and moved into the same positions they held the last time they were sent south to the mine. They were still animated as if there was no seven-mile hump, no bridges, no mud, no jumping obstinate dog, no climb. To them it seemed that all of it was little more than a momentary inconvenience. I turned away from them and looked back down the mountain toward the river scanning first the lower position and then the distant valley we had just scrambled out of.

"Well here you are...Sir. Welcome to the Nam again, yes Sir, welcome to the Nam. Personally, I rather burn the shitters." Lonely laughed and passed on.

"You can't see the mine from up here," a voice said from behind me. "We defend something we can't see."

I turned to answer, but the man was already walking away and because I couldn't remember his name, I said nothing after him. I watched him grow smaller as he moved away. Like the others the vanishing man had discarded his pack but somehow, even with it gone, his shoulders seemed to bend forward against its imagined weight and his head bowed down toward the ground. Like the others he soon disappeared completely into the coolness of the bunkers. When he could no longer be seen, I was alone, perched on the edge of the bunker.

"Balen." Now, the name came to me. It was the bent shoulders and the clearing of lightheadedness that brought it back. One of my squad leaders. And glasses, yes, he wore glasses.

"Damn."

I would have to do better.

"Balen."

SitRep Jan090943: Part of the position was manned by a loosely organized group of Vietnamese, rag-tag remnants of a larger force that once occupied the mountain in its entirety far from the passing of the river below. Now, the few that remained, sat in their dilapidated positions, piles of crumbling rotten sandbags heaped up over holes spooned into the mud that frosted the rocky mountain top beneath, and waited for the comforting drizzle to end. They waited for the Marines to go home and the war to end, and while they waited, they drank homemade rice wine and laughed in high youthful voices.

They played cards gobbling loudly over only the gaming. As in almost everything they did winning and losing was unimportant. Only continuing the game had meaning and periodically when they tired of the play they sold candles to the round eye and sometimes, when no one kept watch, they sold them some of the rice wine or tried to lure them with some success into their card games. And always they tried to trade American cigarettes for 'number one boom-boom in the bush' in red, white, and blue.

I stood at last to move out of the thickening mist. I was vaguely thankful that there was no sun to drill in the unforgiving humidity. I moved quickly at first and then more gingerly taking several steps testing my burning feet and then I stopped. Now for the first time I felt the soft flesh on the inside of my thighs rubbed raw by the seven-mile hump, moisture and the knotty seams of my utilities. I really was soft, softer than I expected to be and I winced as my sweat pushed into the meaty burns making them sting. The light weave of my newly issued jungle uniform stuck to the oozing wounds and pulled away more meat with each move and as I picked up my gear additional raw spots under my arms and on my nipples joined the complaint. And for all of it there was no purple heart. This then was the top.

SitRep Jan090947: While I inventoried my pain, I spotted a rat crouched by the edge of an open garbage pit on the southern edge of the saddle. Grey-brown and the size of small perhaps edible game, its greasy hair was spiked by the rain. For a moment the rat sat listening with its nose high in the air twitching slightly, bobbing and then moving cautiously only to pause rear up on its hind legs and repeat the process. Slowly, it poked at the perimeter, picking things up, spinning them around in prying paws, studying them, dropping them. I watched him as he worked his way toward the abandoned hulk of a truck that hung from the southwestern rim. Its make and age had grown indistinguishable under the array of stolen and home-made parts pressed into service to prolong its now departed life all held together by a cratered frosting of rust. From this distance I was unable to distinguish the rat's shape, and as it patrolled the perimeter through the mist I could see it only by its movement. It disappeared behind the small artillery position on the tip of the higher summit, reemerged momentarily, and then vanished a second time and this time for good either next to or into the bunker manned by the Vietnamese. I couldn't be sure. Sleep would be difficult. I thought back over the past few days.

Horey called them gook domestics; the rats, the big ones, some as large as kennel bred cats. He said they all smelled the same like the smell of moist decay because they all eat dead dogs. When I asked what 'they' he was talking about he just raised one finger to the corner of his eye and pulled it into a slant.

"We have cocker spaniels and they have these fucking rats almost as big. I think that's why they spend so much time in the water up to their knees; the rats don't like to swim."

I looked back up the valley toward An Hoa. Yesterday I stood by the wire at the edge of the airstrip next to Wick while he pointed out the bunkers around the air strip and the village several hundred meters away separated from us by a field and my attention had been snagged by the field, a pretty thing, I thought, covered with small white flowers tended by a scattering of squatting Vietnamese peasants.

"Come on," he had said.

We walked to an opening in the wire and out into the field. Flies rose in small black clouds roaring in complaint with every step. Up close to the ankles the flowers were bits of shit paper and the ground was covered with shit and stink. The people from the ville squatted side by side without shame. Beneath the flies, rats scurried away in front of us as we turned and headed back to the wire...

...And rats, rats, rats, always the rats. It should come as no surprise now.

Sleep would indeed be difficult.

I slung on my pack, tugged its shoulder straps away from the chaffing again, glanced for a last time down the trail I just climbed and turned toward the summit to find my bunker. Sergeant Wescott, my second squad leader, had come up behind me soundlessly and now was standing so close that we nearly fell into a tangle as I turned.

"Jesus," I was startled to find someone so close and embarrassed to have not heard his approach. Wescott registered on my discomfort with a smile and pointed to a small wire enclosure next to the Vietnamese bunker.

"It's a prisoner cage, Sir," he said in his painfully manicured lip smacking English as though he anticipated a question I was about to ask.

"What...?"

"There," Wescott continued, pointing toward the Vietnamese bunker. "There next to their bunker. It's barbed wire. I don't think Geneva would approve."

Wescott fell silent, grinning broadly watching me focus on the small cage for the first time, waiting for me to respond.

"What the hell are you talking about?"

"The Geneva Convention, Sir, and the treatment of prisoners."

"Oh, no," I said after a minute. "No, probably not."

"Twelve," Wescott now said, pausing and grinning, still grinning, always grinning.

"Twelve?" I asked. Suddenly I was beginning to feel very tired and crushed by everything that hurt.

"Men, Sir," Wescott continued. "Twelve men. That's how many I've heard they can get in there."

I looked over at the small cage again. It was a little larger than a large refrigerator knocked over on its side, and it was placed so that when the sun was shining, if in fact it did shine up here, it would receive maximum exposure throughout the day. And when it rained, well, it would be like this, like everything was now. Ankle deep in mud and not a single place to hide.

"Why do you think they allow it, Sir?"

"What's that?"

"Geneva, why do you think they allow a cage like that?"

"I don't know," I said after a moment's weary reflection thinking about the field of flowers. "Maybe they don't know it's here, or maybe it's because they've never had a war in Switzerland, or maybe it's because they all look the same anyway and they keep rats as pets."

"Maybe," Wescott said thoughtfully. "I wonder what they do when they need to eat or take a dump in there?"

I was suddenly not sure I want to spend much more time with Sergeant Wescott and using the resumption of the rain as a cue to move and using the wire from the land line as a guide I started toward what I took to be my bunker. And as I moved the mountain top continued to dissolve into soup behind me.

"We're bunk-mates, Sir," Wescott said happily, pointing to the bunker where the slender strand of com wire disappeared. It was mid-way up the saddle on its northern edge and overlooked the sheer tree-tangled drop that ended in the narrow canyon below where the coal mine opened into a small circle of muddy road. "And that's our bunker over there."

Roofed not more than a foot above ground level it looked like a soggy, forgotten grave and with the exception of wisps of smoke spitting into the mist at one end it appeared to be lifeless or worse, not capable of supporting life.

"Well that is indeed good fucking news."

I breathed deeply and together, we retreated into the bunker out of the rain.

Inside, English had a fire crackling in a makeshift stove cut from a square five-gallon tin can and vented with heavy cardboard artillery round canisters forced together to make a flue that passed through a hole in the wall of the bunker at ground level taking most, but not all, of the smoke from the wet wood with it.

Jimmy English was a beefy Oklahoma Corporal that tossed his feet out in front of him and off to the side like a penguin when he walked, but still, he crossed the remains of the bridge like an Olympic gymnast, and he came up the staggering slope of the mountain like a champion cross county skier.

I shook my head.

He had a man's body and a child's mind. His smooth skin said he was no more than a teenager, but in his eyes he was older and strong and their deep reflection grew at ease somehow in what they saw. Wick called him, "good man."

He called himself, "short."

"Jesus Christ, Wescott, close the fucking flap... oh, sorry Sir." He turned back to Wescott. "See you made it all the way to the top this time. No more half-way Wescott?"

Wescott ignored the comment.

"He usually just stops at the first position half way up the hill," English continued. "Half-way up for half a Marine, half-way Wescott...,Sir. Rico must'a got some good shit on you to get you all the way up here."

He laughed at his own joke while Wescott remained quiet.

The rain that blasted through the small opening with our entry still sizzled on the glowing tin. In the short time since our arrival on the hill, English had somehow managed to assemble a sizeable pile of soggy burnable scrap that he was now trying to coax dry by nestling it close to the rapidly heating can.

"We figured you'd like to be as far away from the opening as possible Sir, so we saved that spot over there for you," Wescott said pointing to the darkness in the far corner.

English whistled softly and relighted his candle, a casualty along with his warmth and comfort, to our arrival. Unable to stand in the confined bunker, I pushed my pack across the dirt floor and dumped it on the slightly elevated wooden platform called bed. 'Over there away from the opening' as it worked out was also over there away from the fire and heat.

I stowed my gear and laid back on my rack watching the fire and listening to the rain while Sergeant Wescott talked and English poked at the stove opening pulling small tufts of smoke back into the cramped dark bunker.

"Is that thing safe?" I asked edging myself around trying to capture more of the concentrated heat from the hissing stove. "I'd hate to die in my sleep my first week here."

When he was satisfied that the fire would continue on untended, English leaned back, pulled a well-used paperback from his pack, thumbed through the pages until he found his place and held it close up to the candle stuck in melted wax on to the edge of wooden platform he claimed as his sleeping space. A melancholy yellow glow filtered through the additional wisps of smoke leaking uncoaxed from the stove and circled his helmet less head. At his feet the comm. wire that I followed in from the storm ended on the terminals of the small land phone. At one end of the platform the radio hummed to itself quietly.

"It's okay Sir, best stove on the top of the mountain."

Because I had just arrived, I had never seen English without his helmet. He had almost no facial hair and now I knew why. It was all on his head in a great black mound crushed down by the web in his steel pot.

I seized a pause in Wescott's endless monolog.

"Has the Gunny seen that?"

English looked up from his book and into my critical stare.

"You mean me Sir?"

I nodded.

"Has the Gunny seen what, Sir?"

"That fine head of hair."

English smiled.

"Hell no Sir, like I said I'm short. I'm so short even he can't see me."

"I would think that when the wind blew through that forest he would hear you coming."

His grin broadened.

"I told him Sir, but you can see how much good it does."

"Ah, fuck you Wescott, I ain't hard core like you."

"How old are you English?"

"Eighteen, Sir."

"What are you reading?"

"The Bible."

Wescott shook his head and picked up where he left off in his seemingly endless assessment of everyone in the platoon. I nodded during the pauses where he caught his breath but said little in response. Suddenly he stopped mid-sentence and turned to where English was again tending the fire.

"Where did you get the dry fire wood, Corporal English?"

"What difference does it make?"

"I may need to send someone like you out to get more."

"No problem, it came out of your rack, firmness or warmth, no contest. The firmness just helps you, the warmth helps us all. And anyway, now it'll be soft and lumpy just like your wife."

Wescott rummaged under the poncho he had spread out over the wooden platform earlier and discovered that several of the cross pieces were missing. I saw that perhaps for the first time since our meeting, the intensity of Wescott's grin wavered and the hint of a frown ran across the edges of his somewhat transparent hazel eyes and up onto his smooth forehead. He looked at English briefly. When he turned back to me his grin had returned unleashing perfect unblemished teeth and he continued his monologue in single-note, half-phrases and thoughts, throwing out 'Sirs' like punctuation. He said he had had the second squad, been their leader, for three months now. He came from somewhere in the northwest, Seattle maybe, where he was an extremely successful contractor of some sort, building things, houses and small shopping centers and upscale office space, from the comfort of an air conditioned office. He owned the company so he didn't have to come, he could have stayed home safe with his wife and his hammers and saws and anyway, in addition to owning his own business he had already served his time; done six in the reserves. Not only that, as English had pointed out so clearly, he was married. But in spite of it all he came back while lesser men ran away. He came back for the war and to get in on the GI Bill. He was going back to school when he got out to complete his degree in something he wasn't sure about yet, but whatever it might be, it made sense from a business point of view to let the tax payers pay for it. He had been half way through school when he dropped out to get married. Now, he said, his wife thought it a wonderful plan and had encouraged him to get started as soon as he could.

When he first arrived he had worked in Da Nang helping to build the PX. But for some reason, they had decided to ship him down to a line company.

He …

I drifted away.

…liked to make decisions he wasn't responsible for; he liked to use his hands to count on his fingers but he failed to use them to grasp the total of things he counted; his friendship was sticky and it drew flies like an open garbage pit or a field full of flowers; and like the bunker, it smelled like it had been soggy too long. With any luck it wouldn't attract rats.

And still, he talked and talked and talked and I listened to the crack of the fire thoughtfully.

Finally, his analysis completed he turned back to English.

"And don't make comments about my wife."

English, his Bible balanced on one knee, had fallen asleep.

Whether Wescott was the reason or not, I wasn't sure, but for certain tonight there was to be no luck. From the growing storm came more rats, running along the log rafters that were laid across the hole to support the sandbags of the roof. When they ran, they knocked sand loose from the rotting bags, letting it sift down on to whoever sat below and into the earth floor. Tonight the 'whoever' was me. I heard the scratch of their passage. I listened to them with apprehension and flinched from the sift of the sand. I shifted uncomfortably to avoid their droppings that I was sure must be airborne too. Next to me, the droning Wescott and the sleeping English took no notice.

"Anybody ever get bitten by those things?"

"What's that?" Wescott asked.

"Nothing," I rolled over to face the wall. I waited and I listened and soon I grew use to their skitter.

And so it was that in this we were all the same; and they really were large too, as large as the one had looked at a distance through the rain, but not as large as cats, Horey was wrong there. More like fast moving possum; healthy, quick-footed, hairless-tailed possum grown fat on the liberal waste of military largess, half-eaten C-rations and other shit. But now up close they added a new dimension; the smell of moist decay. I wondered if the rats ran freely through the Vietnamese bunker as well. Perhaps over time they had learned to avoid the stew pot by living only with Marines who they knew wouldn't eat rat. And I wondered if the natives recognized a rat among them or were they all just brothers in the storm. Was the rat the dragon of the old man's history and did the eating of rat fill them with the seed? They were given away by the field of small white flowers where people from the refugee ville walked and tended to their slight beauty. Up close to the ankles in bits of soiled paper the earth was nothing more than hard ground covered with shit and stink. And so, because of that, it was natural here too. I supposed it would be easy to kill a rat if it came to that.

While the rats ran and Wescott tried to rearrange his air mattress, his rubber lady, to compensate for the missing boards, long soggy threads from the sandbags hung toward the floor and dripped, slowly, dripped, continually.

…and there was no sign over the door here, no sign of a sign that is.

Suddenly I was awake. English was up now too The Bible set aside; he was ripping open the brown carton of C-rations held between his knees. He pulled each can out of the box, held it up to the glow of the fire to read the label and then set it down a new member of the growing line of cans beside him on his rack. Wescott sat quietly at last writing a letter.

"Ham and motherfuckers," English said pulling his dog tags out of his shirt to get at the can opener that shared the chain. "I'm the only one in the Nam that likes them, so I'll never starve to death."

"What," I asked, "other than the obvious, are motherfuckers?"

"Lima beans," English said pushing the blade of the opener into the can and working it around the rim.

"And why are lima beans motherfuckers?"

English stopped for a moment and looked across at me.

"I guess that's because that's what they are, Sir."

He returned to his meal preparation.

"What's that?" I asked watching him make an incision in the next can, a squat gold colored container.

"Cheese," English said and he scraped the contents with the included plastic spoon into the larger can of Ham and, and, and motherfuckers. When he finished, he carefully set the concoction on the top of the glowing stove and stirred it periodically until the cheese was melted and the entire mess began to steam and bubble adding yet another smell to the thick heavy air. Pulling the can gingerly from the stove he plunged the plastic spoon into its midst and attacked the slurry with zeal.

"I think you can take your time," I said. "Not even a rat would eat that shit."

From where I sat, I could see through the narrow gap between the jamb of the door and the canvas cover as the mist and rain and darkness folded over the mountain, obscuring the bunkers I knew to be there. I stood, stooped over, and stepped closer to the door. I leaned forward to flip a spent cigarette, another Marlboro gone, into the wet out through the door pausing a moment to study the growing night. I watched the glowing ash arch into the soggy air and fizzle quietly into the mud. Coming back to my rack I sat and felt the air of my new rubber lady shift easily with my movement. Together, we sat on a wooden platform hammered from old ammunition boxes, listening to the rain. Like English's, and Wescott's, my platform was a foot or so off the damp floor but unlike Wescott's, mine still had all its pieces. Unlike both of theirs, however, mine caught rain water from a leak in the tattered roof canvas that clung to the sandbags. When the air stirred outside, its shredded remains flapped in clumsy quiet under the half-hearted comm-wire lash. Heaving like a hollow cheeked old man gasping for a final breathe it invited the rain to join me and my lady below.

And while we sat huddled against the darkness and the rain others moved quietly through the fluid jungle four hundred meters below.

SitRep Jan091728H: "We're going into the valley tomorrow with two," Captain Delpert said that evening from the far end of a cricket. "It'll be you and the third."

He cleared his throat as he paused. The curl of his lip and the pink of his gums were audible.

"That's it," he said. "Be down here in the morning, ah… at first light, and we'll go over it on the map."

I said, "Yes Sir" and stood next to the glowing stove unaware of the sharp slash of up close heat, looking at and through the now silent instrument in my hand.

"Technically," I said out loud, "it's not a cricket, it's a double-e-eight." I handed it back to English, who hung it back on the nail that had been driven into a supporting timber by the door, and stooped back to my rack.

"I beg your pardon, Sir?" Wescott asked. He hadn't taken his eyes from me since I first picked up the phone.

"Tomorrow."

I leaned back and pulled at the book of matches deep in the side pocket of my jungle utilities. Black letters on the olive drab paper explained their use: For Tropical Weather.

Absently, the first few failed and fell to the floor. Finally, one caught and took to the wick of the candle stuck in the earth over my rack. I lay back again and fished the map out from where I stashed it under my rubber lady. I could feel the short hairs come to attention through the wreckage of hump induced raw skin. A first combat patrol.

"At least it will be in the day light," I said, and again, softly, "tomorrow."

I unfolded the map in front of me on my rack. Traces of the grease penciled route of march of this morning still cling to the clear contact paper cocoon that protected the thin paper map from environmental destruction. Running my finger back up the spotted road that paralleled the river I came to the place where Polo had refused to cross the bridge; the place where Wick and the Gunny had quietly moved the Company off the road while watching the high ground with practiced eyes. And it was there that the stream that skulked in the rut beneath the broken twist of steel, disappeared through a narrow slot marked only by a lone palm tree and then quickly opened into a wide lengthy stretch of valley.

I scanned the rest of the map silently trying to recapture the mountain top panorama and plug the features into the wiggling mass of elevations trapped neatly in thousand meter grid squares.

In the mountainous areas surrounding the coal mine, there were thousands of valleys; small clusters of rice paddies tucked themselves into their relief, set into the rugged folded countryside, and from the top of the mountain, filled them with facets reflecting in the sun, or subdued light when there was no sun, like today. The natives stole every inch of the soil and laced it with flooded terrace and dike and filled the small plateaus with water to raise the slender life giving threads of rippling rice.

From the valley floors, the paddies swept up to the mountains clinging precariously like beads of water kicked up in the passing of a fast moving car to the steep abrupt rise and seemed ready to topple back down at any moment without notice.

But there was only one valley here, or so they said in the quiet moments following Delpert's briefing yesterday, pointing it out with special emphasis, about mid-way down the line of march. It was the Antenna Valley.

It was the largest of the valleys slicing east from the river to the coastal flat-lands and the sea. It was rich, fertile and unused. Once inside through its narrow opening at the river, the wide floor opened into a repetitive labyrinth of overgrown paddies left untended, and deserted villages. People spilled out in uncountable numbers in November, they said, to escape: no one said from what or from whom; and now, except for the few who choose to remain in their homes, the unfriendly remained and flourished. A valve from the east, a route to the north, a place to rest, a pretty place with a pretty name. Into the valley, into the valley with two. Wick said it got its name from gook antennas that were really just long bamboo poles stuck into the ground on hilltops and wrapped with wire, any kind of wire, barbed, comm., any kind. He said they used them for relaying weak radio signals from somewhere to somewhere else; he said the valley was full of them till we, they, went in and knocked them down in November, and then it began to rain. "Jesus. Tacson gooks in that valley though," he said.

Now, while I studied the map I imagined him standing slim and stooped midway down the hill in front of the Company command post chewing on a dead cigar and gazing out toward the valley. He chose his words as he spoke and he echoed, 'tacson gooks out there all right, tacson.'

SitRep Jan100217H: With the loud explosion still ringing in my ears, I swiped at the small bloody patch on my forehead caused by jumping too high, too quickly, in a space too low. Crouching out through the bunker entrance I stopped to clear my sleep filled aching head.

"H&I's, Lieutenant, from the guns on the point."

I recognized Lonely's pronunciation of Lieutenant making it sound like he had just spit something distasteful on the ground. As I approached, I saw the flash of his smile.

"My time for the watch on the walking post." Pow. He set off a hand-held flare so close to me that I felt the heat of its ignition.

"Jesus Christ." I said jerking back out of the way.

"Got to get some Lieutenant, could be some gooks sneaking up on us right now."

The small flare drifted down over the glistening jungle below us. Lonely pulled the pin on a grenade and tossed it over the side of the mountain toward the smouldering remains of the flare swinging under the luminous patch of silk. There was a flash followed by a muffled explosion and then it was quiet.

"H&Is from Lonely, Lieutenant."

"Knock that shit off Lonely," someone called from the far side of the position.

Lonely laughed and disappeared into the shadows.

"Hey Lieutenant," English called from the bunker. "It's the Six."

I gave the handset back to English and stepped back outside into the darkness.

"Hey, Lonely, no targets no more grenades."

"Whatever you say, Lieutenant."

I could hear their laughter. For a moment anyway it had stopped raining. Overhead a small opening in the sky allowed the moon to do a brief recon of the mountain top and the valley beyond.

"She sees the same moon."

I took a quick check of each position and went back into the dark quiet bunker. How the hell did I get here? Least likely to go into the military and now I was a leader of Marines in combat.

SitRep Jan100500H: I met with my squad leaders before first light: bent shouldered Balen, the one who seldom spoke, but smiled now and then through thick lensed glasses, Wescott, and Rico the short dark Mexican, who neither spoke nor smiled. Except for Wescott, the older, they like English were young, 18, 19 maybe. They were alert, skeptical as they listened, cautious as they watched in the dark, my movements; they focused carefully on mechanics as if watching a rookie on his fist trip to the mound. They searched my eyes that still failed clear vision but learned quickly to hear and understand; they searched for the hint of that intangible quality that made them take comfort, that made them trust and perform well. They wanted to know if I would make them safe. They searched and I saw, heard, understood that they were still unsure, that they would probe deeper through the following days.

There was a thick, chewy mist around the mountain again and the filtered moon retreated into the west. It was cold. Wescott because he was from Seattle seemed not to notice. He wore no shirt under his flak jacket and nodded his head to the things that were said. He sought nothing; he brought nothing other than his grin. It was said well as he decided it should be.

He was older. He was experienced.

"Have them down to the bottom in thirty minutes."

That finished it. The younger two watched for a moment, I heard them and I heard them again when they stopped watching, and again,

"Yessir."

In a minute their sounds were lost in the darkness. Balen slogged to the perimeter near the truck and Rico began the slide down the steep slope ahead of me to his squad on the small lower position. I saddled up now and headed out toward the trail and down just behind him. Across the small perimeter new sound returned as Balen and Wescott rousted out those not on watch, kicking them out of the short cat naps that carried them through the night. I reached the trail head and started the slide down the dark badly rutted trail. In minutes I slid into Rico's lower position as the top of the mountain finally came to life. Rico stood next to the 106 recoilless rifle briefing his team leaders. Another volley of artillery fire that belched in a thunderous plume of flame from the far tip of the upper position and headed off in the darkness toward Antenna Valley. I flinched at the crack of the rounds passing over my head and nearly lost my footing. It was still unfamiliar, all of it, and the sky offered little assistance.

"I will never get used to this shit," I said steadying myself on the roof of a nearby bunker. I had travelled barely 30 paces from the top of the hill and I was already a tangle of web gear and binocular case straps and canteens, and my pack wore heavily. I released the bunker and untangled the straps. I rocked the pack forward on my shoulders and continued on down.

Several hundred meters farther down the trail I stopped to listen for what sounded like the gentle swish in the trees behind me moving like a high whisper of wind. When I stopped, the wind ebbed and grew still. I moved forward and the sound followed me like a rippling wave down the side of the mountain.

By the time I reached the bottom, the Company Command Post, the sun was just up over the horizon but still chose to remain sheathed in the grey fissured slate that joined on the mountains and arched easily up over them. The drizzle that started the preceding afternoon returned, freezing captured glimpses of the natives on the far shore through the leaves as they moved in black, mired in chatter. Behind me the low hanging branches were quietly pushed aside and several of the native warriors from the top slid into the mist of the small clearing.

Captain Delpert was waiting. He wore a green tee-shirt, skive shirt, under a half buttoned jungle jacket, his sleeves were rolled to the elbows. His trousers were mud spattered to the knee and his boots turned moist brown. Behind where he stood, a worn puddled strip stretched back and forth in front of his tent; the tent a low lash-up of shelter half and poncho, where, because he was Captain, he slept alone. His hat, his cover, had lost its shape in the rain and pushed down on and conformed to the shape of his skull and forced his ears out away from the side of his head. They looked like receivers anxious to snatch up the meaning of the faint valley signals emanating from beyond his ability to see.

Wick crouched by a smoky fire prodding into a C-ration can of Ham and Eggs that sat in the coals at the fire's edge. Polo, panting over her pink lolling tongue sat across from him, alert on coiled haunches watching, and he glanced infrequently back at her. With equal frequency, he looked at the orbiting Captain too and shook his head slightly into the edge of the fire. He was silent, and except for the glances, he blended into his surroundings like a stone. He seemed to ignore Delpert's passing.

Horey was just crawling out of the sack, his eyes still puffy from sleep. As he moved, I looked at him closely for the first time; his nose. It was true; what Harry said was true, it was a beautiful nose, really, because there was almost nothing to it. I had heard the story over warm San Miguel; parts of it anyway. It had been smashed in childhood and most of it removed so he could continue to breathe. Wick said he had run his face into a tree on a sled but Harry said it was because he got it too far up someone's ass and it had to be sniped off to prevent suffocation and save his life. He also said it didn't make any difference because Horey was an ugly fuck whether he had a nose or not. Horey seldom talked about it saying only that, although it looked quite snoutish removing dimension from and flattening his face for lack of shadow, it worked.

"Of course it works, " Horey said. "What the hell do you think! You're goddamn right it works and besides, it's easier to drink cognac, nothing to get snagged in those stupid fucking little glasses."

I watched him. He stretched, rubbed a sleeve across the nub over his lip, squinted at the sky and turned back into the tent that he shared with Wick. Harry hadn't arrived yet. I watched them and felt more at ease. Just another day at the office.

A night on a hill in the woods had dimmed the long days of anticipation.

"Good morning, Sam," Delpert curled. "What do you think?"

"Sir?"

"The weather," Delpert said.

"Oh, shitty, Sir, I guess, I hadn't noticed."

"It gets worse," Wick said without looking up.

Delpert smiled widening the curl.

Jesus.

"Where the fuck are my C's," Horey said emerging from the tent a second time, pawing through his pack.

"If they was up your nose you'd know," Harry said, joining the group, brushing through the small group of Vietnamese shadows.

Horey stopped and looked up.

"Fuck you," he said, and turned back to his pack.

Harry laughed and nodded a greeting to the rest.

Delpert smiled again looking gee-this-is-wonderful, and unfolded his map. He had drawn a route on it with a grease pencil. It started on the river bank on the far side, followed the trace of the road we traveled the day before, to the north, turned right through the small pass and ended midway down the Antenna Valley. Where Delpert touched it, it fell apart in smears and grew hazy. Several small circles marked check points along the route but their names were washed away by the rain. I quickly copied the single line of the route onto my map. Balancing on a slender thread of runny grease we would find our way into the valley. Along the same spidery thread, I suspected, hoped, we would find our way back out.

Deep in the valley moist shadows moved into the surrounding hills and waited for our arrival.

SitRep Jan100610H: The rest of the platoon arrived and moved through to the beach where it milled around searching for some semblance of order until finally joined by Harry and I and the third platoon. Like the day before, the Gunny moved through the yawning troops whispering threats, checking their gear and moving them into columns to board the barge. When he was done, they were Marines. He came up beside Captain Delpert.

"They're ready Skipper."

He stuffed is hand deep into his hip pocket and waited. Delpert raised his hand and set them into motion. They moved into the Native Barge and headed across, moving slowly in the choke and bang song of the straining engine; singing its single note into the quiet. The man with the yellow hat leaned back by the tiller and again bowed slightly and lifted his hat to me and Horey. I turned away and concentrated on the sounds of the barge as it repeated its chant up through the deep river valley like the beat of a signal drum. It had the sound of a bad beginning, a goddamn bad beginning. When I turned to look back at the mountain I thought I saw Wick standing half-way up the hill by the fire shaking his head as he watched us pull away. He was probably thinking it was a bad start too. He kicked out at Polo because, like him she remained and he missed because he wanted to.

71

I let my hands slip away from the gunwale and huddled down closer to the floor of the barge. The metal was cold below the water line, but it shielded the sting of the breeze and as I looked at the rest huddled around me, the coolness of the metal made little difference. Delpert stood tall in the bow of the boat.

The barge dumped us out on the eastern edge of the river. While the barge returned to the far side for Harry and his platoon, I moved mine through the quickly building throng of hawking children, some of whom recognized Lonely from the day before giving him wide berth, and put them into two staggered columns along the road. And when I was finished, I turned my attention inland toward the small village and the mountains. The village nestled into the lush foliage at the foot of the steep incline had been little more than a blur when we passed through the day before. But now as we waited for Harry it came into focus.

Stagnant water churned up and shit in by water-buffalo stood in purple-black pools in the muddy trace of the road where it ran through the scatter of the village. Along it, the business district stood, close by on either side, made up mostly of thatched huts, but punctuated by occasional masonry half-gutted pink and orange French built buildings. The suburbs lay moored at the river by the strike of the barge. Crowded together the narrow thatched shallow-draft junks steamed and stunk in the growing heat of the day; tethered to sticks stuck in the bed of the muddy, yes, muddy also, slow winter river.

Now, the junks were empty. Women stood waist deep and half naked in the river washing their clothing and themselves, oblivious to the cold and the cat calls and hoots walking along next to them and setting in on the side of the road. While they washed, their children jumped from the sides of the boats and joined the swelling flood of short vendors milling through the Marines, picking up sales pitches from where they had left them in the mud the day before. And still they gave Lonely special attention from a safe distance saying 'you number 10' quietly until he raised his rifle and they scattered, a receding wavelet leaving bubble popped shadows behind in the sand.

Deeper into the ville, movable walls of the clustered hooches moored along the road, that hung on hinges of vine were now being pushed up and set on sticks as awnings and the ville came to life beneath them.

Harry's platoon arrived with the Gunny and tagged onto the end of mine. Now the Company, covering the full length of the village in a long jingling column of twos, began its slow movement north toward the valley.

The natives from the top of the hill that came with us as guides dropped off in the shops as they passed, disappearing into bursts of familiar gobbling and the smoke-filled, 42nd Street stink. I watched them as they smiled and nodded, droppings from the column. They carried carbines and hand-grenades that they juggled to the delight of the young girls that lived there. Slowly they rejoined the end of the column as it passed. By the time the patrol had turned the first bend in the river, however, they had dropped off again, disappearing into the quiet close-in foliage and were heading back toward the ville to await safe passage back to the top of the mountain.

"That's not good," Horey said coming up behind me.

"What's that?"

"Them," he said. "The little gook shit bags want no part of Antenna Valley. When they drop off you sure as shit know its lock and load time."

For the next few minutes we walked in silence.

After a moment he said, "I wonder how many of the little fucks I killed with H&I's last night. They roar out every night and every morning I wonder 'how many? Sometimes I dream about that."

Easy Echo moved like a snake, a column on each side of the cut of the road, while within its bowels the occasional native bearing the sparse commerce of the deserted valley on his shoulders tied to the opposite ends of slender poles, that it, the snake, crawled over, slogged barefoot in the shin-deep muck heading back toward the village.

I walked in the mud next to Horey and felt it cold as it oozed down over my boots.

"What makes this place stink?"

"They do," Horey said, nodding toward the middle of the column. "They're all the same, just like those fucking war heroes that skipped as soon as we turned the corner. It's the essence of rat and dead dog."

I looked across at him for a minute, but he, Horey, didn't smile: he continued to walk looking down at his feet as they slipped from view into the mud.

"Oh," I said, my head joining Horey's in the ground searching for my feet.

The light conversations of the column faded as the last of the barefoot traffic passed into the invisible scenes of the village edge. Except for the hum of the nearby radio and the occasional radio checks between English and Sanchez, the Company radio operator, it was quiet.

SitRep Jan100712H: The Company arrived at the mouth of the valley where it yawned down on the river. Looking into its narrow mouth the small stream bed could be seen meandering peacefully away to the east between the still paddies and small green tufts of hill. It was once a game preserve where wealthy French colonists flew in to hunt, week-end hops that terminated on a small airstrip mid-way up the valley. The airstrip had all but vanished now showing as little more than a dotted feature on the map. The remains of an old fort, the floor plan, broken yard thick walls, stood to the south of the strip on a small hill in the shadow of the towering mountains, a road, punctuated with broken concrete bridges ran down the middle; along and over and through the stream.

Wick said that Foxtrot shot and wounded a tiger here two weeks ago and tracked it for three days. He said they followed blood traces up into the mountain on the northern rim of the valley but that they never found it because they didn't know fuck all about hunting and tracking. Now, as I looked into the valley, the prospect of running across a wounded tiger added to my apprehension. No shit. First Horey said it was lock and load time and now I had managed to remember the wounded tiger. All I needed now was to get shot at or worse, to throw up because I had to sweep up some other poor bastard's remains. Turning to the right we squeezed through the narrow opening, forded the small stream and fanned out onto the valley floor. We moved down the center of the valley along the road still formed as a staggered column. My platoon had the point. I went over it all again to myself, step by step while I walked. Delpert's plan was vague.

We'd move into the valley a couple of miles, 2000 meters, two clicks he said, a long way, longer than it looked on the map; we'd set up on a hill that sat on the rim of the valley floor. From there, Harry and his along with the mortars would cover, while I and mine swept the large village just off the slope to the east. I wondered about that. Inside the valley it was quiet and the chatter of the road churned in the mire behind us; it had fallen through the ass-end of the snake. Here the road was soft and unbroken showing only signs of light traffic and I began to perspire. Was that what it was? Perspire? Yes, I decided, it was alright today to perspire.

Dear Pumpkin,

I can perspire today, later I will sweat. I perspire heavily under the weight of my flak jacket and helmet. They insulate my body but they hold the heat as well and they hinder my movement; they chafe deeper into the pits of my arms, the jacket, and under the stretch of my chin, the helmet; they are bowling ball heavy, 10 maybe 15 pounds.

It is rather pretty inside this valley, pretty and soft and it reminds me of peaceful places we've been before. I'm still not sure how this all happened or if it is even happening now. Yesterday's raw places open up again and begin to complain.

Love,

Sam

The weather grew closer, more immediate. The clouds that had separated the top of the mountain from the river valley tumbled down onto the valley floor now and it began to rain. What had first been a drizzle now increased as we moved further into the gut of the valley.

Half way into half way, we held up. I moved up the column with English and his singing radio slogging along next to me. I looked across the middle of the narrow road that separated us. 'And that ridiculous farm boy walk,' I thought, 'There's no way he should move this quickly.'

"Good man." Wick was right about that. Only 18, yet he was old enough to be called "a good man." But none of it mattered, not to him, when all he could think to call himself was "short."

Together, English, big with his helmet cocked back off-center and his unused chin strap serving only as a trapeze for the pendulum swing of the wired-on radio handset and I consciously shorter and smaller and 'long,' together, we worked our way up the column. The troops watched as we, I, went by, and I was conscious of that too. Rico waited for us off to the side of the road. Rain dripped from my helmet and soaked up into my shirt. It ran down my back under my flak jacket where I felt it spread out along my belt line probing for safe passage back to the ground.

"That it, Sir?" he asked, pointing to a small hillock to our left front. The road ahead was empty.

I squatted across from him and eased my map out of the large pocket on the thigh of my jungle trousers. English stretched out in a dry patch under the spreading leaves of a squat banana, propped back on his radio, the hand set swung slowly to a stop and dangled limply from his helmet whispering quietly into the still air, and, cupping his hands against the rain, lighted a cigarette.

With eyes closed, he batted at the bent broken tape antenna that now buzzed around his ear like a distracted lazy fly. When we moved it strode like a stork above us, pointing into my back shouting 'here he is, here he is.' Now, it was a bothersome thing hanging limply over English's shoulder.

Carefully, so no one could see, I unfolded the map shielding it from the rain and flipped the lid back on my compass.

Silly. In the village back by the river, the kids danced and pointed and called 'honcho;' as if they didn't know. Silly. And the spidery handed yellow hat that ran the barge; they all knew, might as well pin a target on my back and together with the radio pointer they could yell, 'here he is, step right up, three shots for a dollar.'

As I looked at the dark greasy line imposed across the thin printed lines of the map scribed in blue and red and black, it lifted from the page and tried to wrap around my wrist while the contour lines slithered over and through my fingers. The rose garden they called it, a deep Virginia gully full of flowerless thorns. Map reading. I did poorly that day, made mistakes, added the wrong things together and got thirsty and lost. To save time I decided to cut through the gully, through the rose garden. The thorn bushes pushed up over my head and I got spun around in the slashing thicket. The only thing that found its way in through the towering mass of pricker bushes was the crushing mid-day heat. Only by luck did I find my way out, find my way to enough of the proper check points to pass, barely. I struggled back into the Basic School campus bleeding and tired and well after dark with the prospect of facing Pumpkin and a long since cold special dinner. I squeezed my eyes tightly and then looked back to the now quiet map. It was a bad fucking thing to remember now and it irritated me. I knew the science of maps, understood them, but now I would never be really sure of where I was. I envied Boots, at least he got lost in the dark. I was on a fucking road in the middle of the day with no place to hide and I couldn't be sure. I was sure of one thing though, that unlike exercises in Virginia, this problem would probably require more than luck.

Damn.

I slid the map around, oriented it.

The Sergeant in the training said 'orientate' and now I wasn't sure of that either. Damn.

I knelt in the mud by the side of the road and studied it, slowly glancing at the surrounding terrain. It all looked the same, each fold, each an image of the one that preceded and followed. Rolling hills at the edge; sharp uplifting mountains, the paddies flat and laced with tree lines and cane. Small watery graves outlined with a uniform hardened lattice of dike.

Jesus.

"Sam," Delpert said.

I turned and met Delpert with eyes still focused to the map.

"Lost?" Delpert asked.

I shook my head and looked back down at my map. Delpert's being there made me even more uneasy.

Everything about him; the thousand-yard stare, the exposed gum, the way he was dressed, his parallel silver bars, glistening railroad tracks, pulled outside his flak jacket on his collar, catching the flat glare of the valley floor and the shine of the rain squarely. While the rest of us squatted off to the edge of the road, Delpert stood precisely in the middle. Head up, shoulders back, fingers extended and joined in a natural curl, thumb along the seam of the trousers, knees straight but not stiff, not locked, heels together feet in a 45 degree angle.

He marched past me to the point and beyond, sweeping his radio operators along behind him. I watched them as they went by. They looked the way I felt; their eyes strained with the extra weight and the cutting shoulder straps and the growing anxious smouldering heat. They searched the hills around them for the glint and a shadow of movement; the things that would tell them to jump quickly to safety, or to stay where they stood. Sound disappeared in the mesh of the falling rain. English roused up, cast them a scornful glance as they passed and closed his eyes again. His breathing grew easy and the cigarette he had first lighted burned down between his chewed nailless fingers. Sanchez the Company radio operator kicked a rock at him. It missed.

"Get off you goddamn ass," he said.

English opened an eye.

"Fuck you, you goddamn Mexican," he said. His eyes were closed again before Sanchez could answer.

"This isn't it," Delpert said.

He had been scanning the valley to the east through the binoculars that he carried in a large case hung over his chest. As he spoke, he pushed at the map that stuck from his flak jacket just over his heart like a target and slid the glasses back into their case. Turning back he looked down at me and rested his right hand on the grip of his holstered .45.

"No," he repeated. "This isn't it." He smiled and curled his lip back over those moist pasty gums. He nodded to Sanchez and the others. He was ready to head back toward his position in the line of march between the two platoons. They gathered in a tight knot behind him and stood ready to move.

"It's the next one over," he said, pointing. "That one, just there."

I nodded. Quietly, I wondered about how much of my body I could mix into the webbing of my helmet.

Delpert continued.

"I can't understand why they're not shooting at us."

He stood there, looking first down at me and then out into the valley. He was detached, dreamy and still smiling, and as he turned to move back down the column, marching tall with his slump-shouldered radio men slogging along behind him, I couldn't understand it either.

I watched him with better eyes as he left. He paraded down the middle of the road the same way he came, a head-and-a-half taller and three lanky strides ahead of the scurrying Sanchez and the rest of the entourage. And as I watched all I could think of was the spirit of '76. All they needed was a fife and some drums and bloody bandages. And a flag. A flag in red, white, and blue.

After they had moved on out of sight I stood and folded my map deliberately. I pointed and Rico and his squad moved out. I kicked English.

"We're moving, get up.

"Who is that that Rico has on the point?"

He pulled his chin into his chest and glanced through half open eyes at the lead man in Rico's squad.

"It's Morales, Sir. He's good on the point."

Now he stood and stretched brushing the long taper of cigarette ash from his trousers.

"He looked like he was directing traffic Sir, like some traffic cop standing in the middle of the goddamn road."

He hadn't missed a thing even in his sleep.

He stretched, batted at the tape antenna and cursed quietly.

"I was just goin' to have a wet dream too, Sir. You mind if I just wait for you here? Now that I'm awake, seems a shame to waste it."

SitRep Jan100958H: The cane and elephant grass that grew on the small hill was tall and thick and movement was hard and slow. It took us two hours to reach this small objective, and now, with the blistering heat cutting through the drenching rain, we were into our second hour once over, slogging through the mud and thick growth with machetes and heels; some rifles slung, others swung from the shoulder at curtains of vine like baseball bats in the spring.

At the edge of the old French airstrip where I had called my squad leaders up to show them the hill, the growth had seemed unimportant. While I waited for them to come up I crouched in the short grass forming words and sentences to myself, and, for a moment, I thought of the strip at the base camp and the fear I saw in the eyes of the pilot who was a passenger with me when the plane from Da Nang touched down and lurched in the mud. It wasn't possible to hide the fear in your eyes. It just hung out there for everybody to see. When I turned, they were there. Now in the daylight, Balen and Rico watched me more than they had at dawn, and when I pointed to the small hill to their front they glanced quickly and then turned to continue their study of me, and while I continued to talk, Wescott smiled. They knew of valleys like this but they still didn't know me, they didn't know me as I chose my words, they didn't know me as I tried to make things flow smoothly through the five paragraph order, I was the one that held their interest. They knelt quietly and listened and they tried to look into my eyes. Rico slowly running his hand up and down the sling on his rifle and Balen watching, nodding turning his head from side to side like an owl and, when I was done, they asked no questions. They whispered 'Yes Sir' in respect to the small brown bars that they knew I had but didn't wear, and moved to where their men waited for them, waiting for the passing of the word. No one spoke of the jungle. I envied Wescott when I spoke to them then because now I knew why he wore no shirt; it was hot as hell and the long sleeves of my jungle jacket were heavy with the accumulated drench of the rain and sweat.

SitRep Jan101210H: It was noon, and we stood in a small clearing at the top. From where I stood I could see the village, or at least the signs of a village that slunk back from view. I could see the clump of trees, the circular, elliptical stand of bamboo and banana and cane that formed the island in the unused filling paddies where the village, according to the map, should be.

Harry and the command group would remain here, here, on the hill Delpert said again. The plunging fire from here into the village was good. They could get down there to it in a hurry if there was trouble. It made a fine place for the mortars. A good spot for Horey to dump in artillery. I would go down to the ville, sweep and return easily. The Company Corpsman would go with me. And while I thought about that, thought about 'if there was trouble;' Harry and the command group went about the business of preparing support, slinging ponchos to shield the rain and digging small fighting holes for defense. The curl of steam from heating C-rations propped up over blue heat tabs and began to erupt in small plumes across the top of the hill.

I studied the ground where we were to move. At the base of the hill, two rows of trees marked the bed of a small stream. It wound up to the north around a slice of paddy that cut into the mountains from the main valley floor, and then turned east into the village. To the south it curled back to the larger stream in the middle of the valley floor. The slender green rice shoots of the paddy were beginning to give way to the shine and gloss of the rain induced rising water that also erased the intricate lace of dike. But now as I watched, the rain eased and for the moment, stopped. I looked across from the stream to the veiled village. If there was anybody there they were well hidden. Nothing spoke of life. No chatter. No animal sounds. No flicker of motion. No curl of morning smoke. No shit, really well hidden.

"Time, it's going to take time, but screw it, time is mine, time is all I have, plenty of time, and the time it takes is worth it if there's anybody home. Jesus, don't let there be anybody home. That's the way we'll go in, in the cover of trees along the stream so no one will know."

I looked around to see if anyone was standing close, to see if I might have been heard.

"There was, of course, the crossing of the barge and the stroll down the road in the middle, and the high striding Delpert, there was that."

I continued running over my plan.

Where the stream ran through the paddy dike that edged the village, at that point, we'd get on line and sweep. All very basic and bookish, all very okay.

Again I called them up and explained it slowly, taking my time, step by step, still in five paragraph order.

"Are there questions?" I asked when I was finished. I waited. 'I have a couple,' I thought. 'I wanted to know where the Vietnamese war heroes, Horey called them, from the top of the hill were and I wanted to know what we were going to find in the ville and mostly I wanted to know if now that I had started this journey, was it ever going to end, or perhaps would it end abruptly in a flash.'

They looked from one to the other and then back to me waiting to see if anyone was going to speak. There were no questions. I had nothing more to add and they moved back to their squads. As they left, I watched.

They accepted it all without question because that was the Marine Corps way beaten into them in boot camp by a survivor. They accepted it as they accepted being here to begin with, as the spike-nosed pike accepted the hook so that it could be dragged through a hole in the twenty-three inch thick high Adirondack mountain ice on the outside chance that it was record material. Poor pike, how sad it must be when a record becomes a statistic and there is no more to it than that. How much we have in common. If I should die before I wake, who would really give a statistical shit out here. Poor pike, poor, poor pike.

From where I sat I could hear Balen talk to his team leaders.

"We're going down the hill to sweep that ville," he said, "And then we're coming back up here. We're going to move through that stream bed."

Simple.

The rest of the Company had eaten and now the humid gray overcoat the sky had worn briefly following the earlier downpour unbuttoned again to release another gathering of warm pissy rain. Ahead I could see it dashed to mist and swallowed into the camouflage covered steel helmets of my men as we moved down the slope. The rain and the movement drew my gut up tight and things went badly at first. We were confused, there was milling and talking; they cursed at each other and it pissed me off. I could feel the Gunny's fist jamming deeper into his pocket. And, when we finally dropped from the sight of the rest of the Company and moved below the brow of the hill, I was relieved, not happy but relieved. I said nothing.

We moved through the swelling stream and nothing happened. I listened to the swish of the water through my trousers and I felt them get heavy. Small wakes washed off the banks as we moved, tracing lines to our feet and then our ankles and then finally our knees as we slid into deeper water.

Dear Pumpkin,

It is quiet, and when we walk in a line in the water pulled along with the caressing current that wraps moist fingers around strong young legs, coaxing', there is little confusion. No one speaks. Even Lonely has left his monologue on the hill. English is alert and Wescott, who moves several feet ahead walks in grinless silence. This is serious shit.

Ssssssam

Muffled rain fell into the leaves of the tree line and covered our passing.

We moved to the dike in the paddy and much to my surprise came on line easily. The troops hauled out over the dike without words into the deepening water that now threatened the lip of the dike, and swept in a wave of hand signals and silent pointing toward the village. Still there was nothing, no sound, no movement save the mounting fall of the rain.

In minutes, while I watched from the stream bed, they cleared the edge of the paddy and moved toward the first few standing huts of the ville. Morales led the way in, cautiously, pausing, lowering down slowly into a hunch and then motioning the rest to follow. Rico moved to the edge of the ville in precise leap frog moves while Balen spread his squad to the left flank and moved his men forward steadily on line into the sagging stands of banana. I saw Lonely moving quickly into the shadow of the first hooch, nothing funny today. Today it was all business. With one lean brown arm he grabbed at a tree and jumped what looked like a trench. Behind him Stepps leapt but fell short falling back into the swollen paddy. Lonely returned from the darkness, grabbed the balding Stepps by the web gear and pulled him into the ville. In minutes they were all across the paddy and into the trees. The decay and disuse of the paddies crept over the dikes beside them and slid over the ground into the bowels of the thatched houses leaving most of them unused and dilapidated, blown apart by harassing artillery fires, tumbles of rotting straw that steamed in the rain and smelled bad. The smell of tended white flowers and roving rats.

Now I left the stream bed and followed in the ripple of their wake as the damp village began to swallow the last few Marines in the first line of advance. The surface of the paddy quickly grew still covering all signs of their passing. English sailed silently several meters to my right.

I see it, I drink it in as images from a clear mountain pool, and when my thirst is fulfilled, I put it aside.

Now I was into the reflection of the village, and I could see its inverted whole, I stood in its skyline, a ripple of a lofty wall, a spire bearing the flag and the crest of its lord. But there was none. The reflection lay shattered in foam. In front of me the skyline fell flat and even, broken only by supple palm fronds and drooping banana brought to a high sheen in the rain that hid the mountains beyond.

It was militarily familiar and out here in the middle of a deserted valley, unexpected; there was a trench, a deep trench, deep enough to hold men of their stature upright, and it had been dug in a sweeping curve to encircle the entire serfdom and provide an easy view, like subterranean ramparts, over the surrounding paddies. Drains to carry away the always-there rain were bored into the sides of the soft dirt walls at regular intervals. In random selection, stout logs were placed across the trench and earth stripped from the trench itself during excavation, piled high over them for protection. And now, now for the first time I felt the tearing of the tangled wire and bamboo in my legs and I remembered that I had not seen it coming, like piss tubes in the night, when I moved from the stream bed, nor had I seen it when I walked toward it through the reflection in the still paddy and found myself in it where I stood as it chewed into the fabric of my clothing and checked the timber of my skin. I remembered that as I stood there by the stream that the others had moved through it easily because they knew it was there and now like them I knew it too and would not make this mistake again. So, it was fortified as was the friendly village just outside the wire back at An Hoa, but it was deceptive like a well hidden trap ready to spring where that one back at the base was proudly

protective, but, it was fortified all the same presiding over the field
of flowers and so I guessed it didn't make much difference at the
end of the day. Was that the way it went? It all made little
difference at the end of the day. It had a discomforting final
sound.

And for the moment while I stood there registering on the
mounting pain in my leg, I thought, 'the spires shrink behind the
supple frond while rain muddies the banners and crests. The kings
are gone, the serfs are gone, all are gone, gone into restive watchful
watery hiding to blend with the steaming rot of the rain.' It was
fortified and it was feudal and I was glad that they were gone; that
today they chose to be knights errant, to watch from a tower that I
could not see.

"Goddamn it," I said as I pulled free from the last of the tangled
wire apron, jumped the narrow trench and stood fully on the hard
ground of the village. "Goddamn it." Where the wire had held me,
now the fabric of my new issue hung soaked and badly torn, Stepps
stood quietly dripping and watching just back under the trees as I
held the "L" shaped tear up to where it had been and then let it fall
loosely to where it would now stay.

He smiled and said, "You're bleeding Lieutenant," and then he
turned into the village. I followed. Several paces behind me
English cleared the wire and jumped the trench into the ville
without incident.

"You could have told me about the wire."

"I knew you'd find it Sir," he said. "That rip looks nasty. I'd have
the Doc put something on that. Gook wire is the worst shit there
is."

Together we walked away from the silent paddy.

As I peered into the nearest of the broken shelters, the rest of the
platoon began the methodic search without direction, the familiar
systems learned through repetition, the pantomime of prodding
walls with rifles, bayonets fixed and raised, pushing deep into the
steamy thatch, searching, the lifting of mats, the cautious kicking
and prying. Slowly, as locusts they devoured with their eyes the

sculptured mows of shocks of straw. "I build my house of straw, I build my house of straw…"

"They're gook bomb shelters, Sir."

I looked up from the entrance of the hut just in time to see Balen kick at the head high dirt igloo next to the hooch they were searching, loosening some of the slick soaked clay. Like mud beaver dens they dotted through the lush stands of banana adding to the submerged quality of the village.

"We'll need to check those out too. Sometimes they hook on to escape tunnels. I don't think we'll find much here though."

"Why is that?"

"No water-bo. All the pits are empty."

Turning, Balen saw Lonely picking bananas that hung down over the trail.

"Lonely," he called, "climb into these bunkers and check them out."

"Aw shit Balen, I'm strictly an above ground hunter."

"Not today," Balen said turning back to me. "Today you are in charge of the underground railway. Get your ass into the hole."

Lonely tossed a half-eaten banana into the brush and crawled into the bunker.

I shook my head as Balen moved off deeper into the village.

"Hey, Balen," Lonely shouted from inside the shelter. "There's nothing in here but the stink of shit. Balen…?"

I smiled and looked back into the hooch. It was my first smile since my arrival.

The people left quickly or had been taken away. Their possessions remained behind. The household items, handmade clay dishes, large round low lipped rice baskets, an old sewing machine left idle to listen for the gunfire in the high ground that circled the hard old fort; a rusted bicycle left relaxing on a thick smooth-barked palm, the memory of its rider just around the corner, another step beyond the shadows. It all remained while the buildings, feeding themselves on the surrounding decay, collapsed. Scattered in steamy heaps they hid the shame of the abandoned memories until they too rotted away.

"Sir."

"What is it?"

"There are people over here, Sir, a old lady and some kids."

I fell in behind the young Marine whose name I had forgotten and followed him through the tangle deeper into the village. Already, most of the search in that quarter was complete, and as I moved closer, I could smell the faint traces of life, a fire held close by the weight of the conspiring rain.

The old woman knelt by the edge of the fire pit just inside the overhang formed by the lifted wall of the large hooch that filled the small clearing, and did not look up as I approached. The children remained huddled back in the dark wet corners of the main structure.

"Get those little bastards out here," Balen said.

The Marine closest to the opening reached in and dragged three small children out into the shadow of the awning where they stood pressing into the old woman.

Dear Pumpkin,

The children here are dirty and they wear only the threads of sad tattered shirts. Their necks and their arms are hungry and their bellies, full of worms, bulge painfully as if they might burst because the weight is too much for them to carry beneath their small wasted smocks. They wear no pants and because of that they can piss and shit where they stand. Because they are frightened, they huddle and they do not play; because they are frightened and because they are hungry. Horey says they look the way they do because all they eat is rice which looks like maggots and they cannot tell the difference. I say, as I stand here now and I see them dirty and sweat lined and shitty; I say, as I notice that they are not soft-skinned as children should be; I say it is because their father is war and their mother is that old whore death and only dear sweet betel-nutted grannies remain.

Love

One of the children moved now and walked in front of the old lady trying to separate her from the nearest Marine. He looked to be the oldest of the three. His eyes were more oval than slant and he kept them fixed on me as he walked from her side. An angry infection gnawed at his thin shin just below the knee and slowed his movement to a halt step. A brown crusty scab clutched at the sore and there was a hum of flies.

'Jesus,' I thought while I watched him walk, 'the flies are commuters, moving from the mucus of his shin to small pussy deposits in the corner of his eyes.' He did nothing to bat them away, but had learned to live quietly behind them while he stared at me as though it was all my fault.

"Its water-bo shit, Sir," someone said.

I looked up to the voice and met the frosted eyes of Balen.

Several of Balen's men joined the group and now stood back by the hooch watching the other children.

"What?"

"Its water-bo shit, water-buffalo," he said, "rubbed into the sore."

"Why?"

Balen shrugged his shoulders and looked down at the child who now stood closer to the old woman still acting as a shield.

"Because they think it makes them better, I guess," he said. "Because it makes the rice grow. Christ Sir, I don't know, I guess it's just a gook Band-Aid."

I looked to the old woman. She was deeply lined in the face and her startled eyes were set as if punched with an awl over a high, pronounced promontory of boney cheek. Her teeth were rotted away with everything else leaving only reddish stained stubs, pylons driven into pasty shining gums. She leaned forward and spit on the ground next to the fire. Like the remains of her teeth, her spittle was red and it melted into the ground slowly. It was betel nut, nothing more. Balen stood next to her questioning quietly and while he spoke she singled me out and watched me carefully.

"I thought you said the water-bo were gone."

And while I waited for an answer that didn't come I looked around at the gathering Marines. Stepps, the one who had come to get me; others drifting in alone or in twos, leaning in soggy union up against the hooch. 'You were wrong,' I thought, 'when you came to tell me you had found life, you were wrong in calling this life, dead. wrong.'

Balen spoke, "Where are they, mammason?

"They're here aren't they mammason.

"Where are they, mammason?

"Come on mammason, smile that good looking smile again."

Now the old woman moved back off her knees and crouched down on her haunches. She held her hands clasped together in front of her face and shook her head. "No," she said in a quiet voice. "No VC."

Balen smiled and she smiled revealing her badly stained teeth a second time.

She spit and the rest of them laughed. She laughed with them, looking from face-to-face, a stream of red drool following the curve of her lip and down onto her chin where it nestled in and slid down the slender chin hairs of age. She looked back to me.

"No," she said again still smiling. "No VC."

Rico walked into the clearing through the trees and came up beside me.

"We got some tunnels over here, Sir," he said.

English and I went with him back to the trench that circled the ville. Balen talked quietly to one of his men and then joined us. Rico's squad waited in and around the trench in front of the cave. It was cut into the wall in a widening of the trench halfway between the floor and the rim and seemed to go back under the village. I looked at the mouth of the narrow opening and said nothing.

Bates, the machine gunner, "and a damn fine one," Wick said, waited crouched at the entrance. He had stripped off his flak jacket and his helmet and tossed them up onto the edge of the trench beside him.

Bates was married and he had a child, a son. He was 18 years older than his son. "How far back does it go?" I asked.

"Can't tell Sir," Bates said.

"You tried the light?"

"Yes Sir," he said.

I looked at the hole and then at Bates. No one spoke and few still looked at the cave.

"Well, I'm not going to tell anyone to go in there; I wouldn't go in the goddamn thing myself. As far as I'm concerned we can blow the fucker up."

Balen looked across the trench to Rico and Rico smiled. He nodded to Bates who waited in the trench.

"I'll go in, Sir" Bates said. "I don't mind it."

I looked at him and then like Rico, nodded. "All right," I said. "Go ahead on in."

Bates started in. He held the flashlight off away from his body in one hand and a cocked .45 pistol in the other.

'Hold the light away from you,' I thought. 'Hold it away because if there is anyone in there they will shoot at the light you carry and you will be safe indeed. Hold it away because it is written that you should. Because that is a lesson that has been hard learned.'

On all fours, Bates climbed into the cave opening until only his feet could be seen dangling at the entrance. And then it all turned to dreams.

There were no sounds and no longer was there a smell of the smoke from the wet fire behind me. I stood there in the continuing light rain and I watched and I knew that he would soon not be seen and as I thought those things I saw into his eyes and I watched the heaving of his chest and the flow of his sweat as it darkened the color or his shirt. I saw too the dead cobra that lay floating in the soupy mud at his knees and I knew that Wesley the grenadier had shot it dead, that he shot it when it came out of the cave with his .45. I knew there would be no more volunteers today. I knew that Bates was frightened, because he was looking at Piggy in a strange and silent way.

"Jesus" Bates said. That's all he said, just "Jesus" over and over.

Lonely pranced up out of the tree line lured by the sound of gun fire and danced around the edge of the pit pumping more rounds into the dead snake.

"Cobra, that's what we gonna call you now, man, Cobra, you ain't Wesley no more. From now on you're Cobra and that's no shit."

Wesley holstered his .45 and smiled at Lonely.

"Yeah, Cobra, that's cool."

"Son-of-a-bitch, they tied a goddamn cobra just inside the opening with a trip wire. Son-of-a-bitch," Balen said. "Get the old woman, Lonely."

Lonely turned and disappeared back through the trees. In seconds he was back, pushing the old lady ahead of him and at a safe distance behind him trailed the children. He called her an old bitch and when she faltered, he took her up by the arm and threw her along in front of him. He was 21, a draftee and divorced, and I began to see why he preferred Lonely to his real name.

Balen forced the old woman down firmly into the trench and up to the cave opening. Rain soaked into the thinning wisps of her grey hair. She stood there a moment looking in and then up at the men that stood above and around her.

Now away from the darkness of the tree-hidden ville she had detail. She was frail, small and delicate, and the things I mistook as lines by her eyes were finely cast trails left by a spider. By the look in her eyes, she knew what we wanted of her and by the same look she said she would not do it, the smile was gone from her mouth now and the understanding 'no' eyes said please.

"Go on in mammason," Balen said. She shook her head as he spoke to her.

"Get in there you old bitch," Lonely said. He jumped down into the pit and put the butt of his rifle into her shoulders. He pushed her to her knees into the growing puddle in front of the cave. As she folded easily under the thrust, I heard the metal and wood of the rifle grind on the bones of her back, her flesh was thin and papery with age and bad food, or no food at all. She looked up at Lonely and continued to speak with her eyes until she fixed her gaze on me. She had taken no strength from the water.

Ah, Honcho, she was just like the rest, she knew.

"Push her in," Balen said.

Lonely took her by the back of the neck and forced her head into the cave. She struggled and started to cry.

"No," she said. "No." Tears quickly varnished the furrows of her weathered face. "No VC, no VC."

Lonely put his rifle down and took her in both hands.

"In you go you old VC bitch," he said lifting her off the ground. "Get your skinny ass in there and go find pappasan."

She reached out pushing against the sides of the opening. Lonely lifted one hand in a hard brown fist over the middle of her back.

"That's enough," I said at last. "Let her go."

Lonely looked up and brought his fist quivering down to his side. Slowly he released his grip. As he let her sink to the ground he reached out and tapped her back with his still clenched fist as if to say don't forget me old lady.

"You sure Lieutenant?" he asked looking up from the pit. "This old bitch gonna bite you in the ass, Sir."

"We'll blow it."

I called Delpert on the radio and told him we had completed the search and that we would soon be in. Delpert said, "Yes."

Lonely pushed the old woman up out of the way and pulled the pin on a gas grenade.

"Fire in the hole, fire in the hole, fire in the hole." He threw the round grenade in and followed it with a frag.

"Fire in the hole," he said again.

They detonated almost simultaneously; the quiet pop of the gas followed almost at once by the throaty explosion of the frag. The old woman jumped, and her eyes grew large as she watched the dirt blown out of the cave float to the floor of the trench. She began to cry in short shrill sobs; her voice carried out through the village. She continued as we left her alone at the edge of the trench now at last drawing strength from the pool that grew around her ankles. She clenched her hands together in a tight knot and looked up into the trees, waving them slowly over her head as she shuttered with grief. The cave was still and sealed, collapsed by the concussion. Several Marines ran back into the ville to watch for telltale traces of gas popping up from hidden tunnel entrances. They found none.

"Stop! Stop! Stop!"

The rapid burst of rifle fire ripped through the valley stillness and silenced the moaning mommasan. Frozen by the ringing crack of the M-14 she looked through the remaining circle of Marines out toward the far edge of the village. But now I was running toward the sound. At the far edge of the ville, a kidney-shaped paddy stretched farther east into the valley. About 15 yards out, a crumpled pile of black lay motionless in the rain soaked stubble of rice.

"He wouldn't stop Sir, so I shot him. When the tunnel blew, he ran past me like a man on fire and then when I shouted to stop he jus' kep' going, so I shot his ass and right there he is right now, right there."

It was Stepps. He had wandered from the hooch to the edge of the ville looking out over the paddy on Balen's orders. Now he pointed out into the paddy with his rifle.

"Okay," I said. "Let's check it out."

He repeated the story as we moved out into the paddy to the motionless hump.

"We was set in you know, like Balen said, looking out over the paddy when this gook guy just comes crazy running by me, right next to me, bumping into to me and keeps on going out into the paddy and when I shouted he don't stop so I fired that's all."

I knelt next to the small body.

Balen and Lonely came up beside us.

"You numb shit," Lonely said. "How's a old man gonna know stop, stop, stop when you shout it. Shit. Dung Lau you fuckin' dummy, you supposed to say dung lau."

"He just run fuckin' past me."

Lonely laughed and shook his head.

"Get back on the line," Balen said.

The back of the old man's thigh just above the knee was torn open and the labored pasty flow of blood was slowly turning the black trousers to a sticky brown. It ran in small curls into the water, a brown spill mixing with the surface of the paddy and spreading away from the source.

"Get the Doc up here," I said quietly as I eased the wounded old man over onto his back.

"Jesus."

His wrinkled cheeks ended on a thinly stretched chin that boasted wisps of fine, spindly, white hairs like proud pennants highlighted with light brown crusted streaks leading from the corners of his windswept cracked lips. His milky eyes folded nearly shut smiled silently.

English slobbered through the paddy and squatted down next to me.

"It's the Six," is all he said and he handed me the radio hand set.

"No Sir," I answered. "We're all right, we've just got a wounded civilian."

There was a pause.

And while I spoke the Doc wiped off the ragged torn leg and wrapped it tight in a battle dressing.

"Yes Sir, we'll need an evacuation, he's just an old man."

"Just a dumb, fuckin' gook old man," Lonely said form behind me to whoever would listen.

Forty minutes later we lifted the old man on to the 34 and started back toward the rest to the Company as the chopper corkscrewed up out of the valley and headed north to Da Nang.

"He didn't stop so I shot him. I didn't know he was no old man he just didn't stop that's all."

"It's alright Stepps," I said, watching the chopper vanish into the thick sullen sky.

"Fuckin A," Lonely said. "Now he's just another VC, just old that's all, just another old fuckin' VC."

SitRep Jan101356H: By now the small stream was swollen up over the banks and merged into the adjacent paddy. We were thigh and waist-deep and still the rain continued to fall. When we reached the top of the small hill again the light had begun to fade behind the mountains and the third platoon had already set in more permanently. Shelter halves spattered the ridge and the smell of heating C-rats once again filled the air.

"A change," Delpert said. "We'll spend the night here, see what develops. Move your people over to the northern edge and set in, tie in with the third on both ends and then join me back here."

When I came back to the CP, Harry and Horey had made a helmet full of C-rats coffee. Delpert shuffled his maps sitting under the protection of a poncho suspended from several small banana palms. Sanchez sat further back monitoring the radio as evening radio checks from listening posts and platoon radio men began to filter in.

"I think we'll sweep back through that village again in the morning and then move back out toward the river," Delpert said. And then he said, "We'll move out at first light." He turned and took the hand set from Sanchez to tell Wick of the change, and then he asked "How's Polo?" After listening for a moment, he handed the hand set back and smiled into the darkness.

"I'm going to turn in."

Soon he lay a stiff motionless lump in the back of his shelter while Sanchez huddled under the adjacent CP shelter and continued to work the radio.

"Asshole," Horey said quietly.

Harry looked up at him but made no response. To fight off the chill of my soaked clothing plastered to my skin, I sipped at my hot coffee, burning my lips on the tin can when I drank. Even with the following pain, it was damn fine coffee.

Horey continued.

"Do you remember when we were in here last November?"

Harry nodded and then Horey told the story.

"It was our first time in here. We came in on a Company-sized sweep at the beginning of last November, probably around the second week and it began to rain, just like this. It was weird because it's not supposed to rain much in November, but man, that shit came down. The stream in the middle of the valley filled and the paddies filled and the little streams that fed the one in the middle swelled and the Son Thu Bon came over its banks and before the first day was over this place was a fucking lake and we were split up and set in on little islands that the troops called 'Parris' all over the valley floor. To move from one position to the other meant a chest deep stroll through the shit. God it was awful.

"We stayed like that for about three days, hung up on the valley floor surrounded by water. Nobody moved. You remember that Harry? Jesus. We were running out of food and water because nobody could get a damn chopper in here because of the rain. And then finally it stopped and the ceiling lifted a little and shit began to happen. That was on the 10th, the fucking Marine Corps Birthday.

"Teapot had just joined the Battalion so he decides to bond with the troops out in the field and since it's the birthday he also decides to bring a fucking cake. No food or water that's drinkable for three days and the first chopper in brings Teapot and a fucking cake.

"You should'a seen him. He's got this small squad of radio men and security and he's wearing flak panties. It's the first time I ever saw flak panties. I didn't even think they made flak panties. Jesus. Anyway, while he's unloading the cake, this black kid from Kansas City is just coming in off listening post. We had these poor bastards out on these little tufts of high ground that they had to wade out to, listening to the frogs and peepers because nothing else was moving. So anyway he's just cleared the line and he thinks he feels something moving around in his trousers so he drops them down to look and he finds a leech about a foot long hanging off the end of his dick giving him tongue. It looked like two eels in a whore house. Well, then he lets out a yelp like he's on fire or something and takes off running toward the CP, his trousers and skivvies down around his ankles and this fucking leech whipping him on his bare ass with every step.

"Now while all of this is going on, Teapot has taken off his flak panties and tossed them into the chopper, cut the cake and just made some shit-ass speech that 'there's no finer way for Marines to celebrate the birthday of the Corps than by being in the fuckin' field doing what Marines are supposed to do' and wham this kid runs right over the top of him and he goes ass-over-buttkiss into the fucking cake. Man he's covered from one end to the other with 'no finer way' and the kid is gone into the shadows across the next paddy and into the first platoon's position where they tackle him so the Doc can get the now bloated leech off his cock. They get him and quiet him, but now Teapot is wild. 'Who,' is all he can say. 'Who.' The Skipper, who was it, Captain Longfellow? Yeah, Longfellow he's doing all he can to keep from choking on a mouthful of cake and is dancing around Teapot shouting 'Yes Sir, No Sir, Yes Sir.' Sanchez is chewing on the end of his hand set and the tears are rolling down his face and I finally jump up and say, 'I'll find him Sir,' and I head off into the muck toward the first platoon, but before I get to the paddy that separates us I meet the Doc coming the other way with a big shit-ass grin on his face and the biggest fucking leech I ever saw. 'Where you going with that?' I ask him and he says 'I got to show this to the Skipper.' I say 'I got a better idea.'

"Because Teapot is making such a ruckus the chopper pilot walks over to see what's going on. Sooo, we take this leech, cut around behind him to the chopper and make it comfortable in Teapot's flak panties laying on the floor. The Doc disappears back to the first platoon and I go back to the CP with the bad news that the unknown assailant has vanished.

"'I want him,' Teapot is shouting while the Skipper tries to scrape the icing off him, following him around like a beat on puppy. 'I want him now.' Longfellow begins to edge him toward the chopper and gives the pilot the high sign to get that baby cranked up and get Teapot out of there before he explodes. 'We'll find him Sir,' Longfellow says as he eases him up into the chopper, 'Be assured we'll find him.'

"Teapot flops his ugly ass into the jump seat still wiping the frosting off his forehead and collar ranting 'him... him.' And as the chopper lifts off I can see him reach down, grab his flak panties and begin to pull them on up over his decorated trousers. For a minute there's this really funny look on his face and I can see him reach down into the front of his panties feeling for whatever it is that he can feel moving. His face contorts and he shrieks into the growing roar of the ascending chopper as he pulls the blood loaded leech out of his crotch and holds it squirming at an arm's length in front of him. And as the chopper lifts out of sight into the mist that hangs in the mountains, you can faintly hear, 'Him...' echo back through the soggy valley. And for one brief moment there's the fleeting shadow of an airborne leech floating back down to the wet safety of the paddy.

"No finer way."

Horey flipped the end of his cigarette into the soaked brush and climbed into his shelter.

"Asshole." He said as he shifted under the leaky poncho trying to find a dry patch of ground.

Harry and I finished the last of the coffee and headed back to our respective platoons.

SitRep Jan110647H: Captain Delpert stood studying his map in the clearing. "We'll make a quick sweep and go back out the same way we came in," he said. "But from the looks, I guess they don't want to fight today or right now, anyway."

I passed the word and we saddled up. As I started down the hill just behind Balen's squad my thoughts ran along ahead of me.

Slowly, slowly, I watched them to work them, I pushed them and rushed them in groups through the open spaces quickly, gliding through pages and sections in steps to see if it worked to cover our asses be careful in movements; guns up, put them there, now move, slowly, so slowly, I watched them.

I studied the squad leaders as they worked their Marines.

Balen quietly kicked ass for results, while Rico bobbed with his fingers and brows, slight shifts of the shoulders. Wescott sweet Wescott was a head patter and smiler who built things for money before he came here; he moved behind his squad out of their view.

We reached the ville. Moving through the same paddy I passed through the wire and jumped the trench without incident.

"Hey Lieutenant."

It was Lonely calling from several meters to my left past where the trench bent around ahead of the encroaching paddy.

"Hey, Lieutenant, the tunnel is opened up again and the cobra is gone."

I walked back to the widening in the trench. Where yesterday there had been foot prints and spilled dirt from the explosion and the remains of the wasted cobra sentinel everything seemed undisturbed as though we were seeing it for the first time.

"Little bastards was busy in the night," Lonely said shaking his head. "Fuckin' shadows in the rain."

Delpert joined us on the side of the opening. He looked down quietly for a moment smiling at some private distant thought and then turning back in toward the village said, "Blow it again when we leave."

I left Lonely to blow the tunnel again while the rest of the platoon swept through the village with the Company. This time everything alive had melted back into the surrounding rippled high ground. The hooch where the old woman and the children had been was empty and the sorry fire pit was cold, awash in the rain.

We moved through the ville and back to the road. A muffled explosion pushed through the banana trees followed quickly by a second, and together they pushed the grinning Lonely along ahead of the concussion and out onto the road. He joined the rest of the platoon.

"I bet I threw that motherfucker about 30 yards back in there and then tossed in another just to make sure."

Delpert put the Company in a column and sent me to the point again. I staggered the column and we began the slow trek back to the mine. Horey moved up the column and walked beside me.

"I've been thinking about the first night you got here," he said.

"What about it?"

"How come you took my goddamn blanket?"

"Wick gave it to me."

"That son-of-a-bitch," Horey said. "I damn near froze my goddamn ass off."

"Sorry."

"Don't worry about it," he said. "I didn't give a shit at the time any...."

The eagle flew off Colonel, Lieutenant Colonel Teapot's desk and nipped at the words in Horey's mouth.

'There are no such things as accidental discharges here, Lootenant. I will not tolerate accidental discharges. I do not want to hear of accidental discharges in my command, Lootenant.

'If you have an accidental discharge, it is negligence and I will have a full report.

'Lootenant.'

"Now we're in trouble," I said.

"I hope to shit in your mess gear," Horey said. "Get down."

I stood in the middle of the narrow road looking back toward the end of the column.

"But what about the Colonel's report?" I asked.

Another quick burst of rifle fire slashed through the slender bamboo separating the road from the paddy.

"What the hell are you talking about? If you don't get your ass down the only report will be about how you caught one of those motherfuckers right between the eyes."

I looked down to where Horey lay up against the berm of the road.

"The accidental discharges...."

"Jesus Christ," Horey shouted over the growing roar of return fire. "Those aren't accidental discharges, they're occidental discharges and they use real goddamn bullets, so for Christ sake will you get your ass off the road."

"Of course they're real bullets," I said shaking my head.

"Jesus sweet son-of-a-bitch," Horey groaned. "Boots."

"He's right, Sir," English said. "You better get down."

I looked to the sound of English's voice.

"Why would anyone want to shoot at me, for God's sake?"

"Holy shit," Horey said. "Stay there you numb bastard, as long as they're shooting at you they won't be shooting at me."

The chatter of exchanged small arms fire increased.

"Plenty of time," I said looking down at Horey. I scrambled off to the side of the road to get out of the way.

"What the fuck were you thinking about?' he growled shaking his head.

I looked over at English. We were down behind the small berm by the side of the road and now he was very much awake. His splayed feet carried him quickly, and if I had been watching, I would have seen him go first; he and the rest of the short and the shorter. The radio on his back was alive.

I rolled onto my back and let the rain fall on my face. For the next few minutes all I heard was, 'I can't believe it, I can't believe it,' ringing in the distance whispered by someone I couldn't see. An echoing drumbeat played out in slow motion, dreamlike. Shot at. Impossible. Where was the fear? There should have been fear but the ripping of the rounds cracking into the underbrush faded behind silent voices. I can't believe it was answered with no need to believe, there's plenty of time. The firing continued. Sharp sporadic clatter punctuated by more rapid bursts as the machine guns joined in. 'Why shoot at me' ran through me from gut to brain and back again bouncing off bone and muscle until it leapt off my tongue.

"Why don't I get an answer? Why the fuck would someone shoot at me?"

Horey slapped me on the back of my helmet.

"Because you wear a white hat," he shouted. "Now keep your fucking head down before someone puts a hole in it."

I settled down into the cut of the road with English and Horey and began to refocus. My breathing was normal. Heart-rate stable. Just a head full of incredible disbelief that was now being pounded out onto the ground next to me by the chatter on the net.

"Harry," Delpert said. "Is anyone hurt?"

"This is Echo Three," another voice said. "The Lieutenant ain't right here, but there wasn't nobody hurt, Skipper. He's back with the guns. We getting' fire from that fuckin' village."

The radio picked up the clatter of the return fire blocking the understanding of the sounds. I listened. Horey rolled over on his back and fished for a cigarette.

"Nice afternoon for it, slightly overcast and a sure sign of rain," he said. "Those fucking snipers will have us ass up for the rest of the afternoon now that they haven't got you to shoot at, may as well sit back and enjoy it. English, can you get into the arty net on that thing?"

"Yes Sir."

"Good, we'll kiss their ass with fire for effect before this is over. Maybe I'll get a shitload of them this time."

Delpert broke back in on the net. "I'm coming back," he said.

"No shit, help has come from Da Nang," Horey scoffed. He found his cigarettes, drew in on the sputtering match and smoked quietly under the cover of a small bush.

"It was cold as a bitch that night and I couldn't find my goddamn blanket," he said blowing smoke out through his nose.

I looked over at him without answering.

"My fucking blanket was gone and I damn near froze my ass off."

"We're being shot at for Christ sake and you're still talking about that fucking blanket?"

"All the more reason to stay warm while you can. You can just never tell when shit like this is going to come at you."

"I said I was sorry for Christ sake, and besides you got the damn thing back."

"All right, all right," Horey said. "But that don't keep me from freezing my nuts off that night; you can't wrap up in sorry five days later. And by the way, nice of you to finally notice that we're being shot at."

"Okay," I said. "I got the point."

He tossed his cigarette up onto the road.

"Echo One, Echo Six over." It was Sanchez.

"Roger One," English answered.

"Roger One send the arty guy back here, over."

"Roger."

English turned to Horey.

"Sir…, I guess you're not going to need me after all."

Gun fire continued to build from the back of column; the strong muscular report of the M-14s punctuated by the higher sharp crack of carbines. There had been only one at first but now there were more.

"I know, I know." Horey stood in a low crouch, pushed another unlighted cigarette back into his breast pocket and turned back down the road toward the village.

The radio burst into chatter again. Over it, I could hear Sanchez's shrill voice screaming through English's dangling handset.

"He's hit, he's hit, Echo Three, Echo Three."

"This is Three. The actual is still back at the rear."

"Roger, Echo One."

"Jesus Christ," Horey said. He stiffened and began to run back toward the thundering exchange of fire. "It's those goddamn bars. Now what the fuck are we going to do with that fucking dog?"

He looked down at his hands and then shouted again back to me over his rapidly vanishing shoulder.

"Well, come on, we better get back there for sure now."

I yelled to Balen that I was going back, and with Horey and English, I started in a low quick dash back to the rear of the column.

"I'm too short for this shit, Lieutenant," English said, as we ran toward Wescott's squad.

"Me too," I agreed. "And I just got here."

"What's up, Lieutenant?" Wescott said as we passed through. He was smiling.

I shook my head and kept moving.

"That guy's an asshole," Horey said.

English laughed out loud but I didn't answer.

Dear Pumpkin,

I feel the wet in my face and my clothing as jog along stooping off to the side of the road. I feel those things and I feel that the waiting is worse than the doing. The doing is easy and soon it is done, but waiting is counting and the counting won't stop. So I feel these things along with the wet blowing in my face as I jog along on this empty straight road with English behind me and Horey ahead toward the Six who is down.

S

In the distance I saw Sanchez and the other two operators. They had dragged Delpert to the protection of the cut of the road where the Company Corpsman worked over him with flashing hands.

"He walked right down the middle of the goddamn road, Sir," Sanchez shouted, when he saw us coming. "I was just a step behind him and he was right in the goddamn middle of the goddamn road. And then 'bang' I'm standing up and he's flat-ass out in the mud. Bang, just like that."

"You got the medevac in yet?" Horey asked.

"Yes Sir," Sanchez said.

"Get a hold of Lieutenant Bings," Horey said. "Tell him to get the LZ in."

"Yes Sir."

"Where's the Gunny?"

"He's back with the guns."

"He's okay?"

"Yes Sir, he ran back when the first shots came in. He don't know about the Skipper yet."

Delpert lay on his back now, wilted. He held his hands over the gaping hole in his guts, while the corpsman dabbed at the blood that trickled down over the corner of his mouth. I could see his pink, glistening intestines squeezing out between his fingers and in a detached way I marveled at how much they resembled academic picture book perfection and how the pink matched the pink of his gums.

"I hit him with some morphine but there's not much I can do here, Sir," the corpsman said.

"I know, Doc," Horey said. "I know."

"If you want to hold his hands back I'll get a battle dressing over his guts. We gotta keep them wet."

Horey knelt with a knee on each side of Delpert's head and pulled his hands away from the wound. Delpert moaned and tried to pull away.

"Easy big fella," Horey said. And to the Doc, "The round still in him?"

"Naw, it went clean through."

Now blood began to ooze into the dirt from underneath him in a growing dark stain.

I knelt to one side and watched and as I watched the noise grew more distant and the pace of the action grew slower and slower and slower.

His big eyes were closed now, back in the case that lay in the dirt next to him, the strap still around his neck. His blood spattered map was in the dirt under the open flap of his flak jacket. His lip was drawn back over his teeth. His teeth were clenched, and his gums no longer pink were now boney white. And while the Doc worked, his guts shivered and tried to escape the battle dressings like worms suddenly exposed under a lifted rock.

"He's bleeding pretty bad inside Sir," the corpsman said. "We've got to get him out."

"It's on the way Doc," Horey said looking over toward Sanchez.

Sanchez nodded.

"Yes Sir. Emergency; it's on the way."

I watched. The color was gone from his face now and the cords on his neck grew rigid drawing down tighter on his teeth. Now it was quiet. The snipers had broken off and left. Horey told Sanchez to get into the arty net. He called in the fire mission and in minutes I could hear the distant rumble of the big guns in An Hoa.

"Let me know when the medevac comes up, we'll fire until then." He turned to me and then squatted down by Delpert again. "It won't do any good but it'll make the troops feel better, those little fuckers are long gone."

The first rounds, ten at a time, began to pour into the village with muffled crunching explosions sending dark grey patches of smoke just above the tree line where they waited to greet the next barrage. The rounds continued to rain down on the small ville.

"Medevac, Sir," Sanchez shouted.

"Roger, get me the battery."

Sanchez passed the handset across the limp Delpert to Horey.

"Cease your fire," he said calmly. "Medevac coming in."

The guns silenced and now I could hear the pop of the CH-34 as it neared the valley from the north.

"I'm going to die," Delpert said in a choke. "I'm going to die, I'm going to die."

"Bullshit," Horey said handing the hand set back to Sanchez. "You do the things you do too good to die right now."

In minutes, I could see the black forms of the medevac helicopters clearly as they dropped down over the mountains on the northern edge of the valley, swooped down to floor and streaked toward the towering yellow smoke marking the LZ . In the steely grey of the sky, they looked like fat tadpoles in a still, clear pond sunning near the warm bottom sand.

"This is a CH-34," they said in Oki. "It is obsolete in the present military system and has not been used since Korea when they stopped making them. I show them only because you may still see them employed by our Vietnamese allies." Now it was headed in to pick up Delpert while the slimmer wasplike Huey circled above.

"Take his hands while I talk these guys in."

I knelt beside Delpert and took his hands. They were cold and limp and kept moist only by the thick heavy air and patches of his own blood. His guts exposed to the air had started to grey.

The medevac bird circled while Horey spoke to the pilot over the radio.

"Have we taken fire?" he shouted into the hand-set. "Who the Christ would shoot at us down here? We haven't heard a shot in anger in a year. Jesus."

He released the hand-set and turned to me.

"Every once in a while we get one of them won't come in if you tell them there's a war going on for Christ sake," he said. "They don't want to know anything about a hot zone, afraid to lose their precious birds. Think they live in the goddamn States. But that's just a few."

I watched the chopper settle to the ground while the angry Huey escort bird stood guard, above us poised to strike at any movement in the ville.

The village remained quiet.

"Most all of them are good though," Horey shouted over the noise. "Got balls big as a hooch."

When they had lifted off again, I asked, "You think he'll make it?"

"Who, Delpert?"

"Yes."

"Christ no," He snorted. "He didn't have any guts left, didn't you see him?"

I looked at Horey and then at the ground.

"Seems as though they ought to be able to do something about it. They said before I left..."

The helicopters disappeared over the mountains and it was quiet again.

"Where was he from?"

"MPs"

"No, I mean where in the States."

"Beats the shit out of me," Horey said flipping the dial on Sanchez's radio back to the artillery frequency. "Somewhere there though, I guess. But anyway, for now, let's give that ville a little more of our special gift to remember us by."

He spoke briefly on the radio re-entering the ville's coordinates and friendly positions and then he said, "Roger roger shot out." In the distance the guns in An Hoa took voice again like a roll of thunder. In seconds this new volley of rounds whispered over the mountains rimming the valley and scattered through the still smouldering quiet village in compact crunches of smoke and splintered bamboo.

"Roger, battery 10, fire for effect."

The guns thundered again.

"Roger shot out, repeat."

"Add 50 left 50, repeat. Roger shot out."

Systematically he walked the blazing artillery through the village until little remained of the vegetation and the straw huts it concealed. The Gunny walked back to where we stood.

"Not to good huh Lieutenant?"

"Naw Gunny he's deader than that fucking ville. Let's get 'um back on the road."

He turned to me as the last volley echoed away to the south.

"That should do it for them. Get back to the point and let's get the hell out of here."

We stayed off the side road in the low weeds for the rest of the way and no one else was hurt.

Easy – Easy Echo - Eeeeeasy Echo.

We walked back through the village by the river where we left the natives from the top of the hill the day before. I carried Delpert's helmet and pistol and the people that lived there paused as I walked by. They saw the empty helmet and whispered "Honcho" among themselves. They nudged each other and pointed as the helmet that I carried by the chin strap swung loosely in my left hand. The whisper and nudge moved on through the ville ahead faster than I walked and some of them smiled as I caught up.

The barge choked back to life and fired and slowly, as if one at a time, it carried us back across the river.

"That stupid son-of-a-bitch," Wick said when we got back. "Now I got this goddamn Company and I'm too short, too goddamn short."

"You got more than that," Horey said.

"What do you mean?" Wick asked.

"The dog," Horey said through a smile." Don't forget the dog, SKIPPER."

"Fuck you," Wick said, kicking dirt toward the dog.

Polo sat unmoved and looked, tongue lolling, toward the thick glistening underbrush, waiting.

I hiked back to the top of the mountain.

Dear Pumpkin,

Good news, I didn't get sick and throw up.

Think of you often,

Sam

Shadows moved back through the valley. They studied the brown stain in the middle of the road and poked into the pools of the soggy remains of the village. No one had been hurt.

SitRep Jan121056H: It was hot mid-morning and the thick jungle brush on the hill smelled strongly of late-August-back-in-the-world-fresh-cut grass. There were dragon flies everywhere on the top, buzzing lazily in the heat, and the sun, when it broke through, pushed up blisters and burned the flesh on my shoulders. I raced along with Wick toward the top.

My skin grew stiff and brittle in the heat and now, climbing quickly and in stride, I felt it cracking in the movement of my arms and I felt the fluid of the blisters ooze easily down my back. I felt too, the anger that moved beside me while, as pebbles kicked loose, our speed grew with the heat moving up the mountain. I was happy now that my time had begun, for a week ago, I would not have kept up, but now, my legs had grown strong in coming and going off the mountain, and my wind filled the sails of my feet and pushed them easily, even as we met the pillow of the heat that dragon flies carried down the trail in their wings to meet us. Wick beside me did not speak, but the words in his eyes were clear and the sound of the things he said still followed from the bottom, where minutes before we sat talking. I of Delpert who was dead before they landed in Da Nang, and of defence, and he of Jesus Christ. It started well enough, Horey sleeping and Wick passing by and near the fire, since burned out, kicking empty cans with his toe into the cool pithy ashes. It had started well enough, sitting there quietly drawing lines in the loose earth with a stick while Wick kicked cans easily with thought and study. Then, as easily, I was speaking.

"Do you have a defense plan for the top?" I asked.

"No," he said, and I said, "Oh."

"Why," he asked.

"No reason," I said. "I just wondered about it, that's all."

Then he stopped kicking cans and the lines that I traced grew fainter as he watched me and I did not look up.

"Why?" he demanded.

I said, "I just wanted to see it, that's all. I can't see if it makes much difference."

"What you got up there now?" he asked.

I didn't answer. I just let the stick fall from my hands, the flag dropped, the bell rang, the doors of the gate flew open.

At first Wick said nothing. But now as we neared the middle position he spoke.

"How long have you been here?" he asked through clenched teeth.

"Five days," I said. "Maybe six."

"And you didn't think of a defence until now?" Wick asked. "Jesus Christ, that's just what they look for, some simple shit like that. You think your ass is safe up there? Those little gook fuckers could bag your ass just sure as shit if that was what they wanted."

I started to say I hadn't been told but fell silent instead looking down at my feet, matching steps, rematching them and matching them again. We steamed through Rico's squad.

"Every one of these got to be new fighting positions by the book with proper apertures, aiming sticks, intersecting fields of fire. All of it. This ain't no goddamn shanty town. You fucking people are Marines."

I think I can.

I think I can.

I think I can.

I think I can.

Without looking up, we reached the top.

Balen, who heard us coming, stood on the top of his bunker. Wick and I sat at his feet catching our breath in secret. Neither of us spoke.

"Good morning, Sir," Balen said.

Wick nodded and looked away down into the valley where the still river moved without notice toward the south.

"What?" he asked as he followed the line of the river into the mist, "do you defend from here, Balen?"

"My sector runs from that finger, there, to over by those bushes, there." His hand described the arc in the air as he spoke.

"I have one gun," he continued, "It covers the trail coming up."

I looked up at Balen carefully. At first I didn't hear Wick.

"Did, you know that?" he asked again.

I looked away from Balen and then absently back to Wick.

"He knew it, Sir," Balen said before I could answer. "He set it up."

My voice retreated following my eyes down into the valley where it was cool and I noticed that again, except for the buzz of the flies, it was quiet. Wick looked at me closely.

"Let's hear the rest of it," he said.

I stood and followed quietly. As we walked across the top, groups of men cleaning equipment stopped and smiled a greeting.

"Hey Skipper."

I responded automatically and forgot that they were there until another group appeared. While Wick spit words out through his teeth, I glanced infrequently back towards Balen's position. Balen stood on the roof, smiling.

"I may be short," Wick growled. "But I ain't that short. You may think you ain't got to do shit up here, but it wouldn't take much to stick it up your ass. What the hell did they tell you before you got here. Jesus."

Again I had no answer.

The western edge of the hill fell off in a sheer drop. To the east, facing the river, a dirt road that wound up from below and that was only passable when it was dry, ended next to the remains of the truck on a small plateau which served as an occasional LZ.

"What covers this?" Wick asked.

"A walking post." I answered.

"Is that all?"

"Yes."

"Bullshit."

We stood on the western edge looking down into the lush green below us.

"They can get up here, goddamn it," Wick said as we looked down together, down to the road that led into the mine, down into the peaceful trees and bushes where Boots and Harry worked today with short patrols because someone had to.

"Christ, leave your dick hanging out and they'll chop it off and serve it to you on a fucking platter. They'll come out of those huts and holes down there. They'll even come up out of the fucking river and the paddies and bingo, you're dead. All it takes is time, and they got time. That's all they got is time. They don't count the fucking days until they go home from here, this is home, so they just sit down there and wait and watch because they know you're going to fuck up."

I looked down into the tangle of tree tops 300 meters below.

Wick said there were tactics in it somewhere down there, but I thought 'it is only the heat of the day and the climb and perhaps the passing of Delpert that makes him think it.' The rock that I kicked fell untouched by the slope of the mountain and the sound that it made when it struck at the bottom vanished before the soggy air could bring it back to my ears.

I looked at Wick but remained silent.

"I want a position here," he said. "And here." He pointed vaguely as he spoke.

"Cover that road, clear out that shit." He motioned toward the grass growing down over the edge by the wire and it bowed softly in the light river breeze as if it understood the things he said.

"Defend this goddamn hill," he said, at last.

I followed a step behind him as we walked back over the saddle to Balen's position. I stopped there and Wick continued on over the edge.

He was being eaten by the grass because of what he had said. He disappeared slowly as the grass arched over him.

The grass then was to be feared. It had to be destroyed. It was the eyes and ears of the earth where it grew bobbing and watching, whispering as things passed through for hidden messages, as things happened or as they did not.

I turned and looked at Balen who sat on his bunker smoking.

Lonely emerged from a nearby bunker.

"Boy Lieutenant he sure smoked your ass."

I picked up an empty sand bag and threw it to Lonely.

"Get your E-tool," I said. "Your sorry ass is going to dig."

Far below a brown bare foot kicked at the pebble that landed nearby. The shadowy figure stooped to pick it up and gazed up toward the top of the mountain.

After a moment he tossed the pebble to the ground and moved on.

SitRep Jan121710H: By evening, we had five new positions. I checked them through the night and in the darkness I stumbled over things I couldn't see. I met and talked with Balen in the dark of his bunker and together we grew tired and our eyes burned from the smoke of chain-smoked cigarettes. When I returned to my bunker Wescott sat writing letters and English was asleep.

SitRep Jan141017H: I was in the valley with two squads by the mouth of the coal mine and heading in when I first heard the chopper come in through the valley flying down low just over the river. For the past hour we had been on a shit-ass patrol around the base of the mountain watching little men carry more into the mine than they carried out. We broke through to the trail leading back to the CP just in time to see the 34 pick up and head back up through the valley. Balen and Rico drove their squads on toward the hill.

A curtain of dusty pellets blown loose by the wash of the 34 lifted away from the ground and settled again leaving only the straining fading drone of the departing bird and the quiet glide of the river for Captain Flyn-Michael to contemplate. Lieutenants John Brownell and John Fitzlee stood next to him looking first at the pastel plaster houses, then the finger's rising taper and finally, the brownish top.

"Well." Wick said. "There they are."

He stood at the CP looking down at them. Behind him, Gunny Pick sat on a C-rations case looking down too, stroking his smooth jaw with one hand while he looked. Sanchez listened at the buzz of the radio and tossed small rocks at the darting dragon flies.

"Another M.P.," Wick continued. "And two more boot Lieutenants."

"I hear he's a Comm. Officer, Sir," Sanchez said.

Wick looked over at Sanchez and spit on the ground.

"Yeah," he said. "MP, Comm. O, samey-same."

"Jesus Christ," Sanchez said. "That's just what the fuck we need....Sir."

'They are here, at the beginning,' I thought shading my eyes to watch them start the trek up the short rise to the CP, 'finally someone greener than me.' We gained the beach and I followed them up the hill.

Wick told us the night before that they were coming. He told us that the new Skipper was a Comm. Officer. He told us too of the Com Officer at the base camp who had been decorated with the purple heart for wounds received during a mortar attack.

Wick said he was wounded, by the foot-locker he tripped over when he jumped out from between the sheets. We all laughed and Horey said, "I wonder about the fucking truth of things anymore. A VC footlocker. Shit man."

"Anyway," Wick said. "We're fat on officers now." He sat down next to the Gunny and waited while the rest of us circled them for names.

The two new Lieutenants looked at each other and I recognized in their eyes the uneasy glaze that just a few short days ago lived with me.

Brownell was a big man with a craggy broad face and a strong voice that laughed and filled the air around him when he spoke. He spoke and he laughed often and that face, most of it friendly mouth, filled with deep heavy lines when he did. He pulled off his helmet, let it drop to the ground between his feet and replaced it with a highly-starched soft cover that he had somehow managed to get to the hill undamaged. It looked oversized and flared up and out from his head like a papal mitre.

Beside him, kid-faced Fitzlee stood quiet and correct. In his pocket he carried One-Hundred-Years-Of-Our-Finest-Virginia-Military-Schools. There was history in his eyes. Unlike Brownell whose face resembled a relief map, Fitzlee's was absolutely smooth and hairless. His voice was husky and quiet pushing words through his even white teeth with a gentle Virginia drawl. He was indeed someone's fair-haired boy The son of small town Spotsylvania Court House; where no doubt everyone who could attend and still be home by 10 p.m. turned out for his farewell dinner the night before he left. And while he sat at the head table with his father he probably nodded and quietly said, "Thank you, thank you for all you've done for me." And his father beamed, proud as hell.

Beside them, large-eyed Captain Flynn-Michael erupted to a staggering six feet plus, with a large a beachhead of a chest and long striding legs that looked a little too thin for rest of him. Like his eyes, his hair was black and just a little too long to be happy in the Gunny's Company. Today he didn't smile so the fact that his second incisor was missing remained concealed behind large tight and rounded cheeks.

'Today is my lucky day,' he thought. 'Not only have I finally gotten a fucking rifle company but I have also managed to miss meeting Colonel Teapot on check in. I just threw my gear into the hooch and hopped the first chopper down.'

His opportunity to smile passed. Meeting new troops was serious business for now, but he looked like there would be time to smile later. Today he was short on words and appeared to be alone with his thoughts.

"All I can tell you is this," he said finally. "I am a goddamn infantry man. Six years in the Irish Army as a private, a fucking snuffie, and they made me a goddamn communicator, for Christ sake. All I ever wanted to be was an infantry man and now, finally..."

His voice trailed off and he turned to Wick.

"We're going back in tomorrow," he said. "And if it's all the same to you, I'll just be to observing until we get back."

With them too was Doc Peckham a new corpsman just in from the states. Skinny, angular with young shining eyes and hair that was longer than long, his name was Doc. He was a corpsman and because of it he, like the rest shared their common name, Doc. Doc this person or Doc that person, but always Doc. He wore the title like a badge. He spotted the Gunny and struggling under the weight of an enormous mountain of gear easily equal to his weight, he dragged himself across the small campsite and held out a hand.

"Doc Pecham," he said. "I've been assigned to the first platoon."

The Gunny ignored the extended hand and pointed toward me.

"That's your Lieutenant there," he said in a way that told the Doc he was not a special friend. "And that's the Company Doc's hooch over there, you go check in with him and he'll make sure you got what you need although it don't look like you left much behind. And then you'll hump up the hill with the Lieutenant here when he's ready to leave."

The same chopper that carried them in carried Polo out. She sat quietly looking out past the door gunner into the sky and raced back to Da Nang.

"Good fucking riddance," Wick said as he watched the chopper fade noisily up the valley. Next to him a bag of mail sat quietly in the mud.

SitRep Jan141912H It was dark. I checked positions with Balen on the top of the hill and Rico on the lower. It was still chilly on the top, but nightly more stars filled the sky above us and clouds grew fewer. The monsoon was releasing its grip slowly. It pulled off the mountains like the lifting of a sponge removing any remaining water marks from the growths of bamboo and teak and mahogany.

At the CP, Captain Flynn-Michael talked quietly with Wick and the Gunny. And just as quietly Sanchez relayed the information up the hill to English who in turn passed it on to me.

"We'll be going over the river when we get back," he said. "On a search and destroy." Back on the top, I thought about going in while I opened my mail.

Dear S,

Tonight is the first night without you. It's so very quiet and I had trouble trying to sleep so I decided to get up and start this letter. I stopped at the Oceanside beach on the way back and walked out on the pier and just stood there for a while looking west. I think I could feel you looking back east from the plane, could you feel me? At the same time I think I felt the baby move. Now at night it makes me feel better knowing that a little piece of you is still here inside me. Oh S I know you said you'd be back and not to worry, but I've started already and can't imagine I'll stop for the next 395 days until you walk back in that door. Please, please, please be careful and come back to me. I'm going to stop now before I start to cry. I hope you feel how much I love and miss you and that you are able to feel the same. I know I'm rambling but if I stop I feel like I'm letting you go again for the second time today and it makes me feel so lonely. Tia arrives next week so maybe that will help. She's going to look for a job and then we'll have each other for company in the evenings. I know how silly this must all sound and I'm sorry but it really is the way I feel. Good night. I love you. I know how busy you must be but please write soon.

Pumpkin.

Dear Sam,

I'm trying to be strong but it's been almost two weeks now and I haven't heard a word. If you knew how much it makes me worry you wouldn't make me wait so long to write. I don't know if I can do this for a whole year not knowing where you are and what you are thinking. Please, please, please write.

Love.

Oh Sam I just took this out to mail and five of your letters were waiting, so as you see I brought this back in to add to. I've read them all over and over already and now I'm sad again and afraid. I like it when you tell me about what you do and how you feel but it makes me miss you and angry that you are so far away when you should be here. I love you fuzzy cheeks.

P

SitRep Jan150612II. At first light, Echo stood saddled up and on the beach down from the top of the hill. As we moved in pieces to the barge and across, Wick and Captain Flynn-Michael and I stood with the native engineers. Wick talked easily, his hands in his pockets, watching the Company grow larger on the farther bank. Hotel moved across on the return trip to take our place on the hill.

"We got to go back now," Wick said. "We're going 'cross the river next week."

The natives smiled and bowed slightly like small signal flags as he spoke. Captain Flynn-Michael remained silent, glancing first at the Gunny and then rolling his eyes back at Wick. Wick chewed on a cigar and talked steadily toward the river until the barge came for us and then we were across. I looked back across the river and reflected on the past two weeks and while I did so I pulled down on the chin strap of my helmet and we began to move.

There was a new Company there now, and I could feel them watch through the heat as we, Echo, split the quiet in the valley with our movement. The road was finally dull and dry in the sunlight, and, except for the occasional deep glossy pools of shit and piss made by water buffalo, it was brittle to my step. It was changed in texture and in color; light brown at the crown of the ruts, darker at their base where the moisture still seeped in and hid.

I wondered if the new men noticed these things, Brownell who walked taller than Boots beside him; Fitzlee the smooth walking with Harry who grew weary of walking; Captain Flynn-Michael who walked with Wick and watched the Gunny. Probably not. To them, it had always been this way. To me it was different because I had been here longer than one day, truly.

We walked and the base camp grew closer. The pace was stiff and as we turned inland from the river, the heat shifted into our shoulders and we were slowed because of it. Wick cursed at the men who fell down and Harry kicked them in the ass, so they got up and continued, continued until they passed through the wire where, just by the passing, it was considered safe.

"I'm a very cautious man," Captain Flynn-Michael said to his Company when we had rested. "I'm a very cautious man."

I stood against the Company hooch watching my men while Captain Flynn-Michael spoke to the Company formation. I smiled at the flicker of surprise when they saw for the first time that he was missing one of his front teeth; and when they heard his voice, its high tenor brogue.

"I'm a very cautious man," he said again and then he walked away abruptly, as if he was speaking again, soon, in another place. For a moment, no one moved.

"Ten-hut," the Gunny said. And seconds later, "All right, at ease."

The Company relaxed to quiet talking knots and I started back towards my hooch.

"That don't mean no goddamn talking or moving around," Gunny Pick said as he walked behind the loose ranks of the formation, his voice sharp like his jaw. "That don't mean no goddamn talking or moving at all."

"Now," he said, "for some goddamn reason, the General has decided to let you girls into his war."

I walked slowly up the slope that used up the space between the Company area and where I slept, the Q. My pack hung off one shoulder and I carried my helmet. Because it was difficult to carry, I still wore my flak jacket. I passed by the lifeless extinguished shitters and wondered how long it would be before the torch returned. Behind me, the Company laughed.

"All right, all right," Gunny Pick said, stuffing his hand into his hip pocket. "Now I told you girls about these fuckin' wallets. When we go out, you leave that shit here; the letters and the money, all of it. They don't give a rat's ass that mamma misses your pecker and there ain't a goddamn thing you can buy in the bush. And you stay the hell away from those little bastards trying to pimp out their sister. You tie into one of those whores and your dick will go home riding in the seat next to you. You don't need that shit so leave it here."

I stepped around the piss tube and stopped. For a minute I stood looking down at it.

"Missed me," I said quietly saluting it. "That makes us even."

In the background, the Gunny continued, "…and If I catch you out there with that shit, you'll wish to Christ the little fuckers had shot your ass first."

I stood at my hatch, my door, listening.

He was done, and in the minute that I stood there by the door, its screen kicked loose at the bottom and the weather shield drawn to hide the flickering light at night, I saw him with their eyes and I knew with them that he would watch over them and they would feel better about a lot of things or he would kick their ass, their collective asses, until they did.

"Amen," I said aloud, and the piece of rubber cut from a tube slammed the door behind me.

Inside Brownell and Fitzlee were stowing their gear. Delpert's corner was dark and quiet. Tomorrow, first thing in the morning the First Sergeant would pack up his personal gear and send it home to his grieving wife. I wondered if Polo would go home too.

Sanchez rapped on the hatch and stuck his head in.

"Excuse me gentlemen, the Skipper wants to see you all in his hooch."

SitRep Jan151527H Captain Flynn-Michael lay back on his cot, knitting his fingers behind his head and smiling easily at the ceiling. We sat on boxes and on the floor listening to his monologue. From this moment we were his, his Lieutenants, the Actuals, his Actuals.

"It makes a man feel good," he said. "It makes a man feel goddamn good to be doing the things that he always wanted to do. A communicator, for Christ sake, me, Flynn-Michael who came from Ireland with nothing but the education of eight sorry years, and a fiver in her majesty's service."

He reached for the beer that has been sweating on the plywood floor next to him and paused drifting away from us. He propped it on his thick rounded chest and watched the water run down off the can and into the fabric of his jacket. Next to him, also on the floor, the latest selection from his book club lay once read through and half again. Other books and magazines lay half unpacked around the room.

He smiled as he thought out the words that had been foremost with him for the past two days, since they had told him in the Military Police Officers Club where he had simply fucked away half his time.

My Company.

"My Company," he said out loud. "By God that sounds good. Good enough to wipe the slate of all the other shit getting here I can tell you."

He tipped the beer forward and smiled again at the ceiling swiping absently at the suds that leaked from the corner where the can met his mouth. We sat quietly drinking with him and waited for him to go on. He picked up a worn copy of *Papa* and leafed slowly through some of the familiar pages, pausing slightly at the pictures and stopped where he had last left off, his eyes showing little movement as they pulled into their roundness, the words printed on the page. For the moment he seemed to forget we were there and was lost in his own euphoric reverie.

"I wonder what it's like to get shot in the nuts," he said quietly as he came to that part of the book. "Much like being a communicator, I suppose, and that's..."

A brisk, almost timid knocking on the door interrupted him mid-sentence; the clatter of the door to the poorly fitted jamb made more noise than the knuckles of the knocker.

"It isn't locked, for Christ sake," he said, laying the book down open to where he had left off, and noticing casually that we were still there.

"Is that your normal greeting, Captain?" Colonel Teapot asked as he pushed the door open and stepped into the room.

We all jumped to attention. Captain Flynn-Michael forgot the beer perched on his chest and now it lifted off, cart wheeling through the air. It struck first the rail of his rack and then clattered to the floor, spitting white foam and beer onto the highly polished boots and well pressed trousers of Lieutenant Colonel A. Francis Teapot.

"And it gets better, I see," he said looking down at the growing stain as the beer settled through his trousers and onto his leg. "You drink beer," he continued looking around the room. "All of you." He shook his left leg with a slight shift to his right and looked just briefly like a dog coming in from the rain.

"No Sir..., Yes Sir...,That is I can assure you it won't get any better, better than what seems not to be so good so far that is, and yes Sir I am known to have an occasional beer." Captain Flynn-Michael said bending over to right the toppled beer can before it had all poured out.

"It was an accident, you see.

"And can I offer the Colonel one, Sir?"

"I missed you when you arrived and then I thought you would report in as soon as you got back from the mine, but of course that didn't happen, did it. And then I thought I would send for you but I decided no perhaps I would stop on my way to the chow hall, stop in in a less formal way to see if you had settled in yet," the Colonel went on ignoring the offer responding only with a slight wince. "But I see there was no need to worry, you are already quite at home, planning strategy with your Lieutenants. I assume or having something to say about accidental discharges."

He shook his leg again looked around the room more carefully this time recording each of us in turn where we still stood at rigid attention.

"Lieutenants," saying the word as though like Lonely, he found it distasteful, looking from me to Boots to Harry to Horey to Brownell to Fitzlee. "Six of you, my goodness, quite a staff, Captain, quite a staff, and so quickly too."

"Yes Sir, "Flynn-Michael said, his voice beginning to climb through the scale toward high C.

"And, this greeting, it must be some quaint Irish custom?"

"No Sir, I..."

"Think nothing of it," the Colonel said. "Although, it's not often that I bathe in beer spatter, accidently or not. In fact," now his voice increased slightly, "I don't even drink it."

Captain-Flynn-Michael sensing that all was lost could do nothing but relax. His shoulders slumped and he had the air of a condemned man with nothing left to lose as he looked down at the agitated Colonel. From where we stood he towered over him by a head and the breadth of his shoulders masked the Colonel's stiffness completely. He looked us all over again and then as quickly as he came, he departed, the door slamming behind him. There was a brief pause before we realized we could stand at ease and then Flynn-Michael laughed.

"Have you ever seen such an asshole," he said. "'I don't even drink the stuff' he says, for Christ sake. Jesus."

Boots and Horey and I looked from one another and then we smiled slightly and I thought of the new day about to begin.

SitRep Jan151732H A cleaner mc stepped out of the Q and walked back down through the Company area past the Company office and across the airstrip to the perimeter surrounding the camp. Leaning on one of the bunkers I looked out across the small white dotted field. It was better when it was flowers. In the distance I could see and hear Phu Da 2, the buzzing refugee ville. An ant-like line moved back and forth through the opening in the wall carrying bits of possession on their heads and across their shoulders on sticks. Wisps of odorless smoke strained up over the bamboo thicket that enclosed the cluster of thatched shacks. I was right, there was nothing hidden here.

Dear Pumpkin,

Well, Wick is finally happy and for two reasons. First of all the dog is gone and second he goes home in a couple of days so he's done with going out in the field.

First about the dog. We went out on a patrol about a week ago in the rain into this valley where Wick says there are tacson (which means a lot) gooks and we searched this almost deserted village, just some kids and old people one of whom we wounded and had to evacuate, and a cobra tied into a cave like a booby trap that one of my men killed so now they call him cobra. And let me tell you about the kids, covered with flies and sores and… well … shit to heal the sores. And then on the way back in Captain Delpert got shot in the stomach so we stood in the rain and watched him die. I've never seen anyone die before. And did I tell you the good news. I didn't throw up.

Love,

S

6 OPERATION INDEPENDENCE – JANUARY, 1967

SitRep Jan151912H In the evening after chow, Horey and I walked down to the Company area for the briefing on the operation across the river. Fitzlee and Harry squatted under the eaves of the Company hooch watching the Gunny and Brownell pitch horse-shoes. While they watched, they talked of the afternoon's encounter with the Colonel and the platoon that Fitzlee was to take over when Harry left for a special S-4 school on Oki in a week or so. Two country boys, they spoke quietly under the sound of the shoes *whuffing* into the dirt around the pins and the occasional verbal encouragement the players received as they arched them into the darkening sky. Harry pointed to different Marines as they moved back and forth through the Company area and Fitzlee took notes.

"Just a boot up the ass," he said as we walked by.

Wick sat alone on the steps of the Company hooch smoking a cigar.

"He's good," I said as I watched the Gunny toss lazy half turning shoes for point after point.

"Yeah," Horey said. "He's good. You don't know how good."

Five minutes after we arrived, Captain Flynn-Michael strode into the Company area. Again, he had the look of a man with several other engagements after this one. Without speaking we all moved into the Company hooch after him. Boots, who had been made XO to replace Wick with the arrival of Brownell and Fitzlee, was already there going over the Company records with the First Sergeant.

We sat draped around the small office area on field desks and foot lockers and struck matches holding them to candles and cigarettes while Captain Flynn-Michael tacked a map to the bulkhead just next to the door with the butt of his .45. The lighting was bad and from where I sat, the map was difficult to see. I was able to recognize the river, though, and from the position of the map I could see the airstrip, but the other side, the side that Flynn-Michael now pointed to as the objective, that one I had only heard of, that was the Arizona. It was named after the wild and lawless old west and by all accounts it more than lived up to its namesake.

Captain Flynn-Michael put his pistol back in its holster and turned to face us. He looked at us slowly while he drew in his breath causing the candles to flicker, the map now completely hidden behind his rapidly expanding torso. And then he began to speak. He chose his words carefully dropping each one in our midst like a small explosive device the report of which accelerated the delivery of the next until his speech resembled the cadence of a heavily engaged machine gun.

"When we were waiting," he said, "for the barge, I overheard someone tell those fucking," he said fooking, "those fucking gook miners that we were so sorry to be leaving, but that we had to go across the goddamn river to an operation. For Christ sake I thought they were in love. We've got to leave you and go to your fucking war, he said, Jesus. And you can bet your ass right now that the little fucker has told every son-of-a-bitch in 10 miles that we'll be coming over to see them." His eyes which by now had doubled in size and taken on the look of swirling brown bottomless pools blistered when he paused. "Don't say anything to them, not a fucking word, for Christ sake. We'd be a hell of a lot better off if we'd sent them a copy of the goddamn operation order. Nobody can understand the goddamn things anyway, and those that can would die of laughter or embarrassment, or both, Jesus."

He paused again and turned toward the map, stepping back so that a few could see. I looked over at the others in the room.

Boots, Horey, the Gunny, the two new Johns, and Harry who was leaving in the middle, they were all intent, and Wick , he was too short to make this one, he'd stay in An Hoa while we crossed the river and then all alone fly away home.

I turned back to the map.

Wick looked through the map and pulled his knees back under his chin. Slowly, he reached up for his cigar and started spinning it, slowly, slowly, watching the smoke curl up into the bad light. On his thigh, a finger from his other hand worked back and forth over a worn spot on his trousers.

"It'll be a bag of shit, like walking into a fucking cave," Captain Flynn-Michael said. "It's always a bag of shit but, I guess we'll do it anyway and, then we'll talk about it in the club later. Christ knows what will happen."

Like Wick, I watched the smoke swirl through the sputter of the candles and into a "fucking cave."

I remember holding tight at my father's hand when we walked through the large vaulted gates to the Polo Ground, past the rows of boxes that housed fat ticket-takers and thin ones with cast eyes and into the maze of cold pipe corals and chutes, through more pipe turn-styles that were hard to turn, into the crush of cigar smoking cursing men of purpose and hard-mouthed boys who threw popcorn and smoked long cigarettes held awkwardly in cracking miniature hands, past the man who sold score cards two of which my father bought but did not roll and study like the others, walking up the concrete ramps that turned in dark corners that smelled like urine, while my father said 'Hold tightly, hold tightly, I don't want to lose you here;' here sounding like the most unpleasant place in the world, pressing on with the surge of the plaza inside the gate to the point where the concrete in the ramps sang with the pounding feet and the darkness grew with the height.

I remember each step as we climbed higher into the steel frame work and the surprise when we burst into the light and could see the brilliant green of the playing field below still carried on the crest of thousands and millions and billions of people going in an equal number of directions and thinking there is not time, and then sitting down to the first pitch and looking around at all who were settled in the place and father saying, "There," as he freed his hand from mine. "You see there was plenty of time. How Do You Like It?" smiling all the while.

Captain Flynn-Michael pointed into the green part of the map.

"... into the fucking maze called the Arizona, and I'll tell you one thing, it's no fucking place to get lost in the dark. This is the LZ," he said. And then he defined it; he cut it into segments like a pie and passed them out so all might have a piece. "North is twelve o'clock," he said.

A piece to chew on, to digest, to pass from safely.

"First Platoon will have from twelve to four, second from four to eight, third from eight to twelve."

I wrote it down and looked up for the rest.

"We'll be traveling in the finest of 46s," he said. "It'll be a goddamn stroke if they make it in. They should have been in the fucking scrap pile a decade ago, for Christ sake, break apart like eggs they do when the props collide."

"We're to secure the LZ until Hotel comes in and moves out."

Captain Flynn-Michael looked at us for a moment and then turned to take down the map. As he worked at the tacks he had driven in with his pistol, he spoke over his shoulder.

"I'd like to give you the rest of our mission," he said. "But I can't because the Colonel hasn't seen fit to give it to me yet. I wouldn't worry about it though, it's only a war and tomorrow's a long time away, and we can always sit and chat in the LZ, so fuck it. Sweet Jesus, Gunny these tacks must be a meter long, it's a goddamn VC plot, I'm sure of it."

The last tack free, he folded his map and disappeared through the door. I looked down at the two words I had scribbled under the coordinates of the LZ. 'From twelve to four,' I said to myself, and then, closing the book I stood to leave, jamming it deeply into the side pocket of my trousers.

"I need a beer," Horey said as he brushed past.

"Lead on Mac Duff," and I started for the door on his heels.

"You two gents join us in a beer?" Horey asked as we walked past Brownell and Fitzlee.

"Do they have beer over here?" Brownell asked.

"No," Horey said after studying Brownell's eyes. "We're going to use empty glasses and just make believe, Jesus Christ. Where do you think the Skipper got beer? You think he has his own private supplier? Boots."

"What do you want?" Boots asked looking up from the small field desk in the corner of the hooch.

"I'm not talking to you," Horey said turning at the door. "I'm talking about them, and when I said boots, I didn't mean boots with a capital 'B', I meant boots with a capital green, Clear?"

"No," Boots said.

"Let's get out of here," Horey said pushing at the door. "Wick, how about you?"

Wick looked up and nodded.

It was dark outside and I didn't talk as we walked up the hill toward the hooch.

Fifty-seven, fifty-eight, fifty-nine, sixty, sixty-one, sixty-two, step right, sixty-three, step left, sixty-four.

I counted to myself.

"Ow, Jesus," Brownell said behind me.

"Pisstube," I said over my shoulder.

"Why in the Christ didn't you tell me where it was?" he asked.

"No need," I said with a quiet smile. "You found it by yourself and now you know where it is."

Horey laughed and reached for the door pull.

"You know something," Wick said before it was open.

"What's that?" Horey asked.

"That ain't nothing to say the before an operation."

"Aw, who gives a shit," Horey said. "He's right. And besides they already know we're coming anyway, so fuck it."

Wick didn't answer. We went inside. I lighted a candle and then another, and Horey slid a case of beer from under his rack.

"The finest of champagne for the man with the bleeding shins, and bourbon for our gent from the south, and for our dear departing Wick, corn whiskey just like mamma use to make and probably still does. Daddy Warbucks," he said, as Harry entered the hooch, "name your poison, ale of the finest hops, champagne, bourbon?"

"Bourbon sounds good," Harry said.

"Bourbon it is," Horey said tossing a can of warm beer toward him. "And vintage at that, strong enough to kick anybody's ass."

"My favorite," Harry said. "Canned and well shaken."

"Where's mine?" I asked, blowing out a match.

"You drink beer with me, asshole," Horey said. "Only the newly arrived and the soonly departed get the good stuff."

"Is he like this often?" Brownell asked leaning toward me

"Is he like what often?"

Brownell looked at me and then drank the foam off the top of beer can.

"Nothing," he said. "Nothing at all."

"It's his nose," Boots said as he came through the door. "It's so fucking small that he's always about 10,000 feet above the rest of us. Thin air you know."

"You know," Horey said, "I'll bet you're from Chicago."

"How did you know?" Boots asked.

"Because you know so fucking much about nose jobs," Horey said.

"Fuck you," Boots laughed. "Let me have a beer."

"Get your own fucking beer," Horey said. "From up here in the thin air I might fall into a crevice and hurt myself."

"It's a crevasse," I added.

"What?"

"I said it isn't crevice, its crevasse."

"I thought you were an English Major," Horey said passing the can opener to Boots who stood smiling while he listened.

"That's right."

"Well, crevasse isn't English, so go fuck yourself."

Brownell rumbled into laughter, shattering his face along with the conversation. Fitzlee, who had said little, laughed in his thick velvet quiet voice from across the room, Boots sat down on his rack next to Harry who stroked the dip in his cheek with a long fingered hand while Wick blew out the candle nearest his rack and lay down staring at the ceiling; his half-finished beer melted into the plywood floor and...,

...the dish ran away with the spoon.

Horey began to bang his can on the deck in rhythmic strokes. One-by-one we were gavelled to silence. It grew quiet in the room and everyone turned to where Horey sat cross-legged like an Indian, the case of beer in front of him on the floor. He looked slowly from face to face, closing our mouths one by one.

"Who," he asked solemnly, "would care for another beer?"

Boots threw his can at him and the laughter picked up again until soon it was where it had been moments before. Wick rolled over looking away from us and tried to sleep.

Outside in the dark it was quiet. A new threat of rain hissed and listened above us preparing to fall.

SitRep Jan160617H: Morning and Echo stood silently on the air strip drawn in lines fifteen men long. In front of us, down the strip, eight CH-46s, slender pods of green magnesium with a rotor perched at each end, droned in noisy idle discord, their large round exhaust ports popping in time with the sweep of the blades.

I stood at the head of the third line watching the birds rock anxiously on their wheels waiting to swallow me up wrong way to.

'The early bird and all that,' I thought looking back at the forming Company. They watched us as they shifted from tire to tire, dropping their ramps so as to make easy the fact that, the early green birds would eat the early, also green, 15 joint worm.

Behind me, my men stood shifting and pawing at the ground.

And this worm has eaten butterflies for his morning meal and has washed them down with the bitters of memory that recall similar breakfasts in different times, before ball games to be played or sitting in the car in front of the dentist while he watched me from his office window.

I could see Wick as I looked past the choppers to the scatter of hooches where he stood up by the eaves of the Company hooch watching. I could see him standing there like a shadow and I wondered now if he was a little afraid as he realized that the sun was rising and he was growing closer and closer to extinction under his own boots that only a month ago pushed mine with swagger and angry confidence to the top of Mount Nong Son. It made me feel better about things to wonder about him because we stood under the same promise of sun. I hoped it was not going to be a bag of shit because a bag of shit in the promise of sun was bad and worse if the sun, the one we now shared, sank into the promise of rain.

The butterflies were moving now, so as we turned to walk the length of the green panting chopper I decided that any questions I had about all this had no particular answer. Because of that I suddenly felt very lonely and sad.

The Marines around me had each other to turn to and the memories of other waits for other just like this things to take the jitter out of their eyes and let them spit their fears verbally onto the ground with laughs and bravado like so many little brown turds, But Wick and I were lonely because he was at the end of his line and I was at the beginning of mine and we were both afraid.

At the end of the column, Doc Peckham stood alone reaching and grabbing at the tangle of straps that looped over his shoulders and pulled down heavily under his arms. I trotted back and stood before him, arms folded across my chest waiting for him to look up.

"Nervous Doc?" I asked at last.

"A little, Sir" he shouted into the popping noise. "This is my first one you know." He let his hands fall to his sides.

"I know, you joined us at the coal mine the day before we came back in, right?"

Doc Peckham nodded. I remembered his arrival.

Captain Flynn-Michael pulled me aside and said; "For Christ sake, keep an eye on Ichabod there. Where the Christ do they get them?"

I studied him closely now, trying to tie the end of each draping strap to a poorly tied and bloated sandbag.

"What is all this crap?" I asked.

"Things I need, Sir." the Doc said.

"For what? We've got hospitals that stay in one place in the rear, for Christ sake."

"These things will make it better, Sir, if someone gets shot," the Doc said.

"These things will make you slow and they'll probably die before you get to them, or worse you might be the one who gets shot because of it, what then?"

I looked at him again, more slowly now, his trousers, his hands thin and tense.

'You are a fucking spider,' I thought, 'in the middle of a badly made, rancid, with half-spun dead things, web. Your hair is too long and the closeness of these life-giving cocoons prevents your arms, your thin half-rolled-up arms to the elbow, from lying neatly at your sides.'

"You haven't got a goddamn weapon," I said, meeting Doc Peckham's eyes as I spoke.

"I want to be a doctor, Sir," he said.

"Jesus, what the Christ has that got to do with it."

"I thought about it a long time, Sir and I decided I don't need a gun to be a doctor," he said.

"You should live so goddamn long," I shouted over the chatter of the choppers. "You stupid son-of-a-bitch, those goddamn people out there don't give a shit what you want to be back in… where is it?"

"Troy, Sir."

"…back in Troy then unless it's dead. Jesus, Doc, you need a fucking weapon to stay alive."

"It's all right, Sir," Doc Peckham said. I stood in blistering silence looking at him. There was no more to be said.

To our right, the first slice of Echo peeled off and jogged into the rump of the lead 46. I tried to form words spitting them from teeth and tongue and then, without using them I let them fall dead to the tarmac while I moved to the head of my line.

"It's too late now," was all I could shout. "Stay by me and keep your fucking skinny ass down." I counted helmets into the bird.

Inside, the language was the movement of fingers, the lifting of arms and shakes of the head. Through the tube of the belly I could see the hands of the pilots, co and real, moving over the switches, leaning forward to watch the gages move, checking out the systems, making hydraulics squeal, talking secretly to one another through earphones and mikes concealed in their helmets. The crew chief listened in lazily, leaning on the butt of his swing mounted machine gun, watching me and my team strap into the web slings that hung dawn either side of the bird. I watched as the pilot's hands sat back and the crew chief walked between the slings slapping at his buckle and looking into our laps. He moved slowly still looking at each one carefully and then moved on swinging his head from side to side until he stood in front of me. His hand reached up beside him and rested on the switch for the hydraulics of the ramp.

The ramp shook and started to rise causing the bowls of the bird to scream and shake violently.

My thoughts jumped for the ramp as it swung slowly closed. Too late.

I was the last one swallowed up, I would be the first one spat out. Only the Doc beside me made me smile. He took up two seats easily, but tightly he was strapped into one.

In a ripple, the wave of birds lifted off the strip, climbing almost straight up now in tight spirals over the base camp, still one behind the other. As they reached the top of the coil, they leveled and coursed west toward the broad paddies of the Arizona and the mountains beyond; I turned and watched from the round window behind me. The ground moved slowly beneath us and the other birds dotting the sky in the wave seemed not to move at all.

We hung in a bunch like bananas; bright green bananas brought from the tree too quickly and full of brighter greener seed.

Because we moved so slowly, we were woven into the tapestry of the sky. 'The weaver,' I thought, 'is a dragon wrapped in a watery cloak, sitting in the rough unused ground beneath, which I see all at a glance. He studies us quietly through cross-hairs and he muses on the use of round eyes in a tropical world full of water while his thread spreads out below us, quiet now and flowing easily, catching the glint of the occasional dull threatened sun which turns it to ice through the mountains. It laces them and him and us together because without it there would be no here, no him, no bananas, no seed; and he is old, very, very old.'

"But it would be all the same in another place," I said aloud. "So this is just as good."

I looked quickly around to see if I had been heard, but the noise of the bird had eaten my words as soon as they were said. The crew chief smiled and I sat back against the wall of the bird. It was cool where it pressed against my neck and the vibration was steady and soothing.

Across from me, English watched his feet and chewed at the end of a finger. He looked up and out through the partially closed ramp back toward An Hoa. Thinking of Wick, no doubt, standing back up under the eaves comfortably and in the middle of the fleeting thought he bit down hard on the still living flesh. It hurt and he jumped slightly, sucking the small tongue of blood that seeped away from the corner of the nail. He had the look for a moment of someone who had just remembered how short he was growing and then it appeared, he thought no more. We felt the rise in our stomachs as the bird turned and started its decent into the zone. He leaned back looked across at me catching me watching him and then looked back out the window.

I lifted my head from the wall and turned to study the ground as it grew closer under the rattle of the bird. The angle of the window made it difficult to see and I could feel the strain raise the cords in my neck making my eyes water. The river was behind us and the trees that replaced it, lived off it, grew distinct in our decent; hazy grey, then green then patchwork browns and green.

Oh God.

Oh God.

Oh God.

I turned away from the window and closed my eyes. I had seen the sharp bright flash of the muzzle.

And it was a rapid flash, an automatic.

We dropped more quickly now in tightening circles.

And, it was a big flash, big enough to light the world.

The rippling rice in the paddies began to take shape.

...a heavy, a fifty-caliber-heavy.

I swallowed hard and looked down through the insides of the chopper. Some of the others had seen it too and were now nudging the ones sitting next to them that had not.

Last week at Nong Son Horey and I sat by the CP eating chow. He tossed an empty can into the thicket close to his tent and fished for a cigarette.

"You better police that up or you'll be pickin' it out of your ass from some gook booby trap," Wick said.

Horey lighted up and said let me tell you a story and it began like this;

"Once upon a time, in a distant land, a ruler who owned many trucks with bright new .50s mounted on their tops sent them off in a line on a very long road. And the road passed through an evil place for that is where they were told to go. And so it came to pass, as they were on their journey through the evil place, that dark foul things beset them.

"And they ran away.

"Yes, sweet child, ran away, and behind them they left the many trucks with the bright new .50s coolly pointing to nowhere but the sky. And as they disappeared from view, the sly dragon rose from the water smiling at their disarray, and when they were gone he sank back down into river and with him the .50s were gone.

"And so it is here that the story ends.

"And isn't it a funny little tale tiny one, and doesn't it make you want to laugh, sweet child?

"And do you really think I give a fuck about some C-rats can?"

Wick just looked at him and walked away.

I looked back through the window.

It was still there.

'But, if I ignore it,' I thought, 'then it will ignore me and disappear into the bush.

'No one shoots bananas.

'There are laws.

'Bananas that are green must not be shot, they must be thrown back or put on the window sill till they ripen.

'There are laws.

'It is only there because I am new and English is short.

'It is there for no other reason.

'No other reason.'

I looked across to English and smiled. I smiled at the rest, one at a time, looking from face to face until they grew to shadows in the darkness of the insides and the screams of the hydraulics, poorly lighted by the shatter-proof glass in the small round ports that lined the cabin. I was smiling still when the crew chief nudged me, pointing again at my buckle. The ramp of the chopper was down and we settled into the high slender rice shoots of the paddy. The crew chief waved quickly with his hands pushing us out as we ran past him while the chopper danced from tire to tire anxious again to leave.

I stood in the grass at the end of the chopper sucking them out with my soundless voice and the words they couldn't hear. Three of the birds were on the ground, the deck, others were coming in. I checked my compass quickly.

And so the seed was neatly planted.

Tsk, tsk.

Twelve-to-Four, Twelve-to-Four, Twelve-to-Four.

I pointed, that tree line, that hedge-row.

Twelve-to-Four.

The seed was running now.

The banana flew away empty to look for more.

Twelve-to-Four, Twelve-to-Four, Twelve-to-Four.

I ran down in the paddy, in the water beneath the rice grown high and ripe with no one to reap it. It swirled around my thighs in the rotor wash and beat at my groin. Doc Peckham was on the dike running next to me, above me, on the ground beaten hard by barefoot traffic. He ran awkwardly under the weight of the things he carried, but he ran and he stayed even, his head bent to the ground, his rice slender arms pumping around his straps and baggage which trailed slightly behind him, encouraging his untried legs to keep up, to continue.

"Get down," I shouted, waving my hands and pointing down into the high green reeds. "Get down in the paddy."

"Wet, Sir," the Doc called back, shaking his head.

The other two empty choppers lifted off and circled back across the river for another load. They lifted and circled in a tight spiral up and low over me and English and the rest, still running; up over the paddy and the grass, twisting the grain in the shock, whipping it, drumming it into the soggy ground beneath it like a kick-line of fingers as they went; sucking broken filaments and roots behind and up. The choppers lifted; the dead things lifted; the Doc lifted, plucked gently from the hardened dike where he ran, webs twisting under his arms in an independent rotation slowly and down, to be placed again easily like the dead things into the paddy and then out of sight in the grass and the water and the quiet beneath.

"Wet, Sir," he sputtered, pulling himself to his feet.

"Wet to your ass, you silly shit," I said retrieving his helmet and bringing it up laughing.

I stopped beside him, looked back, nodded and smiled. I pointed into the grass again. This time he remained in the paddy next to me without complaint.

It was quiet.

It was cool and quiet and the .50 was gone.

It left with the gunner because we were so many and he so few.

He left taking his heavy stolen precious with him, and as he left, he deployed a rear guard of heat and water to wage his battle for now.

I helped Peckham untwist his straps, and together, we moved into the tree line.

The Company was in; Easy Echo was in without mishap.

The pie was divided and devoured leaving only the crust to sit on as the ferrying choppers returned.

In again,

Out again,

Gone again,

In again.

We sat on the edge of the paddy in a large circle tied in together and waited staring into the tree line as others unseen stared back.

SitRep Jan160815H: "Yes Sir," Flynn-Michael said, turning quickly to leave.

Sanchez walked behind him, and with the last of the choppers out of the zone, it was quiet. Hotel's sweeping units made ready to move out as he passed through them, while Echo sat still around the zone, waiting, staring at once into the bamboo and grass that surrounded the paddy where we landed.

Flynn-Michael stormed into the perimeter. "One Actual, I can't fucking believe it," he said. "That simpering little shit has picked up right where he left off with all his empty chatter about our careers for Christ sake, 'don't have any accidental discharges because it might hurt our careers,' he says, and me saying 'Yes Sir,' just like I did that evening in my hooch when I watched his arm come up over my shoulder while my fucking beer is glistening on the toe of his boot and working into the plywood decking of the hooch. Do you remember it one actual? 'What I really came to talk about,' he says, 'is our careers and how we must work together because we've got the most accidental discharges in the division. We work hard for a lot of things,' he says, 'and our careers are one of the most important and we should be friends, Captain Flynn-Michael,' and me running around him in circles so tight as to break, singing 'Yessir-Yessir-Yessir,' scribbling in my little book energetically adding the days in neat fine columns written sharply and strongly down the center of the page because it is our careers that are important and then, for Christ sake, he says, 'carry on' when he leaves and I feel the weight in my shoulders sink to my elbows because 'Yes Sir' has been said again; 'A sea without waves is a calm one good for sailing and the birds.' Can you fucking believe it?"

From where I sat I could see Colonel Teapot in the middle of the Company perimeter watching Captain Flynn-Michael waving his arms as he paced back and forth next to me. And when Flynn-Michael disappeared into the thicket that ran around the paddy and led him back to the Company CP, I could see that he remained fixed on Flynn-Michael's receding broad shoulders lumbering over the top of Sanchez's radio antenna.

Colonel Teapot broke his gaze and came up behind my position.

"Lieutenant," he said.

"Yes Sir." I jumped to attention.

Teapot looked at me momentarily and then took several steps into the underbrush that still swayed with Flynn-Michael's departure.

"I will keep you closely watched," he said to the shadows.

He turned in time to see the first of the sweeping platoons of Hotel leaving through a vent in the tight chamber of Echo.

"It's been a long time coming," he continued as though I wasn't there, "a long time coming." He watched them leave, his voice softened "…a very long time to get here from there. Starting as a private, two wars and now this, and silver birds just one good tour away. Not to be swept away by a boat rocker. Good sound cautious decisions and except for the birthday incident…"

His voice trailed off and he was wracked with a quiver that started at the very bottom of his boots and continued up until it nearly knocked his helmet spinning.

"Now there was something worth forgetting," he said talking into the quiet of the dense tree line. "Horrible day, horrible day." He paused again.

"Oh my God," he said after a brief reflection. "It was this very Company. Somewhere out there in Echo that cake smasher is charged with keeping me safe and now he is taking orders from that, that, that Irishman. That Captain Flynn-Michael who if he had his way would be on his way here right now, charging toward me swinging a large bloated leech over his head like a bull whip."

The Colonel reached up and rubbed at the bridge of his nose, head bowed and eyes closed. And then aware again of my presence turned quickly and focused on the last platoon as it cleared the perimeter.

"It's going well, don't you think Lieutenant?" he asked as he watched them file past him and a smile grazed his lips. Just as quickly it vanished.

"Damn that leech," he said taking hold of a lone stalk of cane. "Because of it I've left my flak pants behind this time and the thought of not having them makes me just a little more than slightly nervous. That and the memory of the dead ruptured leech make it difficult to smile. And that Irishman, that Captain.

"That Captain makes me nervous; he treads too heavily in the boat."

The Colonel turned as the last of the troops snaked out of sight, and moved back to the center of the perimeter and his command staff.

"Lieutenant," English said. "It's the Six, he wants you up to his CP."

When I arrived Flynn-Michael was still in a rant.

"'We don't want to rock the boat,' he says, for Christ sake. 'We don't want to make waves.'" Captain Flynn-Michael paced in front of the Gunny while he waited for the rest of the Platoon Commanders to arrive.

"'I want to see how you operate,' he says, 'so you'll be providing the Battalion security,' you'll be running here and there to kiss my ass."

"It's gotta happen to somebody, Skipper," the Gunny said striking several soggy matches on the equally soggy book before giving up and tossing it all to the ground.

"He's not fit for command for Christ sake; we don't want to rock the boat. If it was up to me I'd sink his fucking boat."

The Gunny accepted a light from Sanchez, drew in on his cigarette and didn't speak. Sanchez turned back to listen to the radio and Flynn-Michael continued to pace kicking at the small rocks and twigs that crossed in front of him.

"Security," he said. "Security; See the other units out before us. Cue and move off other timid steps, Rity-tidy up the cans and papers they leave behind See-Cur-Rity."

"Bullshit," he said, and then he leaned back and laughed.

"You know something Gunny?"

"What's that Skipper?"

"It's what I've just been thinking about Teapot, Colonel Teapot that is, and about security and the rest and it brings to mind a very old Irish saying that was often whispered to me by my aging dearly sainted grandmother, may the saints preserve her, as she leaned her lean, boney self over my wee-little cradle. 'Flynn-Michael,' she said with a voice that rattled like dry leaves off the bog, 'there's but one thing you must be learning if you're to cut ye a slot in the world when you're surrounded by timid fools, only one little thing.' What is it grandmother I would say with the last few waking morsels left to my command, and she would lift her head and draw her voice to no more than a whisper and say 'faint heart never fooked the pig' and then she'd laugh long and hard, very proud of her sermon indeed and kiss me on the cheek for a night of it. Too bad she can't whisper it into Teapot's ear: Faint heart never fooked the pig. He was the very faint hearted bastard she was talking about don't you see."

The Gunny laughed and Sanchez who had been listening to the story crossed himself rapidly three times and smiled.

Now Flynn-Michael saw that we had all arrived.

"Get ready to move the troops," he said. "We're the fucking security for Colonel's Teapot Pentagon. And for Christ sake don't discharge yourself accidentally."

With the last of Hotel gone, Echo saddled up and followed in trace. We moved to a small ville in from the river about 3,000 meters while surrounding the knot of radio men and Battalion officers that comprised Teapot's command group and set in for the night. Hotel, 600 meters to the northwest, did the same.

I checked my section of the perimeter making sure everyone was dug in. I met briefly with Balen and Rico and Wescott, assigned fields of fire and walked to the near center of the circle to the Company CP.

When I sat down and rested my back against the palm next to Horey the last filtered light of the sun squeezed through the closely knit fronds and raced pale patches across the track laced village floor. I leaned my head back against the trunk. Inches to my right, Horey in the same pose fished for a cigarette.

"Where's the skipper?"

"Getting his ass chewed by Teapot on the other side of the ville." Horey held a match to the cigarette and drew the smoke deep into his lungs. He continued to speak through exhaled smoke that swirled from hole punched nostrils and thickened his voice.

"Teapot has been up his ass since we left An Hoa without a breather. He won't be able to sit down for a week."

A Marine stood in silhouette about two meters in front of us.

"Pill day," he said lifting the bright orange malaria pill to his lips. "Sunday is pill da…"

Crack!

I dove to my left and Horey sprawled in the opposite direction reaching for his helmet as he went.

"Jesus Christ."

I rubbed at my ringing right ear and rose to my knees. The Marine in front of us held his hand out, in slow motion again, toward me.

"I've been hit," he said.

I looked at him and shook my head.

"Why is it always in slow motion?"

The finger, that seconds before had held the pill in his open mouth was gone to the first knuckle and now oozed long sinewy strings of blood to the ground.

"I've been hit," he said again as though trying to convince himself that the end of his finger was indeed gone. "It took the fucking pill right out of my mouth."

"Get down, asshole" Horey said "He's probably got more than one bullet and he may try to take the shit out of your bowls or your fucking brain out of your head."

The Marine dropped down to his knees and began a quiver that started at his tipless finger and ran up his arm to his shoulders where it erupted in violent spasms.

"I've been fucking hit," he said again only this time he was shouting as the corpsman arrived.

"Calm down superman," the corpsman said wrapping the dripping wound in a tight battle dressing. "He missed your social finger."

And while I watched, Horey studied the palm trunk we had been resting against.

"Holy shit," he said softly. "Your ear still ringing?"

I turned and nodded.

"Well, we're lucky that's all it is. An inch in either direction and one of us would have a third fucking eye."

I leaned into the tree. The bullet that had taken the Marine's finger tip had continued on and ripped into the palm bark between our heads. Sticky sap now pushed around and out through the resulting ugly hole.

"Hey Doc," Horey said. "We got a wounded tree over here."

"Yeah, right Sir," he said without looking up. "I'll be right there, but right now we're going to need a medivac first to get stumpy out of here before he goes into shock."

Boots and the Gunny ran up to the kneeling corpsman as he worked on the shaken Marine's finger.

"What the hell happened?"

"Sniper," Horey said. "Tried to kill this tree but that asshole got in the way." He pulled out his K-bar and started to dig into the tree. "I'm taking this fucker with me." And as he spokes the bullet popped out and fell to the ground between his knees.

Boots looked quickly at Horey.

"Sanchez, get a chopper in here."

"Sir," Sanchez said holding the handset out toward Boots, "it's the Six."

Boots took the hand set and listened for a moment without speaking.

"Roger skipper," he said at last. "You can tell him it was a sniper round not an accidental discharge, and yeah we have one slightly wounded Marine. Lance Corporal Willis, one of the mortar ammo humpers in the finger. He needs to be evacuated so we need to get the request in before it gets too dark."

"Where did it come in from?" the Gunny asked.

"Based on the finger and the tree, I'd say from over there," Horey said pointing off into the growing darkness.

"In other words, Lieutenant, you don't know where the fuck it came from."

"In other words Gunny, that would be a roger. We can only hope it was an accidental discharge initiated by Hotel."

No more shots were fired.

Just before dusk Horey called in some willie-peter marking rounds and registered defensive artillery fires around our position.

Across the paddy a lone sniper took note of the slender spires of white phosphorous as they rose into the still air.

SitRep Jan161915H: We set in.

Dear Pumpkin,

The first day is over and the operation goes badly. I am sitting in a shallow hole that I scratched in the loose earth listening to the quiet murmur of my men talking for confidence into the night. We have been sniped at from several places during the day but we are unable to return fire without reports and reprimands. We lose interest in firing at all and merely plod beneath it asking is everyone ok when it stops. The Captain tries to avoid Teapot but so far none on his attempts have been successful. I drink coffee from a C-ration can that came filled with cookies. The Doc heated it over a small fire. It steams into the night and the tin burns my lips but it does not taste bad. In the morning I will tell the skipper that the Doc will be alright. The sun is down now and it begins to rain.

I am thinking of you,

S

SitRep Jan170623H- At first light Hotel moved out and swept northeast through the vacant villages dotting the neglected landscape. Echo sat and waited while Teapot carried on a running dialog with Hotel Six. At mid-morning Flynn-Michael convinced Teapot to let him send a platoon back to the ville where they thought the sniper had hidden the night before.

I took two squads and started out across the paddy. Horey said, "I want a piece of this little jerk myself skipper. I've got a little piece of metal I'd like to jam up his slanted ass."

Now we emerged together from the paddy and entered the tree line that lead into the hidden ville. Balen waited for us where the trail split. One fork ran to the west around the edge of the ville and was tucked just inside the trees that separated the high ground from the paddy. The other seemed to slice into the heart of the village but its true course was hidden from view by a slight bend to the left several meters ahead. Neither was on the map.

"Which way, Sir?"

"We'll go to the right."

"I don't know," Horey said looking up from his map. "I think this edge of the paddy takes us farther away from the village than we want to be. I think we need to check out the one that heads off to the left."

"Shades of the fucking rose garden."

"What?"

"I said 'I think we should take a short recon down the trail to where it hooks off to the left and check it out.'"

Horey led the way. Four steps in and the ground gave way under his foot. With a quick shout his foot disappeared from view into a well concealed punji pit. I ran up and caught him by the shoulders as he started to fall backwards. I looked down into the hole.

"Holy shit, holy shit, holy shit."

"Spare me the sermon, just tell me what you see, I can't feel a fucking thing in my toes."

"It fucking missed your foot."

A barbed hand wrought steel spike stood three inches above the hole in Horey's boot. It had pushed through the sole and ripped out through the top just far enough to the side to miss his foot.

"Holy shit," I said again.

"Get me the fuck out of this hole," Horey said.

He sat at the edge of the trail and pulled off his boot. The spike had grazed his sock but where it passed his foot there wasn't a mark.

"You're getting quite a collection of near-miss hardware," I told him. "I hope this sniper has a big slant ass."

Horey extracted the spike and pulled his sock and boot back on.

"Very funny, let's finish this recon and get the fuck out of here."

We continued down the trail.

As we rounded the bend half of Horey vanished from my side and he was suddenly half a man with his torso protruding from what looked like an open manhole. And then just as suddenly in one smooth blur of motion he caught himself with a hand on each side of a gaping hole that had opened up beneath him and with a violent push he ended in a heap on the far side of the trap.

"Man trap," I shouted. "Are you okay?"

Horey didn't speak. Together, from opposite sides we crept to the edge and looked in.

"Whew," I whistled. "Look at that shit."

Four sharpened bamboo stakes reached up from the bottom of the pit. Each ended in a carved and fire hardened barb which had been smeared in what looked like shit. The sides of the pit bristled with shorter stakes aimed in a slant toward the bottom like rows of shark teeth pulling prey into a gullet.

"Man."

Still, Horey was silent.

We continued to gaze down into the hole. Balen came up behind us from around the corner.

"Who stepped in the…,Jesus," he said. "That's some fucking trap Sir, which one of you found it?"

"Lieutenantt Sills. You can tell because he doesn't have any color."

Balen came carefully to the edge and looked in.

"Jesus," he said again. "Look at that, that fucking thing is wired for sound. That's about a 20 pound box mine wired to those four stakes in the middle. All you had to do was touch one of those stakes, Lieutenant and you both would have gone home in pieces probably all in the same box."

I looked at Balen. All of a sudden I didn't feel so good.

Horey stood and brushed the dirt off his trousers. "We'll take the other fucking trail," he said and without another word he started back down the trail the way we had come.

"Who found the foot-trap?" Balen asked as we stepped around it.

"Lieutenant Sills. It's just his lucky day."

We swept the ville and found nothing.

SitRep Jan171715H: Darkness came and we set in again.

Dear Pumpkin,

Two days have gone by now and again I drink the Doc's coffee. It was hot today and I found several weapons that my men set down and wandered away from. The weapons are of little use to them if they're not allowed to shoot and they begin to show the brownish tint of rust. The Skipper gives little to the credit of Teapot, and while he talks, I wonder what has made him this way. Today shortly after noon, I decided that it was, the system; military lives are not lost to bullets in the battlefield; they are lost to bad decisions, or a lack of one and drowned in a mire of sinking careers. It is sad. Down at this end, where careers are seven seconds short and bullets more real, it all seems very cheap and shabby. But I guess they're important, and who really gives a rat's ass after all because today Horey proved that the only thing you need here is luck.

Love,

S

SitRep Jan180815H: Hotel spent the morning sweeping back and forth through the same village in hopes of catching someone following them. By noon they had two sprained ankles and one snake bite, non fatal. Echo sat. I chewed out my squad leaders about rusty weapons. An hour later I held an informal inspection and found no rust. Horey didn't say much until late in the afternoon.

SitRep Jan181519H: We swept three villages. No enemy contact.

Dear Pumpkin,

This morning a funny thing happened while we milled around waiting to move out. A family of pigs walked past Captain Flynn-Michael. There was a wormy sow with six or seven young that she was still nursing; her tits dragged in the dirt underneath her. Flynn-Michael jumped to attention and saluted very rigidly.

"Make way for the command group," he called over his shoulder. Then rocking forward on the balls of his feet and bending slightly at the waist, continuing his salute throughout, he smiled and said;

"Good morning Colonel."

Colonel Teapot, who stood behind, where Flynn-Michael couldn't see him, frowned and grunted. Captain Flynn-Michael, who turned at the noise, swallowed his smile quickly, puffed his cheeks in and out several times and disappeared a pace behind the pigs. Little else happened during the day and movement was slow.

S

SitRep Jan191427H: The re-supply chopper settled into the small clearing next to the Battalion CP and in addition to C-rats and ammo there were orders for Harry to head in. Harry got mad as hell and said he wasn't going to go. Colonel Teapot told him to quit rocking the boat and to get on the chopper so he did, but he was still mad as hell. Horey who was talking again, said, "See y'a Daddy Warbucks, you old son-of-a-bitch."

Harry said, "Fuck you, I'd like to put a boot up your ass," and then he was gone.

I put my thoughts aside and propped my lip on the edge of my coffee can sipping slowly at the weak brown water and watching over its rim as my men dug in in a native potato patch. The apron of the patch that ran down into a large sweeping paddy was full of pungi stakes.

"Hey, Horey," I shouted. "You want to try these on for size?"

"Fuck you," Horey answered.

"Pass the word on these fucking traps," I told my squad leaders. "They probably won't kill you but they'll sure as hell fuck up your day." I watched them as they went back to their squads. "And they'll mess up the day for those who watch you fall in too," I whispered as they left, "Maybe worse."

No one fell onto to these. They were hastily made with no attempt to conceal them.

While the men dug, they watched the paddies and the trees beyond growing to silhouettes in the twilight. The memory of the finger shot sniper was still fresh. Next to us tied in on the right, I could hear Fitzlee's men, now his alone with Harry's departure, digging into the soft dirt.

SitRep Jan191725H "Hey Lieutenant," Balen called.

"Yo."

"We got something over here, a box."

I stood and walked down the slope to Balen's position. The coffee that remained in my cup had grown cold so I threw it into the ground and hooked the cup into the spoon stuffed into the breast pocket of my flak-jacket.

"What's in it?" I asked when I reached Balen's side.

"Don't know Sir." Balen said. "It looks like a fucking casket."

We looked down at the box in silence. It was rectangular, maybe five-feet long and two-feet wide hidden just below the surface of the loose earth. The Marine who found it had pulled the dirt back off the wooden top and stacked it in neat uniform piles around the perimeter of the hole.

"It was only about six inches down," he said as he continued to clean dirt from the sides.

I knelt by the box.

"Okay," I said pointing toward the shallow hole. "Let's get the top…"

A lone single shot, ripped the air it passed through screaming quietly and rapidly 'move aside, move aside'; crackling curses that it is slowing; puffing proudly that it has struck; burying itself in shame that it has missed, struck the wrong thing harmlessly; inert before it can smile at the fear and suspension of animation that it has caused.

The kicked up dirt landed on my thigh.

"Where is he?" Balen shouted.

"I see him," one of men shouted dropping his small collapsible shovel. "Over there, I see him, in that hooch."

"Roger, got him," another called.

The call of incoming ran down the line of Marines anxious to shoot at something.

Fitzlee's men opened up first; the guns, the M-79. The hooch disintegrated. Another shot followed another.

"He won't survive that shit…"

"He's one dead motherfucker now…"

"He's dragging his skinny ass to gook heaven…"

A second shot dashed into the loose dirt by the box.

The sniper was still out there, he had never been in the hooch.

The Gunny came up to the lines, trotting slowly, hunched toward the ground.

"What in the fuck are you girls shooting at?" he asked.

Several turned and answered together.

"A sniper, Gunny."

The Gunny shoved his hand into his hip pocket and looked at them carefully. His lips moved slowly, slowly tracing the sweep of his eyes.

"You shot all that shit at one fucking sniper? Jesus Christ, I don't want you shooting no more at a goddamn sniper."

As he finished, his eyes passed out across the paddy and back down the line toward me.

"Whatcha got, Lieutenant?" he asked as he approached the box.

"Not sure, Gunny, some kind'a wooden crate," I answered pointing at the box again. "I got the engineers coming up to take a look at it."

A third short nasty plume snapped across my thigh as I pulled my hand back toward my body. I looked up at the Gunny and made a note, no more pointing. The Gunny hit the deck.

"Six inches is pretty goddamn close." I said as I lay next to the Gunny looking out over the paddy. "This has been a six inch adventure."

"Get me a fucking rifle." the Gunny said to Balen.

"They can shoot at the troops," he said softly as he lay his cheek on the stock, "and Lieutenants," his eye closed on the sight, "but, they don't shoot at no goddamn Marine Corps Gunnies." His finger tightened on the trigger.

A Sergeant came up behind us and lay down next to me.

"Scotty," he said. "Engineers."

'You're Scottish,' I thought, 'and a fool to be here now.'

For a minute, a second, we lay still, watching. "There he is Gunny," Scotty shouted. "There he is."

'You burr your r's badly,' I thought.

"I see him," the Gunny said. "Give me a tracer." He worked the bolt back and forward, locking the chamber on the red-tipped round, and nestled the stock again with his cheek. I flinched at the crack in my ear and watched the arc of the tracer as it cleared the trees on the far side of paddy. Directly beneath the path of the bullet, a dark knot sat quietly in a tree.

"In the goddamn trees."

"High," the Gunny said.

"Come down two clicks, Gunny," Scotty shouted. "Come down two clicks."

"Unhuh," the Gunny said, chambering another round.

A second redeye winked back at us. It was high again.

"Bastard," the Gunny said.

"A click, Gunny," Scotty said. "A click."

The third shot was away.

I wondered if the knot in the tree had eyes. I wondered if it could see the redeye coming as we could see it going, arcing slightly over the 800 meters between us, and I wondered if he could hear its whisper. In the morning, the dark knot was gone from the place where he had been tied in the trees. Now, in the silence of dusk he dangled on his rope like a broken yo-yo.

Balen and I turned back to the box.

The Gunny stood, handed the rifle back to the man that had given it to him and looked at Scotty and me.

"Don't let'um shoot at any more snipers. It makes the Colonel nervous and then he's right up the Skipper's ass." And then he left.

SitRep Jan191802H: The engineer Scotty and I sat next to the box and hooked rifle slings together to make a grapple.

"We'll hook these to the lid of the box," Scotty said. "And then we'll get back and lie down and pop it off."

Sergeant Scott pulled sharply on the last sling and the heavy wooden top flopped dully over and rocked still on the little piles of dirt. There was no explosion. It didn't blow.

"For Christ sake," he said. "It's full of dirt."

He called to one of his men and directed him to probe into the dirt in the box with his bayonet. The young Marine engineer knelt by the box and probed carefully into the loose dirt that filled the box to the top, scraping it away with his hands as he went. It was moist and it came up easily. I could hear the grinding of the dirt against the blade as the man eased it in and out looking for concealed explosives.

Six inches down he hit leaves; palm fronds freshly cut and carefully laid under the dirt along with some banana leaves. The man leaned back and flexed the tired muscles of his back.

"What the fuck," he said.

He looked up at Sergeant Scott and then probed again, sticking the blade in up to the hilt, slowly, deliberately. He lifted back the leaves, looked into the box and let them fall back. The bayonet in his hand fell loosely by his side and the probing stopped.

"Jesus," Scotty said pulling the leaves back for a closer look.

"It looks like tears, Sarge," the man said. "His eyes is still open in there and where the cuts is, it looks like tears."

"It ain't tears," Scotty said. "It's fucking dead man's ooze from the slipping in of the bayonet."

The man wiped the blade of his bayonet on his trousers and shoved it back into its scabbard. Scotty had no more to say and together, they left. I told Balen to cover the box and started back to my small CP. By a tree I saw a man grow sick in the dark and I could hear him sobbing softly.

Balen came up behind me and told me the box was filled.

"He looked like a Wall-Eye," Balen said.

"Or a Great Northern," I said.

"I go with the Wall-Eye, Sir. Their eyes look dead even if they're still alive."

I didn't answer and the night closed in around us. In the CP the Doc had the coffee ready and I drank. English dozed by the radio and Balen broke pieces off a small twig and flicked them at the dark where they fell untouched.

SitRep Jan192135H

Dear Pumpkin,

We work very hard. We work as though we think we may finally mark the job done, we may finally turn a corner at last, but once around the corner the job remains unfinished and we begin to understand that there won't be any end to it, not that any of us can see any way. The heat grows more disagreeable each day even though it still rains most nights. Today it was hot as blazes before hardly an hour of morning was spent. The troops all felt fortunate that Teapot let them lay in the shade till after noon, but there's no denying they were miffed at having gotten up so early to do nothing except bed down again and listen to things going on around them.

"Somebody's got to make a decision," Teapot said at one point around ten, but nobody did and the crapped out Marines remained quiet and relaxed, all except the Skipper, who had to hop up and dance around to the Colonel every time he just got comfortable because the Colonel was calling for him to come first here and then there over Sanchez's radio.

A most wonderful thing, Sanchez's radio. Its language is crystal clear, but, fortunately it has difficulty seeing, because it never says 'thank you' for all of the one finger salutes the Skipper gives it.

I rolled over once, to give comfort to my hip which had been in one place on the ground for too long and damn if I couldn't see the place where we had been the day before. It made me sit up and look again, but, damn if it wasn't. And I thought maybe we're not working so hard after all, maybe it's all in my head. Seemed we'd been working like the devil though just the same. We are constantly being deceived.

Shortly before noon, we began to move again, to a new place. We moved very slowly, because I stayed behind to blow up some bombs and things that were left over when we got done. That Scotsman stayed along with me to direct the blowing.

He sings flowing "Rs" like a bird and makes the art of hearing things a pleasure.

Horey was standing along with the CP Marines when I passed through.

"It's a goddamn circus," Flynn-Michael said.

"What the fuck Skipper," Horey said.

"Jesus, Horey these goddamn snuffies, that's what the fuck, these goddamn snuffies."

"All right, Skipper," Horey retreated. "All right."

Sanchez and Horey's radioman looked hard-eyed to the trees like they expected to see something called snuffies attack them across the paddy.

When we were sure the Company was safely out of range Scotty and one of his helpers and I set to sticking charges underneath the bombs and things.

When we were about almost done, Scotty and his helper got into a spat about what time the fuse should be.

"A minute," the helper said.

"Thirty seconds," Scotty answered.

So they set 'um all for 30 seconds.

We each popped a fuse and we walked away to catch the rest of the Company.

At 200 meters I said, "These things have a range of 1,000 meters."

Scotty laughed.

At 300 meters, things went 'Kaboom.' We smiled when I noticed there was shrapnel landing all among us and not one of us was hurt, we smiled and kept walking.

"Should'a been a minute," Scotty said.

I wondered if the explosion had scared the snuffies away or whether Sanchez was still on alert.

When we got back, Flynn-Michael came up to us, smiling more than he had been since the beginning of the operation.

"He hit the deck when they went, for Christ sake," he said.

I smiled.

"I never seen anything like it, all alone and in front of all those goddamn snuffies, for Christ sake."

I smiled some more. I could see Sanchez look over his shoulder convinced that the snuffies were back among us and now not only had he not seen them leave they had managed to return undetected.

"Two-thousand meters away, Jesus, and he hits the deck. Couldn't even finish his question, "Is this clearing big enough Flynn-Michael, will it hold us all Flynn-Michael, we have reporters with us you know Flynn-Michael - Boom - How tall you are from down here Flynn-Michael."

Love,

S

Oh yeah, there's one other thing. We stuck a dead man all over his face with a bayonet and I still didn't get sick. This war stuff is really easier than I thought it would be.

S again.

SitRep Jan200637H: "Isn't that great?" Flynn-Michael said.

Easy Echo smiled in unison and Captain Flynn-Michael smiled back.

It was early morning of the third day when we saddled up to move and it felt good. It was early morning still when we moved; and still again it felt good. It was early morning cool when we crossed a crotch-deep stream; the cold water of the stream felt good, and it washed away the sludge that grew between legs rubbed raw over a week of bitter shit.

Feels good, I chanted to myself as we moved.

Looks Good,

Is Good,

Ummmmmmboy,

Feels Good.

When Easy Echo passed the stream, we slid easily in two-tone trousers, glistening from the crotch on down, we moved easily and we smiled. Safeties off, weapons clean and to the ready, snap, poster perfect. The boot in the ass drowned in the stream and the gesture earned quick response. It all worked well and the Gunny walked quietly beside and a step behind Boots.

I worked my platoon on the right flank and the elation died. Brownell pushed his on the other side, the left flank, and the smiles gave way to serious. Fitzlee moved to the rear where it was quiet and where the foot prints in the damp earth were deep.

SitRep Jan201335H: When we held up for chow, it was early afternoon. I set them in, my people, in a perimeter, a loose circle in the grass just back off a paddy, and I told them to watch.

"It's your ass they're after," I said. "It's your ass."

English walked a pace behind me as we came to the edge of the paddy. The radio strapped on his back had just called us to Flynn-Michael 200 meters away and now it hummed easily while we walked. I paused as we left the tall grass. It was the largest paddy I had seen, stretching 4,000 meters north to the river, gorged to 2,000 meters across at its breadth. I whistled softly under my breath as my eyes moved out across it to where it grew hazy blue and merged with the trees and the sky.

"Big."

"Yes Sir," English answered.

"Lots of dragons in that baby."

"Sir?"

"Nothing."

As we walked, I thought about home.

The land here, the paddies, are like the flat ground around Saratoga, where it runs into the Adirondacks, the sleepy tired old Adirondacks where people, villages of people live like they have lived always, like these, taking food and shelter from the land. The rising is abrupt here, as it is there, but there it is hard and they raise horses; it is a good place to relax and only the flatness is the same. The rising behind the one is the hard blue low ground of the

Adirondacks, here it is trees and the turf is not hard, but sodden from years of flooding. The ground and the rising is frightening here, there it is not. On a stormy night, the old mountains may be fearful but they are not frightening because beneath them it is solid hard and it is calm. The solid brings comfort through your feet and steps need not be led by the toes for fear of falling through into an underwater world filled with dragons and old men.

As we walked through the empty villages hung dangerously close to the shore of the paddy, I could see that these paddies had been worked by hidden hands that now, as I walked by their houses, remained well out of sight.

So they continue to deceive, where it would appear firm and hard, it is fluid with filthy water, where it would look worked, there are no hands for the working. Christ, it is quiet and lonely, and the children? They are hidden in the folds of their mothers eyes and are swept into the gloom of the ones that sit still in the hills.

English fell into a pace two meters behind me, the radio singing idly on his back. He studied the ground with each slap-foot step, finding it difficult to walk on even land.

We followed the trail as it hemmed the paddy and kissed the ankles of the empty villages. It was quiet. There were no dogs barking, no fiddling sounds from the paddy, no snorting and pawing of the penned water buffalo. On our left, a large hedge-grow angled in from the darkness of the village we now passed and paralleled the course of the trail for 30 feet, where it stopped and the trail turned to the left moving on out of sight around the hedge-grow. I turned the corner...,

Unexpectedly your soft cheek brushes close to mine, I look into the depth of your almond eyes and on your breath I smell the lingering hint of dead fish and rice.

...and there we ran into each other, paused for a split second of recognition.

You are so very much different than I pictured from your letters, so very much, really. Fuller in the shoulders, perhaps, broader through the nose more flesh under the eyes, less eyes over the flesh. Much different. Your letters do you little justice really, and it is nice, I think, so very nice of you to say the same of me.

And then it was done...

To the rear march to the rear march march to the rear, march.

"Jesus Christ," I said.

"You should'a grabbed him Lieutenant," English said, coming up to where I still stood now quietly in the spot where a split second ago I had just come face to face with the other.

It-is-very-easy-for-you-to-say-that-but-when-i-turned-to-search-for-you-you-were-gone-and-when-i-turned-back-of-course-so-was-he-so-it-is-very-easy-for-you-to-say short as you are, I thought it but I didn't say it. What I said was, "I 'should'a run a pencil through my ear, too."

I looked at English and could see that he didn't understand.

"Why would you do that Sir?"

I looked down at the ground, then to the empty hooch that faced the trail where the other had been when we met.

"No reason I guess. It's a little late now but there was a time when it all made sense."

."You'd a been a hero, Lieutenant."

"Yes." I said at last. "You're right, I should have grabbed him. I would have been a fucking hero."

I turned and started again down the trail. English waited several seconds and then started along behind shaking his head.

"Too short," he said. "Too fucking short."

We moved quietly and carefully for the rest of the distance to the Company CP. While we moved I wondered how many more there were just off the trail silently watching us pass by.

There may have been other things to see, but we didn't look. When we arrived I choose not to mention the meeting.

English told Sanchez "Right fucking into him, bang, and then this little gook disappeared like smoke. It happened so fast the Lieutenant wasn't even sure he'd seen it."

The rustling of quiet movement next to us wasn't the wind.

SitRep Jan201756H: That night we set in on a gook grave yard. It was in the open and up out of the drench of the paddy, and it was free of tree lines, so the Skipper had picked it. Good fields of fire, he had said as he moved quickly through the graves, good fields of fire.

The graves looked like thick, round pancakes tossed at random on the small dry patch. They were unmarked and whether they held one or 10, I couldn't say. Horey set up shop next to the one closest to the center and registered his nightly defensive fire plan with the battery back in An Hoa.

"Let's see how many of the little fucks we can get tonight," he said.

He paused and looked again at the surrounding graves. "I wonder how many of these have my name on them." He took the radio handset and started through a list of grid coordinates. "H and I grids to follow," he said. "Roger, code sheet Alpha."

The rest of us set in around the edge of the small cluster, dug in, and we watched. From here even in the fading light we could see the river and the fishing villages along it etched in the tree lines like billowed umbrellas of straw but they were beyond hearing and smell. We could see the tree line from which we had just come and the point at which it grew tired and stopped. We could see where the Battalion Command Post was dug in by the constant helicopter traffic, and we could see the paddies all around us, close in, we could smell the thick stagnant air, taste the smells of the ripening and the rotten rice and if we leaned forward from our holes, we could feel them, the ends of their fingers pulling at us from the paddies just out of our reach.

SitRep Jan201843H In the last light of the day, Flynn-Michael told Fitzlee to take two squads and sweep the nearest of the fishing villages.

While Fitzlee got ready to leave, Boots collected canteens and along with Sanchez left the lines for the well we had passed on the way in.

I stood for a minute and watched the coming and going and the preparation for both. For a moment I felt like I had always been there. Compared to Brownell's and Fitzlee's newness I felt older, changed from the first days just a few short weeks before. My men were dug in and I wanted to sit down. Flynn-Michael sat up against one of the graves plowing through a can of C's with a plastic spoon. Horey done with the registration rummaged for a cigarette.

"Balls and beans," Flynn-Michael said. "There's nothing in God's world that can compare. Sit down One Fucking Actual for Christ sake, sit down."

I sat down next to him leaned up against the burial mound that served as cover for the CP and let the muscles in my back unwind.

"It's from the well," Brownell shouted, running past me and Flynn-Michael.

I jumped to my feet and watched the half-eaten can of beans arc through the air past my ear. Horey grabbed his map and began to locate the area of the well.

'Always my ear,' I thought, but now it was full of the chattering noise of rifle fire and the solitary pop of a pistol, maybe two.

In a minute, Boots and Sanchez met us on the run coming the other way headed back into the perimeter at the double quick time. There was no sign of the 18 or so canteens they had left with and the well was quiet.

"Two of them," Boots said breathing hard, clenching his teeth in time with the extension and grip of his fingers, "at sling fucking arms and carrying canteens come from the other direction. I hit the deck and so did Sanchez!"

"What about the canteens?" Flynn-Michael asked.

"Fuck a bunch of canteens, Skipper," Boots said. "I emptied a fucking magazine and missed."

"What in the name of Christ are we going to do for water?" Flynn-Michael said smiling.

"A whole fucking magazine," Horey said. "Jesus Christ, you should'a hit them with a goddamn canteen."

"Fuck you," Boots said.

Now Horey laughed too. "I guess we don't need any artillery now that you've secured the well."

Brownell returned with the fire-team he had taken with him and all the canteens.

"Nothing there now," he said. "We couldn't find any blood trails, the brass was policed and foot prints looked like they were swept away."

Lonely stood next to English listening.

"Sanchez, you dumb Mexican," he said when he was sure Boots wouldn't hear him. "You were just shooting at gook trees. You got to watch out for those gook trees alright. Maybe we can find a place up here to bury all those gook fucking VC trees."

Lonely laughed and Sanchez said, "Fuck you."

SitRep Jan201917H Just after dusk, Fitzlee returned through the lines. He had finished his sweep.

"Goddamn, Skipper," he said softly, "they've been dropping nape over there and big ones."

"As my dear old saintly grandmother used to say," Flynn-Michael started to say.

"I brought some of them in, Skipper," Fitzlee interrupted before he could finish.

For a moment Flynn-Michael didn't answer. He looked down at Fitzlee and then he looked around behind him.

"Is that them?" he asked.

"Yes Sir." Fitzlee said.

Two men stood back among the graves holding a stick over their shoulders, a basket hung in from its middle safari-style.

"They look alright to me, for Christ sake," Flynn-Michael said. "What have they got in the goddamn basket?"

"They are alright," Fitzlee said pointing without looking up. "The one in the basket is the one that's hurt, him and the little girl."

Captain Flynn-Michael brushed past Fitzlee and walked up to the basket. In it, a man sat on his knees, blackened to soot by the fire of the bombs. Only his eyes showed, and against the flaky ebony of his charred flesh, they glittered. He was conscious and quiet and his eyes moved in flashes to gaze fixedly at the one who now looked at him. Flynn-Michael shook his head and looked past the litter to where a man carried his child, a girl of five maybe six. Her leg was badly torn and the jagged shrapnel still stuck proudly from the wound. Like the other she was badly burned, and like the other she didn't cry, she watched the men around her vaguely. Flynn-Michael peered closely into her face and she returned his stare and then he turned back to the place where he had left Fitzlee.

"Why did you bring them in here, for Christ sake." he said.

"I couldn't leave them there, Skipper," Fitzlee said.

"Feed them to the goddamn pigs. Now what the Christ..." Flynn-Michael stopped and looked at Fitzlee and then back at the little girl.

"She doesn't fucking blink," he said.

"Her eyelids are gone, Skipper, burned right off," Fitzlee said quietly.

"All right," he said.

Lonely and English started back to the platoon CP. I stopped and waited with Fitzlee for the chopper. Fitzlee watched Flynn-Michael while together with Horey he plotted the artillery fires on his map and tied them in with the Company mortar defensive fires.

"I couldn't leave them out there like that," he echoed. "Could I?"

I didn't answer right away but just stood there looking at him. Poor Fitzlee, he had been there less than a month, not nearly enough time yet.

He had brown eyes. He was still smooth; He wrote down five paragraph operation orders and read them word for word to his squad leaders. He seldom drank. He was unmarried. He might have had a girl, but if he did he never said, never talked about her. He was from Virginia. His eyes and his bearing and his name said he was from old Virginia. His mother was dead and yet he was gentle still.

"You couldn't leave them today," I said. "But tomorrow, tomorrow it may be different."

"Would you have left them?"

"No," I said. "I guess not, not a month ago anyway, but now I'm not sure."

After a pause Fitzlee looked down at the ground and said, "I don't think so. I don't think it will ever be different not even next month."

I looked at him for just the amount of time it took to turn away and started back to my CP.

'And he is a good man,' I thought. 'He is popular and loved by his troops. He should go home.'

Thirty minutes later, the chopper came in and took them out and I was back at the Company CP, called back for an evening briefing.

It was a 34. Flynn-Michael watched it as it lifted off. I stood next to him.

"Jesus," Flynn-Michael said. "Have you ever seen one of their hospitals, Sam?"

"No," I said.

"They're better off here in the fucking jungle."

SitRep Jan201917H: We were still in the graveyard when it started to rain again. I got into my hole with the darkness. It was next to one of the smaller graves; but between two. Some had been decorated with small smooth river stones, but all were unmarked. When I dozed off I dreamed I was sleeping on a large flat griddle. When I woke I couldn't get back to sleep. My face felt like the skin was growing hard and tight. Did it never end? It rained through the night. I climbed out and checked my positions. All secure.

"LP two, all secure," the radio whispered.

"Roger, all secure."

SitRep Jan210517H; There was a light rain still in the morning. We moved slowly saddling up in the steel-gray dawn, steel-gray from the continuing rain and the slate-like clouds that angled down to the horizon in long continuous sheets blown in from the South China Sea. We were wet, trapped in a cage of soggy, clinging clothes. But the wet didn't matter all that much, it was the cool breeze off the river that made the difference. We moved out and headed north into the village that Fitzlee had swept the night before. One of the bunkers by the trail had taken a direct hit. An old man had been sitting inside on a chair when it came in. He was still in his chair as we passed. There was a hole in the roof of the bunker. The old man's head and shoulders stuck out like a sentinel. So did the top of the chair, and he sat there dead, full of holes like the bunker. I looked at him as I passed. His long white hair was pulled straight back from his forehead and cued in a long braid that snaked down the middle of his back. His wrinkled cheeks ended on a thinly stretched chin that boasted wisps of fine spindly white hairs like proud pennants highlighted with light brown crusted streaks leading from the corners of his windswept cracked lips. His eyes were folded nearly shut and though dead they watched me as I passed for some exchanged sign of recognition. Nothing is different here,' I thought, 'they all look the same.' The sound of the rain on the broad leafed palms seemed to grow louder. In the yard, the livestock was dead, ripped open and exploded with concussion and metal; a large pig, a water buffalo. Their open wounds, unable to hide the escape of their insides, oozed and steamed as the cool rain hit and sizzled in their warmth and they began to smell.

There had been a briefing:

'A Dead Civilian Will Cost The United States Government Forty Dollars Lieutenant.

'A Dead Water Buffalo Will Cost The United States Government Four Hundred Dollars Lieutenant.

'Don't Shoot The Water Buffalo, Lieutenant.'

The chickens lived; the chickens always lived. Some of the hooches still burned, though, smouldered, adding to the gray and smelling of nape. Again by the trail, a woman sat and watched us going by. Absently, she dug at the two inches of jagged shrapnel that stuck from a deep bleeding wound in her calf. I looked down at her and thought for a moment that she must be told of freedom. She looked back at me blankly as if to say Fuck you and your freedom in red, white, and blue. 'She would not understand,' I thought. We passed. Among the dead we counted only the very old and the very young. Those that remained told of the passing of the young and the strong to the mountains in the west. They had gone with the mist and the rain a week before.

From the rear of the column I could hear Lonely. "Look at all these dead VC," he said.

'But just one short day ago,' I added in thought 'the strike had been so very, very necessary, and I think just now I heard someone say it aloud; so very, very necessary.'

"Shit load of dead VC in that ville huh Lieutenant" Lonely said as he came up next to me. "VC Poppasans, VC Mommasans, VC pigs, VC dogs, VC every fucking where."

SitRep Jan211917H The rain continued. It was still raining that night when we set in again. We had been deserted by the promising warmth of the sun two days before. The choppers could not get in and we were without food. We had been without food for over a day. Perhaps it was two, I thought, but tonight I couldn't remember.

Boots and Sanchez went and came bringing the water without incident.

Tonight I don't care, I thought again.

Dear Pumpkin..., I paused and I watched the rain strike into the paddy by the ville where we stayed. In the jungle small streams and rivulets began to slide down the steep slopes toward me and my restless Marines.

Dear Pumpkin,

Where to begin. We've been out on a little patrol across the river around An Hoa in a place they call the Arizona but it's not too bad. A couple of people have been hurt a little. One got a pill shot right out of his mouth, but other than that not much. He was more surprised than hurt. We go into villages and search them but it doesn't take long to search a one room grass hut and what little stuff they have.

I guess they're lucky in one regard if you don't have much then you don't have much to lose. It's raining again. I think that none of us will get shot instead we'll just melt into the paddies and end up feeding the rice. It's amazing really, as we sink down in the muck the locals just seem to spring up out of the same swamp around us.

Are you eating and sleeping the way you should and has Tia made it to the West yet? If so, a Lieutenant that we call Boots would like to write to her if that's Okay.

Boy the weather here sucks.

I think of you most of the time.

S

Dear S,

Tia has been here for a little over a week now, I thought I told you. She has a new boy friend about once a week. T makes me laugh and there are times when I need to laugh. She just left for dinner with a new one tonight. She says she's only going out with Navy guys from now on because she thinks it's safer and then she said sure send his address. Like I said, she makes me laugh.

Love,

P

SitRep Jan221156H:

"I'm Hungry," Private First Class Carroll Stepps said to his squad leader Corporal Balen.

"I didn't think draftees from Chicago got hungry," Corporal Balen said.

"I didn't think they could talk," Corporal English called from where he sat.

"I didn't think they could open their eyes without help," Lonely said. "And I know they sure as shit can't add two and two and get the same answer twice."

Private First Class Stepps looked down at the ground between his feet so his eyes could not be seen.

"Fuck Youse," he said quietly, and the others laughed around him.

"Hey, Stepps," Corporal English called. "What makes you so goddamn dumb?"

"Fuck Youse," Stepps said again, more quietly. "Just fuck youse." But behind it all you could hear the rhythm of his thoughts

Because my eyelids droop strangely as though I am about to fall asleep; Because I was born with this cursed awkwardness that makes me walk as though I stepped from a cartoon; Because people ask me a million and a billion and a trillion questions and my tongue grows snarled when I try to answer; Because of those things and others, they let me out of the school where I could learn things. Because I could not stop them, I said,

Fuck Youse.

Because the pavement of the streets of Chicago is hard when you are fifteen and my hair grew long, I was called a bum; Because I grew hungry and tired, I worked at the labors of the street and I was called a pimp and a hustler and a thief; Because of those things and others, people stepped around me and looked the other way. Because I could not stop them, I said,

Fuck Youse.

Because the only letter I ever received was my draft notice, I came in; Because I read the letter several times aloud and without help, I came in; Because I thought everyone did the same thing, I came in. Because they laughed at me on both sides when I did and they said I had the name of a girl, I said,

Fuck Youse.

Fuck Youse All.

Because I am twenty-five now and my hair, which I remember as full at one time, recedes badly leaving only stubble well back on my brow; and because I groom the stubble carefully because I remember how it once was; and because once a month I go for a haircut because I am told to and the gook natives lather my brow back to my fleeing hair line and shave my stubble off; and because I sit quietly and let them do it because I don't know how to make them stop.

I hate them.

Because I am told to.

I shoot them.

Now I can see that there is a woman here and she reminds me of the many times they have shaved my head; she scatters seed from the folds in her dress to the chickens in front of her and that reminds me that I am hungry still.

Quietly, while I watched, PFC Stepps stood and walked to where a woman fed chickens. For a moment he watched her and she paused, looking up at him. Bending slightly, he snatched up one of the noisy chickens by the neck and just as quickly, he snapped its neck and the chicken dangled limply in his hand. It twitched slightly as he pushed the legs through under his web belt. The old woman cried out sharply when she saw the chicken was dead and then sobbed easily. She wrung her hands together and waved them in front of her clasped. She kicked weakly at the scrawny flock trying to scare them away but they remained scattered around her bare feet in anticipation of more seed. She tried to get between them and Stepps but she moved too slowly. Stepps leaned forward again and snatched another chicken from the ground. He held it in front of him by the neck; in front of her, his arm stretched out to its full length jamming the chicken in her face. There was no motion in his wrist and he continued to hold it steadily. It struggled and squawked loudly and the woman spoke rapidly in a language Stepps didn't understand. As she spoke, she flipped at the folds of her costume and continued to kick at the other chickens trying to scare them to safety. Stepps said nothing.

With his free hand he took off his helmet and dropped it between their feet. I looked at his head, at the even line that ran from ear to ear across the high finely razored forehead, and smiled. The old woman stopped sobbing and looked up into Stepps' face. Stepps looked at her, nodded toward the helmet where it lay on the ground and watched her as she turned back into her hooch. In a moment she was back with a large wicker basket. Carefully, she lifted the small thin shelled eggs from the basket, her spidery hands trembling slightly, and set them into the helmet. Stepps watched her and when he had measured the count long enough or lost count either one, he released the chicken and said thank you. 'The shake-down ends,' I thought. The old woman smiled nervously, but she didn't understand it either.

English butchered and cleaned the chicken; Balen cooked them, the chicken and the eggs. Lonely brought bananas and cut cane from the field by the village. He showed me how to suck it for the sweet juice, how to chew it out until it was fiber and then spit, spat, the carcass onto the ground. In a lot of ways it was the same as a lot of things we did here and with every passing minute it got easier. We ate. The Doc made coffee in his helmet. Horey followed the smell and joined us.

"Nose working well," I said.

The evening passed.

SitRep Jan221323H: I leaned back on a tree. I had finished an egg and now I picked at traces of flesh from a wing.

It looks like a wing, I thought, but it could be something else. This bird like all the others I'd seen was skinny, underfed. Balen found rice in one of the hoochs and boiled it and it helped but the bird was still skinny, a sign of what it was suppose to be, a taste of chicken and nothing more.

I threw down the bones and took my pack off.

But I wear no pack, I reminded myself, only two long socks tied at the ends with string so they hang easily under my arms and across my back. Yet still I took it off, a pack, because that was the way it felt today when I sat down.

I slid from the tree and leaned back on my helmet. There was a band of rubber around it cut from a tube. I carried my cigarettes there under the band; cigarettes and bug juice.

They were C-ration cigarettes, because my precious Marlboros were gone; Chesterfields and Camels, shitty cigarettes, five to a pack. Not To Be Sold was stamped on them; not to be sold because they were stale when they went into the box tasting like day old butts fished from an ash tray sold to the taxpayers at full price no doubt. Nothing to good for our fighting men overseas. Now one was lit, but no, it was not lit, it was lighted, lighted, that was the proper way and wasn't it strange that I hadn't thought of that for a while, the way that she corrected me on that, the way she would correct me now if she were here, no, if I were there, there is nothing to correct here. Here it's any way you want.

I closed my eyes and pulled on the cigarette. I could feel the bend at its middle where the band had laid across it, pressed into it as I drifted away in swirls of smoke and the pinch of the broad rubber band on my helmet.

A thing to remember, a thing to anticipate, a letter is written and I will think of her and the things I did not write.

CANTANKEROUS…

…is what you are, but it is because you are with the child inside you, it is because this was our first Christmas nervously spent making believe in a place where they decorate palms with lights and tinsel and I said they have it made at Easter…;

…and when I tell you there will be no Christmas this year, when I tell you there will be no year this year, and when I say my memory of all there is is this, is the slogging and the misery, is the this I can't explain to anyone because it can't be felt, because everyone feels it too, as to leave it without feeling and to leave it without memory and when they ask me the next time I will say 'NOT BAD REALLY;' how I linger here to cry, to cry and say nothing at all, at my age , really, and after the crying while they have watched to say 'there, now can you see it, now do you see at all; will you cry? And why is none of this written?

I remember that day too, the day that I left and we were divided into groups by division which was the only thing we knew at the time, nothing more and because the buses would hold no more, the buses between which a staff Sergeant stood dancing and spinning and clapping his hands, pointing and chanting while the rest ran by him and filed onto the buses.

"Now the way I see it, that General thought so much of us and where we were going, he sent out the only Captain he had, right then so he could see to it we done things right."

And I stood there with you because I knew the bus I would ride, and together, the three of us, you and me and the Captain, we watched the sergeant spin and point first at one bus and then the other.

"First Divy-div…,

"First Divy-div…,

"Third Divy-div…,

"First Divy-div…,

"Third Divy-div...,

"Divy-div...,

"Youwandoit...,

"First Divy-div...,

"No Sir, the Cap'an, he don't miss a thing, no Sir."

"Goddamn Bluegum," the Captain said under his breath, and then in the same breath he wished me God's speed and I mounted the bus and you went to the car to follow, the car two-months old, as old as the seed you carried inside you for both us. And like all the rest we were suddenly divided, but quietly without ceremony and chant.

I am here before you because you had to shop, 'pick up a few things' you said.

I am drinking coffee in a badly painted public place with a man I never saw, but know well because we are here for the same reason and still you have not come.

I am waiting in the jostle for the phone with one eye on the road while I wait and as yet I have not seen you and I wonder where you are as I look down my arm to where I hide my watch.

I dial the operator abstractly and listen vaguely as after having given her instructions, the call goes through and I wonder after you.

I lean away from the phone to see down the length of the road again and I say 'I'm leaving now' to my mother who has accepted the charge and now says nothing.

'Pumpkin?' I say, I say 'she's fine' and she says 'yes' and I say 'I'm leaving now, in 30 minutes and she says 'then you have a little time.' and I say 'yes, plenty of time.' and I look again at my watch and the road:

Father says 'good luck. be careful.' and I say yes and then I say 'GOODBYE' but neither of us hangs up. After a moment I say 'I am costing you money,' and father says that it is alright, we have plenty of time and then we are silent again. I look first at my watch and then to the road, 'See you next year' and Father says yes and the line clicks open when there is nothing more to say.

I sit again drinking coffee and still you have not come.

I was alone in the parking lot when you drove up and I could see that you had changed your clothes. I smiled because you wore the orange maternity dress I had gotten you for Christmas. You didn't need it yet but I thanked you for wearing it anyway because it made me smile. You modelled it shyly, holding a gather of the full skirt in one hand and spinning lightly in the gravel of the parking lot, laughing nervously.

"You are the 'Great Pumpkin,'" I said and we shared the laugh.

"Where have you been?"

"I brought you this," you said.

"A brown paper bag?"

"Open it," you said.

"What is it?"

"A lunch," "you said. "To eat on the plane."

"They will serve us a lunch on the plane."

"Please take it," you said. "There is an apple."

"An apple?"

"Yes," you said. "Here, do you like it?"

"It's a beautiful apple."

"Yes, I know," you said, putting it back in the bag and she lowered her eyes.

"It took me some time to pick it out."

We walked together out onto the concrete and asphalt air strip. Me with the bag under my arm and you with her eyes still lowered.

"You're not crying."

"No," you said. "It's all worse than that."

"You know that I'll be back."

"I know." you said, your eyes still averted.

"I may hurt badly, I may not look or think or feel the way I do now, but you must know that I'll be back."

"I know," you said softly stopping and looking into my eyes.

As we stood there, the others passed through us in a long shuffling green line that snaked its way toward the plane and the waiting ladder. At the top of a ladder a smiling stewardess stood just inside the open jet liner door.

"I'm sorry about the Christmas."

"You spent too much money," you said. "But it was a good Christmas."

"I'm still sorry."

When the rest had passed, we stood together and held hands.

"I have to go now."

You nodded and let me go.

"Sam," you called after me.

"Yes?"

You ran to me again and kissed me.

"I love you," you said.

I smiled and walked to the plane. Inside, the rest waited with catcalls and whistles. While the stewardess demonstrated the Mae-

West, I looked out through the small oval window to where you stood bright orange. The plane taxied lifted and banked. I could see you, a bright orange dot and then as the plane entered a steady climb toward the west I could see you no more and the ocean peeked through brakes in the clouds over which we flew.

I flicked my cigarette, my Chesterfield, 'not a cigarette, a Chesterfield,' I thought, and listened to the crackle of English's radio parked on the tree three feet off my right hand.

"Put it on squelch," I said

"You can't hear it as good then Sir," English said.

"Put the goddamn thing on squelch. I don't want to listen to it that's what you're paid for," I said.

"Yes Sir," English said. "Bad dream?"

"Just turn it down, okay?"

It was growing dark. I reached for another cigarette and then decided against it.

"Pass the word. The smoking lamp is out. From the distance they look like fucking flares in the dark."

There had been better times, though before all this began, better times in the crooked arm of the Ohio where the water ran wild and fast and big in the spring triggered by the thaws north of Pittsburgh and the valley people lived with the threat measured in feet on a long stick stuck in the muddy bottom.

Not unlike those here though, they lived with it easily enough, naturally enough, tied to it as surely as though it had been a piece of twine, moved back by it once a year, but never forced to leave it, the place where they had been raised, seeded, rooted and raised like plants, because the loss of house was natural enough too but loss of home unthinkable. So they stayed in their thatched huts and they lived there easily in the river's crook where it joined into the Muskingum flowing sluggishly from the north and on to the west to join the Mississippi.

And in the better times too, I remember living there and meeting you so we might love in the fall long before the time of the high water, so we might walk over old brick streets and roads to a place several miles from the town, so we might sit on a grassy hill to watch the sun sinking into it, close together against the chill and sit there still, even after it had grown dark. And after several minutes when we had said nothing we stood and walked back into town holding hands only to find, that now it was dark there too. At first we walked through the puddles in the darkness by mistake but then thinking we could get no wetter we splashed through with purpose and discovered that we had not been as wet as we first thought.

In the spring we lay together on lazy Sunday afternoons and while you slept beside me and the river crested over the undercut banks and spread into the park, where just the week before we flew kites out over Main Street, and the streets of town, dragging unseen underwater sludge along with it, I read aloud from Joyce, my head propped on my arm which the soft down pillow closed around and thought of writing. Most of that that I read made little sense and less to you because you dozed and didn't hear all I said, but the sounds of the words, the sounds, they swelled pounding senselessly into the quiet of the small dusty room. On springly Sundays, I remember too, how sad it made me feel to think of blooms which would flower and die or never flower at all because they had been dragged down by the rising river, and that I was happy that when you woke and I explained it to you you felt the sorrow with me and told me that perhaps if I napped I would feel better and your promising that once we had napped, we would heat dry soup to be drunk from precious plaid cups and sopped with aging matzo spread thick with peanut butter pilfered from the college dining hall because there was nothing else. When it was finished I walked you home in the twilight past the pet shop so you might see the puppies and we both might laugh standing in the darkness at the window. Those were good times then and most of them I remember.

"Sir, SIR, wake up," English said.

"I wasn't asleep," I said and English said "Oh."

"Well," I said pulling myself up on my elbows, "What do you want?" Now I knew it was English. It had grown completely dark. I stood and stretched and looked for English's voice.

"What's up?" I asked again with less edge.

"The Skipper wants you at the CP," he said.

I wiped at the moist stains I could feel, remnants of sleep, and headed for the CP trying to remember just exactly how good the dreamy good days had been.

SitRep Jan221926H; Fitzlee and Brownell looked up when I arrived, and breaking my own rule, I took the cigarette Brownell offered, and sat down next to them. Boots and Horey sat across from us taking exchange sips from a canteen cup of brandy that Flynn-Michael had brought, always brought. He got it from a doctor in one of the rear areas in Da Nang who was beautiful, he said because he was unmilitary as hell.

"I was with him there, in the rear," he said, "And we met these two Bird Colonels, and when the Doc walks by he says 'hiya fellas' and keeps on going. I said 'Jesus Christ, do you know what they were.' and he turns and says 'Oh, sorry,' and gives them a salute with his left hand. They didn't know whether to shit or go blind. Isn't that something? 'Hiya fellas, like he gave a shit about them or their fucking war."

Boots passed the cup to me and I took a long swallow and started the cup around again.

"A damn fine dentist though," Flynn-Michael continued, "and he can get good brandy too. Isn't that good brandy, Sam?"

I let the brandy slide like liquid fire slowly back over my tongue and down into my throat. It was good.

"One canteen for water and the other for brandy," Flynn-Michael said, "The way the Lord meant it to be."

'And damn fine, brandy, too,' I thought, reminiscing in the thick burning taste and a time of being drunk.

"The war is one thing, for Christ sake," Flynn-Michael went on, "but when it gets so bad that there's no more brandy, then it's time to go home, can you think of it, I can't for Christ sake.

"Perspective is what it is, Jesus; and besides, such a shitty worthless little war."

The cup came back past me for the second time, and again I drank and passed it on.

"Fuck it," Flynn-Michael said. "We're not going to live forever anyway, so what the hell."

"So what the hell," Boots said, lifting the cup end draining it down to the bottom before passing it to Horey.

"What the Christ d'you do that for?" Horey asked looking into the empty cup.

"Because it was there." Boots said.

"Chicago asshole," Horey said.

Boots said "Fuck you."

"What the hell," I said again and I thought 'there will be better times again someday when we will sit at three a.m. in the morning with a case of piss warm San Miguel beer on the floor next to us damn fine beer too it will be, like brandy in the field, damn fine beer in the mud by the Wickless candles.' Flynn-Michael was right, what the hell.

"We're going back in tomorrow," Flynn-Michael said, and the meeting was over.

"The end of Independence as we know it," Horey said. "Lift a glass, Independence is dead at last. Long live Independence."

SitRep Jan222113H: I stood now in my own C.P. The Doc was asleep and English dozed by the radio. It was quiet and I hoped that my squad leaders wouldn't come too soon.

The moon was up now in front of our position peeking through the briefly resting rain, the direction was north, and there was a lake. The moon, it was full now, the January moon in the states, the January moon here too, or the Monkey Moon, I wasn't sure. The moon glistened the length of the dragon-shaped lake and cast off in the paddies crazy-quilt around it. To the right there was a cut and a stream that emptied from the lake into the paddy irrigation system. I could only see the trees that edged the sluices now in the darkness, but I knew they were there, the cut, because I had been there, the stream, because I had crossed it several times during the day, days, whichever. Out further on the left, 2,000 meters or so, a village burned, was still burning, where they, Bravo from somewhere had lit it, lighted it, I corrected myself again, still earlier. They said someone died there in the afternoon; a thrown grenade. The thrower died too, shortly thereafter, of natural causes, but still the village had to be burned. And as I watched it, I thought, 'soon there will be no ville left so now he's died nowhere, isn't that nice, and it was, besides, it makes the ones left feel better that nowhere no longer exists.' Now it glowed behind the trees and the vertical stands of the bamboo. I thought I could see people moving in and out of the ville, shadows in the flicker, but because of the distance and the darkness, I couldn't be sure so I stopped trying. But still, I thought, 'it looks that way.'

And I am unable to hear it I continued in my thoughts, the popping bamboo that sounds like rifles, it is all lost in the gentle echo of the night sounds above, the easy sucking, as if air is being drawn in between slightly parted teeth, of the radio. Night sounds; the peeping things that I heard in the swamps around home where I played as a child plays looking for things to look at and pry open. Now they are in the paddies and along their edges, small sentinels that grow quiet when someone is near or among them as they did at home, the peepers and the ground toads. And do they do that now, I wonder, as they did? When they chirp here as they do now are things right in the bog, the paddy and is no one there, no one creeping in on me now, creeping through the peeping and the slimy, slimy bog? Is the old man's dragon asleep?

HA, HA.

If I could write any of this down it would be these sounds and they would make good reading, good listening to sleep by as Joyce did in bed.

The air was clean and the village continued to burn. When I thought I could faintly smell it, I turned and met with the glow of a cigarette tapping easily on a thigh behind me.

"Put that goddamn thing out," I said. "You're going to catch one between the running lights, and if you've got to wave it around like a goddamn signal, stay the fuck away from me."

"Yes Sir," and the glow disappeared.

I recognized the voice as Balen's; the others were there too. I didn't know how long they had been waiting behind me, and now, as I turned back toward the glow of the village, I knew they would be confused by my tone but right now I didn't care. I didn't care if they were confused or if they had to wait for the rest of the goddamn war. Tonight I just wanted to be out of all this rat run shit and ho ….

The dark sodden sky was split by the slice of a brilliant red cleaver appearing out of nowhere and smashing into the ground and seconds later, the quiet was disturbed by a low grumbling roar.

"Jesus Christ," I said thankful that in the darkness none of them had seen me jump. "What the fuck is that?"

"Spooky," Balen said. "The gun ship. It's like an old DC 6 with windows full of .50s. It flies around in circles and pounds the shit out of the ground if some unit is being hit or over run."

"It puts down a wall of lead," Rico added.

"It didn't make you jump did it Sir?"

"No, Sergeant Wescott," I said looking down toward his boots. "I'm just glad it's on our side."

"Some noise, huh, Lieutenant? It sounds like a fucking dragon."

"Yeah, English, just like a fucking dragon. If it doesn't hit them it must scare the shit out of them," and after a silent pause, "anyway…

"…We're going in tomorrow," I said. "Be ready at first light, that's all."

Behind me the night noises in the paddy grew still.

SitRep Jan222240H: That night what little piece of the moon there had been that briefly challenged the clouds fled and it rained again and was cold. The rain water filled up my hole as I slept. My body warmed the water and I chose not to wake hoping instead to rekindle my earlier dreams. I didn't know it had rained until morning. Then I knew that it had grown cloudy and had rained in spite of the stars and the moon that I had imagined to be there; that I had been wet through the night because I was stiff and the evaporation from my clothes made me shiver with the cold. I was disinterested in the movement around me and when the other two platoons had passed, I moved my men mechanically into columns behind them, trying to keep away from the inside of my clothes that hung on me like wallpaper and allowed the damp to trickle down the crack in my ass and set up permanent housekeeping in my bones.

"They're the horniest people in the world, they are," Flynn-Michael had said last night. "Leave just the hint on an opening only once, where they can see it and they'll stick it all up your ass."

The thought of what Flynn-Michael had said jolted me back to the jungle and I forgot the wet misery of my clothes. I moved Balen's squad to the rear to cover our departure and we moved out slowly, cautiously, always cautiously. Around me, men strained their heads back over their shoulders, watching. They studied the ground closely before they stepped, and they were quiet, save the rubbing and stretch of the belts and straps that held them together. Nothing happened.

At noon, we stopped along the edge of a trail grown over heavily from the sides. The sun had broken the clouds and the deep rotting smell of tropical heat steamed up from the ground. I listened to the radio for a minute and then fished for a cigarette from under the band.

Balen came up from the rear and squatted next to me.

"All quiet back there," he said.

"Umm," I said, and then after a pause, "You want a smoke?"

"Yes Sir, thanks."

We coaxed a sputtering glow on the soggy slender butts and pulled hot warming smoke deep into our insides.

"Why do you use Stepps on the point? He's the only person I've ever seen that can trip and fall without taking a step."

"Because next to Morales, he's the best there is, Sir. He sees shit that no one else sees. And when the shit hits the fan, Sir, you wouldn't believe it."

"You're probably right," I said. "I wouldn't."

My cigarette went out. I reset the cigarette and reached for my matches, and as I struck the match, things fell in hard beside us.

"Incoming," someone shouted, and I held the smouldering match between my fingers, studying the sounds. These were new. Sounds I hadn't heard before. The explosions sounded like fire-crackers on the fourth wrapped in a sock; they were sharp but muffled, not like the rolling big booming thunder in the hills when the fliers dropped the heavies and you could see the high pillars of smoke rising over the peaks; nor were they like the distant artillery that Horey poured into unfriendly remote villes, but more of a cracking, sharp yet muffled at the same time. Sounds that you felt rather than heard.

'I do not recognize these sounds up close,' I thought as I ran from the road, 'but someone will shout and then I will know, as I know now they are unfriendly, because I remember unfriendly whispers from before. Until then, I will continue to run from the nameless sounds.'

"That's incoming, Sir," English called from the ditch as I jumped in beside him.

"No shit," I said, feeling the crunch of my boots digging into the dirt as it bounced past my locked knees and up into my back. "I knew it was something unpleasant."

"Mortars Sir," English said.

"Right," I said.

Now that the sounds had names, I sat back to listen. I studied English closely.

"How the fuck do you do it, English?"

"Do what Sir?"

Another volley of rounds smashed down into the twisted jungle farther up the column.

"Nothing," I said. "Just thinking out loud."

'The difference between the quick and the dead,' I thought; 'be first and be ready to be first, but be first first. That's the secret of being short.'

Balen dodged from one side of the trail to the other as he moved back to his squad.

"Turn up the radio," I said. English, who had been cursing the elusive cigarettes sunk deeply in his pocket, paused and fumbled with the volume knob over his shoulder. I pulled another cigarette from under the band on my helmet and together we listened. The remains of my first half-finished cigarette lay unlighted on the trail.

"This is Echo Six Actual," it said in high Irish. "We're taking incoming mortar!"

"Roger wait," another voice said.

"Wait, for Christ sake."

"Echo Six Actual?" the Colonel said. "This is Samantha Six... Actual."

"Tah fucking tah," English said.

"That's not incoming," the Colonel said as another round crunched in close by and sent dust and fine bits of metal spinning over our heads.

"Roger," the radio replied and the net grew silent.

I flicked at my cigarette and continued to listen. The refrain of thuds made me wince and I wondered where the whizzing shrapnel that I could hear all around us in the trees ended up.

"Echo Six, this is Bravo Six," the radio said, speaking again after the pause.

"This is Echo Six, over."

"This is Bravo Six Actual," the radio crackled, "I just wanted to come up on your net to tell you not to worry about that mortar fire, no cause for alarm."

"NO CAUSE FOR ALARM?"

"This is Bravo Six Actual, that's right, that's ours, so you see, it's friendly."

"FRIENDLY?"

"Bravo Six Actual again, that's a roger, apparently," the radio said with a chuckle. "A little screw up on our part."

"SORRY?" the radio said approaching a high tenor shriek, "A LITTLE SCREW UP!" it squealed, but there was no answer. The mortar fire ended.

"Echo Six, Samantha Six, over."

"Echo Six," Sanchez answered.

"Echo Six this is Samantha Six Actual again, put Echo Six Actual on, over."

Flynn-Michael took the hand set from Sanchez and listened and while he listened I could see him pace in large deliberate strides up and down the small trail dragging Sanchez behind him on the short tether of cord that connected the handset to the radio strapped on his back.

"Roger," he said at last and then again after a short pause, "roger, out."

"'No need to be upset,' he says...; 'these thing happen in war,' he says...; well he can fuck himself and his accidental discharges."

Flynn-Michael threw the handset back at Sanchez who caught it on the rebound like a runaway paddle ball.

"Get on the horn and tell them to saddle up. Tell them these things happen in a fucking war for Christ sake. Tell them Accidental discharges won't be tolerated by the Teapot."

I retrieved my half cigarette from the dirt when we got back on the trail and shoved it back up under the rubber band. Like the rest of the Company, it had escaped unscathed. In an hour we were back at the Landing Zone. CH 46's swallowed us again in a hail of noise and dust, and when we landed at Battalion, I felt different than I had on the steel-grey day a month ago when I stepped off into the mud and the country started to suck me into it.

"It wasn't Christmas Eve, thank God," English said.

"I wasn't here then," I said. "I am now."

I counted them off the choppers and watched as they ambled in small chattering clots to the Company area. Even the Doc, I thought watching Peckham struggle with the mass of straps and strings slung back and forth across his back, even the Doc has managed to get back unhurt.

We would drink beer and wash out the dust and the grit; or just grit perhaps, the dust would come later. It was done. I looked under the eaves for Wick and was happy to find him gone. Now we would have only the deep thud and boom of the artillery as it fired H and Is through the night, that and the beer; and I knew as I looked up through the rows of hooches that marked the Company area, that when I walked into the hooch, my hooch, I wouldn't notice the sign over the door this time and nothing would feel strange.

"Yes Sir," English said. "I guess that's right."

7 AN HOA – JANUARY, 1967

SitRep Jan241853H: Phu Lac 6 was to the north, six miles up the road, Liberty Road, a thin stretch of dirt that was a life-line, an umbilical connected to the Battalion area, and it sat on the river, the position, a small hill on the bank. There was a barge moored in the river across from it, and during the days, the barge drifted slowly back and forth with trucks and convoys of trucks from the north. The river was the Song Thu Bon and the area around it was nasty, but no one said why. They said that Christmas Eve was spent across the river and they shook their heads and grew silent. I thought of Wick rubbing the worn Band-Aid on his thigh. "Tocsan gooks," he had said. "A nasty-ass place." Echo was going there again. We would relieve Hotel, who was coming in, in place.

Flynn-Michael let the door to the hooch slam on his heels again this time leaving the map on the wall. For a moment we studied it, taking notes, and then we left. We had been back from Independence for less than five hours and now we were going out again in the morning. Brownell and Fitzlee started up the hill toward the Q and soon disappeared.

SitRep Jan241939H: When the meeting ended Horey and I went to the club. We went for two reasons; we went because it was new and we hadn't seen it or been there before, and we went because we felt we should, because the beer wasn't enough, it was good, but after nine days in the wet, not knowing from day-to-day if the next one was coming, the worry for the 55 kids who said they didn't give a shit but did inside, after that, beer was good for throat thirst only, but for the memories and futures, and to celebrate our good luck, it wasn't enough. So for that reason, reasons and maybe more, maybe because remembering was painful now and anymore pain might make us break, or because we really never knew how many of the little bastards we killed till we met them in our sleep, or because the position in the north was a nasty-ass place, maybe for those reasons too, but not for those admitted reasons even though we knew they were true but denied them, we, Horey and I, with Horey leading the way, went to the club.

"Watch out for man traps," I said.

"Fuck you," Horey said. "You watch out what tree you lean back against, I've still got that fucking round in my pocket you know."

The club had been built, stocked and built, during the nine days while we were away, out across the river and while Colonel Teapot, who didn't drink anything stronger than native water and who would never approve, was away too.

Horey lead and I, who was junior, walked beside him without further conversation, but Flynn-Michael beat us there, and his large oval eyes, brown, and high pitched laugh said he'd been there two maybe three drinks before us. Earlier, before the brief meeting he had been in the enlisted men's club trying to buy beer. The troops had loved it, and they were beginning to love him and when the bartender threw him out because of what was on his collar, the bartender, a Gunny, the troops, his troops, laughed and shouted, and even when he bought a beer for everyone in the house he was thrown out anyway, so he left cursing and smiling pushing his headlong strides ahead of the thunderous happy clamor of the men around him. Now, he had come here to the new staff and officers club, so even though Horey led, he was several drinks ahead of us and it showed in his eyes, his deep Irish brown eyes. When we came in he was talking loudly.

"I've never seen a worse group of pogues, mortared the shit out of us for Christ sake, but I'll tell you one thing, it beat the shit out of being with that fucking Colonel Teapot, Jesus, there's a pogue, not fit for command is he, Jesus.

"Horey," he said as we entered the room. "And One Actual, One Fucking Actual, I thought the goddamn war would be over. Get them a goddamn drink and forget these goddamn pogues Gunny, for Christ sake."

Horey and I sat down across the table while the smiling Gunny behind the bar mixed strong whiskey with stronger slightly clouded water. Flynn-Michael watched the condensation form on the glass as the ice was added and for a moment I thought I could hear the ice crack in the alcohol over the noise of the club.

"Pogues," he said sipping cautiously at his drink and looking out at the people around him. "These goddamn pogues haven't missed a fucking night since it opened, and they won't either by Christ, like that fucking little communicator over there, Jesus. I'll bet the son-of-a-bitch closes the club every night because he gets so much rest during the day. I suppose it's the nature of his work or perhaps the nature in which he approaches his work. That's the way it is when you're a fucking communicator. Listen to the son-of-a-bitch talk about the war and his heart with a capitol Heart, awarded for heroism and bloodshed at the hands of a fucking VC foot-locker, for Christ sake. He does it with bravado, with acumen as it read, but foremost he does it with knowledge, above all, a knowledge of the rigors of war. Pogues; a fucking communicator for Christ sake, I was a communicator you know, can you believe it me a fucking communicator but not like that son-of-a-bitch over there I can tell you that. It's a goddamn bone-pile of pogues talking at a 100 miles an hour about their wars, the big ones, the ones they don't fight except to themselves and among themselves over earphones and headsets; the ones they have fought with trepidation, thinking to themselves of themselves, and how will this all look on film mate, and how shall we discuss it to the very rightest people mate, and how to the wrongest too; catch my style, mate? The slight twitch in the wrist as I draw the slashingest of slashing grease lines on the map, mate, and how rapidly I can erase them, moving units miles like pesky flies on a cow's assey; very neatly done mate, very neatly done. And do you give a rat's ass all things considered, do you really give a rat's ass, for Christ sake?

"Blessed are the fucking pogues," he continued, lifting his glass up over his head. "Blessed are the meek fucking pogues, for they shall inherit the club. I was one of them you know, did I tell you that's what they made me, a fucking communicator."

He drained what remained in the glass and brought it down hard on the table.

"More," he shouted, and the club grew quiet. Because he had shouted and because Horey and I were late and dirty and still unshaved, the smiling Gunny brought three more drinks.

"Is there Vodka?" I asked looking at the murky glass in front of me.

"Yes Sir," the Gunny said.

"Then take this shit away, it's rotten."

"Me too," Horey said. "But make mine Bourbon."

"And Brandy," Flynn-Michael said. "Serve this swill to the pogues, mix it with coke or some other fucking thing."

It was still quiet, and I thought of the peepers and strangers among them and the effect, these people here sensed danger; and I thought of Flynn-Michael and his size and I decided to relax with the enemy among us. Someone at the table across from us offered to buy drinks.

"And bourbon for you," he said, looking at Horey.

"CC," Horey said in a humorless tone.

The man looked into Horey's glass a moment and then said, "all right."

After he had turned for the bar, Flynn-Michael leaned across toward Horey.

"That shit isn't CC," he said.

"I know," Horey said, "but it's his fucking money so what the hell."

"He's a pogue," Flynn-Michael said leaning back on the bench.

"Of course he is," Horey said. "The poguiest."

"The most poguey," Flynn-Michael said.

The man returned and set the drinks on the table and quickly returned to the far end of the club. Horey grabbed his glass and drew long and hard at the drink. He choked and spit it out on the floor.

"That's not CC."

Flynn-Michael laughed and lifted his glass into the air again.

"Blessed are the fucking pogues," he said, and he threw his glass. It shattered on the wall next to the table where the man who had purchased the drinks sat. He rose quickly clutching the table and then sat down slowly looking at Flynn-Michael. Flynn-Michael returned the stare watching him closely, his large brown eyes dancing with laughter.

"Not to worry," he said. "That's not incoming, that's just a little friendly fire. Nobody's ever been hurt by friendly, fucking fire. These fucking things happen in a war. But in spite of it all, you're still a hell of a fine fucking communicator, mate." Now he was shouting and the man sat down. "A hell of a fine fucking communicator."

"I've got to take a piss," Horey said. He pushed his way toward the door and left.

And it was at that moment that Colonel Teapot entered the building. Flynn-Michael brought the curtain of his mouth down on his laughter and turned to quiet conversation with us and the rest sitting at his table in the dimly lighted room, about ice and where it came from and God bless the CB's and their ice-machine and how they would never be classified as pogues.

The Colonel had difficulty making out the faces of the men sitting there drinking. Drinking. He stood in the doorway and looked like he was trying to remember the events that had lead to this. When he left for the field this had been nothing more than an empty hooch.

The smiling Gunny came from behind the bar to greet him, his grin widening as he strode down the aisle between the crowded tables.

"We followed your orders to the T, Colonel," he said as he drew nearer. "How does the Colonel like it?"

"My orders?" Colonel Teapot asked somewhat perplexed and further taken aback, as he sorted it out, to the accompanying sound of Flynn-Michael's voice whining somewhere in the darkness.

"Yes Sir," the smiling Gunny said. "About the club."

"Oh," the Colonel said. "My orders. Yes, it's very nice, just as I had wanted, as I had thought it should be, as I had ordered."

"Yes Sir," the Gunny said. "Even to the stock, the finest to be bought in country, and not cheaply Sir, you have my word on that, not cheaply."

"Fine Gunny," the Colonel said quietly. "Very fine. It was my decision that..."

"Yes Sir," the Gunny said. "We're all aware of that and we all appreciate it very much, the men do, your staff and officers, all of us, very much, Sir, to be sure."

The Colonel grew silent and gazed around his new club. The rigors of command, and of combat, appeared to have drawn him thin, drawn him very, very thin. He had made it through the big one and then Korea and now he was in the middle of this. Deep lines of thought eroded his forehead and he looked like he was trying to recall again, the very day, the very moment that he had called the smiling Gunny, who stood before him now and who he felt he was meeting for the first time, called him into his office and said, 'What this command needs is a club and this, I have decided, is the way it shall be.' It was obvious to those of us who sat quietly watching that he couldn't remember it in all its detail, in fact he probably couldn't remember it at all, but still the look in his eyes seemed to confirm the fact that it must have happened for here he was standing in the club that had taken form in his absence just as he had no doubt decided it should.

At last he relaxed and looked relieved, glad that he had decided to do it, relieved that his decision had turned out as well as it had. Everyone in the small club knew that that was not always the case in the combat zone where decisions went sour more often than not. Where negligence caused accidental discharges.

He followed the smiling Gunny to the bar at the end of the room and ordered a ginger-ale. He passed the length of the small building like someone on parade sensing that every eye was on him, watching him very carefully.

"On the house, Colonel," the Gunny said pushing the Colonel's paper nickel back across the moist wooden bar. "Surely you must remember, Sir? The day you decided we should have a club I promised you the first one on the house."

"Of course I remember Gunny," the Colonel said stuffing the soggy paper script back into his pocket. "But I certainly didn't expect to hold you to it."

"Hold, me to it," the Gunny said, his smile broadening again. "But Sir, I insist."

Colonel Teapot leaned back against the bar and sipped at his ginger-ale. Now he looked content and proud. As his eyes began to adjust to the smoke-filled darkness, he looked at our shining bloated faces, our eyes bulging with happiness and gratitude for the new club he had provided. He scanned us, ticking off the names, pausing at each face in turn, looking more proud at each one he remembered. Flynn-Michael, he mouthed silently as his gaze continued its sweep across our table. He paused in his scan. The sudden taste of the name caused him to repeat it, Flynn-Michael, who at this very minute was smiling back at him over the rim of a glass which sparkled with ice and a refracted light brownish hue. The smile vanished from Colonel Teapot's face and he tipped his head back draining the ginger-ale at a single breath. He looked toward Flynn-Michael again and Flynn-Michael nodded, slowly. Colonel Teapot returned the nod, set his glass down and glanced at the toes of his highly polished boots. He turned to the Gunny, ordered him to keep up the good work and left.

"What the fuck is wrong with Teapot?" Horey asked sliding back into his seat.

"Every fucking thing you can imagine," Flynn-Michael said resting his head on his hands.

"No I mean right now, I was out there taking a piss and all of a sudden he comes reeling down the steps and sucks in a tank load of fresh air and grabs onto the guy wire of one of the foul weather flaps, and mumbles like he's commanding his head to clear. For a moment I thought that maybe the Gunny put something into his drink. He looked like he thought he was the victim of an enemy agent that had been sent here to poison us all. His forehead got all glisteny with sweat, and he reeled back like he might have been poisoned already, and then he began to mumble 'Flynn-Michael is their leader, a foreigner, he is a foreigner, sent here to sabotage my unit, to assassinate me and throw the entire unit into chaos, jeopardize the entire war effort, deal it such a blow that it would rock the Pentagon to its very five pointed foundations and ruin my well orchestrated career. They had been unable to kill me with leeches and cake but quite clearly they haven't given up. The magnitude of the very idea makes my blood run cold.' With that he rumbled off down the pallet catwalk toward his tent getting louder with every step.

"But how had he managed it I wonder, all the way from Da Nang?

"I must take steps to initiate an investigation tomorrow. I can't take my eye off him now.

"How long has it been after all since we received a thorough vote of confidence from Ireland? Whose side are they really on anyway, and with all the North and South business, does anyone really know? It is worthy of an investigation to be sure, and if it is true, if Ireland is really the enemy within, it will make me famous. I'll be

respected and honored where ever I go. And best of all, there are
the silver eagles sitting precariously on the edge of my desk in their
plastic eerie, but even better than that, at last I would be rid of that
dreadful, beer-spilling Captain Flynn-Michael.

"There will be parades, lots and lots of parades and Walter
Cronkite, and... say, what about that Gunny, isn't that Gunny
some sort of Mexican?"

"And then I heard the door of his hooch slam and that was it."

SitRep Jan242151H: Shortly, as the Colonel dozed uneasily in his
quarters under the eider down quilt he had had shipped from the
States, there was running in the club and the solid, stupid tempo of
impacting mortar.

Krump.

"Jesus Christ," I said.

"Sit, for Christ sake, One Fucking Actual, you're not a virgin any
more," Flynn-Michael said. "It's only mortars, and besides we can
only hope they're like those fucking goddamn clowns under the
splendid command of Bravo fucking Six fucking Actual who
couldn't hit shit with a sledgehammer, and anyway, if it's the local
gooks with their bamboo tubes we're just as safe here as in some
goddamn bunker. They only hit their targets by mistake for Christ
sake; it's something about their goddamn watery eyes."

"It doesn't make any difference, Skipper," Horey said, lifting his
glass and spinning the clear, stiff ordered liquid. "You're probably
right. It's friendly and no one will get hurt."

"Or perhaps it's not incoming at all," Flynn-Michael said.

"No," I said. "I guess you're right, it really doesn't make a
difference after all."

We had had too much to drink for anything to make any
difference. We forgot about it, and while everyone else ran and
shouted and shoved for the door we sat quietly and drank, the

three of us only, with the sound of the mortar fire growing more intense and impacting on the northern end of the strip.

Krump.

"They're after the ammo dump," Horey said.

"Umhumm," Flynn-Michael said.

"They won't hit it?" I asked.

"No," Horey said.

"Their eyes?"

"Their eyes," Horey answered.

We sat there and counted them in; 10, 20, into the 30s. I could hear them coming out of the tube, the whoosh, the sound of a pea-shooter held close to the ear, the sound of a quickly moving train. I could hear the quiet while they arced over the camp, 40 to 50 seconds depending on how far out they were, the muffled crack when they hit, impacted. I could feel the concussion on my ears, on the back of my neck, and then the noise, sharp and muffled.

Krump.

We drank. It was still too much. Forty, 50; they were still coming in in unperturbed rhythm.

Krump.

"That's 51," Horey said.

"Fifty-two," Flynn-Michael corrected.

"Where the fuck are the counter mortars? Jesus."

'Be first,' I thought.

"Soon," Horey said.

What we drank now wasn't ours, now we drank what the others had left behind when the club emptied, when they ran from the hooch without their fucking courage, left it on the table, left it alone and on ice for later; ran from the hooch without their hooch. Hoochless from the hooch. We drank what remained, listening, just the three of us.

Krump.

The Gunny had done a good job with the conversion, rounding up tables somewhere; building the bar to run across the narrow way on the far wall, the added back wall that separated the club from the small store room where he kept his cot. The walls were burned plywood varnished. He had louvered the screens with wooden slats to cut the noise and the light. It was nice, restful, I noticed it; noticed it all, while I wandered from table to table gathering the fruits of our bravery, the glistening sweating badges of courage that waited in the muted light of the darkly shaded wall lamps. When the artillery fired, my count was to 60, 65.

"Got them on 68," Horey said. "There it goes."

"Will it hit them?" I asked.

"Shit no," Horey said, "They're gone, they were gone 10 minutes ago."

"Oh," I said spinning a glass in my hand holding it up to the dim light. "That's too bad."

"It's all right," Horey said. "It doesn't make any difference anyway."

"I suppose not," I said.

Flynn-Michael stood and walked to the door.

"We can leave now," he said. "The world is now safe for democracy. I'll bet that fucking Colonel couldn't get into his flak panties quick enough."

Flynn-Michael laughed loudly when we walked out into the cool night. It had little effect. We carried as many drinks as we could hold and staggered under the weight. The booty jingled on the ice. The ice although it melted slowly to nothing had come through. The CB ice had survived.

Half way to the hooch we were stopped by a running man, jingling.

"What do you want running man?" Flynn-Michael asked.

"What are you doing out here?" the running man shot back. "We're in condition red."

"I hope to shit in your mess kit we are," Flynn-Michael said.

"Fuck you," Horey said.

"Jesus Christ," I said.

"Sorry Sirs," the running man said. "I didn't see..."

We continued to the hooch and the running man dashed off away from us into the safety of the darkness and condition red.

"Thought he was fucking Paul Revere, for Christ sake."

We drank and it grew late. 'Not grow,' I thought, 'wrong word, late doesn't grow, it over comes,' and as I thought it through, the lateness over came me. The attack was over, and I observed that it had never really begun. I forgot about it, forgot the running man, forgot the mortars, forgot about Teapot, forgot all of it. I stopped thinking about anything and joined with the others in the destruction of the empty glasses, helped with the hurling of the empties down the length of the hooch where they smashed against the wooden door and sign above it. Fitzlee and Brownell were there, so was Boots. I thought they helped too, or maybe they weren't there, maybe I forgot them too along with the rest.

Perhaps I remembered instead another night before Independence when I found Brownell alone in the hooch with a fifth from the States lying across a rack with his head propped up against the wall drinking. Perhaps it was that night.

"It's my anniversary," he said.

"Congratulations," I said. "Where'd you get the booze?"

"Wife," he said. "She sent it in an Ivory Detergent bottle, plastic, so it wouldn't break.

"Some day we're going to have a shitload of kids.

"But not tonight.

"Want some?"

I said, "Sure.

"This shit tastes like soap suds."

"It's my anniversary," Brownell said again.

I took another swallow, handed the bottle back to him and left. It tasted like soap suds anniversary or not.

The glasses smashed on the door exploding a fine brown mist that speckled on the Fuck Communism sign and the ice melted into the rubble that rose slowly on the floor.

"It's bleeding, for Christ sake," Flynn-Michael said. "It deserves a fucking heart."

We laughed and threw more glasses. It was very late now and we were thoroughly drunk.

The water from the ice soaked through the floor and dripped into the earth below.

8 PHU LAC 6 – FEBRUARY, 1967

SitRep Jan250539H: At first light, we were on the Liberty Road and already it was growing hot in the late January sun. The monsoon was lifting and the road was starting to decay into dust, kept moist and down by the less frequent afternoon rains. It was hot and the now released dirt of the road was kicked up into liberated angry swirls under our feet. Like the rest, Flynn-Michael carried two canteens. Like before one was filled with water, and the other, the still fine brandy that we drank when we broke, passing it from one to the other around the small circle of officers.

"It's damn fine brandy, isn't it?" he said.

It always was, I thought. On a hot dusty road, it was fine, damn fine. Before, in the mud, and it was a sea of mud then, it helped. But it wasn't as fine as it was now, because nothing was fine then. In the midst of the monsoonal downpours when I got here and in early January when I was here and down by the coal mine, when this road, the Liberty Road, was not a road, it was soup. As deep as a man in places or at least up to his armpits. The troops didn't walk to Phu Lac 6 in the monsoons, they rode on amtracks. They burrowed through the muck that they themselves had churned up the day before and the day before that, and the road, the mud, that at first would support a man, the weight, several men, walking, knee-deep perhaps, but still support them gave way, gave up trying until finally it would not even support the amtracks because they

211

had churned it to soup. And when it was unable to bear the weight of their walking and churning machinery, they continued the assault, sinking deeper and deeper into the mire making it an all day trip that began at first light and it ended at dusk. The mud worked up into the road wheels of the bulky track vehicles and they threw track so that it had to be replaced before they could creep another several hundred meters where it happened again. Men replaced it standing their full length deep in the muck and they cursed; they did it often, several times a trip every trip until the sun, the late January, early February sun dried it completely and the water gave up its hold and returned to the paddies on either side to wait. Now, with the monsoons ending, it was more dusty than wet and we drank brandy, damn fine brandy too, and we humped.

The pace we set was good and we were in by early afternoon.

Fitzlee dropped off on a small platoon position on My Loc just to the south of Phu Lac 6 while the rest of the Company moved on to the main position a click to the north. From his position, Fitzlee could see the road to the south; from the Company position, we could see the mile or so stretch between the two positions and the short run that wound down to the river and the river itself and the road beyond that snaked north toward hill 55 and Da Nang.

The Company position covered the top of a hill, not a high hill, but more like a mound, no higher than burial mounds, not like the ones here, more like the ceremonial mounds that some ancient Indian built and scattered into the Ohio Valley. But the ground around it was flat, so it was adequate. It was loosely shaped like a "T." The shaft ran from west to the east, where it tapered to a point. The cross of the "T" ran north and south along the western end of the shaft forming the western slope. It edged the east-west drift of river, the same river that continued to bend south past An Hoa and on to the coal mine, and commanded its junction with a smaller, less thought of river that flowed, unobserved from the mountains to the north and west. Fitzlee's position ruptured. the earth in a similar fashion and sat quietly in tree lines by the sluggish dirty river water and a small village.

I would defend the shaft. Brownell the cross of the "T."

Dear Pumpkin,

When we got there, we relieved ourselves in place. I relieved a Staff Sergeant, 'a hell of a good man,' they said because he kept a bottle of scotch which we drank, he and I, in the cool of his bunker out of the sun after a brief tour of his lately, my newly, portion of the shaft. 'The hill wears your bunker much like a king might wear a crown,' I said. 'Squarely on top and. in the middle.' He said, 'Yes but that it didn't make any difference anymore.' When I asked him why, he said, 'Because it wasn't his bunker anymore, it was mine.' Mine and the rats that we could hear and smell running in the walls as they had in the south. 'This ain't a bad position, though,' he said, 'because the natives has never manned it so it don't stink.' I smiled weakly and filled my cup again with the scotch he offered while in the Command Post, Flynn-Michael sat on a box behind his large oval eyes and listened to the other Company Commander talk happily of the afternoon sniper and how he was later than usual today.

Love.

"There never was a bigger asshole," said Flynn-Michael after we set in and joined at the CP. "Field grade material for Christ sake. The biggest fucking comedy I've seen. Bunkers all on the top of the hill to give the 'afternoon sniper' a sporting chance, while he sat and smiled like an idiot here in this fucking cave. Jesus."

I looked around the CP. It was carved into the highest natural earth on the hill, roofed with rail road ties and timbers and recovered with sandbags and earth. It had several rooms stacked into themselves shotgun style, the farthest back of which already held a sleeping Horey, and three other empty racks nailed into timbers by their feet. Bat cave was an appropriate name.

"... and beer, for Christ sake," Flynn-Michael went on. "We can't fight a war without beer, now can we. We've got to have beer."

He passed the brandy. The last of it.

"Two cans a day, and in this heat too, the work of a pogue grown bloated with air conditioning. Two cans. I piss more than that in my dreams for Christ sake. We've got to have beer."

I passed the empty canteen back around the circle and looked at my watch. The first report of the 'afternoon sniper' still echoed in the mountains across the river and now the second skittered across the river and chased the first into the valleys we hadn't been to yet. It was followed closely by a third. Flynn-Michael took the canteen and shoved it back into the pouch on his belt.

"He's late," Flynn-Michael said, looking down at the wide dirt covered planks in the floor. "You can't count on a fucking word that asshole said."

The meeting had ended when the brandy was gone and I walked back to the rats in the growing darkness. With the sniper song ended it was quiet and the night sounds started again, lifting off the paddies like a harmonic fog. 'It is good,' I thought, 'and all is right with the world.' Later on that night the paddies grew still.

SitRep Jan252114H: The Shitter. The shitter is normally a box, I mused, built from old ammo boxes, with one, two, three or four holes chewed into its top and set over a dark not so deep fly humming hole. Some are built modestly into small green buildings, others, such as this one, the one at Phu Lac 6 are open all around, save the sandbag wall tossed up enemy-ward. Beyond the wall, the wire of our position sags and leans into the rotting bags. Behind, the hill rises and I can hear people moving. Over the wall there is a small paddy that waits between me and the river, and it is wet, still, from not being worked, like those of the valley; it is wet from the climate and the damp and its closeness to the river; the river gives it swamp and the land gives it life and its song which when written must sound like the sounds of a party. I know it is there because when it is light, my head sits on the sorry sandbag wall like a melon, a huge smiling jack-o-lantern and I can see clearly to the river and the trees along the bank. Curious that the wall should be made as though its builder suffered from hemorrhoids and shat with his chin on his knees, or perhaps he grew weary and decided to watch.

The flies that had buzzed when I sat, fussed again at my shifting to restore the circulation in my legs. It was the new moon. Occasionally, I heard whispers drift from the bunkers up on the hill where I knew they would sleep. But they won't sleep tonight, I thought, not the first night, not where they were sniped at in the daylight, not in a nasty-ass place like this. But tomorrow, tomorrow they will sleep at night because it will seem familiar and perhaps some will see, as I had seen today, that the sniper shot high. When they learned that they would sleep and I would not. I moved my head on my fist and the flies jeered me from beneath.

Balen and two of his fire teams filed quietly past me as I made my way back up from the shitter, and continued on out through the wire to set in an ambush on the small, well-worn trail that ran along the south side of the river. In the growing dark I could just make out Doc Peckham striding along next to the stoop shouldered Balen.

"You'll be glad I'm with you," he whispered as they moved by.

"Yeah, yeah," Balen growled. "Just stay down out of the way and shut the fuck up. And is there any way you can keep all that shit from rattling? You're like a fucking rag man."

They moved around the edge of the small paddy and disappeared into the far tree line.

Echoes of the muffled explosion still hung in the thick air and the radio sprang to a chatter of confusion. I ran up over the berm of the hill toward the river pulling Lonely behind me.

From the tree line there was a short burst of fire and then quiet.

"Fucking grenade," Balen panted into the radio. "Wired to a tree knee high with a trip wire. Two down. We're bringing them in."

I stood next to Balen watching the lights of the medevac chopper fade off to the north.

"Nobody else was hurt?"

"Just the Doc," Balen said. "A small piece of shit over his eyebrow. But he pulled it out and fixed it with a Band-Aid. He's alright."

"And the other two?"

"Lucky, couple of stitches and they'll be back. Fucking booby traps. I guess this is the way we're going to play the game now."

Balen gathered up the two rifles and started back toward his squad's area.

"At least these won't be Charlie Med souvenirs."

SitRep Jan252319H: Later that night we came under fire again, better fire this time, low to the ground, just clearing the hill, grazing, meant to bite and stab at the knees and the groin or rip through the head if you got to the ground.

Now, as Flynn-Michael had seen earlier, I saw clearly that they, the bunkers, had to be moved. I stood hunched at the door of my bunker and watched the tracers criss-cross the hill, crossing not five feet from where I stood. Between the ones I saw, there were five that I couldn't. I heard them though, as they struck into the walls of the bunker, and others as they rattled off what sounded like one of two tanks I saw this morning when we arrived. One dug in at each end of the hill. It was the one by the water hole that I heard because it was closer. I walked by it with the Staff Sergeant I replaced, on the way to the water hole, where, he explained we could wash and swim.

I stood and I watched but I didn't go out and it stopped. Only a probe. It had come up from the south; from a tree line 100 meters out. No one was hurt. I called and told Flynn-Michael, told Sanchez, who told Flynn-Michael but he already knew. Horey was asleep, as was Boots. When I finished I lay down. Several yards away the Doc talked quietly to the dozing Lonely.

"I mean booby traps in the middle of the night, can you believe that shit, our own grenades. What kind of person does shit like that?"

"Fucking gooks," Lonely said through his half sleep.

"I just can't believe it," the Doc continued. "I just can't believe it."

"Ummm," Lonely said. "You will." The Doc unable to sleep continued talking into the dark.

The rats moved over my head and as I went to sleep, like Nong Son, I wondered again how they kept from falling from above, and if maybe they didn't. We hadn't discussed them with the scotch, just recognized them as being there and nothing else.

SitRep Jan260617H: At first light I checked on Doc Peckham. A small ooze of blood seeped from under the reddened Band-Aid just above his left eye.

"You okay?"

"Yes Sir, it burned for a while but there's just a little stinging now."

I watched him for a moment and then turned back to my bunker leaving him to finish filling his .45 magazine.

SitRep Jan260729H: When we finished eating, we razed the bunkers and burned them to drive the rats away. We moved off the top of the hill to the slope and dug in, and while we dug, I removed my shirt and the hot sun chewed the flesh from my back.

SitRep Jan261114H: At mid-day, a convoy came through with supplies for the base camp at the air strip.

It was dusty when they arrived and I tasted the dust before I knew that it was landing into the open sores on my back, which I tasted later in the evening.

They had beer too, a shit load of it, under tarps headed for the clubs at An Hoa. While Flynn-Michael dickered for two cases with the Convoy Commander, Horey briefed and led a backside raid that brought the total case tally to 12. Flynn-Michael talked with rapid animation while they slid the brown boxes from under the tarp and ran with them into the bat cave where they wouldn't be seen. There was no ice, but warm beer was better than no beer so we drank it warm. The Gunny went in with the trucks to meet his wife in Hawaii. It made little difference, we still had no ice and the beer remained warm.

"There's mail," the Convoy Commander said as he climbed aboard the lead truck. "We'll drop yours off on our run back through tomorrow." The convoy left sucking the northern dust after it into the south.

From the paddy near the closest tree line a black clad farmer thigh deep in the stagnant water paused and noted the removal of the bunkers. He saw too their new positions, remembered them, and went back to work.

SitRep Jan261414H: Sergeant Jones was a member of the command group. He was short in stature and he talked like they talk in the hills; any hills, West Virginia, the Adirondacks, just the hills; and he laughed too much. When he didn't laugh, he spoke seriously about things that no one else dared to or cared about and nodded his head up and down while he spoke as if it were all the original truth. Other times he spoke from the sides of his eyes, when it was secretive, with the hint of a grin.

Flynn-Michael drained a can of warm beer and tossed it out of the bat cave into the dust. He reached for another of the pile between his legs and paused to watch Sergeant Jones appear from one side of the opening, scoop up the empty can, smile and disappear out of sight on the other side of the opening. He tapped absently on the top of the beer can and smiled back, continuing to smile long after Sergeant Jones had gone.

"Did you see that?" he asked.

"It was the fifth day of Independence and me and the Gooney were standin' at the place we had to move into, and this roving mushroom is flittin,' around all over the goddamn place behind us, when I spin in my goddamn tracks and say; 'Just who in the name of Christ are you?' 'Sergeant Jones,' he says. 'Well,' I says, 'what is it that you do besides follow me around the goddamn country, for Christ sake.' 'I got the weapons, Skipper,' he says. 'You got what?' I says. 'The weapons platoon,' he says. 'I got command of the weapons platoon.' And I look at the Gooney and he nods that he sure as hell does. Up till then, I didn't know who the fuck he was; I thought he was a mascot or a spy, for Christ sake. Then he says, 'I carry the flag, too.' 'What?' I says. 'The Flag', he says takin' off his helmet, 'I carry the colors.' And then he holds up this postage stamp flag that he's had folded and tucked in his helmet. 'I'll be a son-of-a-bitch,' I say and he smiles at me and the Gooney shakes his head.

"Watch, he's like a fucking trained dog."

Flynn-Michael tossed another empty into the darkness, and we all waited for the scrabbling Sergeant Jones as he trotted over to pick it up. After he left, Flynn-Michael said, "How long has the weapons platoon been broken down to squads and joined with the platoons?"

"As long as I've been here," I answered, "I didn't think we had a weapons platoon."

Sergeant Jones made the coffee and followed Flynn-Michael around the hill picking up after him. Most of the troops laughed at him, some to his face, and when he pointed out that he was the only one on the staff list with brig time, the Gunny shook his head and jammed his hands deeper into is hip pockets. He watched him closely and kept him from following too close.

Once we were set in, Flynn-Michael seldom moved from the radios. Sergeant Jones settled into an easy routine of coffee making, pick-up playing, and smiling.

SitRep Jan261524H: My new bunker was going to be a split level. I carved two shelves of different height out of the side of the hill and piled sandbags that came in large bails on the convoy with the beer from the north. I filled and piled steadily into the sun. Stepps, who sat on the top of his bunker watching the paddies, turned a critical eye on my progress.

"Lieutenant," Stepps said. "You doin' it wrong."

I dropped my shovel and looked towards where I had heard the voice; shading my eyes from the glare of the sun with my arm and feeling the grit rub into my forehead.

"What?"

"You're doin' wrong with the sandbags."

"Oh," I said.

"They got too much sand in them."

"So…," I said.

"Fill them not so much and they lay flatter more like brick. Then beat them in."

I filled the bags with less sand and the walls went up more slowly. Stepps sat on the bunker and watched closely as it grew. He knew sandbags. All privates knew sandbags, but Stepps knew them better than the others. He hadn't learned about them anywhere that he remembered, that someone had told him, he learned it by doing it here, not in Chi' where it might have helped too, but here where he had to because it made him safe and because it chewed into the flow of his time, his days, when he might have thought. Besides, he was told to do it and it was better than burning the shitters.

I had learned of, all about them, the sandbags, and how they were filled as well. But I learned it in a school in an air-conditioned room that was clean and well lighted, so I forgot.

Lonely, who had carried the radio since English left for home following Independence, scrambled down the hill from where he had been tinkering with the handset in the shade and grabbed a shovel.

"I'll help," he said.

"They don't know shit from sand in Philly," Stepps said. "Cause in Philly they only fight with the shit that's in their mouth."

"You, my man, are the only one in country with a mouth full of shit," he shot back at Stepps.

Stepps looked out over the paddies and didn't answer and together, Lonely and I, filled bags three-quarters full. Even though he is full of shit, I thought, and partly because he is from Chicago and partly because he was drafted, we filled them three-quarters full.

By dusk, before the good sniper returned, the walls were half up. We would have them finished by morning, in the morning, the next day. I had blisters on my hands and sunburn going to blister on my back that hurt like hell under the plastic plates of my flak jacket.

Earlier that afternoon when the three o'clock sniper had tried for a second day, his rounds plastered the side of the hill harmlessly. Others still ran high and easily cleared the top. No one was hurt.

SitRep Jan270913H: "What's he hurt," Horey said in the morning. "He can't hit shit."

"He hits us every time he takes a shot up here and gets home in time for tea," Flynn-Michael said. "The little fucker's got to go."

SitRep Jan271914H: That night, the snipers came back again. The good ones. They caught Sanchez out taking a piss off the side of the hill. The first rounds out chewed into the dirt between his feet. He ran up the hill and the chattering rounds followed him. He pissed on his legs and was mad as hell when he stumbled panting into the cave. Flynn-Michael laughed and the beer tasted good even warm.

"Don't get worked up, Sanchez," he said. "It's not worth it for Christ sake, a shitty little place like this."

"But they tried to shoot it off Skipper. Jesus Christ."

"You're a plot, Sanchez," Flynn-Michael said. "A fucking VC plot."

Then he turned to us again and said, "They've got to go."

SitRep Jan28   Over the next two days Brownell and I swept through the villages surrounding Phu Lac pushing deep to the south and east searching for some sign of the snipers that plagued the hill. Fitzlee patrolled along the river and moved through the scatter of villes between Phu Lac and My Loc and those necklaced around My Loc to the south back towards An Hoa.

SitRep Jan281427H: Stepps was on the point and half way across the paddy when the first rounds snapped through the early spring rice and buried into the mud and trees behind us. He dove for a crossing paddy dike firing as he moved, spraying the small palms that circled the village in front of us. He rolled to his left switching magazines and sprayed the trees to the other side of the small trail that wound up into the ville. And before I could shout 'get down,' it was over. Stepps was back on his feet rocking from one foot to the other grinning back at the rest of the small patrol. Behind him, two snipers hung from ropes tied to the tops of the palms their lifeless bodies swaying like fruit in a soft river breeze.

"Holy shit," I said.

"I told you Sir," Balen said as he ran up toward the ville.

"I don't believe it."

Balen shouted at Stepps, "Keep moving, keep moving you can smile about it after we get off this fucking paddy."

Stepps turned tripped and floated from the small dike into the paddy.

"Jesus Christ," Balen said grabbing him by his flak jacket and pulling him back up onto the dike. "Get on the fucking point and move."

"He looked like John Wayne," I said as we pushed into the ville.

Lonely came up carrying the snipers rifles.

"You want to cut'um down Lieutenant?"

"Naw," I said. "Maybe a month ago but now, just leave them there to welcome their brothers home."

As we left someone burned two of the hooches. The two squads formed up two fire teams up and one back, abreast of one another and swept out to the east and then turned north and headed back to Phu Lac.

Across the next paddy four young men dressed in black sat in the water to their necks and watched the smoke pouring from the small ville.

SitRep Jan282247H: Night. I finished my check on the Marines standing guard and headed back to the bunker I shared with Lonely and the Doc. It was quiet, and for a moment I stood just down off the top of the ridge and enjoyed the peace; no movement, no low whispers, no night sounds. "Shit, no night sounds," I said out loud and as I finished the sentence I heard the first rounds out of the tube. Mortars.

"Incoming, incoming!"

As I ducked into the half-completed bunker I thought I caught the glimpse of a flash in the trees near the village we had swept earlier that day. "Can you believe this shit?" I asked as I stumbled into the shallow bunker. As I spoke the first rounds landed. They walked across the saddle from the tank at the end of the tee down over the edge and beat into the edge of the surrounding paddies. Shrapnel whizzed through the still night air like locusts and sizzled into the mounded sand bags that separated me from the paddy below. I counted them in as they fell.

"They're 60's," Lonely shouted over the muffled explosions.

I scrambled across the hole and grabbed the radio hand set out of Lonely's hand.

"Roger Six," I said. "In the ville where we got the snipers this morning."

"Roger, wait one."

I pulled my map from under my poncho and held it up to the glow of Lonely's dying cigarette scanning for the ville's grid coordinate location.

"917432," I said finally. "We saw flashes in the tree line there before we went to ground."

A second volley began its random march across the small compound.

"Roger Skipper, I should be able to adjust from here."

I crawled to the front edge of the bunker and rose up to peer over the short wall and as I came up on one knee.

The flash and concussion were simultaneous and the loosened dirt fell on us like gentle rain.

"Jesus," I said rubbing my hands over my ringing ears.

"Anybody hit?"

"Not a mark Lieutenant," Lonely said after a minute.

"Doc?" I said.

"You won't fucking believe it, Sir," the Doc said. "But I've got another piece of metal in my head just over my ear opposite the hit I took two days ago."

I crawled over to the Doc and twisted his head so that I could see the wound.

"It's the Six," Lonely said.

"Tell him we're okay, and tell him the Doc is going to need another Band-Aid." I pulled the hot piece of metal out of the tight skin just above the Doc's ear and handed it to him.

"You're going to need a trophy case to show all these souvenirs when you get back to New York."

"What I need," he said, "is a fucking M-14."

"What you need is luck," Lonely shouted. "Luck is all it is. That's the only thing that gets you out of the Nam. Luck. You ask me Doc I'd say you ain't got none. You been here just a minute and you got two hearts already. Hell, I knew you didn't have no luck the first time we played cards. What do you owe me now, 200 dollars? Shit, I guess you ain't never had no luck, jus' look where the fuck you are."

Lonely paused and looked over at the Doc who was smoothing a small Band-Aid over the wound.

"Hey, maybe you got some luck after all. One more of those cheapies and you'll be on the way home with my two Franklins. Maybe you got some luck or maybe you're just another dumb white boy with a plan."

Doc pulled the top of his Unit-1 closed.

"My only plan now is to get an M-14. Then we'll see who's got the luck."

"Yeah, well make sure you don't plan yourself into a bag and a tin box with my money, that's all. Maybe you better pay me now."

In the distance the guns in An Hoa began to fire the counter mortar fires.

"That's a waste of the tax payer's money," Lonely said as we listened for the artillery rounds to pound into the ville. "Those fucking gook gunners were smoke before the last round came in and kissed the Doc over the ear. But what the fuck do I care."

He looked back at the Doc.

"You can be smart and you can pray your ass off but out here all we got is luck. You remember that because that's all that's keeping your skinny white-ass alive."

One by one the crickets in the paddy began their song.

SitRep Jan 290816H: That morning I stood in front of the bat cave next to Flynn-Michael.

"So, the Doc took another piece of shrapnel last night. The son-of-a-bitch must have a magnet in his head"

"Each time the Doc gets hit," I told Flynn-Michael, "more of the medical gear is displaced by the tools of war. Last night he wanted an M-14 and this morning I caught him with three frag grenades in his Unit-1. Healer heal thyself."

We left the wire and followed the road south for about 1000 meters before turning to the west across the paddies. Today, Morales had the point. We moved through a ville and then another and another. In each we found only bowing mamasans and smiling pappasans but little else. No hidden food, no signs of recent foot traffic just the repeat of sameness and the crossing of vast rippling paddies that covered the murky water beneath. Today we found the booby traps before the traps found us. Three hours into the patrol and no one had been hurt. The sun grew hot. We crossed another small paddy and entered the ville in the opposite tree line. Morales raised his hand and our movement stopped.

Lonely and I came up next to him.

"Looks like the ocean," Lonely said as we looked out across the uninterrupted sea of green.

"We'll hold here," I said dropping down to one knee. Balen and the Doc came up behind us.

"Set them in around this ville after they've done the search."

Balen took Morales turned and left leaving Lonely, me and the Doc at the edge of the paddy. I pulled out my map and slid my binoculars from their case. I slid down the small incline that ended in the paddy and studied the distant tree line. I adjusted the binoculars and scanned the far tree line laying the map across my knees looking for some feature in the distance that told me with reasonable precision where we were. As I looked I listened to the chatter of my men as they poked through the deserted ville. Far to my left a swirl of dust marking the arrival of another convoy from Da Nang at the Phu Lac ferry crossing drifted in a sullen mass above the green of mixed palm and banana. A little higher up on the knoll Lonely and the Doc knelt behind me.

"This all looks the same," Doc said.

"You got that," Lonely said as he shoved the radio handset up under his helmet and lay back into the shade. I continued to scan out across the paddy. Balen came up behind us and settled into the shade next to Lonely. "We didn't miss them by much," he said. "There are cooking fire pits all over the place."

"Okay," I said carefully folding my map and sliding the binoculars back into their case I pulled off my helmet and leaned back into the small banking bumping into Doc Peckham's knee. I looked out across the paddy. '... the dragon sank back into the paddy resting, waiting, spreading his seed throughout the rivers and streams to the sea...' and then turned to look at the Doc. "We're too close together," I said. "I'm going to move." In the time it took me to turn and lean away the Doc was hit. I heard the shot at the same time that I felt it crack across the back of my neck, plowing a bloodless crease through the short hairs just above the collar of my flak jacket. I dove head first into the paddy, embracing the warm shitty water. 'Head shot,' I thought. 'Fucking head shot.' I pulled myself out of the paddy and looked up to the higher ground where the Doc had been. Gone. He had rolled down the small embankment behind me and now he lay across my legs at the edge of the paddy. The round had ripped through his knee peeling back the lean red meat that made up most of his upper leg. When the round hit, the Doc shot straight up in the air and landed in a squirming rolling heap across me holding his split leg. Blood spilled between his fingers and turned the dirt of the nose we sat on a soggy dark brown. "Corpsman," I yelled "Corpsman." But all Doc Peckham said was "Sorry Lieutenant but I can't help you much right now." And then he said "Man this hurts." Lonely pulled a large battle dressing and morphine from the Doc's Unit-1 and while he wrapped the wound I gave the morphine injection. A second battle dressing filled with blood.

"Shit Doc, I don't know if this is luck or not. You're going home but you ain't gonna be chasing no women for a while, spending my two Franklins on 'em but at least you still got the equipment."

"I'll leave money under your pillow," the Doc said through gritted teeth.

"Sheeit, you won't even remember old Lonely once you get those nurses rubbing your leg and you'll still owe me 40 years from now. But as long as you owe me I'll never go broke."

He laughed and pulled down on the third battle dressing.

"Oh Jesus that hurts," he said with a half laugh cry. Tears streamed through the grit on his cheek.

"Give me another and get the choppers on the way."

Balen scrambled to set in an LZ while Lonely began the medevac process speaking quickly into the radio. After a moment he paused.

"Emergency?"

"Emergency," I said, "I'm on my forth dressing." And to the Doc "how you doing?"

"It still hurts like a bastard."

"Lonely's right, that's three," I said forcing a smile. "You're going home."

Lonely kneeled down closer by the Doc.

"Home, you son-of-a-itch. You really are pulling this shit just to beat me out of that card money."

Doc smiled weakly his eyes beginning to sag under the morphine.

"Don't make me laugh, you know what they say, it hurts when I laugh? It's true, it does."

"You want some more?"

"Yeah, maybe."

Lonely fumbled through the Unit-1 looking for another shot of morphine.

"Hey man, you been selling this shit to the gooks? There's only one left in here. That and a bunch of clips."

"That's because he's already had one," I said. "Think twice before you pop another Doc."

"It really hurts, Sir."

Lonely pulled the last vial out and jammed it into the Doc's left cheek. "One of them should hurt, you skinny fuck."

From the north the approaching roar of the medivac choppers grew louder and they were soon circling overhead.

I guided the 34 in while the Huey guarded from above. I grabbed the stretcher from the door gunner and ran to where Lonely waited with the Doc. Together we rolled him onto the litter and ran him back to the waiting chopper. We lifted him to the small side door and slipped him in past the door gunner.

"What about the goddamn gooks?" he asked.

"What about the doctor from Troy?" I answered. That was the last time I saw him.

We watched the chopper lift off and head for Da Nang.

"What do you think Skipper?"

"I think he's headed home and with any luck at all his leg will be under him and not in a bag beside him."

"I'm gonna miss the coffee."

"Yeah," I said. "Me too."

"And I'm gonna miss him, too."

"We all will," I said.

"Balen," I shouted. "Get them formed up and let's get the hell out of here."

As the squads got ready to move I noted the location the shots had come from. The shadowed tree line shimmering in the distance, but I was unable to see the quiet movement.

"Lonely, give these coordinates to Lieutenant Sills, let's leave them a little gift from us to them. Tell him to give it a battery 10 fire for effect."

As we started back toward Phu Lac the distant rumble of the guns at An Hoa bumped against the heavy air. I paused and watched the first rounds flower in an orderly row through the tree line in the distance. By now the shadows had melted away sliding into the lush green of the paddy. What remained of the Doc's blood sank into the moist earth and leached out into the paddy and the rice shoots continued to grow undisturbed.

"He was a good shit, wasn't he," Flynn-Michael said again that evening in the cave. "A fucking Ichabod but as good a shit as they come."

SitRep Jan292014H: I was going out again in the morning with two squads and the guns. More endless patrolling finding nothing but booby traps and sweeping them clear with hands and bits of leg.

We were going to work to the south, into the other villages, two or three clicks away, and we were going to look for the snipers and the gook mortar-men and the ones who set booby traps yet again. We were caught in a loop. As usual, Brownell would be out too, to the west, a click or so away anyway. He could help if we got into trouble, and so could I if the opposite occurred.

The awkwardness of the Antenna Valley and Independence faded into the ripening rice. Over the past six days we had worked contained within ourselves. Now we worked together, daily, in tandem in the heat, because it was hot now so we learned to get use to that too.

Balen and Rico would go. So would Lonely. Wescott, because he had been in construction, would stay back on the hill and fill sandbags. He would make decisions and question them, discuss them, smile over them, and no one would be hurt.

Balen and Rico and I sat in the bunker and drank piss warm beer. In the candle light, we studied the map, the route we would cover, the terrain, what to look for. I showed them where I would be. I said it was important that they know. I told them what I expected, what I had learned from English and the rest, how it would be, of things they already knew, and they took notes. They told me what they needed. They spoke freely, with animation, and they kept their eyes to themselves. Even Balen, the spy. He sat quietly and listened to the things I said.

He looks younger, I thought, when he doesn't watch so closely, he looks his 19 years and sometimes he looks afraid, he looks as though 19 years is not a long time really, like silent, nodding Rico, both of them, not a long time really at all.

When the questions had been answered, the maps folded and jammed into pockets, we relaxed, and drank more of the warm beer.

Rico and I listened while Balen talked of the high country around Boulder where he lived back in the world; about the women and the crisp cold, air; about getting back. He talked about riding bulls and playing baseball, and while I listened, I watched his mustache grow.

When they left, I crossed off a number on the calendar I carried. I had crossed them off since I had gotten there and I counted them like others count words or cars or pages in books, I counted the days. They counted slowly. I enjoyed it when I forgot them, and then, when I remembered again, I could cross off more than one at a time. It didn't happen often. I always remembered. I remembered the nights too, but they were all part of it so I just counted the days. A year ago, two months ago, it had only been two months; I had counted the white lines in the passing zones on the highway as we drove West. They went by quickly. Only dots. Now, all I had left were the days, an endless wealth of days in fact, all neatly numbered waiting to be counted down to the end of the road and crossed off.

"You want coffee Lieutenant?"

I took the cup from Lonely and sipped cautiously at the hot tin cup. The sorry taste cut through the lip burning liquid and I spit it out on the ground.

"Jesus, Lonely, you trying to kill me with that shit?"

"Hey Lieutenant, I told you we'd miss him."

I handed the cup back to Lonely and the darkness closed in around us.

I lay on my rubber lady and listened to the wind that blew up off the river. It blew when the rain stopped, hot and dry. It started in the afternoon and turned the hill into a swirl of dusty rivets. The mud was gone. Now, at night, it blew off the river in a quiet familiar air.

In the North, in the old Adirondacks, it blew in in August, a pre-autumnal chill. I remembered it in the pines; up high in the pines because the boughs grew high, not low where there was no sun and they died. There were no pines here, just the dust on the tin roofs of elsewhere. I heard record players too. The troops; they carried them everywhere a reminder that they were not alone and that they were still alive even though it was night. They stopped. I heard Balen's voice chewing ass and I slept.

While I slept the snipers crept in close enough to listen to the music that again drifted from the bunkers that ringed the hill.

SitRep Jan300514H: When everything that moved was still a shadow, at that time of day or night when it was at last certain that the sun was coming but was not yet there, I along with two squads and the guns saddled up. We moved off the hill and through the wire. We checked into the net; Lonely did. Sanchez was on watch in the cave; he had been unable to sleep. He acknowledged our entry into the net and then mumbled something to Lonely that I couldn't hear. Lonely laughed.

We moved down the Liberty Road quietly and when the sun caught us, came over the rugged ridge of mountains that separated us from the coastal flat-lands and the South China Sea, we moved off the road to the tree lines. We swung north through the trees along the paddies, through the villages and we listened to Brownell as he rattled through check points 2700 meters to our south and west.

SitRep Jan300610H: Balen's grenadier Cobra was there now six months. He could fire his weapon from the hip without sights and hit a target at 100 meters. I knew that; I knew his name was Wesley but that the troops still called him Cobra because of the way he had killed the snake back in Antenna Valley. 'Now,' I thought, 'he should have been named something else.' I knew that he carried a lighter because I had seen him playing with it, and I knew that he didn't smoke, because I had asked. He had carried it for as long as I had been there, clicking it open and shut like a castanet in his pocket while he walked. I could hear it now behind me as we approached the first of several small hooches tucked in the tree line back from the road.

There were people there, a man and a woman, and it smelled like they had lived there since before Jesus. The hooches around theirs were no longer lived in and had long since fallen into decay.

Cobra took out his lighter, clicked it several times, flicked it into flame and held it to the eaves.

"Where VC, Mammason?" he asked. The edge of the roof began to smolder.

"No VC," she said.

The old woman pulled the smoking straw from the roof and stamped it out in the loose soil close up by the wall. Cobra pulled out his .45 and lit, lighted, the hooch again. Again she pulled the straw from the roof and snuffed it out while he watched.

"Plenty VC," he said. "You VC. You shoot Marines."

She was small, very small and gray; frail. She wore black silk pants and shirt. We called them PJ's. I wasn't sure what the gooks called them. I wasn't sure these were gooks. She was a peasant, perhaps, a serf. They both were, but how could you tell them from gooks.

"No VC, VC number 10," she said.

Cobra looked at her and flicked at and then ignited his lighter. He held it into the already singed roof. He watched her as the yellow flames popped in the damp straw and when she reached to grab it again he pushed her away. The old man put his hand on Cobra's arm. It was an old hand, old from age and work in the paddies, and the sun. It was cracked and the veins and cords to the fingers stood out on its back like dried twigs. Cobra struck him with the .45, a neat back hand to the hoary old chin. The old man fell unconscious by the house, blood soaking his beard. I looked down on the crumpled heap. His wrinkled cheeks ended on a thinly stretched chin that boasted the wisps of fine spindly white hairs like proud pennants highlighted with light brown crusted streaks leading from the corners of his windswept cracked lips. His eyes folded nearly shut. The old woman cried and stooped by his side. She stayed there and cried silently as Cobra lighted the eaves in other places, clicked the lighter, closed it, clicked it again and then put it in his pocket. The house burned well. I stood quietly and watched. I hadn't stopped Cobra when a word would have done it. I hadn't stopped him because now I had been there for two months and Cobra had been there for six. That was the difference. I stooped over to get a closer look at the old man's familiar face. I splashed him with some water from my canteen and then moved on. The water ran off his face through deep grooves and cracks and mingled with his blood in the fine dry dirt.

SitRep Jan300847H: "There ain't no good guys in the war zone," Cobra said as he moved past. I watched him walk away looking carefully from side to side with each step. And as I watched I thought, 'Cobra is a good name for him after all.'

We continued north. I could hear the bamboo popping behind us. I had seen it before from the distance, but the smells and the sounds were new. The land didn't burn it never did. Only the hooch burned and it gave off a luxurious thick white smoke when it did. They always did that too.

"Let that be a fucking lesson, a gift from the Doc."

Flynn-Michael's voice cracked in my ear, "One Actual, that you?"

"Roger," I said.

"Roger," Flynn-Michael said.

Behind us the old man stirred and smiled wiping at the water and the trickle of blood.

SitRep Jan300859H: To the south of the position, the islands of trees were distinct. They began and they ended in the paddies. The paddies were at their sides, their flanks again, but always there.

In the paddies, a machine-gun could put out grazing fire for 1,000 yards and it would be uninterrupted. It would strike the rice grain where it grew and cut it down and then continue on.

I preferred to move in the islands and where it was possible I demanded it.

When there was no other choice, where the islands ended, and the paddies ran on out of sight, we held up and we watched and then we went quickly and a few at a time, into the paddies, across and into the trees on the other side where we waited again and then moved.

We were waiting, or had been when we first took fire. Five of my Marines were up and moving. The paddy was small; 75 meters across. The fire had come from the trees on the other side. The five that were moving took cover in the ruin of a broken stone house that had been left by the French. One of the five, Cobra, lost the tip of his finger; a scratch. While I studied the tree line, Doc Wilson, a new arrival, patched Cobra. The rest set in, waiting.

There were two this time, a carbine and something heavier, probably an AK-47. The light high-pitched pop of the first the throatier crack of the other gave them away. By now I knew the loud pop when they came close and the way they whispered when they went high over our collective head. As before, these had been close.

The big guns. I called in the coordinates, the range, the direction, to Horey up on the hill.

"I can't see you," Horey said. "Are you sure you're right?"

"I'm right," I said. "Fire it."

My stomach tightened when I heard the boom from the base camp and for the minute, the second, my thoughts wandered back to the pissy hot Virginia afternoon in the rose garden.

"Shot out," a voice called over the radio.

The shells, 105's, went over my head and I smiled when they hit where I wanted them. I adjusted and walked them through the trees by the small village. The sniping stopped, and I had done it all from under a tree. I could do it with my eyes closed, or while I ate dinner or had a drink.

'Easy. Stick that up your rose garden ass.'

We moved, still with caution, still quickly. I was half way across the paddy when it went. An explosion in front of me, to my front.

Booby traps.

A black plume of smoke leaped and hung over the ground.

"Jesus Christ," I said.

Two of Balen's men; 'Men? No. Boys. Now they were boys, boys when they were hurt. They had been men before though, just seconds before this, but now just limp children scattered on the ground. Blood from the wounds of boys turns the green of their clothing crusty brown,' I thought, 'and thank God, thank God they were running, if that's who you thank when you're here, if that's who listens. In any event it was damn good luck. They had run through most of the damaging blast suffering only slight penetrating wounds. Carnal wounds, penetration no matter how slight.'

The chopper was there in 20 minutes; a routine for the bleeding, a priority for the pain, an emergency for the delay. It made little difference, the time was the same. They were still 34's, they still flew the same distance from the north and they still flew it the same way. Twenty minutes R, P, or E.

They were out.

When we started to move again, I watched Cobra, looked at him closely and then looked down. Balen came up beside me as we walked.

"That's what they mean by nasty-ass place Lieutenant." he said.

"Yes," I said. "I see."

I took the cigarette that he offered and smoked it. I pulled the smoke slowly into my lungs and began to focus on the hooch we now stood next to. Another old lady lived there alone with her chickens. The booby trap, a grenade, a U.S. grenade with a trip wire had been in her front yard.

Had she known it was there?

She said no.

We took her for a guide through the village and didn't step on any more.

When I walked by her hooch I turned to Cobra.

"Burn it," I said.

Cobra held the lighter in his left hand and clicked it up under the eaves and soon it was ablaze. Then we burned the rest of the village too. I smiled, and wished that I could be there to see the old lady's face when she got back to her pile of ashes.

'Ha. Cobra was right. Not a good guy in sight.'

I called Flynn-Michael.

"The answer is yes," I said.

"Yes?" was his answer.

"Yes, just yes" I said.

Dear Pumpkin,

It isn't bad here really, it isn't. Not nearly as bad as I thought. It might even get to be fun.

S

But it got worse. I didn't write it, it had no address, I just thought it. We passed through the burning village and moved to the northeast coming to the edge of yet another broad, rippling paddy.

SitRep Jan300947H: Lonely was the first one to see them up ahead in the paddy. There were two of them moving away, trying to run, but the litter they carried slowed them. The two men I sent caught them easily and brought them back. They were women, three of them. The one on the litter was the youngest, not young, not a child, but the youngest. The other two were older and like all the rest, their teeth were red and wasted from the betel nut. The girl's teeth were uniformly white and intact. She, the one on the litter was not. Her guts had been ripped by the earlier artillery. Shrapnel had cart wheeled through her midsection like a gymnast and disemboweled her.

She was pretty. The wound wasn't, but she was. She wouldn't be soon though, she was dying and she was young, as young as the men that stood around her watching her bleed out. That young but no younger. No older either, but old enough for this. It made the new Doc sick, not wretched, but sick. Not from the wound alone either, but from the age and the sex and a total of the three. 'Perhaps he has a sister,' I thought, 'a sister like Peckham, a sister from Troy, a Trojan sister.' The one on the ground began to turn gray. 'Be thankful, Doc Peckham is gone or you'd die alone.'

The Doc sweat freely as he worked over her.

"She needs help, Lieutenant," he said without looking up.

"Jesus Christ," I said.

Now the Doc looked up.

"She's going to die if you leave her here," he said.

"She's going to die anyway," I said. "She's dead already."

"She's a good looking bitch, Skipper," Lonely said.

"Alright," I said. "Put in the request."

Lonely started the form.

"Request Medieval, can you copy...

"Roger, understand, need priority, wait one...

"What priority you want on this, Lieutenant?"

I looked at the Doc and the girl. He was packing her guts back into her, trying to keep them moist where they protruded darkening the weave of the litter. I looked at her and saw the rest of them; the old ladies where they knelt on the other side of the litter, across from where the Doc worked. I looked at the few young Marines who stood like gawking spectators at a gang-bang while the rest were beginning to form the LZ perimeter.

"Routine," I said.

Lonely looked at me.

"Routine?" he echoed.

"That"s what I said, goddamn it, routine."

"Right, Sir," Lonely said and he called it in.

The old women began to howl, like the old lady in the valley when we tossed the grenade into the cave. One of them held her hands to over her head, waving them in air.

"Lonely," I said, "shit-can that request, she's gone, and tell the Skipper we're coming in."

Lonely spoke the words quietly into the hand set. I called Balen up. We conferred momentarily and then he turned back to his squad. Seconds later Cobra knelt over the litter between the howling women and went through the pockets of the lifeless young girl.

"Just a shitload of papers," he said holding them up for me to see.

"Take them," I said.

Cobra handed the papers up to me and we moved.

"Will they bury her?" the Doc asked.

"They can dip her in goddamn bronze for all I care," I said. "She shouldn't have been here with those teeth; with the old ones it's alright, they don't give a shit, but not with the young, she shouldn't have been here. And besides," I held the papers up, "these probably aren't the funny papers."

The new Doc didn't make the coffee that night. Like Peckham he was going to be a doctor and as it had been with Peckham at first, to be a doctor meant different things.

'He will learn,' I thought as I watched him sitting alone on the top of the bunker, 'he will feel steel himself at some point, maybe not the trifecta like Doc P, not three times in a month but it will come because it can't miss and he'll go back home to the world to think about it forever.'

'He was a damn fine corpsman, the old Doc, eh Sam' Flynn-Michael will repeat and I will agree, they all were.

But tonight the first lesson was hard and the Doc didn't make coffee. I did and the Doc carried it off and drank it quietly alone.

SitRep Jan302117H:

Dear Pumpkin,

FM excels without Col T around his neck like an oversized dog tag, and he forgets about the pogues. So do the rest of us. He is the Company. He can out drink and out cuss us all. He is Irish, you know, and he can lick our collective asses and we know it and he knows it but it makes little difference. We, me and Brownell and Fitzlee are the Actuals, one, two and three, Boots is the Skippy, Horey is Horey and the Gunny is still on R and R so the men grow face hair. Jones makes the coffee and carries the colors in his hat. We drink beer and grow tight, all of us because we are the Actuals. We lead and grow savvy. We are taut. This nasty-ass place shows us the way. It's great fun really.

Your forgotten friend,

S

SitRep Jan302201H: In the cave that night, I spoke easily of the day and the dead girl. Her papers were on their way to the S-2 in An Hoa.

"Booby-traps," Flynn-Michael repeated after I had finished. "For Christ sake."

"They're everywhere we go out there. This one was an M-26," I said. "And trip wire; wired for sound."

"One of ours," Brownell said. "We've seen 'em out there too".

"That's right," I said. "There's not a ville out there without them."

"How do you know it was one of ours?" Flynn-Michael asked.

"By the size of the wounds," I said. "Small, and the big noise."

"One of ours, for Christ sake," Flynn-Michael said again.

"Okay," he said. "And them?"

"Lucky," I said. "They were running. They beat most of it; only hit a couple three times."

"Good," Flynn-Michael said. "Tomorrow?"

"Sure," I said.

SitRep Jan302218H: The day had been hot. I bent over the case of beer and fumbled in my shirt for the C-rats opener that hung on my dog tag chain. When I stood up, Wescott stood in front of me, silent and for the first time as far as I could remember, not smiling. I pushed the beer toward him but he shook it off.

"Well?" I asked.

"I need to talk with you, Sir?" he said.

"Go ahead," I said.

He remained silent and looked at the people around us.

"Okay," I said, placing the unopened can back in the case I followed him into the night.

SitRep Jan302230H: "It's Ham," Wescott said once we had left the cave.

'Hamling,' I thought, 'big and gawky and good.'

"He says he's not going out," he continued. "I've spoken to him at length, but he still says he's not going out."

"Spooked?" I asked.

"Yes Sir."

I tried to remember what I could about Ham. On the first trip out, during Independence we found a scalp, a shock of black gook hair still hanging on the skull bone clipped clean by the arty. Ham, didn't know what it was when I tossed it to him and when I told him he dropped it quickly. 'Good God,' he said and his eyes grew round and white as hell. 'The goddamn thing's got bugs in it,' he said. It did. He laughed when we laughed but his laugh was hollow. He looked at it lying between his feet. 'Good God,' he said again.

"Why?" I asked.

"It's this place; he was hit here at Christmas, hit in the ass by a booby-trap just like the one's today. If you didn't know, Sir, they hurt like hell in the ass. Now, he says he doesn't want it in the ass again."

We turned and walked up the slope to Ham's bunker without anymore talk. In the distance, I could see the white of Hamling's eyes looking down on me.

"I ain't going out, Lieutenant," he said.

"Why not?" I asked.

"I don't know," Hamling said. "All I know is I ain't going out."

We talked into the night about the good things now, the why of it all. It was all first class classroom stuff and tonight on this night after this day and the ones before the ones before, it sounded a little putrid.

"I ain't going," Ham said at last.

"Okay," I said. "Okay for tonight, okay, but you'll go in the morning or you'll go to jail, you'll understand that and fuck the rest of it that makes no sense, you will go to goddamn jail."

When we walked away from the bunker Wescott said "Shouldn't we bring him up on charges now, Sir?"

I stopped and turned back just able to make out Hamling's silhouette.

"And replace him with who, Sergeant Wescott. Replace him with whom?"

I stepped back into the cave and looked at map tacked up on the wall.

"What we need," I said, "is a goddamn flag."

"A what?" Flynn-Michael asked.

"A flag."

"A flag," Flynn-Michael said again. "Like the one inside Jones' helmet."

"That's right," I said. "A goddamn flag; something that tells these young Marines why they're here getting the shit shot out of them and blown up in the ass. Something that tells me the same thing. What the fuck else are we doing here?"

"But there's the rule," Brownell said.

"Ah yes, the rule," I said. "No American flags in country. In the beginning there was the rule and the rule said...

"Fuck the rule. The rules are bird-shit for people like Teapot and the rest who have never been on the ground without one, a flag. It was a flag that carried them all up the goddamn hill, made them all such bad-ass heroes. Back in the world, in the States, they don't give a good rat's ass about us or it, but here it's different, so fuck the rules."

"Bravo," Flynn-Michael said clapping his hands.

"Besides," I said. "I know where we can get one. The barge."

"The barge," Flynn-Michael said quietly.

"And I'll lead the raid," Horey said jumping up for another beer.

The barge lay moored across the river off the northern edge of the hill. It was a 'Mike' boat, a naval vessel that carried the convoys, truck-by-truck, across the river. The Seabees were building a bridge, Liberty Bridge, but now they needed that barge.

That night, we stole the flag.

In the morning, Horey and Brownell and Boots and I put up the pole. Christ, it was high, 30, 40 feet, and bamboo. Horey trotted into the cave and soon reappeared with a beer can to substitute for a ball. It went up on the top. Boots worked the lanyard and at 0800 colors went. At 0810, a stiff backed Navy JG marched into the cave.

"What flag?" Flynn-Michael said innocently.

"That one," the JG said pointing to the top of the new pole.

"Fuck you," Horey said. "We found it."

"On my goddamn ship," the JG said.

"Ship!" I said. "You've been out in the sun too long."

"Listen," the JG said turning back to Flynn-Michael. "That Mike Boat is a Commissioned Vessel in the United States Navy, that flag is my ensign, and I'm going to get it back if I have to go to the Fleet."

He turned and marched back down the slope to the river and his waiting gig.

Within minutes Sanchez trotted up to Flynn-Michael with the radio. "Cassandra Six Actual," he said.

The colors came down and were returned.

"Can you beat that shit for Christ sake," Flynn-Michael said. "A commissioned vessel in the United States Navy is it; that goddamn little tub, Jesus Christ."

"Commissioned my ass," Horey said. "Now we need another flag."

Jones stood by the coffee and smiled.

"Jones," Flynn-Michael shouted.

Jones continued to smile.

"Well break it out, for Christ sake," Flynn-Michael said.

Jones pulled the flag from his helmet.

"Forty-eight stars, Jesus," Horey said.

"It's still a flag," I said.

"I always knew you'd be good for something Sergeant Jones," Flynn-Michael said.

Jones smiled.

Colors went again at 0830. This time they stayed. Sergeant Jones smiled from the corners of his eyes as the flag inched its way up the long pole.

"It's too goddamn small," Horey said. "You have to know it's there to know it's there."

"It's there," I said.

My patrol saw it when they left and they knew it was there. So did Hamling. He was with them. The patrol went quietly. When Wescott got back he returned with his smile.

"No sweat, Lieutenant, no sweat," he said."

SitRep Jan310850H: Lonely said I'm glad to be on this hill because:

On the night you got drunk in the Base Camp, the night the mortars came in and you held and later broke the glasses, me and Morales, Jesus Christ Morales, Lance Corporel, went into the ville just outside the wire. We got drunk there too and mean or meaner, on bad rice wine and tiger beer. We took it out of some gook store there with our bayonets and scared hell out of the little gook bastards that owned the place. When we left they was nothing but a pile of gobbling yellow huddled in the corner. Teapot went ape shit. It got worse when he couldn't get our names. He screamed for the Skipper but the Skipper just shook his head. And he said it was a shame. 'A shame,' Teapot said. 'Goddamn a shame. I want the names. Do you know what a thing like this can do to me, to us?' But that was the way the skipper left him; a shame.

I said:

I knew who you were. So did Flynn-Michael. He called you in for office hours and fined you 25 dollars each.

"You better snap out of your shit," he said.

I relieved you, talked to you, chewed ass, and reinstated you. That was where I needed you, not in a goddamn courtroom; there was no time for that shit. There was another reason why Flynn-Michael didn't give the names too, it was because it was Teapot that wanted them and that made a difference. Jesus, sleeping on post in the zone is court martial stuff too, but we never did it if we caught them, we passed on the judgment. A little primitive I guess, but right. There wasn't a jury to screw with and it didn't go in the book. Balen was the brig. Besides, some of them did it to get out of a fight so it was the worst you could do to them to keep them there. It wasn't that way with these two though, they just wanted to raise a little hell like the rest of us but they didn't do it as well. Their shoulders were too light.

Lonely said:

Light hell, light in the pockets too but it was worth every goddamn dime, every 'P', yes Sir. But it's good to be back to working now too. And my man Morales feels the same way.

I watched them work like Marines.

SitRep Jan311349H: When Morales walked up front on the point, he was light foot and the grass gave in easily to his step. He liked it there on the point as few others did, so Balen left him there more often than Steppes where he liked to be and I said 'okay.' Balen wanted him to lead a fire team but he wouldn't stay off the point so he, Balen, let someone with less balls or more sense or both be the leader.

"Why?" I asked.

"I can't let someone else up there to get killed when I know I do it best, Sir," he said. "And I don't like to tell them to do it. I feel like rotten shit when they get it and I put them there."

"Jesus Christ...," I started.

"It's okay for you, you're the Lieutenant," Morales continued.

I agreed, "Yes", and left him on the point, for that and because he was good. He found the traps before they found him, or the others that followed.

"How do you do it?" I asked?

"I don't know," he said. "I just do. Maybe it's 'cause I'm scared to get hit. I don't know but I find them. My fear tells me where they are so I stay up here where I'm safe."

"Yes, you stay up here, but we won't call it fear."

SitRep Feb010653H: In the morning Balen went out with the engineers. They went out every morning, the engineers, and they swept for mines down the Liberty Road. They swept the small stretch of road from the boat landing to the hill too, not much, just a loop that you could see from the top of the cave, that ran down by the river. They swept it for drill, because everyone knew it would never be mined.

But that's where they were.

I didn't need the radio to tell me what it was, not anymore, because now I knew by the screams of men running. It sent up its pillar, a balling, black column of brackish smoke when it went, and now I was running with the rest. There were others running with me down the slope in the road, but I didn't know who they were until I got there and saw that it was our new corpsman, Doc Wilson.

Balen met me coming up the other way. The wire was 50 feet behind us. He said "Morales." And I said "Bullshit." But he was right. Morales lay on the ground up ahead. He was on his stomach, his head down on his cheek and his knees; one of them was pulled up toward his guts underneath him, the other was twisted back broken, his foot, the one I could see rested in a shallow lap of the river that licked and pulled at the growing brown stain.

"Grenade…, trail…, trip wire…," Balen said. And I said "Yes, he always finds them first."

He was breathing. It was bad breathing though, heavy and full sounding. He was unconscious. I said "Now you can call it fear."

The Doc was kneeling beside him. He had been joined by the engineer corpsman.

"Who gave him morphine?" the engineer corpsman asked.

"I did," the other said.

"You stupid fuck," the engineer corpsman said. "He's got a piece in his fucking head. He's out."

"I'm new," Doc Wilson said.

"NEW," the engineer corpsman shouted. "We're all fucking new." And then he said more quietly, "Yes, new." and he stooped to bandage the wounds.

All were in his legs but one, and that one the one that missed his legs, that one found his eye before he could see it and made a nest in his brain.

Lonely came down the hill, accompanied by the forward air control radio man, the bird man.

"The dirty motherfuckers," he said looking down at Morales' tangled body.

"You want this emergency, Lieutenant?" the birdman asked.

I said "Yes."

The request went in, Balen set the LZ. The time went by, slow motion again.

"Where the fuck is the chopper?" I said, kneeling down at Morales' head stroking his forehead with a shaking hand.

"I don't know Sir," the birdman said. "They said it was on the way."

Morales's breathing was getting too heavy, chunky and slow, slowing within the life rush around us. The corpsmen stayed with him kneeling with little else to do but to watch him pass. A 46 floated by slowly.

"What about him?" I asked.

The birdman talked into the handset watching it head farther south. After a moment he said, "He says he can't come in."

"Why not?"

"He says, because he's got the mail."

"Fuck the mail."

The bird man said "I can't tell him that Sir."

I looked up and shouted, "You get a chopper, you shit one, but you get it now somehow or I'll shove that radio up your ass and fly you to the hospital."

He looked back helplessly and said "Yes Sir." But we both knew it wasn't his fault.

The chopper came but it came no faster still moving in slow motion.

"The dirty motherfuckers," Lonely said.

Morales was still breathing when I pushed his hair back for the last time and we, Lonely and I and the Doc and Balen, carried him to the chopper. He was still breathing when I gave the pilot thumbs up and watched them lift slowly and nose around back toward Da Nang.

"I want a rifle," Lonely said.

I said "You carry the radio."

He said, "I'll teach the motherfuckers."

"No," I said. "No, that's all, no, no, no, no."

Later when we were back in the bunker he said, "My man Morales. Just last week got lit up for 20 and five for a drink."

I said, "That's enough."

"… and look at him now," he said.

I said, "Shut up, just shut the fuck up."

He said, "yes Sir."

SitRep Feb011329H: "Oh," Flynn-Michael said. "Did you hear? We just got the word on your man. He died you know, and a damn fine man too, wasn't he, and married did you know? Neither did I. What was his name?"

"Morales," I said and then I left. I got Balen who was back now from the sweep and told him, told them all. I told Lonely too, with the rest. When I told them, my voice was thick and I had to swallow. They sat there when I had finished, and looked at me waiting for more, for the rest of it to be said, but there was nothing more to say.

"He's dead," I said. "That's all, just dead."

In the silence that followed I looked from one young face to another. I thought back to a more recent summer. I was walking on the beach at the lake in the quiet Adirondacks and I met a young child from the camp next to ours. He walked with me for a while, and after we had walked some distance, he told me that his grandfather had just died. I told him that I was sorry and we once again fell into silence. Finally, he said it was time for him to go back. We said good bye and he turned to go. He took several steps and then turned back to me. 'Mister,' he called, 'we don't worry when our friends die do we?' I looked at him for a minute and said, 'No, we don't.' He smiled at me and ran off down the beach for home.

"Just dead," I said again. "Just fucking dead."

SitRep Feb011926H: In the evening, Balen and his squad, Lonely and I walked slowly up to the cave. Flynn-Michael moved one of the tanks up onto the high point of the hill and directed the big guns onto the tree line near where Morales had been found. For several minutes, the tank pumped 90 mm rounds into the line. One of them hit a tree; it lit, lighted up for a whole second and then fell apart. In the morning the tree line was gone. We all felt better to see that it was no longer there. Balen and his men moved back into their positions for the night. I stayed at the cave and drank beer.

Dear Pumpkin,

So that's what it was, instant old age in the shape of a round or broken metal bit that let the years ooze out through a hole in your head or your guts. It doesn't take long to ooze when you're 19, there's so little life there and it was easier for the one doing it, engaged in it, hard, slow breathing and then done. So that was it and like Lonely said it was all about luck. But we won't worry when our friends die will we, oh no, Morales is gone but we won't worry at all. We'll just get angrier, and angrier, and angrier.

Love,

S

SitRep Feb011956H: When the evening sniper came, we were waiting. We knew the tree line, the spot. We knew it lay across the southern edge of the 'T', 100, maybe 200 meters out. We knew it was darker by his spot than in the rest of the tree line. We knew he would come and we knew he would be on time.

The tanks trained their 90's on it; the spot. Right where he had always shot from, each night, and shot high to boot. Besides the 90's the tanks had their 30's and 50's. They aimed in on it too; the spot. Flynn-Michael had the mortars lay their tubes in; the 60's, on the spot. The line aimed in and they waited.

"When he fires," they whispered.

The word passed. We waited. The sun was sinking; a shimmer, a smudge now behind the spot. We waited.

He was on time, not ready, but there.

He fired. It was high.

"Poor bastard," I smiled.

The sniper didn't fire any more that night and the spot was out damned out.

"Did we get him, Lieutenant?" Ham asked.

"I don't know," I said. "But we sure as hell scared the shit out of him if we didn't."

"Poor little bastard," Horey said like an echo.

Flynn-Michael laughed and sliced open a beer.

"Beautiful, wasn't it," he said. "And. Jesus, those tanks. God, those big, beautiful, fucking tanks."

'And we won't worry, anymore,' I thought.

SitRep Feb020845H: The Gunny returned. The mustaches that had sprouted and flourished in his absence, now departed in turn.

"What's the story on the mustaches, Skipper?" he asked. He said Skippah.

"I don't care, for Christ sake, Gunny," Flynn-Michael said. He still said Gooney.

"Goddamn it Skippah, I don't want no mustaches in my Company."

"All right, Gooney," Flynn-Michael said. "All right."

It took an hour and they were gone.

SitRep Feb031059H: The day the first M-16's came in, Boots took one to the top of the bat cave and knocked a suspected VC down at 1500 meters.

"Now fuck you and your canteens," he said to Horey who had been watching through the glasses. The rest that stood watching laughed and said they looked good.

When the rest followed they didn't look so good; assembly line shit full of the usual economy cuts, probably the subject of a hard fought bill to save a nickel or a dime, based on the premise that pine boxes were cheaper.

"I want to keep my M-14, Lieutenant," Hamlin said.

"But you can't," I said. "It's got to go in."

"Why?" he asked.

"Because," I said. "That's the fucking rule."

SitRep Feb031237H: When Foxtrot got in trouble in the valley and 48 were killed, they found them bent dead over jammed up weapons, shot at close range in the head. They identified them with their tags because their faces were gone. The rest, to a man, were wounded.

"I'd rather keep my M-14, Sir, with all due respect, Sir, I'd rather, Sir," Ham said.

"No," I said.

That night the troops spoke of how Foxtrot got the shit kicked out of them, of how they were all zipped up in the valley. They talked until dawn. Flynn-Michael and I and the rest all drank beer.

"It's not the goddamn weapon," Boots said. "It's good. Fifteen hundred meters and I got the little asshole."

"It's the system, for Christ sake," Brownell said. "You can't beat a man with an M-14 in boot camp and tell him it's great and then say it isn't worth a shit in combat and give him something new and untried. Jesus."

"Long live the system," I said in a toast.

"They don't even know what to clean the fucking thing with."

"Jesus."

"It isn't here, it's all of it, a nasty ass place."

"Amen."

"Please Sir," Hamlin said.

"I said no dice, Hamlin. No. no, no, no, no."

SitRep Feb032215H That night, I sat on my bunker and listened. Lonely and a new man, a replacement part, talked inside. They talked in darkness and were unaware of my listening.

"Hey man," the new man said. "You know what they talking about in the States?"

"Back in the world?" Lonely asked. "Yeah, pussy."

"No, man, no shit, no shit, not that," the new man said. "All those motherfuckers talk about is puttin' a man on the moon, ain't that some shit?"

"A man on the moon?" Lonely repeated.

"Yeah, man," the new man said. "No shit, a man on the moon."

"Yeah," Lonely said. "That's some crazy shit I guess."

"Some shit," the new man said. "Those motherfuckers are gonna put a man on the moon; they sure got'um."

It grew still, and remained so for several minutes until Lonely spoke again,

"They forget, though," he said. "And then they won't give a shit about the man or the moon or the man in the moon either."

Dear Pumpkin,

People just vanish here. One minute you're walking with them next to you or sitting drinking shitty coffee and the next minute they're gone, just gone. Funny. Someone talking here in the night just said it doesn't matter though because we all just forget. So I guess that is it, they will all forget or have forgotten. I envy them that; they, with their fingers, extended and joined; a mythical they, but 'THEY' none the less because to give them all names might be treason, so it is better 'THEY.' 'THEY', again extended and joined, 'THEY'll' tire of it and forget and those of us that live through it to see the casting of seed on the ground, will sneak home to remember. Patsies. Framed. There are no heroes here, only murderers; murderers who have no feet left on which to sneak, but must wobble sorely on stumps that will not sneak again; what of them; and what of me, and what of you who must remember, because when THEY say it "is" or "was" or "has been" a mistake; WE will have made no one happy for any of it and maybe at last we'll be sad for our friends.

Sleep well,

Sam

'Fuck it,' I said to myself.

Dear S,

I don't go out alone a lot these days because everything seems to be in such a state of shambles there, and everyone here is so angry. Even though most of the people here are Marine wives we only feel safe when we go out together in groups. Fat pregnant me, and them pushing their babies. We try to keep busy together but in our hearts we're looking back over our shoulders for that damn brown car. I guess we're lucky to have each other though because everyone around us seems so angry. They're angry at the government and at soldiers here and at you that are there and it's all so very confusing because they all seem to think it's all your fault. You're supposed to be home in just a very few short months and I don't know where you are. I was up all night again worrying. You must promise not to wear your uniform out off the base when you get home, please, it's important.

Love,

Pumpkin

SitRep Feb040648H: It was clear the morning that Wescott went out on patrol, clear and hot as a bitch. From the top of the hill, I could see them; with the radio I could hear. They moved well, with caution and knowledge. I could see the guns and the knot they made when they walked, because they had to, because they couldn't get separated, because one had the gun and one had the tripod and the others had the ammo; so they must walk in a knot, and I cursed.

Wescott moved them well, though, I had to admit he was good. Two up and then cover, now move, now fast, now slow, then stop and look, listen for the dogs and the bark, for the sound of a bolt going home, the sound of the spoon when it pops off the grenade, small things in a swamp, and then, move again.

I watched. It could be ballet when it was done right, when things clicked. It could be a goddamn mess too, when they didn't. Today, because Wescott was short he was careful and the men in his squad were good, it was ballet, except for the guns. Jesus, except for the guns.

I sat and watched them and I listened when they started through the tree line.

"Stay off the trails," I said in a whisper.

I watched the first smoke and I could see Hamlin running. It, the smoke was yellow, and I watched when the white smoke started, and I could see Hamlin running the other way. I heard the dull explosion both ways and I started to run. As the white smoke came, I was running and the radio was alive. There was another explosion and the radio started to scream and I was still running with Balen close behind me. My boots were unlaced but I ran and was first to arrive. Five of them were down. One of them, a fire team leader, was hit in the legs, high in the legs.

"Well," he said calmly, quietly. "Check my nuts."

"You're all right boy," I said.

"I know Sir," he said. "But I wanted to be sure."

"They're there," I said without looking.

"Yes Sir," he said. "They had it rigged to a stick of bamboo; Stupid."

"You looked good, though," I said. "But the guns."

"I know," he said. "Too close, they hit it."

"I know," I said.

The young Marine's cartridge belt lay by him smoking. He had been carrying the gas grenade that had been the white smoke, and the yellow from the signal grenade. The blast set them off, and now the belt still burned.

"Get gassed?" I asked.

"A little," he said.

"Get the magazines out of this Marine's pouches," I said.

Someone did.

Balen set his squad into a loose circle around the wounded while Lonely started the call for a medivac.

"Where's Wescott?"

"He was back by the guns."

"Over here Sir."

Balen stood next to part of what remained of the motionless Wescott.

"He's gone."

Half of Wescott from the belt on down lay in a tangled heap of broken bamboo thicket and web gear.

"Where the fuck is the rest of him?"

"That's what I mean, Sir, he's really fucking gone."

"Hey Lieutenant," Lonely said quietly from behind them. "Look up there."

He pointed up into the thicket of bamboo up over our heads. Wescott's arms and torso clutched the slender green shoots as if afraid to fall.

"Jesus."

"Oh my aching ass, Sir, there's no fucking head."

Hamling walked past them moving cautiously down the narrow path through the tree line.

"Oh shit, goddamn."

He leaned down picked something up and started back toward me, Balen and Lonely where we stood looking up at the grisly piece of meat above us.

"Sir," he said quietly. "Here he is."

In his left hand he held a badly dented helmet. The camouflaged cover was burned and tattered and waved gently with the shift of his gate. He stopped next to them and lifted it even with our eyes. Staring back at us from under the helmet's shadow were the empty features that had once been Wescott.

His face was slack and gray and his lifeless eyes looked past us into the distance. Balen and Lonely turned away but I continued to look into the dirty blood smeared hollow portrait looking for some hint of his smile. There was none.

"Put it down in a poncho. No smiles today."

We pulled Wescott's remains from the trees and together with his head and bottom half, reassembled him in a waiting poncho and wrapped him tightly in a cocoon.

"Choppers coming in," Lonely said.

I looked around to the rest of the wounded, and then turned back to Wescott. I hadn't been fond of Wescott but no one deserved this.

"Did it hurt?" I asked quietly. "You're done; you're going home early, back to school and to build little buildings all over northern California."

The ponchoed remains sat motionless in the middle of the small LZ.

"You're going home," I said again.

"Bullshit," I said at last. "You're really going home."

"Yes Sir."

I stood in the middle of the zone when the chopper came into view. The squads, Wescott"'s and the one I brought with me, Balen's, together they made a squad; had formed the LZ.

"Hey, Lieutenant," Hamlin called, "I want them."

"Are you ready?" I asked.

"I want to have this squad," he said.

I looked down at the motionless mound in front of me for a moment, and then looked across to where Ham was setting in his men.

"I know," Ham said when he saw me watching. "It don't make no difference, I already got it."

"This mess gave it to you," I said.

"No," Hamlin said, "I took it."

"All right," I said. "Just don't get shot in the ass and fuck it all up."

"I won't," he said. "Don't worry."

"I do," I said.

"I know," Hamlin said. "So I won't."

He turned and ran back to his lines as the chopper made its approach. I was alone in the zone, standing up; waving my arms downward, setting it down. Over my shoulder I could see my men, again men, shooting rapidly; high volume and fast. The pilot who sat in the bubble in front of me looked excited and mouthed 'Hurry Up.' I brought the chopper in and the Doc and I ran the litters, four of them. It was noisy and dusty as hell. Now all the zone was shooting.

The crew chief leaned down from the bird.

"How many more?" he asked.

"One," I said, and calling to Hamlin I said, "Let's get him on."

We looked at each other briefly and then hoisted the poncho into the side door of the chopper. The crew chief watched us and then turned to scan the tree line that surrounded us.

"Be careful with this one, he comes apart."

"Yes Sir," the gunner nodded. Ham and I stepped back from the bird. I raised my arm in a slow silent salute and then they were gone.

"That zone was hot as hell, Lieutenant," Ham said.

"Was it?" I said, watching the bird climbing hard for the blue.

"Yes Sir," Ham said.

Bates, who still had time to think things over well, had the guns.

"There goes one," he shouted.

He put down a burst as he swung the gun. The man that had been running, taking a hat, they said, flipped up and fell lazily behind, what looked like a grave.

They always flip that way, hit by nothing seen, hard, and then down; on both teams, the same.

Cobra came up and fired from the hip; his third round hit behind, the grave. I could see the man's arm flip up and then fall hanging over the grave.

"It's the finger," one of them said. "He's giving us the finger."

We laughed.

I worked artillery into the village that stood behind the grave where the fingered one had fallen. There was nothing there worth killing, I knew that, but it made the ones still there feel better about it. Today, it made me feel better about it as well. We left when the arty lifted, and we went back in Indian-style. Hamling had the point and Balen's squad followed along in the rear. Balen walked at the head of his squad next to me and Lonely.

"You know," I said. "That was one of the things I worried about before I got here."

"What's that Lieutenant?"

"Seeing people, good Marines turned into chopped meat, you know what I mean? I had this fucking nightmare vision of a situation just like now and somebody saying 'Hey where's the Lieutenant?' and someone else shouting, 'Aw he's over in the pucker brush puking his guts out, again.' I thought about it when Delpert got wacked but then that wasn't so bad and now with little pieces of meat decorating a fucking palm tree even though you still feel bad about it and it gets into your guts and your head there's nothing more to it, there it is and you just look at it and that's all there is. And you say man what shitty luck."

"Yes Sir," Balen said. "That's all there is, but it always comes back to bite you in the ass."

"It's the stuff dreams are made of."

"Yes Sir."

Lonely checked in with Sanchez as we passed through the wire.

The patrol was over.

SitRep Feb050630H: In the morning we went out again. Balen's squad moved out ahead and Rico's fanned out to our rear. We were going to make one final sweep of the small ville next to the tree line where Wescott had been blown to pieces. In the cool morning air I could hear Cobra click his lighter open, close, open, close while I walked along behind him. We moved off the road into the tree line, leap-frogged across the next small paddy, and then we were in the village. Several hooches remained standing in spite of yesterday's artillery barrage. There were no people. We walked cautiously up to the first hooch. It was dark and silent.

"Cobra wants to know if we're going to burn these stragglers, Lieutenant?" Balen asked.

"Yes, but tell him to wait until we've checked them out and are headed back. I want him the last one out so we don't get cooked by his fucking fire."

Five hooches remained. We were done with our search in 30 minutes. All were empty.

We stood at the edge of the tree line and watched as Cobra leaned his M-79 against a palm and pulled out his lighter. We could see his smile as he reached up with one hand to lift a small section of roof while flicking the lighter to life with the other. The small yellow flame flickered as it arched up over the adjoining hooch still clutched in Cobra's shredded hand. The explosion tossed him like a rag doll and he landed on his back next to his resting weapon. Like falling dominoes the remaining hooches exploded in a hail of fire, each detonated by the one preceding.

"Holy shit," Balen shouted.

Battling the blistering heat from the burning hooches we ran forward and dragged Cobra back away from the flames. Lonely grabbed the resting M-79.

"Sonof-a-bitch, both his fucking hands are gone," Balen said looking down at the freely flowing blood that gushed from the tattered stumps.

"Get me two rifle slings," I shouted.

Lonely grabbed the two slings and handed them to me and Balen. I wrapped one around his arm just above the elbow.

"Tourniquets," I said. "Pull them tight like this, like you're tying off a steer."

Balen pulled his tight on the other arm. Slowly the river of blood slowed to a dribble.

"Medevac?"

"On the way Skipper," Lonely said.

Twenty minutes later the chopper came in and hauled Cobra away. No shots had been fired and now all that remained was the snapping confident pop of the burning hooches.

"What do you think?" Balen asked as we saddled up and headed in.

"He was still breathing when they took off," I said. "But his career as a drummer is over."

Balen looked at me and then we moved out.

Dear Pumpkin,

The hardest part of all this is wondering where they went and then caring about it. Why do I care? They come and they go so quickly. Blank skinny faces of so many different colors that I can barely tell one from the other. I don't get to know them very well. They arrive. I tell them to get on the point and then they're gone, blown up because that's where I put them and that's the way it is here, BANG and they just vanish and then I have to figure out why I should care about this one or that one or why anyone should care. It's not like we're wasting any grownups here. Just another one gone, pieces swept up and recognized only because the Marine next to him knew who it was a minute ago. And that's what I care most about, another lost Marine whose name may or may not be on the tip of my tongue. But if I don't care who will. The families for sure or some families anyway will grieve the loss but I'm not sure grieving is caring. So I care about them as Marines even though caring may be the first sign that it's all coming apart. I care that Morales is now just a shadow on the point and Wescott, poor irritating Wescott was shipped home like some discarded fucking jigsaw puzzle. And I care that Cobra has no hands and that Doc Peckham wasn't here to make coffee today and he won't be making coffee tomorrow or the day after that and that the minute before he vanished bleeding in a 34 on his way to Da Nang he preferred a bag full of hand grenades to a Unit-1 and it was more important to bring death to the people that live here than heal the sick of Troy, New York.

Sam

SitRep Feb051429H: New word came out with the convoy. It was time to go back, we had gotten enough; we had come here and listened to the sounds of Phu Lac 6 and we had learned the lessons it had to teach so now we could go back.

I lost 23 men on the hill and around it. They were lean and they were young and they were men, the ones lost and the others, men and more than that they were Marines, I was sure of that.

We walked back down the road, Liberty Road, and we knew, I knew, when we left that if the future proved to be the same as the last few weeks, the same Company wouldn't be back. And even if some of the people remained they would see the world through different eyes. We walked back quietly and well. We had kept the mines off the road for a month, and no one other Company could make that claim, and that little fuck the afternoon sniper was history because of us, no, one else could say that either.

"Asshole" Flynn-Michael said thinking about going back in. "Asshole."

He had fresh brandy. No one knew where it had come from, we didn't ask, because it didn't matter; we drank it. It was good, damn fine brandy, here, and from a canteen, and when we got back, Flynn-Michael, the actuals, and the finest goddamn snuffies in the world, all of us, we were ready to go to war.

9 OPERATION NEWCASTLE – MARCH, 1967

SitRep Mar192016H: There was thunder in the air that night; it was night when we kicked off; distant thunder. And lightening; long veins, fingers of lightening that wandered slowly across the sky, not quickly as it does when the storm crashes in on top of you, but late-August slow. When it lighted the sky, I could see the Company stretched out ahead of me moving, slowly, quietly, moving, and when the lightening didn't come, and it was dark, they were only there because I knew they were there burned into my inner eye by the last flash like an image on an exposed piece of film. As I walked by my Corpsman I strained briefly with the night sounds between the cascading thumps of the thunder. Satisfied, my thoughts trailed off behind me.

It seemed so long ago. Off the hill for three, was it three? Yes three weeks now. More days ticked off.

A week before we left, the day after we shipped the puzzled Wescott home, the Chaplain flew out to the hill for services.

"Let's get them there, for Christ sake, for the Chaplain. He's a good shit," Flynn-Michael said.

My troops went because they were told but for no other reason.

And me…

"What about you?" Balen asked.

It was true the Chaplain was a good shit. On the bad operations he stood at the Battalion Aid Station, where it wandered through old white-washed French storage buildings, and met the dead and the dying and gave them comfort. He stood by and watched when the doctors lashed them up with loose broad stitches that left mountainous pink welts the size of your finger when they healed but kept them living for the time being. And he watched too when they failed to remain alive, but, he was a good shit nonetheless.

"Bullshit," he said. "That's what I give them, Bullshit and God." And he went into the club, and there he got drunk.

'A drunk Chaplain fights all the battles of all the wars and suffers the most in the guts, right here,' I thought. 'And for that reason perhaps and because he was a good shit and because Balen had caught me, and maybe because I felt guilty because I hadn't been too fond of Wescott, I went too.'

Someone hung a rifle on a tree so that its shadow coupled with that of the tree cast in the shape of a cross onto the service, across the floor, the deck, the ground of the tent where it was held. So I missed all that was said and while I missed it I watched all the others that were missing it too.

I said thanks to the Chaplain when he finished and left and congratulated him on being such a good shit. When I got back to my bunker a letter was there waiting.

Dear S,

I can't imagine how you must feel when one of your Marines gets killed or badly hurt. I wish I were there to hold you safely away from all that horrible world you're in. I know of the pain it causes on this end because every time someone falls there another brown car rolls slowly down the street here and I can see the man in dress blues leaning down to see out the window to read address numbers. He comes at the same time every day, the same slow casual drive and each time I hold my breath and say please don't let him stop here. And when he passes I put my hands on our growing child and close my eyes and then step outside to see where

267

he stops. We're all the same here so we have to be ready to catch the bits of someone's broken life. I have a hard time sleeping. I'm sorry. I shouldn't say that, I don't want you to worry, I'm fine, really. T got her first letter from Boots today and I think she enjoyed the attention. She read it quietly and smiled a lot.

I write to your mom and pop often and so should you. All they can do is worry, it's all any of us can do even when you say 'remember how safe I was last week well I'm even safer now.' They say some of their friends look at them like they raised a serial killer. So they need to hear from you to know you're okay. Because we're mostly Marine wives here we feel safe in the neighborhood but even so we don't go out for our walks down town as often.

I think of you all the time. Stay safe.

Love,

Pumpkin

We walked south on the road toward the mine and I wondered if the chaplain was waiting at B.A.S. tonight. I worried about that because my shoulders shone and I knew more than the ones moving with me in the dark did. I worried because I was the one that had to tell them where to go.

Then I thought about rubber boats.

I could see the muted lights of the base camp behind me as we climbed through the pass in the hills that separated the air-strip from the road. Outpost Zulu , on my left now, was a worthless piece of cupped ground that looked like a blown-out volcano in miniature where morning fog paused, held gently in the cup, before it fled to the river beyond and then sank into the ground. It was manned daily for denial and nothing else. There was no one there in the night, no one friendly anyway.

SitRep Mar190516H: Earlier that morning, a squad of men had left for the launch site with the road sweep. They had been sweeping the road to the south for a week so it wouldn't look different today. They never swept the road to the south before.

While the sweeps proceeded, the Company practiced with rubber boats in a tent; taught their use by professionals sent down from Da Nang along with the boats - dip, stroke, out, dip. Now it was dark and the squad from the sweep was still there along the road setting in where they had slipped away from the rest, still there resting in the night and guarding the launch site.

SitRep Mar192137H: We arrived. A large beach had been chosen for the debarking, large for a river anyway, with steep sandy banks to either side. The river opened up in the front of us. We couldn't hear it or see it, but we could smell it and we had seen it before, swam in it, hooted at saggy-titted gook women naked to waist to wash in it, so we knew it was there.

On the white of the beach I could see my men moving like ghosts; their movements exaggerated in the bad light, but slow, quiet. The river was black behind them. So was the bank on the other side.

The bank on the other side had to be there: memory put it there, fixed it in place, but what if the river had swept it away in the dark while the squad dozed on the opposite shore. What if the place where it once sat firmly anchored was now a yawning sea with no banks, no end, full of large jawed monstrous things that waited patiently just at the edge.

"And they rose from the water," the old man had said. "And it was to the water that they returned to wait."

I moved them into the side of the bank, slowly, easily. From where I stood they looked good, damn good. But as I watched, a small knot of people began to form in the ranks.

"Who the fuck is this?" I snarled, moving in closer.

"And who the fuck is smoking a cigar?"

The voice that said 'me' said he was a Major. He said he had come to watch, to observe, to snap in.

He had come all the way from D.C. just to watch us perform, to witness the third battle of the water bull run. Washington, where they made signs of support and carried parasols to stave off the harsh heat. No parasol today, today it was replaced by a Thompson and the stub of a cigar.

I took his hand and was not surprised to find it smooth and moist like lips.

'Welcome, welcome to the Nam you poor son-of-a-bitch,' I thought and wanted to say.

"You need to put the cigar out, Sir," is what I said. "It can be smelled for miles."

"Sorry."

He buried the short blunt butt in the soft sandy ground, grinding it in with his boot.

We waited. It was quiet. We were quiet and we waited.

Two trucks halted on the road next to us. They had pea lights on like they'd driven straight out of a Bogart movie.

We had heard them coming through the quiet, gunning, jamming gears on the bad pieces of road. The road they couldn't see because their lights were so secret and small and the lightening had stopped. They had tarps pulled up over the boats.

"Is this where you want the rubber boats," someone shouted out from the truck.

I scanned the far bank straining for a sound or a flicker of movement. There was none. In spite of the announced arrival of the rubber boats our secret seemed intact. I hoped it wasn't that they were better secret keepers.

Now, Flynn-Michael checked with the squad leader that had been sitting in the weeds around the small beach head since the morning sweep. Nothing to report. No traffic on the road. No traffic on the river. Charcoal burners higher up on the mountain away from the river earlier in the morning but their telltale wisps of smoke that mimicked the beards of the old as they snaked up out of the thick canopy chin had drifted away with the rising of the sun toward noon.

We had eight boats, LCR's, landing craft, rubber, to move us all, 150 plus across. It was slow, but we moved. I watched them go in waves until they disappeared in the darkness, and I saw them, the boats, when they came back empty. A second wave shoved off. Mine was next. When I lost them in the darkness a second time, I heard a splash. One of Fitzlee's men had dropped his helmet into the shadows of the slow moving river. Fitzlee gave him his.

"And they will rise up out of the water and take hold of them and drag them down." I could hear the echoing thunder of the old man's voice blasting away at the back of my head.

Now I crossed. My boat leaked and made me wet and cold to the crotch reaching up around my legs, pulling at the tails of my T shirt. 'Oh, that's just fucking wonderful,' I thought, 'But what the hell, better now than later, after all, what the hell. You smile you old gray haired fuck, you smile and fade back into the mist.'

On the other side we waited again, listened, strained to see. While the Company waited, I tried to pull my body away from the cling of my soaked trow. And then we moved.

When Flynn-Michael gave the operation order earlier that afternoon he said, "The Big Picture, says:

We will move all night and block in the morning 5,000 meters away. We must be there at first light because at 0800, or there abouts. Fox loaded amtracs will crank up and leave An Hoa and go north along the river on the other side, just as they have been doing for a week, secretly. They will go past the Duc Duc District Headquarters, past the refugee village where the stench is so thick it cannot be withstood by mortal man and flies cluster at the festers in children's eyes and threaten to carry them away. They will pass it all. They will cross the river and all the little foxes will sweep into echo. easily done."

Dear Mom,

Pumpkin says I should write. On the ground here, you should know, it is a bitch, a moist alluring bitch.

You remember I hunted the Adirondacks in the winter deep snow. Together and in parties, you remember father and I hunted. With the parties, we set in a watch; the drivers circled out ahead and walked back toward us. We hunted deer then in the pines and the snow. Sometimes it worked, usually, it didn't. At noon, or when we met, we built a fire and drank hot coffee from tin cups that melted down into the deep snow from the heat of the thick liquid inside them when we set them down and burned our lips when we touched them to drink. We ate the cold sandwiches that you made and packed the night before and we listened to unclean stories. Some did, anyway; father and I stayed away to ourselves. When we were done, we posted and drove again until dark.

Love,

Your Son

I tore up the letter in my thoughts and slogged on.

When we moved, we moved Indian-style, American Indian-style, in a queue, a tail, and we moved quietly or as quietly as we could move in the dark in a place where we'd never been before through off-trail jungle. The earlier thunder storm had given way to a moonless, starless night.

The tributaries running full from the morning storm cascaded down into the river that now drifted by on our right flank, and cut, had cut, deep ugly gullies into the banks. The jungle, ashamed of its scares, concealed them in vines; a hellish verdant washboard painfully twisted and choked, slippery with the recent rain. More jungle flowed down with the cuts to the river at night to drink.

We flailed, slashed at the growth. It was rotten still and men cursed, as blisters grew under the handles of their machetes. They cursed too, because they couldn't smoke and because, at night, it is difficult to keep a secret.

Teapot said, "The Marines own the night." But, suppose the others just don't want it, suppose they have seen it and found it less than good and by their peculiar preference prefer to stay at home asleep with mother leaving us to be the proprietors of darkness.

We moved. We crept and we hacked at the growth that bathed in the river by night with our blisters and we cursed. We went down through the gullies and up, through the streams at the bottom. The rest got wet and I smiled, smiled at the streams while others who had tried to stay dry cursed at that too. We grew tired, very tired. It was late. First light was coming too fast. We moved.

SitRepMar200200H, I stepped off the bank smartly pushing past the small knot of Marines hesitating at the brink.

"Get through it," I snarled softly as I brushed by. You're already wet. Move, move, move."

They remained and watched as the soft muddy ooze at the bottom of the gully pulled me down to my waist. Unable to move, I cursed and waited for two already across to help me free. It happened to others, to all, and as it happened, the queue disintegrated into two's and three's, lost in the dark in a nasty ass place called bad.

'Tacon, tacon., tacon, tacon, tacon, tacon, tacon, tacon, tacon, tacon, tacon, tacon, tacon, tacon, tacon, tacon, gooks out here in the dark,' I thought.

"VC mud," Lonely whispered.

It took an hour to get the column back together; an hour, with first light sliding towards us; an hour lost.

We put it together, slowly piece-by-piece and we moved. Flynn-Michael stalked through the night raising hell. We were tired and we moved, in step, easy Echo, we moved through the night, owners on the prowl.

It was quiet; there were no night sounds other than ours. We were the night sounds now. The small creatures heard us coming and left us to produce our own sounds. We did so credibly, yet the sounds we made were unusual when wrapped in secrets and darkness and dreams where they didn't belong. We didn't drink the brandy that Flynn-Michael carried that night.

"What's the name of this son-of-a-bitch?" someone asked in a whisper.

"Newcastle," another voice said.

"Nice name," the first voice said quietly.

No one heard them; it was all swallowed in the fatigue and the dark of the night. We humped.

At first light we set in. We were there. I noted that the Major had made it. I set my men in and slept.

SitRep Mar200615: I didn't sleep, I tried to sleep, but I didn't. There was a shot, one single shot. A man was down, hit in the leg.

"I going home," he hollered. "That's three, that's three, I'm going home."

When the chopper came in he ran to it and then as it lifted off, he waved.

"I'm going home," he shouted down, but no one heard him because of the chopper, it was a 34, its prop wash made too much noise.

Christ, the idea of home sounded good, yet, it took him three. 'Say 'hi' to the Doc back in the world,' I thought while I watched the chopper slip away. 'Ask him if he can run and wave yet. Ask him if the people of Troy give a shit about having one less doctor that might have helped them all. Ask him if three's a good way to go. 'Bullshit, no, three's no good,' he'll say, 'the whole tour's easier." And like before, back in the world, when it was easier to go than to stay, now it is easier to stay than to go.

There were no more shots fired and I slept, a cat nap propped in the roots of a tree. Alone in an Eden wondering perhaps if life in the world would soon begin.

SitRep Mar200916H: We trapped nothing, sometimes it worked, usually it didn't. We spent the day drying in the sun. The pull of the old man's night weakened and steam rose from the fabric of my legs while bits of caked mud flaked off and fell into the dirt where I sat.

Now there was more word, new word, new plans, new orders; the same Teapot though, just another glimpse of the Big Picture, different angle, more exposure; Flynn-Michael listened, took scribbled notes.

"We're to move again," he said. "Now, saddle up."

We moved 2,000 meters in from the river, and set in. It was the same place I had stood during Independence watching while Company B from somewhere burned the village. Just ahead was the same place that night sounds came in from the lake and talked to me. I had been there once and I knew it, like I knew that we shouldn't be there twice in' the same month because by now everyone knew it. The word was passed; touch nothing, booby traps. I stayed in the same hole; the dirt in it was still soft so I kicked it out and climbed in.

The night sounds from the lake spoke in the quiet murmur of watchful waiting voices and mingled with the whispered talk of my Marines as they found where they had been and settled in telling the boots what Independence had been like. It would be drier this time and Teapot was with the sweepers over on the river, that was different, and the days, they had changed too, like fallen Marines stricken from the list in an endless succession, but other than that, it was the same only not quite as good.

We set the CP in on a small hill and then the three of us, the actuals, gathered together. We talked of the night just passed, and we had the brandy now, here, where things were familiar, but not as good; we had the brandy and talked. The helmetless Fitzlee leaned back into the shadows.

"I wonder if there are snakes out here?" he asked.

"Now that's a happy thought," Brownell answered.

"Jesus," Boots said. "I hate fucking snakes."

"I thought you didn't like beetles," I said.

After a momentary blank stare he remembered and said, "Fuck you."

"We've no snakes in Ireland, you know." Flynn-Michael said, "Thanks to that fucking St. Patrick. Got rid of every last snake except one. The dreaded sand snake. Those bastards are everywhere. Christ, the Gunny tells me you can even find them out here in this God-forsaken land as well."

"What the fuck is a sand snake?" Boots asked.

"Boots," Flynn-Michael said. "I'm shocked, a man of the world like yourself and you've never heard of the dreaded sand snake. Probably the most deadly snake there is; feared throughout the civilized world. Terrible they are, about two feet in length and the color of the ground they crawl on. And smart. Oh, Jesus, there are none smarter. They work in pairs, you see."

He paused and looked slowly around the circle. Boots leaned forward.

"And while you're walking by not paying attention to the ground you walk on, one sneaks up and ever so quietly winds himself around your feet to bring you crashing to the ground and as quick as you can blink a blue Chicago eye the other is on you, and before you can use your last breathe in a cry, he rams sand up your ass till you suffocate."

"Jesus," Boots said.

"Aw man Boots," Horey said. "You are the dumbest fuck in South East Asia. Sand snakes. Jesus Christ. What the hell do they teach you in Chicago."

Brownell rolled back with a deep rumbling laugh and Flynn-Michael slapped Boots on the back.

"You're a plot, Boots," he said. "A fucking VC plot."

Boots stood up and kicked at the dirt.

"Fuck you all," he said. "Just fuck you all."

The soft -handed Major sat at the edge of the circle and listened. We planned and we talked and every now and then we all, including Boots, laughed and the night passed quietly as it had before.

SitRep Mar210529H: At first light, we were ready to move, but more word came in, more changes, more Teapot. The Big Picture grew in bounds, by bounds, but from close up, on the ground where we stood, it grew vague in its size and gave us all headaches caused by the blur.

"Not yet," Teapot said.

Flynn-Michael said, "Jesus."

We would wait. We waited. First light melted into a robust dawn and we waited still. We watched and we listened for change. There was no change, we would wait. We continued to wait. The sun crested the low ridge in the east and grew large and red; from morning, to mid-morning to zenith. It was hot, hot as hell, and now we finally re-saddled up and moved.

I watched them move.

Christ, they moved well, it was ballet again, even the guns. They had learned and they moved in precision, ballet by the lake, duck lake through the stream bed that traced in the trees.

And that was the reason that we continued to live, to go on; we moved by the script; we were grown experienced by rehearsal and previous performance. We no longer lost our place in the score. Choreography, by things hidden just below the surface. We knew that strict adherence to the ballet of battle was the one thing that coupled with luck would keep us alive. The response to the laws of movement, cued on the sounds of the surrounding natural orchestra, the meaningful flicking of fingers and arms, all of it rooted in the discipline of the ballet, for when that was gone there was nothing left and we were dead.

Dead and scattered through the trees dripping back into the soil. And even though some of us might still walk, it was only the time that made us walk because our lives were gone and we were really dead and only the curtain stood before us waiting for us to bow and lie down. And maybe it was the ballet that killed us after all.

We moved through places we had moved before, in this month, not in names, but in days, in the days, less than 30 that first flowed by and now hid under the marks on my calendar.

We moved in jumps and bounds through the heat in the stream bed. We moved into the ville where we had been without food. We walked past the hooch where we had gotten the chicken and the eggs. We passed the old lady, and I wondered if she remembered. As we filed passed her, she drove the gathered chickens into the house bowing and nodding as she went. When she saw me she paused and then continued into the shadows and safety of the small broken hooch, backing in, her hands held together as in prayer bowing repeatedly as she went. We moved to the north and west, the same routes, the same landmarks. We moved.

I wanted to tell her about Stepps. Balen's squad had gone out by the river before first light when Stepps got it from a booby trap, a big one that knocked them all on their asses, their collective ass. In our night, in our dark, what balls. It took five, and Stepps was one of them. When the chopper lifted off, Stepps was gone. She would probably want to know.

We moved. I went first and moved onto the right flank. Brownell moved through and onto the left. I covered while he moved. Fitzlee with the third platoon, was back. We moved through what had been a tree line, a village.

We continued to move slowly, poking through the line of trees. It was quiet, just the people watching, and in the distance, a water buffalo snorting from its pen.

Caution.

"For I am, above all, a very cautious man."

We were all cautious men, very cautious men. Cautious because of the steps we had taken that hadn't gone well, because of the steps we would take. Cautious because the delay in the morning could be deadly, because the big picture was slow in developing, too slow when things went fast as hell on the ground; because some of us remembered Morales while others remembered Wescott and we shared our memories with the new boots as they arrived.

SitRep Mar211327H: At mid-afternoon, we took a prisoner. He was young, in his twenties and he was strong. He was a gimp. He held his hands in front of him like flippers and he wobbled when he walked, from side-to-side, but he was strong and his teeth were white and straight. So, we took him. And we took him because there was nothing else to take. Lonely pushed him along in front of him. Again, he used the butt of his rifle as he had on the old woman a century before, one day in a valley. Today I let it happen naturally.

SitRep Mar211346H: We reconned with fire as we pushed along the tree line. Short bursts then move. Caution, nothing to chance, no mistakes, fire, test it, move into it and search. Jet aircraft circled above us. On station. The pilots glided their birds through the sullen air doing nothing, watching the war in an air conditioned cabin. The seat is hard though, or so it is said, so that makes it better. No arty though, not with them up there.

We fired again. I watched the tracers disappear into the tree line across from us.

"Hey Skipper," Lonely said. "It's the Six."

I took the hand set and listened.

"You're shitting me," I said.

I listened again.

"Balen," I said. "Secure the recon by fire."

"You mean it?" Balen asked.

"That's right," I said.

"None?"

"None, it makes the Colonel nervous."

I watched Balen move back down the line and talk briefly to Bates who looked back in my direction and shook his head.

'Nervous,' I thought, 'Why not, I was a little nervous myself. Not about a career going down in a hail of gunfire perhaps but about less important small details. I was nervous because someone shouted is this where you want the rubber boats in the night. I was nervous about leaflets dropped from a plane that said 'here we come'; I was nervous about a broadcast into the night over a PA system that announced our planned morning arrival, nervous that we were the only ones that followed the rules. Nervous my ass.'

We moved now in silence. We moved and we watched and we waited. We moved more slowly without the guns, in quiet unaccompanied bounds. A silent ballet was all we had left.

SitRep Mar211355H: "There'll be amtracs across your front, Sam," Flynn-Michael said. "Stop them and give them your prisoner then send them over to me. We must have 50 of the little bastards in tow. It looks like a goddamn parade of rags, for Christ sake."

I said, "Roger."

The rest of the platoon set in in the trees back up the finger we had just swept. We had moved 1500 meters past Phase Line Rook. Lonely and I stood out in the open in a potato patch and waited for the tracks. I could see them coming, plowing across the paddy that ran to the east where it stopped at the river.

SitRep Mar211356H: Potato patches were small little snatches of turf too dry for rice and too small for graves. They were furrowed about eight inches deep, the crests of the furrows separated by 12 or so inches more. I noticed them first in the valley, and thought what a nice place to hide. That was then, in the early days when I was interested in such things. That didn't make as much difference any more. I kicked the dust in the furrows as I waited while Lonely tossed hardened bits of dirt into the air behind me.

SitRep Mar211357H: "Here they come," Lonely said.

"Yes," I said. "Here they come."

Then I said, "Oh shit." And as I went to ground I fell through the days and the months and the years again back into Antenna Valley back into the eyes of a knee-high child. I was young, or younger, less than a child, a hand holder. I fished with my father in the pools of a river in the woods. We walked in on the narrow needled path, and while father laid out his fishing things on the bank, I tossed stones into the pools that remained in the river bed every time they closed the big gates in the dam back at Conklingville, where we had come from.

Father said:

"In the pools is where the fishing's good, good trout, browns and rainbow; some carp. The carp aren't so good, but they fight like a skunk on the hook.

"Mind your step and stay close by."

We walked out to the middle on the big smooth rocks. Father cast easily out into the largest pool and snatched the fly back in gentle steady snaps of his wrist. The fly skipped and then sat quietly for a moment, waiting. Father and I watched it until my eyes tired and I turned to search for smooth flat skipping rocks and small fresh water crabs.

Father said, "There."

The fly disappeared from the pool and the pole bent down close after. The clacking whirr of the reel broke the stillness of the valley. Father shifted his footing in the rocks and settled his attention to where the thin line cut through the water.

"Big one," he said, working in the slack of the line before the next run.

It broke the water quickly and ran for the other end of the pool. The loud crack of its body flopping on the water startled me and I turned to watch. It was then that I heard it.

"Father," I said.

"Yes," he said, "You're right. They've opened the gates."

I turned for the bank. The bite of the water grew louder through the mountains and the clean air like thunder. I scrambled over the smooth stones toward the trees. When I stopped to breathe, Father was not by me, he remained in the middle fighting the fish.

"Father," I called. "I can see it up at the bend."

I stood and watched him alone in the middle and I heard him when he said 'darn.' I watched him strike the carp in the rocks and toss it back into the pool. He picked the things of fishing up deliberately and walked to my side.

"Plenty of time," I could hear him say. "Plenty of time." And we walked slowly the little remaining distance to the shore.

We sat up against the trees as the roar grew down the valley. We sat where we could see it, a white line of foam devouring the rocks in the bed and the pools. It came on quickly until the roar was all there was and it was very loud because I was small and the waiting for fish was over.

SitRep Mar211358H: "Lonely," I shouted as I hit the deck. "LONELY."

Lonely was back in the trees. 'The quick and the dead and the difference. Jesus, I'll never learn it all in such a very short time, really.' And now it looked like he would be the quick and I would be the dead.

Hornets buzzed and landed with the close precision of circus thrown knives. They landed all around me, pinning me to the ground like a laboratory bug.

They landed all around me, but they didn't hit. I lay there and I didn't move because when I did, more hornets, more instant old age in a jacket of steel, impacted. Minutes went by.

It seemed like minuets anyway but more probably seconds, yet laying there it felt like minutes or hours or days. And all I could think was 'Why am I not dead? Why haven't I felt the burning that they say I will feel when it comes?'

More minutes flicked by, and more rounds poured into the small little patch of brown. 'Prayer, there is that, and thoughts of my unborn child and my wife who expects me home just now, but what prayer and to whom.

More lead skipped past, long, long, short, inches right, inches left, come down two clicks, come down two clicks. When I raised my head to see, the rounds filled my eyes with dust. 'How in the hell do they miss?'

I must not die, not now like this on my stomach in the dust, for the Chaplain, as we are friends, will meet me at the aid station and say a few words and then he will certainly get drunk and that would be bad, I would not like to be responsible for that for truly, he is a good, good shit.

I began to pray. This is my rifle, there are many others like it, but this one is mine. I know that this one in mine for I landed on it when I fell and now it massages my groin with its hard parts, but I don't feel the pain.

More minutes leaked away. This must be a trick. Why in the name of God don't you hit me? I know it will come and when it does it will let me relax. I know I've counted 20 minutes now or 30, perhaps, or maybe it's just two or three. I haven't moved and it all starts to ebb into monstrous monotony. My ears wandered back to the tree line behind me to listen to 'he's dead, he doesn't move.'

"No, no, in the high ground, there, just there," I shouted from my arm pit. "That's it, that's it." There's a flash and a second. I am zip. I am gone.

Now, for a minute, just one, I sat sucking in large pieces of stale humid glorious air. You owe me just this brief pause, just one for my youth, for I have come back from the dead.

I sat behind a rock sweating heavily. I looked up at Lonely who still held the M-79 at the ready and nodded. He smiled and lowered the weapon and handed it back to the man who had replaced Cobra who in turn fished two fresh rounds from his ammo pouch.

"You all right, Skipper?" he asked.

"Yeah, great, you fuck. But the next time you use my body for cover, I'll shoot your ass."

"Sir?" Lonely said through a lip smacking grin. "I just saved your life."

"You bastard," I said.

SitRep Mar211402H: Now we moved on the run, forward, toward a growing clatter of small arms fire. The prisoner who was still with us ran too, back toward the rear of the column, now with Hamlin.

Mid-way across the paddy where we ran, there was a small tuft of land laced with trenches, trenches that hadn't been there the first time a month ago. They ran in rays from the middle of a clearing to the trees along its edge at the north and the west. Up there, by the trees, Brownell and his second platoon were in the shit. Flynn-Michael with Boots and Horey, 200 meters behind Brownell, was deep in it too. Screwed up.

I reached the tuft. From there, I turned to watch Hamlin cover the paddy on the run with the gimp in front of him.

He ran well for a gimp, hands swinging like flippers or vacuum run wipers, in front of him with Hamlin down on him, encouraging him, massaging his shoulder blades, as he ran, with the butt of his rifle. And then he faltered and Hamlin rammed the muzzle of the rifle into his back. With new found energy, his hands flipped rapidly. They covered another 20 feet and there he was done, the remaining 25 yards was too much and he stood motionless, fagged. Hamlin brought the stock of his rifle crashing down on his shoulders and he fell. Hamlin hit him again. He held up his flippers to ward off the blows but they were of little use and they wilted back to the ground. Hamlin grabbed him by the collar now and he was running. The motionless gimp bounced along behind him like a morsel of trash. They gained the tuft.

Through it all the roar was around us. It persisted. Instant old age. We moved up the trench and stopped. I listened to the radio.

Brownell, just ahead, spoke calmly from an open place 25 feet from the flood gates as they opened in the trees.

Brownell said, "Echo Six, Two Actual,"

"Echo Six Actual Over," Flynn-Michael said.

"Skipper," Brownell said. "I'm pulling back now."

"Roger," Flynn-Michael said. "Air will be in soon, but no arty because of it."

"Roger," Brownell said.

Water-buffalo were kept in underground corrals; square holes maybe around 12 feet to a side dug about four feet down. Their floors were six inches deeper in a muck of shit, piss and the nervous tramping of a 1,500 pound animal. They were unpleasant to look at and they smelled of stagnant rotting things. Into one of these corals, Flynn-Michael plunged headlong, Sanchez tumbled in after him, and now they sank into the stink of the stagnation. When Flynn-Michael took the hand set from Sanchez who had jammed it deeply into the mire in his fall, and had pressed it up to his lips, he said, "Jesus Christ Sanchez you're a plot, a fucking VC plot."

Horey didn't make it in. He lay face down and flat a few feet behind. When he moved and he only moved once, a bullet split open the fabric camouflage covering his helmet. He didn't move for the rest of the afternoon and he said "fuck you" when Flynn-Michael called for him.

"Echo Six, this is Echo Two," Brownell said.

"Roger, Echo Two," Flynn-Michael said.

"Anything on the air yet?"

"Soon," Flynn-Michael said.

"Roger, wait one.

"Jesus. They're coming down the trench after us."

A pistol popped, it popped twice more.

"I think I got one, Skipper," Brownell said. "I'm going to pull back again, it's getting a little hot out here."

The jets rolled in. A pilot clicked into the Company radio net.

"Where are the good guys?

"Where are the bad?

"Mark your position.

"Roger.

"Have you located.

"Coming in."

They came in.

"Can make one drop.

"Am almost out of fuel."

"Roger," Brownell said.

"Am dropping stick."

"Roger."

The roar continued.

"Echo Two, Echo Six Actual Over."

"This is Two"

"How was that?"

"Beautiful. Pulling back."

"Roger break,

"Echo One, Echo Six."

"Roger, One," I said.

"Hold, what you've got, Sam," Flynn-Michael said. "I'll have something for you in a minute."

"Roger," I said.

We held.

I stood in the trench and listened to the war progressing without me. I sent Rico with his squad to a small piece of high ground to the rear of the Company. They set in and they watched down the small paddy that ran back to the south from the trench. That was our ass. Across the paddy Flynn-Michael moved cautiously back and forth in the bull pen.

While I listened and watched, a small cloud of black-orange in the shape of a ball popped over the paddy, 50 meters out. I checked with Rico up on the hill. They had seen it but they hadn't fired it. Another ball formed half the distance from the first closer in to the trench. The noise of it was still lost in the roar and the talk of the war on the radio. Brownell was still pulling back and the amtracks now panted close by the trees and the trench.

"No," Rico said again. "It wasn't us."

I hit the deck in the narrow slit trench, twisting onto my back as I fell. Above me, the thin line of sky was blue veiled in dust. The clotted dirt of the trench rocked loose by the last explosion stuck to my face. My face, my God, my face, too good, too pretty to get screwed up in this, after all, when it comes to that, it's time to go home.

The exploding rounds crashed in on the berm of the trench just above my face cutting out the blue completely and filling the trench with more dirt.

"My Face." And I began to laugh.

At the place where we went fishing and spent long easy kid summers in the low Adirondacks, Father decided we needed a well. So he began to dig. For several weeks he scratched through the rock-hard surface of the mountain until he was unable to throw the small shovels full of gravely dirt out of the hole. That's when Mother went to work. A piece of clothes-line was tied to the handle of an old, galvanized bucket. Mother lowered the bucket into the hole. Father filled it. Mother hauled it to the top, emptied it and let it down into the narrow pit for another load. Hour after hour the process repeated and slowly the well got deeper and deeper. It was just before lunch and Father was now about 14 feet down.

"It's time for lunch," Mother called.

"Okay," Father shouted back, "Just a couple more."

Mother hoisted the next load to the top and as it was just about to clear the rim the edge of the pail caught on a small vicious root. It tipped, and the contents including a rock about the size of a grapefruit rained back down on Father. The rock bounced off Father's head and hit the bottom of the well with a thunk.

It was quiet. And then Father, who never swore, began his lament.

"Son-of-a,-a,...Skunk," he said starting up the ladder. "Son-of-a-skunk, son-of-a-skunk, son-of-a-skunk."

His bloody skull cleared the rim.

"Son-of-a-Skunk."

And Mother began to laugh.

I laughed again. I rolled over in the narrow trench twisting the belts and straps of my web gear tightly around my arms and chest until I was barely able to move.

"Son-of-a-skunk," I said as more chunks of earth and small pebbles gave way under the continued mortar assault and rained down on us.

"Son-of-a-skunk."

And then we started to crawl.

"Echo Six, Echo One,"

"Roger, Echo Six," Flynn-Michael said.

"Mortars" I said. "From behind us somewhere and they're pounding the shit out of us."

"Roger," Flynn-Michael said. "I wish I could help but as you see it's a bag of shit in all directions. And by the way Sam, Faint heart and all that, you know."

"Roger," I said. "And thanks."

"There isn't much else, really, is there."

"No," I said. "There isn't."

We crawled up the trench, still crawling, still low, and still the rounds came in, following us, hitting into the trench where we had been. My ears rang with the concussion.

We crawled.

And then just as quickly we were up and running. Without command, we stood and ran down the trench all at once all together toward the fire in the tree line ahead and through and away from the incoming shells. The mortar fire lifted. For no reason, they lifted. The power of prayer I thought.

And mom, and apple pie. This is my rifle, there are many others like it, but this one is mine.

They had lifted.

I pulled my knees up under my chin and pushed closer to my father under the trees. Together, we watched it rush past us, sweeping away the pools and the fish.

Faint heart and all that, and all that.

"Echo Two, Echo Six."

"Echo Two."

"We're sending the tracks in to pull you out."

"Roger, we're still pulling back."

"Roger."

The pistol popped again.

An amtrack fired up somewhere behind us and began the trek along the trench to join us. The roar, some ours, some theirs, still ruptured the normal rural silence, but the roar coming from out of the trees towards us seemed less than before. That's was nice. There was still plenty of time.

SitRep Mar211650H: Another amtrack churned back to the tree line where we stood, its big engine straining with the neutral steers, spraying dust out behind the biting track. When the ramp came down, two of the walking wounded helped Brownell out of the track, his arms draped over their shoulders. His green, jungle green utes were mottled with the crusty brown that said he was bleeding. The blood of the young.

He had been hit when the first shots were fired and no one had known.

His voice was steady, easy and calm, it gave no hint of the pain or the fear, yes, there had to be fear. It was a good voice and loyal and strong and it hid the fear well, yet, now, his eyes betrayed him, for there deep in their sockets the remnants of fear remained, settled in so that those of us there would see it and know once it got there it would never go away.

There were two rounds still in him and a grenade had gone off between his legs. They helped him down off the ramp onto the ground. He shook them off at the bottom and walked toward the second amtrack that had come up behind us. Its ramp lowered.

I met him half way across the small space.

"Hell of a good job," I said.

"Yeah," Brownell said. He draped one arm over my shoulder and leaned into me hard. "But they got me, they got me good."

I looked down to where the brown was brownest and, then looked back up to his face.

There we were, the two of us, standing there talking while lead splattered on the hulls of the tracks beside us, and I thought, 'What do you say to someone who has just been shot in the nuts. And to his wife, what do you say to a wife. Like Pumpkin, she'll sit at home with the other wives watching every day as the brown car comes slowly up the street, the driver reading numbers off mailboxes, slowly one at a time and she'll say 'don't stop here oh please don't stop here' with her eyes closed tightly and then when it passes she'll rush to the window to see where he stops and she'll begin to think of things to say to her friend who has just become a widow and she will wonder 'what do you say' and then she will do it all again tomorrow, and the day after that and like her man she will stack the days up behind little x's and marks on the big calendar next to the map.' Jesus. .But today, like Brownell's, her counting will stop, her wait will be over. They'll give him a medal, I suppose, and a new pair of sneakers or something real neat. And a plaque that will tell her, 'Your husband has just been shot in the nuts, sorry.'

"You're looking good," I said.

"Yeah,

"But listen," he said. "I got a dead Marine out there."

"We'll get him," I said.

"Yeah," he said.

"Yeah," I repeated.

"Alright then," he said.

I helped him up into the second amtrack because I wanted to and because no one else would. The troops wouldn't believe it could happen to an Actual, so they made believe it hadn't happened and I helped him up the ramp. The incoming fire increased slapping all around us. We stood there a moment and then shook hands. We had known each other well for only two months. And even so, by the end of it all we would never forget.

"The dead man," he said.

"God's speed." I said.

Brownell walked alone to the back of the second amtrack where the Battalion Surgeon, a fat, little guy from the Bronx with balls bigger than he was, waited.

When Brownell eased down on a pile of sandbags stacked up against the back wall the Doctor shoved a small vial of Brandy into his hand. Damn good though, damn fine brandy for a place like this, medicinal of course, in two ounce drams.

Brownell drank one and someone handed him a lit cigarette.

He smoked it quietly. The Doctor was already beginning to cut. With the ramp still down, small arms rounds snapped in and out like angry hornets bouncing around the insides of the track. The Doctor knelt calmly and lifted his voice over the roar in tongues of acute Bronx.

"The dirty sons-of-bitches," he shouted. "Close that fucking door. The dirty-sons-of-bitches."

"It's not a door Doc, it's not even a hatch," I said unheard in the din. "It's a ramp."

The Doctor knelt by Brownell and cut smoothly, draining the blood from his ball sack, and he continued to curse like they do in the streets of the city when it is summer and hot. The ramp horn sounded and slowly the ramp lifted closed in a screech of hydraulics. Now I was alone. I noticed the roar and the snap of the rounds as I walked slowly back to the trench.

"You better get down Lieutenant," Lonely called from the trench

"Fuck the quick and the dead," I said. "He was shot in the nuts. Jesus."

SitRep Mar211854H: Hours had passed since the first rounds had been fired, and now in the twilight it was silent again. Ham bounced a bloody gimp down in front of the S-2 intelligence Sergeant.

"What the fuck is this?" he asked.

"VC," I said.

"Christ, Sir, he is what he is, a fucking gimp. You can cut him loose."

When we let him go he scurried off into the twilight tree line like a wounded animal.

SitRep Mar211935H: "That night, because it was ours we closed the roaring gates. We had lost only one dead, the one that had been out in the forward trench with Brownell. We found him where he had been left, where Brownell said he would be, half-in, half-out and all dead. He hadn't been touched, there was that, and he was dead, they said, the ones who had been there with him, because he hadn't stayed down as he was told. There was that too. That should certainly be comforting.

The dead Marine and the wounded were evacuated. Horey registered night time artillery targets. FItzlee and Flynn-Michael and Boots and the soft-handed Major sat with their thoughts. No one spoke.

"Boots," Flynn-Michael said finally. "You got the Second now, you know. Be ready at first light."

SitRep Mar220510H: I stood by Flynn-Michael and the rest at dawn.

"But we're ready to go now," Flynn-Michael said into the hand set. "Sir? Sir?"

He handed the hand set back to Sanchez and turned back to where the rest of us were waiting, listening.

"We wait, for Christ sake," he said. "Wait, wait, wait."

So once again we waited.

Horey said, "Wasted a hell of a lot of arty last night if we don't move now, Skipper."

"What the fuck would you have me do, Horey? That fucking Teapot says wait, so we wait," Flynn-Michael said. "Goddamn it Horey, we wait."

"All right, Skipper," Horey said throwing his hands up. "All right, I'm getting tired of it all anyway."

At noon, the word came to move across Phase Line Queen. The Line of Departure, the LOD. A jumping off point marked by a lazy curl of half stream half irrigation ditch. Where we entered, the slope was gradual but where we emerged, the bank was steep and about four feet high and made slippery by the exiting Marines. 'They should be ready for us by now,' I thought as I watched my platoon check magazines and hook grenades to web gear.

We saddled up.

Fitzlee on the left flank.   Me on the right

Boots moved with the Second

Brownell back in Charlie Med

We crossed the stream and approached the next tree line.

The air strikes and Horey's arty had torn up large chunks of earth but as though nothing had happened people moved with disinterest in the shadows of the hidden ville. They were hollow-eyed and quiet, but unhurt and moving, as if there had been no war here the day before. They looked away when we passed through them hiding the wounds in their eyes, wounds that we shared. Like us, when it was finally over, they would be left with the chore of putting it all back together.

Where the ambush had been, there was nothing, no brass, no spent cartridges, no blood other than ours. A battalion of gooks had been there, one of the hollow-eyed people said, and now they were gone without a trace, not a broken twig or fallen leaf, not a print.

"Ghosts," Lonely said. "They didn't leave shit."

"No," I said. "Not even that."

"Hey Lieutenant, over here."

On the trail just past the ambush site we found the gimp. During the night he had been badly beaten and dumped to die.

"Why the fuck would they do that?" Ham asked.

"Because he spent the day with us I guess," I said.

"Yeah, but we beat the shit out of him too."

We left him cowering back in the shade of the palms.

SitRep Mar221218H: We moved through the ville and on the far side Fitzlee took fire. I didn't. When we first heard it, we like Fitzlee were through the village but farther to the east on the edge of an island where it disappeared back into the paddy. Another stream, a tributary on its way back to the river 2,000 meters away, cut across our front as we looked to the north. It cut the paddy in two. It was a small paddy. On the other side, a new island of firmer ground took shape and disappeared into yet another distant tree line.

On the Big Picture a grease line followed the trace of the stream. Large letters called it Phase Line Rook. Here on the ground, it was only a stream in a nasty-assed place.

I got to the phase line first and reported no grease. I held up, and listened. Fitzlee bogged down on the western flank. He had run into snipers. He moved slowly, returned fire, and then crept forward. No one was hurt. The snipers had been spotted near a small hooch on the far side of Phase Line Rook. Fitzlee requested arty. Horey called for it. It went in. It whistled over our heads, and crashed into the tree line across the stream. I couldn't see where it hit from where I held. I waited. I strained to pick up some movement caused by the attack and I listened.

SitRep Mar221245H: The sun shone on the green nose of our finger that angled out north and west to the stream, Phase Line Rook, and disappeared. The cane and brush thinned, had been cleared from this end where we set in. In its place, the earth had been pushed into mounds to form another grave yard. We sat there and waited while Fitzlee moved up on the snipers. The mood was light in the sunshine, and when the arty lifted, it was quiet.

We leaned back on the graves and rested in the warm sun. Some of the troops smoked and crossed their feet. They looked up at the sky and closed their eyes. Others, still smoking, looked out across the paddies watching. We all listened.

'They are all such sweet young things,' I thought. 'But then, so am I, 22, 23, somewhere in there, but young still; very, very young. We swagger like men and use the vernacular of men, the hard words of men, but yes, still we are young in the eyes. Too young to be here in this x-rated thing.'

The radio hummed and sounded like air being sucked through gaps its teeth.

Funny, it never exhales. It just sucks it in until there is nothing left for the rest of us to breathe.

I lay back up against one of the graves drifting. It's always the waiting that's the hardest part. Once we get going, war isn't all that bad.

Fitzlee went out to check the arty hit. I waited in the sunshine.

Out into the paddy he went with a squad, he left two behind him to cover.

I could see him without the helmet now, walking quietly like he spoke and proudly like old Virginia.

'I don't even really know who he is,' I thought as I watched him move.

'He is another young one like us, I know that. But unlike us who are held together with hard sun cracked dirty hide, his skin is soft and unblemished. His eyelashes proud signs of his youth are long almost feminine. He looks the part of youth while the rest of us begin to take on the wrinkles and bowed shoulders of old men so he may be openly called a youth or perhaps just young.'

Dear Pumpkin,

Wars aren't so bad really; always had them always will. And anyway, what about the hammer, that was probably used in a war before we learned how to use it for building. So all in all, wars per se, are pretty damn good. It's the 'ME' in them that's touchy. But war, as war, is just dandy, it keeps us honest like church. Lonely likes it very much, but, then, he's from Philadelphia and I guess that makes a difference. Doc Peckham came to like it too. He began to understand that we live comfortably with love, so why not sit back and enjoy the ride of hate and war.

S

Fitzlee moved, without his helmet, with his squad, he moved across Phase Line Rook. I composed letters in the sunshine and watched and listened to the radio sucking wind. Lonely smoked.

I am One Actual, One Fucking Actual. Fitzlee is Three Actual, Three Alpha and Bravo are those left behind to cover. Two Actual who was Brownell is Boots. Horey's with Flynn-Michael the Six. We all hail from Echo and today we are all so young, so very, very young.

"Bullshit.

"Bullshit," I said.

"Sir?" Lonely asked.

"Just Bullshit," I said. "That's all, just bullshit."

The sun was still shining and we were still by the brook warm and thoughtful. In the brook small eddies and reflections watched and waited.

SitRep Mar221257H: "He's hit, he's hit, Oh, Jesus, he's hit."

"Echo Three, Echo Six."

"He's dying, hurt bad, we need help. Oh Jesus."

"Echo Three, this is Echo Six Actual, what's going on up there, over. Echo Three, this is Echo Six Actual. Do you copy over?"

"Hurry."

"Echo Six, Echo Three Alpha, Three Actual is hit. I've lost them."

I jumped up when it started, the noise, a round, a bullet burned across my bicep. I grabbed at my arm and slowly peeled my fingers away sure that I was not going to like what I found. There was no blood, only a single, ugly, red welt the size of a finger marked its passing. The skin had held together. "No blood," I said. "No blood at all."

'There is no time Father,' I thought, 'for they have opened the gates all at once and now the roar is on top of me and beside me and all around me, and surely I shall be dashed to death on the quiet smooth rocks.'

Dust plumes launched by automatics weapons danced across the ville like small brown flowers. The radio ran along before their bloom panting for breath.

"Echo Three Alpha...., Echo Three Alpha...., this is...., Echo Six...., Actual over."

"Skipper, I gotta go get them. I can hear them calling out there. They need help."

"Where...., are you...., Three Alpha...., What...., is your position?"

"Skipper, they're screaming for help, you gotta let me go get them."

"Echo Three Alpha...., this Is Echo Six...., over...., what is your position...., for Christ sake."

"I can hear them out there Skipper. I'm going out after them."

"No...., what In the...., name of Christ...., is your position?"

"Oh.

"Jesus, Skipper.

"We're mortared.

"I've got them hit.

"...all over."

I listened quietly while I rubbed away the burning pain in my arm. The air around us was electric with the roar and the dust. There was pity on the net, pity and despair. I held.

"Echo One, Echo One."

"Echo One. Over."

"Sam, get over there."

"Roger."

I stood and pointed and people began to move around me. There was no pause, no time for thought, just movement, action, action, action and reaction; the inertia of waiting was broken and for a moment there was a pause in the laws of nature.

Phase Line Rook; now it was just a stream. I could feel the tug of the current as it wandered back toward the river and as I reached the far bank it pulled, holding me back. I broke loose and scrambled up the bank. Now we were across, the balance of things, the natural laws, appeared to be restored.

But it is nothing but bullshit, smoke and mirrors, there is no law when men fight. They either win or they lose. There is no room for law here and there is no need. There are laws in other places, and that's good, but there is no law here and that's good too, because without law we can be winners and not losers and when we are done only the memories will remain. A law would punish us and remove the need for memory because in it men would pay for their crimes and be done. Memories can't be bought off, not by men, so we remember. And the memories remain, they endure.

And we can never run away.

We were up now, running. We ran like hell.

The quick and the dead and the difference. We moved well and with knowledge.

Arty came in, lots of arty, and we ran.

Horey was working his ass off, or perhaps it was his balls, It most certainly wasn't his nose, but, nevertheless, he was hurting them and he was saving us. He was good.

We came up over another finger. Flynn-Michael was there.

"They're over there," he said.

He pointed toward the next tree line. He displaced, he pointed and displaced again.

"Mortars," he said. "Never put a CP by the fucking guns. Jesus."

The guns chattered and then displaced along with him.

"Get going," he shouted.

We ran down off the finger. The soft-handed Major huddled down by a grave next to Horey and chewed at the end of a cigar. He nodded at me and I nodded in return. Horey was on the radio moving, adding, shifting left, shifting right; the arty came in, continued to come in, 10 rounds at a time. A barrage hit in close and filled the air with shrapnel and my ears with the pounding concussion. Pieces of body flew into the air weakly twisted, and I smiled as I ran toward the mayhem.

'Well now,' I wondered, 'I wonder if they're government inspected too, like us Choice grade A, and I wonder if they have laws when they get home, and are they young.'

One thing is certain, though.

Once they might have been quick.

But not now.

Now.

They're dead.

No question about that.

Very.

Goddamn.

Dead.

Horey leaned back and admired his work.

"How many of those little fucks do you think I killed today?" he asked that evening

"I don't know," I said. "How many?"

"I don't know either," he said smiling through sad eyes. "But it's got to be a shit load."

We ran and we did it well and the arty came in, kept coming in around us. We churned through another stream and sent angry wavelets rolling up on the further bank.

SitRep Mar221258H: "Get a hold of yourself, Captain," Teapot said from the river. "You're not being shot at. I can't hear it."

"'Get a hold of yourself.' Jesus," Flynn-Michael repeated. "'I can't hear it,' for Christ sake," he exploded. "How in the fuck can you not hear it." He held the handset up in the air.

The Major behind the grave confirmed the tussle and Teapot answered, "Roger, still..."

In the rear, we were told later, a Major who had been in the field as a Captain wrote 'shut up' on a post in the Combat Operations Center, the COC, in pencil. He didn't write it to anyone in particular, just to everything as it stood while he listened, just 'shut up' in pencil on a railroad tie stood on end to hold up the roof and painted white.

As a combination of the two, or, perhaps for no reason of any obvious sort, Teapot, Shut Up.

SitRep Mar221303H: And as we sat and watched it, Father and I, we, safe with our trees, I felt that my small ears were no match for the roar and that soon, it would sweep through my brain and tear at the back of my eyes and that it would sweep me away, grab me from the bank and dash me until there was nothing left. The thought of it frightened me and I moved closer to Father as if he might make it stop. 'Plenty of time,' he said.

There were five of them down with Three Alpha. They had been up and moving toward Fitzlee when it came in and cut them down like the guns cut down the rice. The Sergeant in charge told me that they had once been up on their feet doing things, that they had not always been like this. That there had been a time when they were good, young, strong Marines

Because he was a man, he wanted to cry while he spoke. Because of this and because of who was dead now and because of youth, he wanted to shout and swear and stamp his feet at the ground on which he stood. Because he was a Sergeant of Marines and because he could not remember things being any different, he did not, he only allowed his voice to grow thick.

The Gunny was there, kneeling by one who still remembered a different world and could allow himself to cry. The Gunny knelt by him and held his head and talked softly.

"You're alright, boy," he said. "You're all right now, you're all right."

And I noticed that this young Marine was no longer a girl nor was he a man, he was a child who was hurt and had fallen and now the Gunny knew he had to give comfort as though he were his son.

"Take it easy son, you're all right," he said.

"But he was so young Gunny," the boy said. "As old as am, just a kid. Oh, goddamn it. It hurts Gunny, it hurts."

His wounds were small but his memory bled freely and the things he remembered hurt. But, still his wounds were small. They would heal. So why then did they cause him to shake with anger and cry? Did he know that the wounds on his body would heal but that the wounds on his memory would remain open forever?

"You're all right, son," Gunny said.

I stood over him and echoed the words quietly. It did no good and he, the man on the ground, continued to cry and shake and swear because now, there was no reason why he shouldn't.

The others lay beside him and were quiet. Their faces showed nothing except the relaxation, perhaps it was relaxation, of one who has waited for something he fears and now it is finally over. Like going to the dentist.

"They're in shock," the Corpsman said.

"No, they're not" I said. "It is nothing of the kind, they're relieved."

They lay quietly and waited for the birds they knew would eventually come.

Why don't they call them doves? I wondered. Was it because they looked like guppies, and for no other reason, or was it because they haven't been made since the early '50's.

One of the downed Marines had been hit high in the thighs. His trousers were ripped to the crotch to show him that he was still intact, that they were still the there.

Another, the corpsman, had been wrapped in 123 battle dressings. He had counted them one-by-one as each wound was covered with 123 separate fucking battle dressings. A piece of the metal had ripped through his throat. When spoke he whispered,

"Hey Lieutenant," he said.

"Don't talk," I said. "What do you want?"

"Come here and take my picture," he said.

"What in the name of Christ for?"

"For my mother, so she'll see that I'm alright, and so she won't worry. Funny, she always worries," he said.

I took the picture.

The others that had been there that were still able to stand took prisoners, three of them, two men and a woman. They were young and tied by the feet and the hands, with comm. wire. A third piece pulled their hands and feet together behind them and they lay trussed up face down by a tree. I stood by them as the ones that had been with Fitzlee in the killing zone came in carrying extra rifles and the three bodies. They, like the man on the ground, cried. They cried quietly and they cried without shame.

'And if I could write,' I thought while I watched them, 'this too, the sounds of confusion and hurt and hate, not the words, the words are easy and always the same, and fear, yes, that too because fear has a sound of its own when you stand next to it and it is the same in the eyes of all animals, but the sounds of grown men crying.'

I stood by the prisoners as they, the others, came in. One of them walked over to where they were tied. He cried and he swore as he looked down at them. He swore while he raised his rifle butt back high over his shoulder.

"Put it down Marine and keep moving," I said.

The man looked up and through me. He hadn't noticed me there, or hadn't wanted to, or had but didn't give a shit. He stood with the butt poised up over his head, aimed at the people on the ground, and said nothing. Tears ran easily down his cheeks.

"Put the fucking thing down and move away or I'll shoot you myself," I said raising my rifle. The man looked at me closely now, lowered his weapon slowly and moved on.

"They're no fucking good," he said.

It happened again, and again after that. Fitzlee lay next to the others covered with a poncho. Like them he waited quietly for the incoming birds, peacefully, without urgency.

I watched Fitzlee lying, still, in the mud. He didn't move. I looked back down at the three next to me and then back to Fitzlee and it made me sick, Lord so very, very, sick.

"Why don't you get up," I asked. But there was no movement only the slight flap of the covering poncho in the evening breeze and the background moans of the wounded. I looked again at the three and kicked dirt at them and then I kicked them.

"Lonely," I said. "Come here."

"Sir," Lonely said, moving up to where I stood.

"Watch them," I said. "And keep them alive."

"I'm going to kill their moldy gook ass, Sir," he said.

"I said keep them alive," I repeated vacantly.

"Yes Sir," he said. "But Sir," he called as I walked away. "I'm only doing it because you said to. I want you to know that."

I paused.

I watched from the distance. Lonely stood over them. When they moved, they felt more boots in their ribs. This time it was Lonely's hard Philadelphia boot.

After a while they stopped moving.

I stood and waited in the clearing for the choppers.

They were 34's, and the pilot wanted to know if the zone was hot. After they landed, the crew chief asked how many more? I held up my finger, one, and shrugged my shoulders because I knew there was no end to it in the succession of days. There would always be one more, and one more, and one more. So I gave him the finger, popped him the twig, because that was the only true answer I could give, and he flew away with all the wounded but one. They would be back for him along with Fitzlee and the rest of the dead.

Because we had pulled back, the stream, Phase Line Rook, was in front of us again, to our front. The village stood around us. There had been people there and they had let Fitzlee and his squad walk into a battalion hidden just across the paddy in the trees. They had hidden the luring sniper and they had let Fitzlee and his squad pass through.

And like they smiled at us now, they must have smiled at him, as he walked through, because they knew where he was going. There was a time when I thought it was a good thing to be here and although I knew that it was their war and that we fought to help them and that they had asked us here as guests that all fell away when they let young Fitzlee, not even as old as me and whose mother is dead, walk into a battalion that they knew, had to know was there. A battalion that they fed, no doubt, in all things including chickens and eggs. How long ago, four hours ago, five, had it been that long face down again. But then, maybe Fitzlee had failed to ask them for help in their war. Maybe he expected them to be on his side. The old man was right, their rice would grow tall next year for we made the land fertile, irrigated it in blood, in the blood of FItzlee and his blood was young and good and government inspected. And that will be the extent of our accomplishment here.

I watched. Still no birds. It made little difference now.

Balen reported all set in and stood by me as we waited. We stood quietly, the shooting had stopped, the artillery silent. The only noise was that of the one wounded boy who cried and swore in the middle of the clearing. There had been no room for him so he waited to ride back with Fitzlee. He shook now, violently, like one with Malaria, a shaking he couldn't control but that went well with his crying and the things he said when he cursed.

A single machine-gun cracked a quick burst to my left. I ran to the lines at the sound of the shot. Balen followed. In the paddy that opened out to the west, a water buffalo sank, his front legs buckling first as if in prayer and then his hind quarter, shining, falling slowly to the west. He disappeared into the rice that grew taller than his crumpled body. He died without a sound and fell with slow dignity.

"VC water-bo," the gunner said.

'Do that again,' I thought to the man behind the still smoking gun, 'and I'll wrap the fucking thing around your skull.'

What I said was "That will cost us 400 dollars."

"Yes Sir," he said, smiling.

SitRep Mar221632H: When we moved back to Flynn-Michael's position, we burned the village. The bamboo popped around us and it was hot.

"I want these bunkers blown," I said kicking at the one closest to me. "I want this goddamn village levelled. They can blame it on their goddamn war, or they can blame it on invitations, all of them."

"There are people in some of the bunkers, Sir."

It was Lonely.

"I said blow them," I said again.

"The people in them, they're women and kids, Sir."

I looked away over the stream and rice paddy beyond and finally to the tree line.

'What the fuck am I going to do here,' I thought. 'I can see it in his eyes, that son-of-a-bitch, and I can hear it in the way he speaks. He's only 19, what does he know. Who the hell does he think he is to stand there and wait with that look. God damn him, goddamn the look in his young eyes.

I'd felt that look in my eyes too once or twice before; but never for this, not when people were dead, good people, young people, people who will be cried for tomorrow, never for this.' Shit blows through my mind, bits and pieces of memory; 'judge not..., I answer only to one judge..., here comes the judge...'

He stood there with those goddamn eyes.

I turned back toward the bunker.

"Blow them," I said again. "They're all fucking VC." And as I said it I took the grenades from him.

"Yes Sir," he said backing away as he continued to watch.

I walked toward the bunker. I pulled the pin on the first grenade and stood for a moment looking in.

When I am out of this shit and I am with my wife and my son, we will go to the edge of the sea and we will live there because there are few people there during the year who know of this and it is crowded only when there is sun. We will not live in the mountains, for although they are good, their valleys fill with the fearful roaring torrents of spring, and during those times they are only for the very old who cannot hear and the very young who live without memory; they are safe from lack of use and wise with age but the sudden noise of spring.... It is by the sea that is best for it is lonely and the water takes back the land and is wild but the sound of the sea is constant.

So that is the way it will be, and when the summer is dead, we will drive on Route 28 or 6-A and we will find ourselves alone like ants on strips of sandy ribbon that lay loosely in folds along the ragged coast of the arm. When it is cool in the Fall, the Indian Summer, because there it still exists, we will walk on the dunes and the beach by the point or down by the light-house that continues to fall off into the sea. There will be a stiff breeze, fresh and clean, and a sunset, and the silhouettes that move ahead of me will be of my wife and my child, my son. And he will discover things, hermit crabs and sea stars washed ashore. He will discover things that are alive and good brought up from the depths by the running tide. He will notice that the strong eat the weak, but he will save it for another time by himself.

My hands will grow cold and I will put them quietly in my pockets where I can feel them, the pockets of the rough wool plaid coat from Afton, Oklahoma because it was snowing the day we were there. They will feel rough too, because I will work with my hands and the wind burn on my cheeks will not bother me because my work will be done outdoors. I will work with my hands because my mind will not yet be whole and my memory will still bleed.

Later, in the dark, we will walk home and meet no one. The fresh smell of salt air will fade and the rancid smell of blown bunkers will return. My son will ride on my shoulders with his small, scorched hands wrapped around my head and I will say 'thank you' and he will hold my ears so that I may not hear.

Plenty of time.

I threw the first of the grenades into the dark recesses of the bunker. The thud of the first explosion rocked me back with its closeness. I could feel the heat of the blast mixed with the damp of the day bury itself deep into everything in me that was still alive, and I could see through the scattered palms and banana trees the cloud of twisted dirt and debris and what might have been the burned and charred parts of the hidden. The scene faded into the glitter of the eyes of the young girl carried by her father to the waiting chopper only this time she reached out to me with charred smoking fingers trying to grab at my hands, to touch my face. This time there was no Fitzlee to plead for her evacuation because the many shes like her had let him die.

I threw the second grenade in as far as I could. There was a second explosion and then it was still. I let my hands fall to my sides. I looked down at the mud caked on my boots. I felt at the ugly red welt raised on my arm as I rubbed my index finger back and forth over the complaining flesh. Now, in the final quiet of the cooling day I began to sweat and I couldn't stop shaking.

Lonely turned and walked back to the CP and the security of his radio.

SitRep Mar221851H: The hooches still burned and it was beginning to grow dusk. When the burning stopped sometime in the night, there was nothing that said, I-Am-A-Village-Where-People-Live left, only the clearing, the ashes, the name on the map, but nothing more. The graves. The radio sucked wind again as though nothing had happened, nothing had changed.

We set up close to Flynn-Michael's position, where we had set up before, and we met, while Horey continued the guns, working them into the area to our front, 3,000 meters out all around. He fired them on through the night.

"I'm going to kill them fucking all," he said. "Every fucking one."

"There was never a finer man," Flynn-Michael said. "Jesus."

He went through the day, reliving each step. He told it in detail explained it all, as though he had been there alone.

"Never a finer man," he said at the end.

For a while, we did things differently, for most of it we were quiet, looking down at the feet that we couldn't see in the dark but knew were there because now we could feel things again.

That ended it. We drifted away without speaking into the comforting dark, and the night sounds of Horey's artillery pounding the shit, if that's what it was out of the earth. Not the world, the earth, the wet soggy earth.

When I got back to my own small CP, Balen and Hamlin and Rico were there. They were quiet and looked away when I sat down with them and they mumbled when they spoke. Lonely dozed to the pleasant, now pleasant quiet sucking of the radio that leaned against a tree and supported his head.

"Get ready to move," I said.

"Yes Sir."

They sat not seeming anxious to leave.

"Lonely.

"Lonely," I said again.

"Yes Sir," he answered.

"What happened to the three gooks I left with you?"

"They happy motherfuckers now Sir," he said.

"I suppose they are but I guess it doesn't make any difference now anyway," I said quietly.

Again there was silence.

"What about tonight?" Balen asked at last.

"What about it?"

"Do they expect any shit tonight?"

I could see his eyes plainly now as he spoke watching me in the growing dusk.

"Christ no," I said. "No sweat, we own this night, remember?"

"And the days?" Balen asked.

"Ah, the days," I said. "Yes, the days are still a bitch."

SitRep Mar222018H: We picked up the pieces and moved out, Indian-style again in the dark. Teapot had called us back over by the river. It was over. Tonight, right now, the Big Picture didn't look as bad to me on the ground as we trudged east.

We walked back through another burning village. There were guides there to lead us back into the Battalion area. It was hot as hell, the whole village burning at once, the guides silhouetted in the red-white glow of popping bamboo and straw. The stink filled my nostrils. Following a turn in the rutted path, I tripped over the remains of a short, stout pig ripped open by artillery fired throughout the afternoon. When I sat up I came face-to-face with smiling lifeless eyes. An old man peered over the top of the village water buffalo pit. His left shoulder pushed down into the rubble and his bowed back crumpled down onto his mud soaked knees, bent as if in prayer. His wrinkled cheeks ended on a thinly stretched chin that boasted wisps of fine, spindly, white hairs like proud pennants highlighted with light brown crusted streaks leading from the corners of his windswept cracked lips. His lifeless eyes folded nearly shut and the shreds of his long queue wrapped around his neck liked an angry cobra.

I scrambled back to my feet, returned the smile and hurried on to catch up with the column as it wound its way out of the village.

Turning a corner I looked back at the old man and smiled a second time. The roar is always with us, someway, somehow, it's there. But tonight it is not the sound of water. It is this, a roaring fire and no more. A damn hot roaring fire boiling the water just beneath the surface. We moved into a clearing by the river and set in. For several hours, I sat alone and drifted in and out of sleep. I hadn't slept for four days.

It was quiet. A dead gook lay in the middle of the clearing we surrounded. His left leg was bandaged at the knee. He was twisted and had not been touched since he fell the day before, and now he began to stink. There were flies beginning to gather at the openings, eagerly buzzing, landing and flying away. He had died with his eyes closed as though he hadn't seen it coming but flickering distant firelight made him look like he was winking as though acknowledging some great secret conspiracy.

The little, fat Doctor from the Bronx said, "Yesterday, in the morning, this little bastard comes up with his knee all fucked-up and says we did it and that he's a civilian. So, I bandage the little asshole and clean him up. Then, the next thing I know, the little shit pins me down in the paddy like a fucking rat in the afternoon, trying to kill me. The little sons-of-bitches."

"Maybe you charged him too much," Horey said and for a moment I thought I could laugh.

"You assholes can laugh" the Doctor said. "It wasn't you that he..." He paused.

"Yes," he said when he spoke again. "You can laugh can't you? You got to laugh, we've all got to laugh."

That evening, Lonely seemed to have forgotten the events of the day. He danced around my little CP chanting and laughing.

"Two Actual the first day, Three Actual the second day on the third day we rested, huh Skipper? And on the third day we rested."

Some people drank for relief, Lonely did this.

I stirred at the fire and didn't answer.

'Somewhere, in the world,' I thought prodding at a simmering can of balls and beans. 'Today is the Thursday before good Friday, but here it was just a day, not even today but day, a day in the wonderful succession of days. Sunday will be Easter. Sunday is always pill day for the Malaria, but this Sunday will be Easter too. The Chaplain will be sober and those of us who are left will go to the service because he's such a good...'

I drifted off to sleep. The merciful dawn came quickly.

SitRep Mar230805H: In the morning, we got on amtracks and crossed the river again going in. It was quiet as it had been the night before. I rode with Horey and the Gunny. None of us talked. When we reached the refugee village, I took my helmet off. The breeze from our moving felt good. Kids from the village ran along next to us shouting at us as we rolled on into the base camp. When they ran, the flies stayed off their eyes.

"Honcho," they said. "You give me one cigarette?

"Hey, Honcho."

"Hey Honcho yourself, you little shit."

"Hosanna.

"To the skies Hosanna.

"Hey Honcho yourself.

"You know too goddamn much for such a little shit.

"Hosefuckinghannah."

The tracks rolled through the flower field at the edge of the wire and the flies swarmed and buzzed with anger.

SitRep Mar231705H: We ate hot chow in the mess hall that night, Horey, Boots and me. The soft-handed Major said 'well done' and sat next to us. Teapot came in smiling and spoke loudly to those that were there.

"Don't get close to me," he said. "I've been in the field. I stink."

"I'll drink to that," Horey said into his coffee.

The soft-handed Major smiled slightly and busied himself with his chow.

SitRep Mar232115H: That night we did it. We got very drunk on bad wine. I finally got sick and puked in a bunker. I went back into the hooch and listened to the others. I still felt sick and I knew my head would hurt in the morning. I hoped she would understand and know that I was suddenly for the moment anyway just afraid.

SitRepMar240832H: That morning Boots and Horey went down to the airstrip and hopped a chopper for Da Nang. Boots went to pick up the Company payroll. Horey went because he said that if Boots could fuck up getting water he would need help to keep from fucking up all that money.

I took a shaky walked down to the home of 'Fightin' Echo' past the Company office. Inside I could hear Flynn-Michael recounting the battle to the First Sergeant. I continued on to my platoon's hooch. Balen sat shirtless on the front step cleaning his rifle while Lonely could be heard somewhere in the distance trying to hustle a game of cards. I looked at Balen and shook my head. Balen shrugged and returned his attention to his M-14. I turned and walked back toward the Company office. Inside, Flynn-Michael looked up from the small field desk where he sat writing letters.

"One Fooking Actual," he said as the door slammed closed behind me.

"One Fucking Only would be closer to it," I said.

Flynn-Michael put his pen down and leaned back knitting his fingers behind his head trying to read my expression.

"You okay?"

Now I shrugged.

"I'm better than Fitzlee and Brownell."

Flynn-Michael grunted in response and turned back to his writing.

"You know Sam," he said without looking up. "I've got to write these sad, fooking letters home you know, and the Goony's got the troops in hand and it strikes me that that fooking Horey could use the help of a man of your caliber keeping track of Boots and all that money."

I caught an afternoon chopper and caught up with Boots and Horey at the Freedom Hill Officer's Club. That evening we went to Charlie Med to find Brownell. When we went onto the ward we found him tubed up and asleep.

"I'm outta here," Horey said and he left me and Boots at Brownell's bed side.

"He looks smaller," I said

Boots took off his glasses and wiped them on the loose end of his sleeve.

"I'd rather get my fuckin' face blown off than end up like this."

"He doesn't know about Fitzlee."

"Probably just as well."

After a few minutes we left Brownell sleeping and found Horey playing darts in the doctor's lounge.

"I need a drink."

"I think I need more than that."

By nightfall we were in the big MACV club in the MACV compound in downtown Da Nang, The Stone Elephant.

"Can you believe this shit?" Horey asked as we walked up to the long polished bar,. "There's no fucking war here. Look at these pogues. They're all fucking civilians."

One of the 'pogues' turned from the bar and gave me, Boots and Horey an up and down. When he saw the shoulder holstered half cocked .45s he slowly lowered his drink and turned full around from the bar.

"You can't have those in here," he said. "You need to turn them in at the door."

"Fuck you," Horey said. "And turn your civilian ass around. Where we are so are the .45s."

The civilian raised his right hand and pulled his wallet out with his left flipping it open to his military ID, Colonel USAF.

"The MPs are on the way gentlemen. You either check in the weapons, or you're gone."

At 7:35 the next morning Boots picked up the payroll at the division pay office while I tried to focus on anything that would hold still.

"Where the fuck is Horey?" Boots asked coming out of the pay office.

"I'm not even sure where my feet are," I said and together we climbed into the jeep for the bumpy ride through Dogpatch to the Air Viet Nam terminal. Had it been only three months? I scanned the smoke-filled, noisy room. Nothing had changed but nothing looked familiar.

"The last time I saw him he was trying to convince a nurse that he was a jet pilot."

I said, "yeah," and we walked through the building to the waiting chopper.

SitRep Mar261000H: The sun broke hot for an Easter Sunday and we all went to the service offered by the red-eyed Chaplain. He spoke with resonance and he spoke of crosses and sin and forgiveness. Again, I couldn't follow it. I looked out through the screen of the white painted hooch they called the Chapel. I could see Outpost ZULU and the snake road that led through the pass and south.

"Crosses," I said.

The inside of the chapel was done in pressed bamboo. It was stained and the prominent color was brown, sanctuary brown. The Chaplain spoke through a portable electric PA system that had been placed on the bar. He spoke over his little, baggy, red eyes. 'What a good shit he is,' I thought, 'but I won't find forgiveness today.'

The benches that had been moved in the night prior were white and had no backs. We sang the Gloria and bowed our heads to pray. I watched the heat simmer off ZULU.

We will all go home someday. We will shoulder our little crosses and sneak back home and we will stand there quietly and be overlooked while people in high places and low places race to Pilate's Bowl.

I watched ZULU.

And before the water has dried from their hands they will turn back to where we are standing quietly, and they will waggle their fingers and say there must be some reason for all of it and they will look disparagingly upon us. Some will admonish us and when we come to the bowl we will find that it is empty and that our hands must remain as they are because we have gone where we were sent and we have done what we were told to do, what we had to do; and in some cases we have done it too well and gladly with hardened hands because that was what you have made of us. We will not be allowed to wash because we will be the necessary lava for cleansing the others and they will leave us happily rubbed raw.

Bullshit.

Bullshitus.

Bullshatum.

The service ended.

Boots and I walked back to the hooch alone. Horey was back and already nursing a bottle of bourbon.

"I don't want to talk about it," he said raising his hand. For several minutes, while our eyes adjusted to the subdued light, we sat on our cots in silence. Two empty racks remained untouched looking as they had when we left them just five short days ago.

Boots slapped his thighs and stood and as if on cue Horey and I stood with him.

Now there was only one thing left to do, to look at their things, all that was left of Brownell and Fitzlee, paw them out and count them like the days, store them under 'X'S and ship them home, days spent. We counted them, looked at them, touched them held them up to the light and then locked them away.

"Now," I said. "I suppose we will never be done with the counting."

Boots looked up from the things he had in front of him. Horey looked across his bottle.

"What?" Boots asked.

"I said...," I said.

"I know what you said," Boots said. "But what do you mean?"

"I don't know," I said. "I don't know what any of it means anymore."

"You're full of shit," Boots said and he returned to the sifting and sorting. I watched him as he sorted through the gear, Fitzlee's and Brownell's.

"I've got to piss," Horey said.

He rolled over, dropped his bottle next to him and pissed on the floor.

"What the fuck did you do that for?" Boots shouted.

"I don't know," Horey said quietly. "But what the hell difference does it make anyway?"

I looked at Boots and smiled.

"He's right," I said. "It really doesn't make any difference today."

"Well, who in hell is going to clean up this mess?".

I looked at Boots and then down to the things he had been counting.

"I don't know," I said. "I truly don't, there's so much to count."

Horey cleared from the bottom of his throat and spat into the center of the already stained piss-puddled floor. Boots studied him silently and then looked back to me.

"You're crazy," he said "Both of you, just fucking crazy."

Horey and I laughed. After a moment Boots laughed with us. It felt good to be crazy and to laugh, and besides there really wasn't anything else to do.

10 FREEDOM HILL – JULY, 1967

SitRep July142110H: I stood on a small porch at the front door of the large cabana-styled building that served as the quarters for the Commanding General, First Marine Division. From here, high up on Freedom Hill, I could look down on the vast lighted Da Nang airbase and watch the waves of jets taking off for night bombing missions somewhere to the north. Next to me the officious Major who had driven me to the top of the ridge shifted from foot-to-foot as we waited for the General to come to the door. 'Fookin' Pogue,' I thought watching him from the corner of my eye. And then, I thought again, 'just like me.' Four months had passed since New Castle. Flynn-Michael and Horey were back in the world and I had been transferred from the Company into Battalion Operations where I spent most of my time 12 feet underground watching the slow progress of grease pencil lines as they crawled from check point to check point across the large map screwed to the wall in front of me, and Boots... At 1029 hundred hotel all hell let loose. The daily road sweep from An Hoa to the river was ambushed and in a twinkling, they were all gone, and Boots.... Boots was with them taking the pay to the troops of Echo Company out guarding the river crossing at Phu Lac 6.

The door opened and the General stood silhouetted against the light from the room behind. Reaching across in front of the Major he put his arm around my shoulder and pulled me inside.

"Come on in Lieutenant," he said, and to the Major, "be back in an hour." With that, he closed the door in the Major's face.

"This place is too damn big for one person," the General said giving me a quick tour of his quarters and then motioning toward the bamboo, pillowed couch in the middle of the spacious living room, he said. "Sit down over there, Lieutenant."

For the first few minutes we talked about nothing, the where you from stuff. I told him about the pumpkin that I left growing by the side of the El Toro airstrip and he told me he understood about that kind of thing.

"Can I get you something to drink?" he asked.

I sat and shook my head 'no'.

The General looked down at me for a moment and then dragged an easel and large map of the An Hoa area in front of the couch.

"Okay, Lieutenant," he said, pulling a dark brown cigar from the box on the table next to the couch. "Why don't you tell me what happened."

I looked at the map, swallowed, and leaned forward pointing at the old railroad bridge where it crossed Liberty Road.

"It happened here," I said softly. "And I didn't recognize his voice. I was talking to Boots and I didn't even recognize his voice... the last thing he said was 'where the fuck is that artillery' and I said 'it's on the way' and then 'shot out' but when I asked for an adjustment there was no response, nothing, just silence... I tried to get the Green Beret birds sitting on our strip to go up but they wouldn't go so I got mad as hell...and then someone came running through and said 'Boots was with them'... and I said they're gone, they're all gone...Boots is gone and I'm the only one left."

The hour passed. The General finished his cigar and placed the stub aside in the ashtray. The Major returned, and an hour after that, I hopped off the chopper back in An Hoa.

SitRep July271848H: I sat in the COC again watching more fuzzy lines of grease pencil crawl across the large map in front of me. The newly arrived Major, my new boss, had just come into the bunker when the small land-line phone next to me began to buzz. Nodding to the Major I pulled the phone to my ear.

"Grasshopper," I said without interest.

"Grasshopper this is Isherwood, wait one…," and as the division operator spoke the connection dissolved into broken static punctuated with fragments of spoken word.

"Lieutenant Sam…

"…Red Cross…

"…boy…

"…and to tell you that your wife…

"…fine… "

And then the line went dead.

I slid the phone handset back into its narrow case and looked across the cramped COC to where the Major stood next to a large coffee urn.

"I think I just became a father," I said.

The Major smiled.

"Congratulations. Let me buy you a cup of coffee."

I accepted the hand-shake and the coffee poured from the large, olive-drab urn brought over from the chow hall, I returned to my seat and gazed at the map.

"Just in case I forget where I am," I said.

Two days later, I was called into the office of the smoot-handed Major and told to stand at ease.

"The General," he said, "has directed me to give you one of these."

From the top drawer of his desk he pulled a dark brown cellophane wrapped cigar.

"You must recognize this," he said.

I took the cigar.

"I thought I was the one who handed out the cigars."

"You're a Marine," he said. "You do what the General tells you to do."

I put the cigar in my breast pocket.

"I'll save this," I said, and left.

"Sam," the Major called through the screen door. "Life continues its flow all around us."

Dear S,

Your flowers arrived today and they're beautiful. Throw away all the lousy things I said in the last letter I love you, oops we love you. I held him in front of the big map of Viet Nam that's up on the wall over the dining room table and pointed to the pins showing where you are and I said you send my daddy home. I dream about that every night and I still have a little trouble sleeping but don't worry about us, we're ok. You just be careful.

Love,

Pumpkin and Gerald!

At the end of the month the Battalion saddled up and left An Hoa to the Army. We loaded everything onto 46's and in two days we were in Phu Bai.

11 – CALIFORNIA – FEBRUARY, 1968

It was night when the big Continental, fly the golden tail, came to a stop on the far end of the quiet El Toro air strip. For the past hour we had flown down the coast looking at the brightly lighted night-time California landscape. Inside the initial shouts had given way to assorted "wows" and "look at thats" and "man, I'm back in the worlds." Now, as we began to taxi back toward the main terminal it was quiet again.

The pilot who had announced the arrival of the flight back over California to cheers and shouts came back up on the cabin P.A. now for a second time. All he said was "Welcome home." This time there were no cheers. The 275 returning Marines moved quietly about the cabin gathering up their belongings and began to head to the front of the plane where they were greeted by the stewardesses that had been with us on the flight home, since Oki. They too said welcome home and smiled as the deplaning got under way.

I returned the smiles and said, "Thanks."

At the bottom of the roll-up gang-way two Sergeants wearing MP arm-bands waited for us as we descended into the cool February California darkness. A gentle mist muffled their voices.

"Customs," they said and they began to herd the new arrivals toward a make shift shake down area to go through sea bags, to ask questions, to make sure all was in order.

"Yeah, we're back in the world alright," someone said.

"Boy it didn't take long for this chicken-shit to start," from another.

"Chicken-shit doesn't start," the first Marine said. "It just is."

One of the Sergeants approached me.

"Do you have anything to declare, Sir?"

I shook my head 'no,' and then I remembered the cigar.

"Does this count?" I asked fishing it out of my top pocket. "It's about all I have, everything else was blown up."

The Sergeant leaned in closer to study what I now held up like a torch in the light.

The cigar was badly twisted and broke but the cellophane wrapping had held and now it glistened reflected light into the mild California darkness.

"It's a cigar," I said. "Life continues to flow all around us, you know, like a river"

The Sergeant pulled back away from me.

"No Sir" he said. "There's no need to declare a cigar."

The Sergeant saluted and said, "Welcome home, Sir." There was nothing else to say. Moments later I was on the phone.

"I'm home," I said. "You can come and get me." And just like that it was over.

The next day was a blur and by the time I was through it, I had only embarrassed myself once. At a downtown intersection, while we waited for the light to change, a car had pulled up next to us and back-fired. Before I could stop myself I was out to the car and down on the pavement.

"It's all right," Pumpkin said. "You don't have to do that anymore."

"The quick and the dead," was all I said as I sheepishly climbed back into the driver's seat. "When you just get somewhere, when you're brand new, sometimes it just takes time."

In the back seat Gerald gurgled over a mouthful of fist.

12 QUANTICO – JULY, 1968

"Because they're glad you're home, that's why, and we haven't had a chance until now," Pumpkin said that evening when I got home. "For the last five months you've made excuses to avoid them so this time I promised so that's why we have to go. And because they cared while you were gone. Besides, most people will be celebrating the Fourth so it won't be that bad and before you know it, it will be over. Anyway, I told Bill and Leeanne it would be okay."

"Oh God" I said. "Tell them to leave their fire crackers at home."

So now we are at the Welcome Home party that I'd managed to put off until now. I am quiet and the darkened room is full of talking people, most of whom, like she said, I don't know.

"They're friends of Bill and Leeanne and some are people I work with," she told me when we arrived. "Just try to relax and enjoy them. We're done with all that other stuff now."

I nod and wander off across the crowded living room. Midway to the sofa I am stopped by one of the smiling friends.

"So," the friend askes. "Are you a friend of Bill and Leeanne?"

"Yes Sir," I say. "I'm the 'Sam' in the 'Welcome Home Sam' sign up over the door, in red, white, and blue."

The friend's smile slips away.

"So it's you," he says. "What must it be like, all those poor people dying because of…"

Suddenly, over them all I hear the following roar of a jet from the base and seconds later the thundering boom as it breaks the sonic barrier. And as the lingering roar echoes through the room I throw my glass against the opposite wall and pull the broken cigar from my pocket and point it around the room like a pistol.

"Don't move," I shout, against the backdrop of ice glittering and rattling in brown sweating glasses.

"That's incoming," I say more quietly as no one but the quickly retreating smiling friend appears to notice.

"Condition Red," I whisper. And finally.

"It's not incoming, it's friendly fire." I mouth the words without sound. "No cause for alarm."

"Morales take the point," I say more urgently. "Be alert, watch your step, be cautious, be afraid, find them first…

"Pick up Wescott's head, silent at last…, grab it with Cobra hands.

"Where is Fitzlee?" I say looking around the room. "Where is Brownell?"

"Boots, I can barely hear you. I don't know who you are standing tall next to Delpert."

And a minute later I say, "I can see an old man."

And after that, "I've heard the roar of the dragon."

And finally, "Where the fuck am I. Please, don't let the rain fall on me again."

SitRep July042235R: In the darkness, Pumpkin reaches out to me, and by her side Gerald our son lunges up in baby spasms and jerks, swatting at my face like a young cat. Others crowd around me, reaching to touch me. Their features melt away, their hands and arms turn black against dimly lighted walls of the room and their eyes glitter like bright pinpoint stars. While the party goes on around me and Bill sweeps up the broken glass, I sit on the edge of a stair and weep. Single, small teardrops fall and drive deep into the fabric of my civilian jeans leaving small ghostly traces behind. In front of me Pumpkin squats, still, and rocks back on her heels watching me, like a gook.

GLOSSARY

ACTUAL: radio call sign for unit leader prefixed with unit number

BIRD: fixed wing aircraft or helicopter

BOOT: recruit or someone inexperienced

BUNKER: fortified structure either above or below ground usually constructed with sand bags

CLICK: a notch of adjustment on a rifle sight; a 1000 meter grid square on a map (see klick)

COLORS: the flag; or the ceremony of raising or lowering the flag

C-RATS: C rations, canned rations

CORPSMAN: Navy medic serving with Marines

COVER: hat.

DECK: floor

FIRE IN THE HOLE!: shouted warning that hand grenades or explosives are about to o off

HAM AND MOTHERS: "Ham and Motherfuckers;" name given to C-ration meal ham and lima beans.

HATCH: door

HEAD: toilet.

HOOCH: shelter or place of domicile

HONCHO: the leader

INCOMING!: fire being received; it may be either enemy fire or friendly fire

KLICK: a kilometer

PISS TUBE: field urinal; often made from artillery round casings buried to about half their length

POGUE: usually someone in a rear area that fights his war from behind a desk

RACK: cot, bunk

RUBBER LADY: rubber air mattress

SEABAG: duffle bag

SHORT: nearing the end of a tour of duty or enlistment.

SITREP: Situation Report, situation updates given to higher command by units operating in the field

SKIPPER: captain; commanding officer

SNUFFY: derogatory name for sloppy lower enlisted man

ABOUT THE AUTHOR

A 1965 graduate of Marietta College, Marietta, Ohio, Mr. Newton worked as a reporter for The Marietta Daily Times before entering the United States Marine Corps in March of 1966. He earned his commission as a Second Lieutenant in June of that year and served as an infantry platoon commander and Battalion staff member with the Second Battalion, Fifth Marines from January 1967 to February 1968. Following his release from active duty Mr. Newton and his wife moved to South Chatham, Massachusetts on Cape Cod where they raised their three children. During the years following his release he worked as a manager in a retail lumber chain. In 1992 he became a certified teacher. He finished his professional career as a special needs teacher working with incarcerated juveniles. He retired from teaching in 2005 and now operates an ice cream parlor, Short n Sweet, in South Chatham with his wife.